# CALL OF THE
# TREE OF DEATH

OTHER TITLES IN THE FAITHWALKER SERIES
BY DARRYL S. MARKOWITZ

*Call of the Tree: Book One*

*The Sacrificial Wood: Book Two*

*The Dead Forest: Book Three*

*Succession: Book Four*

*Unnatural Disaster: Book Five*

# CALL OF THE TREE OF DEATH

## THE FAITHWALKER SERIES BOOK SIX

### THE LEGACY OF THE TREE OF LIFE
### AS PASSED DOWN TO THE LAST GENERATION

# DARRYL MARKOWITZ

FaithWalker Publishing

**The Faithwalker Series**
**Book VI: Call of the Tree Of Death**



*Published by:*

Faithwalker Publishing
An imprint of Darryl Markowitz

Cover and Interior Design: Creative Publishing Book Design
Cover Art: Amelia M.

ISBN Paperback: 978-1-7374936-6-2
ISBN eBook: 978-1-7374936-7-9

Printed in the United States of America

CHAPTER 1

# Nothing Stands
# Without the Smallest

*Walking alone down a sideroad of polished, many colored stones, Marta paid no mind to the wonderful scents of the various fruit trees at each side. Normally, she would have stopped at least thrice to sample her favorites then toss the rest to seriously waiting squirrels, racoons, and possums who knew her by first sight. Her three long, shiny, light brown braids dangled and bounced around in front of her so she threw them behind to alleviate the nuisance, then smoothed out her brown peasant dress and tried not to appear too upset because you never knew who you might meet even on a road hardly ever noticed.* I'm in Heaven, I shouldn't be upset, no matter what. *But she also knew that over the past few Earth years, upset happened more often than not, but that was because of what she was watching* down there. *This time, however, she mumbled to herself about something up here:* I don't understand. A *substitute* teacher? For me? *Indefinitely?* What did I do wrong?

*Though having been up here for a while, fifty-seven Earth years, to be exact, she still only looked the fourteen Earth*

1

*years that she had lived* down *there. Well, maybe a couple years older now, but age is quite hard to decipher in Heaven. Nevertheless, her identity up here to all, and very much to herself had developed into the teacher that everyone talked about, especially after it was* her *class whose prayers made* the *difference for Lady Stephanie and King Vaughn.*

*Mafferan, decked out in his usual brown tunic and pants, with neatly trimmed square, white and brown beard suddenly appeared beside her with a slight head bow to* her! *"Teacher Marta, the Lord requests your presence in a very* special *way, in a very special room."*

*His whole presentation, from an amazing head bow from* him, *no matter how small, to the fact that the Lord summoned* her *in person, and. . .* Special way? A very special room? *It sent goose bumps all through her, but in the next moment Mafferan placed his hand upon her shoulder and they reappeared in . . .*

*Everything was so still it was like time stopped, even though Heaven, in general, is eternal, but this far exceeded anything Marta had ever felt before. She could barely see through the intense golden glow all around but she discerned that Mafferan was already on one knee and Marta quickly fell on her face not feeling worthy at all. But then . . . the Lord spoke directly to her! It was like the whole room was the Lord's voice. "Marta, of your own free will you have honored me above all others!"*

*She could hardly believe that! And before she could call back her words, she said, "Oh, not so, Lord, I'm really not even that much of a teacher. I'm just sorta repeating what your goodness shows me inside." Then she realized she was actually* contradicting *the LORD!* "*Forgive me my foolishness, but I don't understand.*"

"*No one is as small to themselves as you are, and so you honor the smallest of My Goodness above all others. And when I'm honored thusly in the smallest, the greatest of Me is perfectly honored. Rise!*"

*And Marta found herself standing, and the Lord spoke, "What I tell you here is to be only between you and I and Mafferan. No one is to know of it up here or down there. . ."*

*And then Marta found herself upon an endless bridge suspended in Heaven made of infinite stones of different colors shining with a golden hue. She was still dazed from all the Lord had told her but Mafferan poured a bottle of the golden Oil of Peace over her head, and said, "So you can travel,* down there!"

*And she looked down upon the Earth and saw great darkness swallowing it up except where Lady Stephanie and King Vaughn ruled. She looked into Mafferan's glowing rare brown eyes, and blurted out, "But what about the Truce?" What the Lord had given her clearly violated it, the Truce between Heaven and the Ethereal.*

*Mafferan leveled a deep gaze into her which had begun imparting understanding even before he spoke. "It is insane to think anyone could make a fair deal with the devil. I only made him believe that's what I did. In truth, there never was a Truce. The ruse was but a tool to slow him down a bit, to give them time."*

*And Marta knew that the word them meant all humanity but her attention was immediately drawn to the Holy Mountain where three little girls and one little boy slumbered together in a circular cabin.*

This should have been the best sleepover ever, but Lana lay in the soft, round bed unable to sleep though the meager light from the curtained window was hardly a distraction. Her sharp gray eyes just stared upward, while her light brown hair spread neatly over her pillow. Lady Stephanie used to lavish her with such hair care when putting her to sleep when she was only five-years-old. Now, a whole eight-years-old, Lana was careful to remember all that Stephanie had done to her and taught her. But with absorbing such depths of *personal* responsibility, she now felt more and more responsible for Rebecca and Lynnara, though she was only a year older than them.

Rebecca, her long dark brown hair splayed everywhere, was now turned on her side sleeping deeply with her little hand over Lana's heart. Lana looked over to her right where Lynnara was also turned on her side facing Lana, but she clung to Lana's arm. Lynnara's rich brown hair, though long, curled up so much it was like a big fuzzy ball. These were her two bestest friends *ever* and the love she felt for them weighed on her little heart because Lana sensed she was about to have another terrible vision, but somehow she knew this one would be far different than anything before.

Lana looked back at Rebecca remembering Rebecca's descriptions of how she had saved Lynnara's life. Then Lana turned back to Lynnara and remembered how she described saving Stephanie from a real live, no, dead, no, well, it was a real demon and Lynnara had saved the *faithwalker* from being eaten and then gave Stephanie her life back. Lana hadn't done anything nearly as important as her two friends. And after all, Lynnara was now like Stephanie, a *faithwalker* because Queen Stephanie had bonded with Lynnara right before Stephanie died in the Dead Forest.

Yet, even though only a single year older, Lana felt practically grown up, at least right now, and then the vision slammed into her:

Alone in the darkness, in a deep forest. *Fear!* Overwhelming, suffocating fear, but not like any of her other visions, because now, she felt herself trembling and was in the back of her mind worrying she would scare her friends. And then panting, but it wasn't just her. There were others nearby, running. And then a child ran right into her and knocked her over and Lana screamed in the vision but the child, a boy, no, a girl, no . . . crawled on top of Lana and put its hand over her mouth. "Shhhh, they'll hear you." Even though the voice wasn't deep like a man, Lana knew this was a boy, but a good bit older than her, maybe twelve.

Then more running, and another child dove onto them. "Don't make a sound, or they'll hear you." This was a girl, maybe ten or eleven, but. . . only by the voice. The girl seemed like a boy. But the boy seemed like a girl. The deep sense of a twisted reality pressed upon Lana and she realized it was *this* sense that was causing all her fear! Then both children pleaded with her. "Help us. You *have to* help us."

Ferocious dogs growled and howled and barked but not like any dog Lana had ever heard. The other children said together, "Be still. Don't even breathe!" And the beasts burst from between the trees and ran right up to them. They had glowing red eyes, pointy ears, and one of them laid a heavily clawed paw upon Lana's shoulder.

She should have been terrified by now, but as soon as this demon dog touched her, Lana got angry. She remembered when she had bit Jargono's hand, and at that time he was a very evil man with powers, but she didn't care about that. She bit him because he was hurting her Mommy. Lana reached up and grabbed the demon-dog's ear and she snarled at it. "Leave us!"

Lana sat bolt-upright in bed but the other girls were still sound asleep. Understanding flooded her like never before and tears ran down her little freckled cheeks but she gathered her long light brown hair in her little hands and did it up in a bun just like Stephanie had taught her. There was work to be done now. *Serious* work. She shook Rebecca. "Wake up! We have to *go!*"

Rebecca opened her dark brown eyes, rubbed them, then said, "Go where? This is the best place in the whole world." And that was very true. They were in one of the many round Appendaho cottages upon the Holy Mountain where the Tree of Life now grew and where King Vaughn and Lady Stephanie had created a whole town because Jesus gave them the power and showed them how to do it. Many truly holy people resided here.

Little laughter came from the crib and the girls looked over to see Michael, now two-years-old, standing up in his little blue jammies and peering over the top rail at them. His adorable reddish brown curls always made the girls hearts throb but now he glowed golden with goodness all around him like never before.

The story Lynnara had told of how she and Stephanie had fought a whole bunch of human demons immediately came into Lana's heart and mind. They had badly wounded Lady Stephanie while Michael was still inside her and the demon's poison was killing them both. Lynnara had tried to heal her third Mommy, her bestest Mommy ever, but she couldn't. *That's* when King Vaughn took his special staff and laid it on Stephanie, his Queen, and God turned the staff into a serpent and it sucked all the poison out. But little Michael was gone and Stephanie hurt so bad she told God's serpent to take her life, too, if she couldn't have Michael back inside her. So the serpent breathed really hard on her and Michael came back. Then the serpent looked over to Vaughn then turned back into his staff again.

Michael giggled again then screeched in joy and it brought Lana back to the important, *super* important task at hand. She shook Lynnara and she opened her soft brown eyes, eyes that had gold flecks in them so the soft brown was so beautiful. "Is it time to eat?" Lynnara asked.

"No. It's time to *go*! And you have to take us!"

Now Lynnara, fully awake and recognizing the call from the Holy Spirit, sat up straight and tried to pull her long but curly brown hair out of her face. She understood Lana wanted her to use her *faithwalking* ability to travel. Recently, she no longer needed to hold Stephanie's holy hair ribbon to do it. She could do it all by herself just like Mommy.

Rebecca jumped down from the soft bed and went over to a nightstand and got her hair brush and ran it through her long, straight, dark brown hair. Ever since Ranger Vaughn had rescued her and buried her Mommy and took care of her and showed her how to brush her teeth and hair every day, she never missed her self-responsibility. "There. I'm ready. Where're we goin'?"

Lynnara looked over to Lana, too, with the same question in her now glowing eyes. She was gathering power for the journey. But Lana didn't know, not exactly. Then she made the girls sit back down on the bed and told them her vision. Their little eyes went wide. Then Lana explained, "It's real! I *know* it is. It's a *real* place. And those are *real* people, like us, ahh, sorta. But they *need* our help *now!*" Lana looked over to Lynnara for the answer because *Lynnara* was a *faithwalker* now.

Lynnara bowed her little head and placed her hand upon Lana's head. She *knew* how to do this! It just came to her! It was knowledge about *faithwalking* that Lady Stephanie had placed inside her for when she needed it, because Lady Stephanie had thought Lynnara would be the new keeper of the Seed to the Tree of Life right before Stephanie had died.

Lynnara, with her hand on Lana's head, now concentrated into Lana's vision that lived inside Lana's heart and mind. Once there, Lynnara gained the feeling of the place where the vision was located and she was about to transport them all straight there when Michael screeched again and broke Lynnara's concentration.

Michael was beckoning them to come to him. "Come. Come 'errre," his little two-year-old voice chirped. The three girls looked at each other then bounded over and kissed him all over his head and face but his little hands kept pushing them away. Then he held his hands out and so Lana picked him up from the crib and was going to hold him but he immediately fought to be put down, so there he stood in their midst, and raised his arms and began to glow. Then he touched each of the girls hands and they began to glow, too!

Michael, *everyone* knew, was a *very* special child. All of the ethereal demons were going to go to war just to destroy this one child, so when the girls saw the surprising blessings that went out from him, they were in awe, but not surprised. In fact, they were jubilant, jumping up and down along with little Michael.

Lana said to Lynnara, "Ok. I think that's like a sign that we're ready." So Lynnara began to concentrate again but then realized she should tell her Mommy first because even Jargono had told her not to do these kinds of things again without telling Mommy or Daddy first. So Lynnara began to concentrate on where her Mommy was so she could quickly pop in on her and tell her the plan, and *then* go.

But the girls heard the door to the cottage open then softly close and when they all turned around, it wasn't Stephanie as they had supposed, because Stephanie always seemed to know when they were up to something. It was Carla! She looked so very humble in her brown peasant dress, but when she pulled her long, dark brown hair behind her and leveled the gaze of her soft brown eyes into them all, they all recognized her serious look. She *knew!* Carla motioned them to get up on the bed so they scampered up and Carla pulled over a wooden chair to be at eye level with them.

"You can't tell your Mommy, or your Daddy!"

Rebecca threw her hand to her mouth remembering. Carla had visions, too. But she was a lot more grown up than Lana. The girls now all remembered how three years ago Carla told them how Ranger Vaughn had rescued her, and she had said to Vaughn, "I know you. God showed me you would come." But Carla had never met Ranger Vaughn before that! But not only *that*, It was *Carla,* and *only* Carla, who knew the horrible evil that trapped Lynnara *and* Lady Stephanie *and* that *only* Rebecca had the chance, the *only* chance to save them all. It was Carla who had warned her now husband Ranger Larson to secretly make sure his men didn't interfere with Rebecca getting into the evil building where Lynnara was trapped.

Lynnara said to Carla with wide eyes, "Mommy's gonna be sooo mad at me."

Carla straightened in her chair. "You know we're sisters. Mandy, Stephanie, and I."

Just then, Mandy, now seventeen-years-old and Carla's younger sister by two years, opened the door carrying a long knapsack and plunked it down on the floor, saying, "I got everything Sis. Are you *sure* about this?"

Carla turned back to the children. "If you tell Mommy and Daddy, they'll immediately go to where you were going to go. The enemy will know they're there, and. . ." Carla grimaced, bowed her head, and couldn't speak any further. Her long, straight, dark brown hair hung over her face.

Mandy pulled back her wavy, long, reddish brown hair and put her hand on her sister's shoulder, but hiding things from Stephanie just didn't seem right. Mandy loved Stephanie more than *anything*. It was Mandy who stuck right by Stephanie's side through her terrible ordeal because even though Mandy had treated Stephanie *horribly*, Stephanie had found a way to redeem her *anyway* and save Carla, all while Stephanie had been in utter despair. Mandy squeezed Carla's shoulder and she looked up at her, and Mandy had to ask, "What is it Sis? This really is just like before, isn't it?"

Carla sighed but managed to speak. "Worse! *Much worse!*" Then she raised her head and steeled herself to speak to the children. "I'll take responsibility for all this so you won't get in trouble. And Mommy and Daddy have way too much important stuff they're doing now, and they can't be distracted. *But* you can't just go without an adult. *Mandy* will go with you."

The girls then turned back to Mandy and noticed she was wearing a lady's ranger uniform. *That* meant this was *really* serious. The girls had often delighted in watching her train when they were all back at the castle where Vaughn and Stephanie lived. Mandy reached into her knapsack and pulled out brown girl's ranger uniforms for them, but to Rebecca she also gave a small archers bow and a special quiver with special arrows like King Vaughn had.

"Wow!" Lana and Lynnara both said at once.

But Rebecca smiled proudly at them, saying, "Ever since I went into that bad building and that *bad* man grabbed me, I wanted to know how to *fight!* Mandy's been teaching me, ahh, in *secret!*" Rebecca went over, put on her new uniform, and slung the little quiver and bow over her shoulders. "I'm *ready!*"

Mandy pulled out her own bow and quiver with similar blessed arrows, then she strapped on two simitars which criss-crossed behind her back. Lady Stephanie had gifted them to her when Mandy officially became a ranger. Tears welled in Mandy's eyes at the memory, at the *meaning.* These swords had originally belonged to Queen Karen who died while protecting Stephanie with those very same weapons. Queen Karen actually chose to die in Stephanie's place by stepping between her and the enemy in a split-second decision. Then Queen Stephanie, in a rage, took Karen's swords and vanquished the enemy from their castle. Hard to believe Stephanie and Karen had been arch-enemies for most of their lives. Mandy checked her knife and hatchet at each of her sides, and then said, "I'm ready, too."

All of them stood up and then turned to Carla, who had tears in her eyes. "It's time. But what I mean by this is that the end has come. *This* is the beginning of the rise of the Tree of Death. God has called each of us to do our part for goodness sake. Because there are people that need our help, people that if we help them, won't be lost to the demons, to the Tree of Death."

Lynnara had power suddenly surging all through her little body and she glowed for the first time, like her Mommy sometimes did, in rainbow colors. She held out her arms and they all squeezed in so she could touch them and they vanished.

Carla remembered the wonderful letter Stephanie had wrote to Vaughn that all we can do, is do our part. We're not assured of any outcome, but we won't have failed if we do what we can, if we fulfil the love God has given us to *be*. And that's all we can do. Just our part. Carla knew this was as true on Earth even as in Heaven above. She buried her face in her hands, went to her knees, and wept. Little Michael turned somber and sat down at Carla's head and placed his little hand there.

# CHAPTER 2

# The Short Life
# of Democracy

*Facing each other while hovering around the orb in the center of the Father's darkest room, HrorrarrAggrang snickered as the Father crossed his very long deepest black tail over his massive arm. The arm protruded from an immense deepest black serpentine body that had grown way past its original size, the Father having consumed all of the original tribe except for HrorrarrAggrang. The room was so dark, the four walls weren't even visible, but the Father's new orb that Queen Karen had supplied cast a pale blue light upon them.*

*It was only by mere accident that the Father had discovered the orb still functioned properly. Actually, in a fit of rage he'd slammed it around his ethereal room but then noticed the faintest change in its utter darkness. Remembering exactly what he had done, he realized he had touched a hidden brightness switch. He had shaken his huge bulbous head at himself, at his stupidity and the brass that Earth boy Vaughn had to trick* even the Father of the Ethereal into thinking the orb no longer worked. And, of course, it was no surprise that Vaughn had been using it to spy even on the Ethereal!

The Father asked HrorrarrAggrang again why he was so sure his plan would work and why the so-called holy prophecy would actually fail. This time the Father expected an answer. He was beginning to question whether he should have vomited HrorrarrAggrang back into existence. Love him, or not, consuming HrorrarrAggrang had been the best meal the Father had ever eaten, especially when HrorrarrAggrang had actually tried to consume the Father! Unbelievable!

"Free will," HrorrarrAggrang simply said until the Father grew irritated at the vacuous, over-simplified answer.

HrorrarrAggrang lifted his tail tip to scratch the upper corner of his now ever-itching Great Eye in the center of his bulbous head. They had managed to return it to almost a perfect ocular circle but it still had the slightest vertical oblong shape. It was supposed to be horizontal, but no matter, it functioned perfectly. Hard to believe, though, that a mere two Earth years earlier, Jargono, that traitor, had literally blown him to smithereens all over the Ethereal Corridor and the Father had to literally put him back together piece by tiny piece.

HrorrarrAggrang figured he'd gotten away with the utmost stall and irritation before the Father might explode even over him, so he explained, "Free will means that ultimately nothing is set in Ethereal Stone, so to speak. Freedom is freedom and even their Father in Heaven can't trespass that. What I have devised, after considering past failures but being so very close *to victory, well, my plan can't fail. And we really have Vaughn to thank for it. I knew if I merely acquainted him with where the true history books for the former United States were, he'd do all the rest I needed him to do without any prodding at all. Remember, from the very start we always had felt that way about him, that he would do what we needed him to do without us even touching him at all. I can see what he plans to do and I'm waiting for it."*

James brought their breakfast to the ornate, oblong, mahogany dining table, one of the few things Jargono had created that still remained in his former castle, and James placed their plates at the respective table heads. He *still* always dressed properly in his butler uniform, even though a whole year ago after he had received the Holy Ghost, Vaughn and Stephanie had told him none of that was any longer necessary. But it was the *way* James had set their eggs, pancakes, sausages, and fruit bowls down. There was the slightest bit of *bang* to it and the *meaning* seemed to ring out through the whole castle, perhaps even through the entire North where they now resided.

Vaughn, in his usual brown shirt and pants and Stephanie in a brown peasant dress sat together comfortably at the *horizontal* table side, even though James delivered their food to each *proper* table end. Both raised their eyebrows at each other. Stephanie swished her hand and their food easily slid across the shiny table to rest before them, and Vaughn said, "James, you *know* you can always speak freely to us. We love you dearly. We're *family* in the truest sense."

James studied the lad, now twenty-years-old and Stephanie now nineteen. His heart pounded for the love of them and what they had done for the country. King Vaughn and Queen Stephanie, if history could ever compare it, were unquestionably the best rulers the world had ever seen, but they were about to throw it all away. But all James could muster was, "Are you sure *Sire?*" And when he asked the question, they both could *swear* his temples seemed to gray just a bit more!

Vaughn grimaced and Stephanie chuckled because she knew Vaughn *hated* to be addressed like that but she also knew James meant it and *particularly* meant it at *this* time. She understood his meaning quite clearly. "James, why don't you think what we're going to do is a good idea? It's never too late to hear wisdom, *especially* from you! In fact, none of this would have been even close to possible without you."

That was true. James, together with Jargono, had designed the sophisticated technology that interfaced with spiritual powers, particularly *faithwalking* powers, that now propelled their kingdom into the fastest recovery from disaster ever to be imagined. But even more importantly, it allowed them to see into the Ethereal fairly well, although, lately, Vaughn began to question exactly *how well* that really was.

Yet, all this technological marvel was the *least* of what made the recovery fantastic. James knew it was the impeccable character of these young rulers that made the important and vital difference. Their love and integrity seemed to infect the whole country, and its whole disposition began to mirror *them!* So James straightened, squared his shoulders, tugged his butler's black vest to make sure it was smooth and proper, then spoke clearly, respectfully, "No offense meant Me Lady, and Sire, but you be like my very own children and my heart pains for you. You both have ruled *excellently.* The country prospers and you are about to reunite the *whole* United States. But *both* the North and South *gladly* recognize you as their rulers, their King and Queen. *Even* the judges down South have likened you to King David, of all people, and have found a Biblical way to justify you ruling as their king while embracing what you call *constitutional* changes. But more than that, they truly love you and respect you both." He couldn't bear to speak the rest so he just let it be implied.

Stephanie squeezed Vaughn's arm, which meant he should speak up, though he always hated to contradict or disagree with James. James was clearly his elder, even if he was his butler, and James now being holy made it even more difficult for Vaughn to speak even though Vaughn was dead sure he was right. Vaughn sighed, then said, "James, our rule is from the top down. That's the way royal rule works. *That* creates certain processes within the people to merely absorb, even emulate from the *bottom up.* But *democracy* engages everyone *equally.* They *all* become an *active* part of governing. My dear friend, don't you see the added power to that? And we *need* all the power we can get to face what's coming. Not to mention the *true* freedom such a government supplies. Free oneness knit together by a common love is more powerful even than rulers who are beloved."

Lady Stephanie beamed at her King. She couldn't have said it any better. She tossed her three red braids behind her and sat up straighter. Her rich brown eyes shined golden light but their warmth radiated to James as she implored him, "Tell us your heart, James. We are way too young for all this. Give us your wisdom by the Lord."

James paused to make sure he was careful enough. But what his Queen asked for was *exactly* the problem. Wisdom always comes late, and just because it's spoken doesn't mean it will be received, though he was sure these young souls would appreciate it. But he was sure they wouldn't follow it. Nevertheless, James gave them deference, and spoke, "You're trying to implement an *ideal* into a *practical* situation where even at their best, the people as a whole are simply, well, *not* ideal. Which *means,* someone who appeals more to their practical side, or, well, some *other* side, no matter how far from that ideal they are, has a better chance to win their support than you do! Why would you put yourselves to a *vote,* and not even as King and Queen but merely what you call a *President?*"

Vaughn pushed his plate of food away, not even having eaten a single bite. Stephanie studied him but then began to wolf her food down. For some reason she was ravenously hungry. After quickly finishing what she had, she glimpsed at Vaughn again then snatched his plate and finished his food as well! Both Vaughn and James turned to look at her but she scrunched her shoulders with an I-don't-know expression.

Vaughn turned back to James and James steeled himself for what he knew was coming. "I understand what you mean, James. I thought about that, too. But I don't see how being King and Queen could protect against that kind of undermining either."

James became quite frank. "*Sire.* You are *King.* That gives you the *force* you need to fight such a battle that a *President* simply does not have." And he did in fact spit that word *President* out with disdain, perhaps from his old English roots, for Jargono had found him in what used to be the country England. And with that, James collected the empty plates and left.

Vaughn sat back in his elegant table-matching padded chair and sighed then looked over to his wife, his Lady, his Queen, and Stephanie picked up on the full meaning of his searching eyes. She looked down, then back up. "You know, as much as we meant it, could we really put drug dealers to death? And women who have abortions? We have the power. Not just because we *personally* have so much power, but simply because we rule."

Vaughn nodded. "Well, I think the people actually believed our threats. As far as I've heard from our intelligence folks, drugs have practically gone non-existent now. And abortions have all but ended and adoption way up."

Stephanie shook her head remembering her former gang and how they operated. "Until someone overcomes their fear of *us* and listens to the demon's seduction. Then they challenge us, and then what? The rule of law has more *meaning* within a democracy than a royal rule."

But Vaughn mumbled his reply, "If it's enforced."

And to that, Stephanie replied, "Then law enforcement becomes the bad guys. But. . . at least it's the *law* they are fighting, not merely a King and Queen."

James, now sitting at his neatly arranged desk in his study, waved the controller at the computer screen that filled the whole wall across from him. The screen where he had been watching his King and Queen went blank. He knew they spoke truly, even with true love, but he also knew they simply weren't wise concerning this. He flipped his screen to *External Monitoring* and then split it to reveal the public squares across the twelve largest cities in the North. They were all filled with demonstrators, each advocating for their particular group and what *rights* they wanted under the forthcoming new government, though, as yet, no candidates had been put forward. They probably didn't want to do that before the official proclamation in case their King and Queen had second thoughts. But for a whole year now, Vaughn and Stephanie had been educating the people about *Democracy.*

James redirected his screen to show the public squares across the twelve largest cities in the *South.* These weren't at all like the North. Their religion, Christianity, and even more importantly, how the current holy people had helped make their religion a lot more pure, obviously provided them the meaning, the value in life they need, so there were hardly any groups advocating for *anything.* There no longer was *any* rivalry between Christian *factions.* In fact, those divisions had been consistently dying over the past two years. Except there was one predominate group that seemed to come out of the closet, so to speak. These *funny* people who had affinity for the same sex were advocating in every single city. And they were all asking for the same, seemingly innocuous thing: equality. And also stating that God is love.

James scanned back up to the North and found those same *funny* people up there, too, with the same exact signs and statements: God is Love. Equality. We fought and died alongside *you!* We have a RIGHT to a free life. Support the DOWNTRODDEN. But up North, there have been *many* groups of downtrodden, and they all now seemed to be banning together with the *funny* people joining with them. James sighed because it appeared to him that it wasn't equality these people really wanted. Their angry faces portrayed vengeance. As good as Vaughn and Stephanie had been to everyone, well, that didn't seem to touch *these* people at all.

Shaking his head with foreboding, James went to his messaging application and sent the confirmation for tomorrow's ceremonies celebrating the rejoining of the North and South into the United States and then the implementation of elections. In the pit of his stomach he knew this was very wrong, but he would stick with his beloved King and Queen no matter what. No matter what, they would always have his full love and honor.

⁓

Lana, Rebecca, Lynnara, and Mandy appeared in a small hollow in the midst of a thick forest in the middle of a moonless night. Cool forest dampness filled their noses while their feet sunk slightly into the soft ground. It seemed as if it had just rained. Goose bumps went up Mandy's arms and she took her bow from her shoulder and knocked an arrow. Seeing that, Rebecca did like her mentor and armed her small, yet, effective bow, for the arrows were all blessed with King Vaughn's battle oil he brought back from the underground ancient tomb. And there they waited in silence, none of them daring to move because Lana's vision played in their hearts and minds.

Mandy motioned to put a bit of distance between each other but as soon as they did, Lynnara suddenly shrieked and threw her arms wide and a glowing golden dome enveloped them just like it had automatically done right before the human demons had attacked her and her Mommy two years ago. A beast leapt out from between the thick woods and slammed into the dome but then proceeded to pass right through it, albeit it passed through the shield in slow motion. Mandy put an arrow through its head and it dropped dead at their feet. The girls looked into Lynnara's eyes. Rebecca asked, "Was that supposed to happen?"

Lynnara could only shake her head. She looked over to Lana. "Was that supposed to happen?"

Lana shook her head and then they all looked up to Mandy. "Well, keep your dome up, anyway. It slows them down." Mandy slung her bow back over her shoulder and drew her blessed simitars and the girls all waited in silence, again. Which, moments later, was broken by snarls and howls from all around them. Mandy looked at Lana again. Even though Mandy was indeed a holy young woman, and even though, she, too, was there when the human demons first attacked Lady Stephanie and Lynnara, Mandy couldn't help feeling they might be overmatched here, at the least. But, frankly, the rank abomination also made all their flesh crawl.

Suddenly the growling turned into roaring as several more beasts leapt upon the dome and began passing through. Mandy spun from beast to beast like a ballet dancer and their heads all came off, their black blood squirting at their feet. Then several thuds hit the top of the dome. Squirrels, sort of, began scratching right through the shield. They had black fangs and long black claws and red eyes. Rebecca shot three arrows faster than any of them could believe and all three demon squirrels fell between them. She smiled broadly. "I've been practicing that!"

Lynnara lowered the shield and they all looked over to her. "I'm *done* being nice!" Something had come over her, again, just like what had driven her Mommy to actually grab the demon's throat when they were in the Dead Forest. The other three girls were all about to tell her that dropping the shield might not be such a good idea but five demon dog's charged from the trees from all around them. Mandy knew she couldn't get them all but she was determined to try, and Rebecca, too. But Lynnara clapped her hands and bright blue, compact fireballs laced with silver sped past them all and blew all the demon dogs to hell!

Lynnara had remembered seeing how her Mommy had fought Demon Fred, Stephanie's father, and she remembered how they fought the human demons when Stephanie was pregnant with Michael. Somehow Lynnara just knew this energy combination would work. Then ten more demon dogs slowly walked into view and circled them and then suddenly the tree branches above teemed with demon squirrels, but none attacked . . . yet.

Mandy tensed, asking Lana, *again*, with urgency, "*Lana is *this* supposed to happen?"

Lana was holy, too, but still just a child. Tears began to cloud her eyes. "Nooo. I mean, I don't know."

Mandy began to wonder, *Maybe her vision was just the demon's trap to lure us here.* "Lynnara, get us out of here."

But Lynnara suddenly became inundated with anger. She was a *faithwalker.* Not holy like Lana and Mandy, but one day that would come, too. She knew Mandy's thoughts. "Lana's vision was *real.* We're *staying!*"

But even Lana began to wonder, because, "Sometimes the visions are just right, but sometimes . . ."

"*What?*" they all asked.

The snarling began to increase in intensity and Lana had to shout over it. "Well, sometimes they're more, like, in *meaning* than just right."

Lynnara grew even angrier with power swirling inside of her. She didn't like these damned demons scaring her friends. It was just *wrong!* She felt the good *purpose* inside of her and the *worthlessness* of evil was apparent. Why should *evil* have its way? She wasn't holy and she was only seven, almost eight-years-old, but she prayed all the time. She called out. "Lord Jesus, help me know what to do." *Lynnara* was the *faithwalker.* She knew it was *her* who was responsible for everyone just like Lady Stephanie is. And Lynnara was tired of being threatened by evil, *tired* of just waiting to be attacked. She threw wide her arms and knife-like sheets of thin blue-silver energy went out from all around her, jumped over the girls then came down and sliced all the demon dogs to pieces. Then she raised her little hands over her head and a silver-blue mist sprayed upward and shriveled demon squirrels fell from the tree limbs and piled up around them.

Lynnara's eyes glowed red-gold with power. "We're *staying*. Lana's vision is *real.*" *Nothing* could shake the faith she had in her friends. She loved Mandy dearly, too, but *nothing* compared to the bond she had with Rebecca and Lana.

No one could believe what Lynnara had just done, but then they remembered that she had actually been wrapped up in the coil of an actual demon and that she stood up against the demons when they wanted to eat Stephanie, her third and best Mommy ever. None of them had such bravery or experience as *that* little girl. They all marveled at her through the peace she had just created around them.

Another sound drew their attention and Mandy raised her swords and Rebecca her bow. Two children about twelve-years-old dressed in muddy black clothes crept out of the woods and bowed to the ground to them. They were speaking but in a language the girls couldn't understand. "That's *them!*" Lana cried out. And she waved them to come closer. They both ran together and fell at their feet, in fact, *holding* their feet but their words sounded like babbling. The girls looked at each other but then Lynnara remembered that a *faithwalker* walks in meaning. She put a hand on each of the children's heads and bowed her head in concentration. Moments later, she had their meaning. A bit after that, she understood their language, and a bit after that, both children raised their heads in amazement. Lynnara smiled broadly at them, "I'm Lynnara. This is Mandy, Rebecca, and Lana. She had a vision to come here for *you!*"

The child that sounded like a boy said, "We had visions to come. I'm Shara. This is Sam."

The girls looked at each other, again, because the boy clearly had a girl's name and the girl had a boy's name. Upon closer inspection, the supposed-to-be boy had long, straight black hair but the supposed-to-be girl had very short black hair. The boy even wore a dress! The girl had pants. All four girls couldn't help being clearly revolted and the two children at their feet perceived it.

Sam, the supposed-to-be girl, looked upon her saviors, saw how they were all dressed in clearly feminine uniforms, and that they all *clearly* acted like girls, well, Mandy like a woman, and Sam wailed with a tortured cry, "Forgive us, We're *hideous!*" And she bowed low and covered her head with her hands out of pure shame.

Shara leveled his dark brown eyes into Lana's, saying, "Many of us, even most, don't want to be like *this.*" And he spread out his hands to openly show his wretchedness.

Sam sat up and immediately followed up, "But we have no *choice.* They *make us* be this way."

"Or they do even more terrible things to us. I'm actually *still* a real boy." And he stood up and began to lift up his dress.

All the girls shouted, raising their hands, "That's OK. We believe you. We don't need to see!"

The two children looked confused and looked at each other.

Mandy just had to ask, "*Why?*"

The two looked at each other again, then Shara said, "To prove our love for everyone!"

Then Sam said, "If you're a boy and you *truly* love girls, then you have to become what you love! A girl. And if you're a girl and you love boys, you have to become. . ."

Shara said, "A boy. But, we don't know. It just seems so *wrong*. They try to make us feel and think like the other."

Sam's eyes went wide for emphasis, saying, "*Everything*. Feel, think, sound. And if you don't do it so well, well, if you don't *really* feel true love, then they operate on you and change you for real into the other!"

The four girls mouths had all dropped open. They'd seen demons and abominations but *never* in their wildest imaginations had they *ever* seen *this*. The three youngest looked up to Mandy for help.

Mandy remembered the underground she used to go to in the South and that there were a few *funny* bars where those who wanted to be with the same sex hung out. She remembered a few stories about those places, and even ran across a few who were like that but the girls still were girls and the boys were still boys. Now maybe that was because the United for Christ had rules about dressing and behaving but in the underground you pretty much could do *anything*, and Mandy never heard of *anything* like *this*!

All Mandy could say to everyone is, "I don't know. Liking the same sex like you would the opposite, well, that's never been for me, and I think that's really confused, messed up, but *this*… I don't know."

But Lynnara got that determined look about her, and said, "Well, I do know *this!*" And she stretched her hands over their new friends and the girl suddenly had long hair, a new clean brown peasant dress, and the boy had short hair, with brown pants and shirt. The two stood up and beheld themselves then each other in amazement, clearly loving the transformation but their joy was cut short.

The sound of something large running through the woods right at them drew all their attention. Lynnara created a large fireball in her palm, Mandy raised her swords and Rebecca her bow. A moment later three deer, normal deer, burst from the woods and practically ran them all over. Everyone breathed a sigh of relief but then they heard hideous wailing from behind them. And an odd sound of zapping noises.

In the distance they could see what seemed like sparks. Mandy squinted then ran into the woods. Everyone else took up defensive positions again but it wasn't long before Mandy returned. "You're not going to believe this. One of the deer tried to jump over an *electric* fence but didn't make it." Everyone else just had blank stares, so Mandy repeated, "*Electric fence*, as in a *border* fence!" She pointed back towards it. "*That* has to be the United for Christ, *on the other side!*"

Lana looked back at the two children. "Where do you come from? I mean, where's your home, what country, what part of the world?"

Sam said, "South America, well, *we* fled from there, but it's really the same all through the whole continent. We thought Central America might be better, but it's *worse* there. Then we heard rumors about North America, because many had escaped to there in the past. So we were gonna try."

Mandy shook her head. "We're just on the other side of the *southern* border for the United for Christ. Lynnara, can you just pop us over to the other side of the fence?"

And *that* got Lynnara to thinking because she *hadn't* thought of where she would go after saving the children. She looked over to Lana, but Lana shook her head and looked up at Mandy, saying, "Carla said King Vaughn and Queen Stephanie can't know. That means *no one* can know because if anyone besides us knows, then *they'll* know. Besides, King Vaughn is also *Ranger* Vaughn. Rangers patrol the border."

Rebecca came over and took Lynnara's hand and looked up to Mandy. "Do you really think that fence could stop those demon animals?"

Shara came forward. "It won't. *Nothing* has ever stopped them until now! They were sent after us! *No one* escapes the New International Rules Based Order. No matter where you take us, they will come."

Mandy looked into the two children's fearful eyes. "Then how did you get this far?"

Sam said, "We ran. We had a vision *together* to come here. *And* we heard whispers there's, well, someone called God, called Jesus, who loves us, who created us, so we prayed to Him instead of the King of This World."

Mandy smiled and began to glow golden, the first time they'd ever seen any manifestation from her, and she said, "Well, the Lord Jesus Christ, he *is* King of Kings, and Lord of Lords, and he is *all* Goodness, and *all* powerful, and He's also going to judge everyone and every *thing,* and *no one* is able to escape *Him*. God didn't send us here for you to lose you."

Lynnara shrieked again, threw her arms wide and blue and silver energy sheets went over them. There were so many beasts this time! Many were blown up, but there now seemed to be big cats, too, with flaming eyes, and they either ducked or dodged Lynnara's attack. Rebecca quickly shot three. They didn't seem to pick up well on her smaller arrows. Mandy still had her simitars in her hands and had no time to switch to her bow. Lynnara kept shooting fireballs from her hands but more cat beasts came and many of them evaded her fireballs, too.

Mandy hollered, "Get us out of here, Lynnara."

But she screamed back, "I can't. They're too fast. If I stop firing. . . I can't!"

It was the same weakness Stephanie used to have in battles. Transitioning from one mode such as attacking to shielding and even more so to transporting took time. True, only a few seconds, but with *these* beasts, in a second or two, they'd all be dead and Lynnara knew it. So did Mandy, so she quickly flipped away from the others because one thing Mandy understood about *these* beasts: They knew she was the biggest threat to them because she was the oldest, the largest. Even with all the power Lynnara demonstrated, these cat beasts weren't scared of her, but they were of Mandy and she could feel it. So she used herself as bait to lure them away.

And *all* the beasts went after her. But the simitars she had weren't just average swords. They had been Queen Karen's and blessed with the sacred battle oil King Vaughn had brought back from the mediaeval tomb. In short, the swords had a battle mind of their own! And so she danced with devils and they began to die, but they also began to get past even the swords and their poison claws began to slice into her.

Mandy screamed through the battle, "Get them *out of here* Lynnara,"

But Lynnara cried out, "*NO.* I'm *not* leaving you." And she hurled more fireballs and blew up more beasts because they weren't watching her now. But for every beast she destroyed, two more seemed to come from the woods and also went after Mandy.

But Mandy knew as soon as they killed her, they would turn on the rest. She also knew that from the very first scratch from these demon beasts that she was doomed. She could feel their poison working its way into her. All that mattered now was the other's safety. Through her tremendous efforts to stay alive long enough, she scolded Lynnara, "Don't be a *brat* this time. You *know* you're more important than me. Do what the *Lord* sent you to do, *NOW!*"

When the human demons had attacked Stephanie and Lynnara, Mandy, and Carla, Stephanie had immediately transported them all to safety but Lynnara had refused to go and stayed by her third Mommy's side to fight for her. *That* time she proved successful because little Lynnara helped buy just enough time for King Vaughn to arrive and save them. At *that* time nothing and no one was more important than Lady Stephanie and her unborn child. But *this* time Lynnara knew Mandy was right and she could feel the two escaped children peering deeply into her, begging her to save them. But Mandy and Carla and Stephanie had all become sisters and they all mothers to Lynnara.

Rebecca remembered Mandy's very first lesson when she began to train her as a junior ranger: *We fight because we love. We hurt because we love. Don't let the pain be more important than the love.* With tears streaming but her head held high, Rebecca spoke to her bestest friend, "Lynnara, we have to love *first*, hurt *later!* Mandy wants us to *go.* Jesus wants us to *go.*"

"No, no, *nooo*," Lynnara wailed with tears streaming down her cheeks, her little chest heaving and her little heart breaking. And she could feel Mandy dying, even as she stopped firing and opened her arms for everyone to squeeze in. Sam and Shara were put closest, then Rebecca and Lana behind them, everyone touching each other. Lynnara could feel the poison in Mandy already killing her just like it did to Stephanie and Michael when she unsuccessfully tried to heal them. Images flashed in Lynnara's heart and mind, memories passed to her through the bond between her and her Mommy of when Stephanie had lost Arlupo and the Appendaho but also how Stephanie rose above the pain in order to fulfil what *only* a *faithwalker* could. And with one final cry of torment that even most adults could not bear, they all vanished to the only place Lynnara knew they could go and be safe.

CHAPTER 3

# Best Intentions

*The Father, in his usual place by the orb, shook his bulbous head and wondered how such stupid humans could even taste good, but he wanted to hear the explanation from HrorrarrAggrang as to how he accomplished it.*

*HrorrarrAggrang's Great misaligned Eye smiled in delight. "Equality. To their immature malfunctioning minds they think the word* equality *has the same meaning as the word* same. *So to be equal, everyone has to be the* same. *The same economic status, the same attractiveness, the same power, same intelligence. I also threw in* equity, *which sounds great to them because it sounds like equality and therefore the same. Except that equity means you* don't *treat everyone the same, but, you're unfair so everyone can be the same, so everyone can be equal. And HrorrarrAggrang began to snortle and quiver in demon laughter, because of all things, same intelligence was the most absurd. For Alpha, everyone prided themselves on their own uniqueness, and a special intelligence unique to each demon. That* was *their main hope to rise to the top, that their unique intelligence could best all the others.*

The Father simply couldn't believe the worthlessness in such ignorance, no, stupidity. But one thing amazed him even more than that, so he asked, "But how are you getting them to actually hate themselves and destroy their sex? What does that have to do with equality or equity?"

HrorrarrAggrang's arm tip brushed black tears from his Great Eye then managed to answer. "Because in order to prove each sex is equal to the other, you have to give your utmost love and praise to the other, which, of course means you have to become the other. How dare a man act like a real man, because that's not respecting being a woman. Respecting being a woman is to become a woman. That's true equity. Because when a man gives up his conflicting differences with a woman, he becomes the same as a woman and therefore equal! Same with economic status, power, attractiveness, and intelligence! The rich must give up their wealth, the intelligent must become dumber, the beautiful must become ugly, and those in power must give it up to those who haven't had any, yet. And what better way to do all this than to make laws enforcing it!" And he fell apart at the absurdity and quivered and snortled even more.

Then HrorrarrAggrang said, "And the beauty of this is that real women, who crave attention from truly masculine men because that is their true complement, true affirmation of being a woman, they will feel cheated by men and hate their femininity for giving them a desire these self-destroyed men can't fulfill. It also infuriates them that efemininity is held to be the same as true femininity. The same is true the other way around when women become emasculine. But this gets even better when dealing with intelligence and power because once you hand over rule to morons and those who don't know nor understand power, all hell breaks loose." And that was just what the Alpha desired because all that suffering made the humans far more tasty.

But the Father still couldn't understand this illogic. "But sex. . . they can't become the other sex. All they can do is just destroy their own sex. Lacking masculinity, even cutting off their member, well, that doesn't equal being a female. Same the other way around for females."

But HrorrarrAggrang turned deadly serious. "Ahh Father, but equality and equity isn't so much about their mind's reason, but about their feeeelings. All those who destroy themselves, whether they are male or female, they all have the same feelings. They all feel equal in self-destruction, so they band together in brotherly love. They love the commonality! But even more goes on here because the glow is still ever-present around them and they feel condemned by it. So they hate the glow. Their common hatred binds them all together even more so than their common self-destruction. And right now, that common hatred is focused on the United for Christ because there's so much glow there now besides the mere name of Christianity, which in and of itself is also worthy to be destroyed."

The Father put his tail-tip under his supposed-to-be chin, and rubbed it while deeply contemplating. "No more Christians or Christianity."

"When my plan comes to fruit, then none. Oh, except for the new churches I'm starting. That's even better than no

Christians. I'm having them call it, The Church of True Love!" And HrorrarrAggrang fell apart again, black tears streaming, snortling so hard even the Father's ethereal room began to shake a bit. "That church is a church supporting all perversions of their humanity. All destruction of their humanity. To prove your love for everyone as their God demands, they must embrace all perversions, hence becoming the same, and hence becoming equal and fulfilling equity. They call this, of their own accord, loving diversity. In fact, they say diversity makes them stronger."

The Father could actually follow the illogic of all this up until that last description. His Greatest Eye bleared. "But how can diversity be the same?"

"Let me explain it another way, Father. The glow has given everyone their unique structure both in body, mind, heart, and spirit along with unique abilities. They feel having such structure and uniqueness is unfair, restrictive, so even though they are diverse, they are the same in hating their own structure and uniqueness, in hating the glow. Diversity makes them stronger because it gives them all unique chances to destroy themselves! To all prove they love one another like that."

And that made sense to the Father. That was a value he could identify with and the humans regained their tastiness to him. "Well, with us, we actually found a way to improve upon our structure and abilities because we're Ethereal. But the humans need our help because when they try to improve themselves, all they manage is self-destruction. Let's give them something of us to make them stronger, then we can really enjoy consuming them."

*"Ahh Father, that is already being done. But Father, I thought you kept track of all this."*

*"No time! All my efforts have been in studying what's happening way up* there! *It turns out Karen's orb can do that!"*

There had been much discussion as to where King Vaughn and Queen Stephanie should personally attend the ceremonies. It had been a long time since they had been to the South, to the United for Christ, and since they were as much a part of unification as the North, and since Vaughn and Stephanie now lived in the North, they felt it was wise and necessary to have the proceedings on the very stage where Stephanie used to speak to all the people of the South, in the very town in the South where they had lived and fought to defend, where Stephanie had built the very first castles.

This was the very same stage where Stephanie had fought Demon Fred, her father, twice. The first time he humiliated his daughter, but the second time she *finally* put an end to him. It was the same stage where Captain Joshua died defending Stephanie, his wife, and the very same stage where in his dying breaths, he joined Stephanie and Vaughn together as true husband and wife. It was the same stage where Judge Matthew had humiliated Stephanie, and the same stage where she had bested him in having him marry Stephanie to Joshua instead of Judge Matthew marrying her. It was the same stage where Joshua's funeral was conducted and where Colonel Asa, Joshua's brother, had revealed Stephanie's secrets to the whole world and where he joined Stephanie and Vaughn in holy matrimony. It was also the same stage where Vaughn was promoted to Captain in Joshua's stead, a position King Vaughn never relinquished, and none inquired as to his intentions.

When they arrived early in the morning via their *faith-walking* ability to ethereal travel, they popped straight over to the senior judge's headquarters. Queen Stephanie wore her original Appendaho dress of royal blue with Appendaho golden embroidery around her neck and at the hems of the long sleeves and full length dress bottom, while King Vaughn insisted he simply wear his smart black Captain's uniform. Supreme Judge Samuel, in his righteous black robe, promptly called both the military and the rangers to come join him. Such comradery hadn't existed until after the truth came out about all Stephanie and Vaughn had suffered at the hands of corrupt judges. But ever since the evening when Lady Stephanie preached the undying perfect love of the Lord Jesus Christ and the true nature of the Holy Ghost, and how we share far more in common than not, ever since *that* evening when she couldn't help weeping before the whole nation because of such love for the people but simultaneously being overwrought from the severe danger to her unborn child which she had hidden from everyone, ever since in the midst of such turmoil little Michael, still inside his Mommy, began to glow for all the world to see, *then* the people began to understand what she suffered for them, for *their* welfare and not hers, because she could have abandoned them at any time to save herself. The people as a whole, both judges and military and common folk all clung tightly to their TV sets weeping, too, and ever since then when *all* people pledged their undying love for Stephanie, the people became more and more united in the true love of their Lord Jesus Christ. 'Our lives for you. Our lives for you and your child,' they had chanted as one, willing to give up their own lives for them! It seemed like just yesterday even though two years had passed.

Stephanie hugged Samuel and tears flowed down her cheeks. When the military and rangers showed up, Vaughn went out with them in pure joy as one of them, because he was still a ranger, too, but there was also much to catch up on.

Stephanie sat with the judges discussing the spiritual developments of the country. Neither of them had a word to speak about unification because they first needed to catch up on current events. But when that topic finally came about when Vaughn returned, both Stephanie and Vaughn were both shocked by the answer. The heads of the rangers, military, and Judges all said together, "We trust you. Whatever you think is best!"

In the back of both their hearts, Stephanie and Vaughn felt uneasy but since there was so much propelling them forward to unification and elections, they couldn't bring themselves to heed any possible warning or trepidation. Besides, it was natural to feel uneasy with anything new, though more than once Stephanie had checked all around her for transparent gray or black arms but saw nor sensed none.

Judge Samuel, in his righteous black robe, head Judge of the whole United for Christ, whose short-cropped temples had been fully white for some time, yet the rest of his hair was still solid black, put his arm around Stephanie and hugged her like a daughter as they now slowly walked down the sidewalk of the Judge's compound to the stage, yet a good ways away. "I never thought I would say this, but *you*, a *woman*, have made as much difference to our country, a *fantastic* difference, as our founders of the United for Christ."

Stephanie just shrugged her shoulders. "What do you *really* think of the original founders of the United States? Did you read what I sent you?" The book, one that had been found in an ancient museum, was quite thick, and though all Stephanie had to do was put her hand on it and absorb its meaning in total, she knew Judge Samuel had to read it page by careful old page.

The old judge rubbed his chin then stopped and took Stephanie's arms then turned her to face him squarely. "Every single page! Benjamin Franklyn and the rest, and Thomas Paine's commentaries are seriously impressive. Their discussions about their Constitution, their careful reason is all impeccable, as well as their heartfelt desires to get it right. And sad to say, what they were trying to guard against, that being corruption taking hold of government, well, even we, the United for Christ, were almost destroyed by the lust for power. Having three branches of government instead of our two, may have been better and might *now* be better than what we currently do. Although, being *head* Judge, I am reluctant to divide power by three instead of two, and actually, we Judges, to be honest, had more power than the military, quite a bit more. But I also feel that the way the Constitution of the United States of America designed the judiciary, well, I truly feel *that* is our current judges best calling, a *true* calling. And being so partitioned will help to keep our focus where it should be. I only hope the North won't reject us as their Judges."

Stephanie replied, "I've explained to the North quite clearly that being Judges constrained within the Judiciary of the United States Constitution will be far different than your rule in the United for Christ. They all now recognize the need for such Judiciary."

As they all began walking again, Vaughn looked over to Colonel Asa beside him. The Colonel's straight posture, short dark black hair, and perfect, unwrinkled, dapper black uniform all radiated authority and respect, though Asa's humility was well known and regarded by everyone. Vaughn asked, "Are we to accept having no role in government *at all?*"

Colonel Asa immediately noticed the *we* in Vaughn's question, meaning that though Vaughn would no longer be King, he was *still* very much Captain, and, in fact, had kept in close contact concerning those duties all the while being King. Asa responded, "Well, as long as *you* run for President, as we agreed. I feel only *that* would give us the transition we need to make all this work."

Vaughn shook his head. It was the *only* thing they changed in the constitution, that being the age required to run for President. And *that* was a special accommodation solely for him which both sides had agreed upon. Vaughn said, "Sir, you are assuming I will *win* the election. I haven't even formally declared my candidacy yet. We only floated that to the people as a possibility. Plus, we don't know who else will run for the office."

Judge Samuel had to butt in. "King Vaughn, don't let your humility turn into foolishness. Everyone still wants you as King and Lady Stephanie as Queen, both in the North and South, so we are *sure* everyone would have you as President." And Colonel Asa agreed.

Vaughn ran his hand through his close cropped dark brown, almost black hair, as his stomach lurched but he didn't know why. Stephanie's heart began pounding and *she* didn't know why. Both of them suddenly felt overwhelmingly small. And so the rest of the walk was in silence with both Judge Samuel and Colonel Asa deep in prayer.

When they ascended the stairs to the outdoor stage, which was fourteen-feet-deep and twenty-eight feet long with a podium dead center in the front and seats behind, both the Colonel and the Supreme Judge walked Vaughn to the pedestal, each flanking him at his sides. Stephanie stood just behind her husband but to his right a bit and behind Samuel.

The large courtyard was packed with seating extending as far back across the grass as possible and many standing on the sidelines. All the Judges from across the country were there in the front rows, and all the military leaders behind them. It was a beautiful early summer afternoon, still cool but the sun warming everyone comfortably. Vaughn cleared his throat and began to speak.

"It is with great pleasure and reverence that I and my Queen stand before you today in the company of such wonderful souls," and he crisply saluted Colonel Asa and bowed his head to Supreme Judge Samuel. Asa returned the salute and Samuel nodded to Vaughn and they took their seats in the front row behind while Stephanie came to Vaughn's right side.

Vaughn continued, "I am so very proud of my wife, my Queen, my Lady for all that she has done to help you all recover from the war." Cheers went up so loud and deep they seemed to shake the stage. Everyone up North felt the same way and shouted for joy at their TV sets. There seemed to be the Spirit of Love uniting everyone, it was that palpable.

Vaughn continued, "It was not easy at all for me to come to the conclusions that I have already shared with you, that a constitutional government is far better for us than a monarchy, that such government would engage you all in a much stronger, more beneficial way than just being loyal subjects. It was not easy to decide to relinquish the power, the authority we have as your rulers because *we* know what it right for you. We know we do. But there is great love and talent amongst all of you, also, and to allow you all to take a far more active role in governing your lives is simply stronger and better for all. It is with no further ado that I declare that firstly, the North and South are reunited to be as they were, the United States of America."

The cheers went up all across the country. Much had been taught to everyone about how such a new government would work, how representation would work from the local levels on up. Many people waited with excited anticipation, as well as others who conspired to gain power and influence. They all cheered their King and Queen for their own, very personal reasons. True, life was unbelievably better than two years ago.

With King Vaughn and Queen Stephanie's *faithwalking* abilities, they were able to aide immensely in rebuilding even the condemned big cities that were quarantined due to the plague from the Great Religious War over a hundred years earlier.

Vaughn held up his hand and the silence was immediate. "The question is now before us as to who will run for the very many offices of our new governments. To all local municipalities we have designed generic paper ballots for you to use in your elections. All you have to do is just write in who you want to vote for. We have also provided to you state and Federal ballots that enable you to do the same, *and* we have in place election workers in every locale to collect and count the ballots and how they should verify and report their results. All that is left to be done is for people to declare their candidacy for the various offices."

The people all cheered raucously again but this time Vaughn let it go on for some time. It was right that deep celebration should be held at this moment. Then Vaughn raised his hand again. "Elections shall be six months from now, whereupon I and my Queen shall step aside from being your monarchs."

Someone in the audience shouted, "Declare! Declare you're running!"

Another shouted, "King Vaughn for President."

And a wave of chants erupted in King Vaughn's favor, whereupon he held up his hand and once again received silence all across the country. "It is with great respect to you all that I declare I am running for President and my lovely wife, Stephanie, for Vice President of the United States of America."

Cheers erupted again but King Vaughn quickly cut them all off. "Now, according to our new Constitution and its guidelines, please be advised that even for President, there can be those who desire to run for that office."

The sound of sharp clapping came from behind them. In fact, it was so loud everyone in attendance could clearly hear it and saw King Vaughn and Queen Stephanie turn their backs on the crowd to see who it was. The sound of the clapping didn't exactly have a celebratory ring to it. It had a tinge of challenge, even mockery, but it was so subtle it likely went unnoticed by most people's minds except their hearts would definitely register it at some level. But to *faithwalkers* the meaning was clear.

Stephanie and Vaughn searched between those sitting at the back of the stage, who were all shaking their heads in denial. The clapping continued but no one was there . . . except, slowly, an image began to materialize, and then a figure, and everyone on stage had their mouths drop open, not knowing what to make of this, nor what to do.

Part of Stephanie and Vaughn wanted to rejoice and run over to him, but part of them knew it *couldn't* be him. Part of them wanted to raise every defense they could muster in power, but part of them longed for it to be true. How could it be? They and the whole country, both North and South saw the recording when he blew himself up along with Hrorrar-rAggrang, the huge demon.

Jargono, well combed straight black hair, same rare brown eyes as Stephanie, and in his standard Appendaho tan tunic and brown pants came forward to them and hugged Vaughn then Stephanie. "I know you missed me, so I couldn't stay away." They hugged him back with an odd mix of mere reflex, trepidation, inner cringing, yet hope. That odd mix left both King Vaughn and Queen Stephanie, as it were, frozen in time, almost as if some kind of power held them in place, but it was probably just the sheer incongruence of these events. Jargono smiled deeply at them then went to the podium.

"Surprise!" he said, and stretched out his arms wide to everyone, who all began to slowly cheer him. The people were also digesting incongruity. Then someone shouted, "Remember how great Jargono had made us?"

And another shouted, "He gave his life for us so we could have a better one."

And someone else shouted, "He was gracious to Vaughn and Stephanie. Even let them rule in his place because Jargono thought he was going to be dead. He became noble, our *best* leader."

Another shouted, "Vaughn and Stephanie are great but *only* King Jargono could *kill* a demon. Run for President! Run for President!"

Someone else shouted, "No! King Vaughn and Queen Stephanie deserve it!"

Someone else shouted, "NO! We have a *new* government now. Let's *celebrate* it! What better way than to have *elections?*"

And *that* idea actually took hold, *especially* because King Vaughn and Lady Stephanie had taught them to love the governmental processes of democracy, well, a representative republic. And so, excitement suddenly built up and people began to chant, "Run, Run, Run. . ."

And so Jargono held his hand up and got immediate silence. "Alright. Begging your pardon Vaughn, Stephanie," and he bowed his head to them but then turned back to the crowd, "Since you desire it, let's have a *real* election. I declare my candidacy for President. I'll name my running mate later."

Cheers went up across the North while not so many cheered in the South because they still remembered the evil Jargono had forecasted against them. But more than that. In the pits of their stomachs they knew something wasn't quite right.

Jargono held up his hand, then declared, "King Vaughn and Queen Stephanie have done the impossible. They have brought back the United States of America!" And Jargono threw his fist into the air. "No longer will we be just the *foot* of the world, to be stepped on, takin' for granted, mocked, and abused." And a huge TV screen appeared mounted on an iron stand on the stage beside Vaughn and began to play news scenes from the old USA depicting protestors burning the American flag. "Those people were coerced by foreign countries who *hated* us. Well I say NO MORE!" And he threw his fist in the air again and people started doing the same until everyone, well, most everyone threw *their* fists in the air, and likewise, everyone watching TV.

Jargono held up his hand for silence and immediately received it. "I propose a new flag, to go along with the stars and stripes." And the TV showed the old United States of America flag but then a fist superimposed over it. "So everyone can know *not to mess with us!*"

Back at the King and Queen's castle, James was shaking his head, then folded his hands on his desk and bowed his head upon them in prayer. He wanted to turn the TV off but knew he needed to at least hear it in the background.

And while everyone still had their fists in the air, Jargono disappeared! Seeing *that*, the people began chanting his name and pumping their fists, and repeating his last words, NO MORE, NO MORE . . .

Vaughn and Stephanie looked at each other. They wanted to tell their audience that they didn't think that flag concept was appropriate, but now just didn't seem like the right time. Vaughn remembered James's warning about someone appealing to the more practical rather than the ideal. *But this* fist *isn't practical. It's inspiring a false sense of pride.*

Knowing her husband's thoughts, Stephanie sent him her own, *Inspiring* pride, *true or false* is *practical, if you want to win an election! It gives everyone an inflated sense of value that will last as long as the illusion can be maintained. And that* feeling is very *practical to them. Who doesn't want to feel powerful?*

Stephanie stepped forward and Vaughn stepped aside. She remembered all the times she was caught unprepared and how painfully foolish she looked to everyone. *Well, not this time!* "Dear People here and all across the country." Everyone immediately hushed in the South, for they *knew* that Dear People salutation was going to be followed with a depth that would sink deep into their hearts. But the people in the North begrudgingly lowered their fists, flattened their mouths, and tried to pay attention. They didn't like having their good feelings diverted.

"We've been through so much together." And she waited for people to focus on their memories. "I've wept with you, felt the depths of your suffering, and we have worked tirelessly to *utter* exhaustion to raise all of your standards of living. King Vaughn has singlehandedly guided our economy to be one of the strongest in the world. If you can remember, the word *hope* wasn't ever spoken, nor even dared enter our minds let alone out hearts. I remember when even I used to feel that way. But King Vaughn changed *everything* for me, and for you, too!"

The crowd immediately started cheering, as well as everyone in the South. The ones in the North nodded to the truth of that. "As you know, both King Vaughn and I were born in the North. But we weren't *privileged.* I was born into a poverty that aged my mother beyond her years. Because of our former governments' corrupt support for mind altering drugs, at a young age I was *destroyed* by them. They supported my gang that sold them but when I wanted out, they intended to brutalize me. And when they had trapped me, I wanted to die. But more than that, when I wept, *cornered* in a *stinking* bathroom, I suddenly realized that what if I *didn't* die? What if they brutalized me and I still lived? And I had decided to *make them* kill me."

No one had ever heard this part of the story before. *This* even grabbed the rapt attention of the Northern people. In fact, many women there painfully understood such feelings. Stephanie continued, "But right after those thoughts, my dear King Vaughn appeared at a *second* story bathroom window straining to hold on, standing on the tiptop of an old rickety ladder that was too short. But he had seen me try to jump out that window and decided he had to try and rescue me."

Everyone, North and South, were silent. All focus of minds and hearts were waiting to hear more. "He told me to climb onto his back and he would lower me down. I couldn't believe it, how I could even do such a thing, how *he* could even be strong enough. But when my old gang began to bang on the bathroom door for me to come out, I rushed to escape. I climbed out and put my feet on his shoulders because the ladder was too short and that was the only way to make it work! But as he tried to lower me so I could grab hold of the ladder, too, I fell!" And Stephanie paused to let it sink in. People's hearts were in their throats as if they themselves were out on that ladder.

"Without thinking, Vaughn bent himself so I would fall onto his back, and I *did*. I slammed down onto him and I grabbed hold of his neck with my arms with all the strength and fear that I had and I held on for dear life. But the momentum of my fall caused the ladder to pull away from the house and it went *completely* vertical!" And she paused again.

Wives and girlfriends listening to the story squeezed their men's arms, and even they had a tear in their eyes but so very inspired by such bravery. "I cried out then because I didn't want Vaughn to get hurt. *Me?* I was *worthless* to myself back then, but *Vaughn,* he didn't deserve to be harmed. I cried out to God when the ladder began to ease *the wrong way.*"

And Stephanie spoke very softly now, yet made it so everyone could hear. "Right now, *all of us* are at the top of that ladder!" And she paused again and the revelation sunk into *everyone*. They could feel it. Wives and girlfriends nails dug into whatever they were holding on to.

"God heard my prayer and sent the ladder banging back against the house instead of falling. My prayers today are the same, but for all of you. We need the ladder to fall in the *right* direction. *Our* hearts, King Vaughn's, and mine, you *know*. And we have helped you become strong but *not* through some trick, not with our *fists* pumping in the air like some *stupid* adolescent *boy* trying to make up for his *lack* of manhood with such vacuous displays." And the *meaning* of her sternness was now *clearly* felt by all, and those up North hung their heads even though many didn't even want to.

"We all have seen in these last few years things we never *ever* thought possible. *That* man, though he looked like Jargono. . . Well, all I can say for now is that he is *not* the Jargono Vaughn and I came to love!" And with that, Stephanie looked at Vaughn, then at Judge Samuel and Colonel Asa, and all four of them disappeared!

CHAPTER 4

# The Times
# Are a Changin' Again

*This time the Lord allowed Mafferan to finally share knowledge with Yinauqua, his wife. She knew something was up just from her husband's demeanor and she had immediately began to investigate by pumping him full of well-intentioned questions. When the Lord saw it and that this time Mafferan couldn't escape, the Lord popped them both into his very special room. And the Lord said simply, "Tell your wife everything!"*

*After Mafferan had finished his long explanations, Yinauqua went to her knees and bowed low with tears shining rainbow colors amidst the golden glow of the room. Mafferan knelt beside her and put his hand on her back. "Now we are finally together and you know all of my secrets. And you know why I had to keep them."*

*Yinauqua sat up and they stood up together, arm in arm. She looked deeply into her husband's eyes and asked, "Do you trust me, husband?"*

*"Completely," Mafferan replied.*

*And after she sent him a huge telepathic picture which he couldn't immediately decipher, Yinauqua disappeared!*

Marta knew she had to time this perfectly. The beasts had ravished Mandy but rather than just consume her, they all backed up and waited for her to be fully converted by their poison. The demon dogs howled and the demon cats screeched like demonic infants. Mandy lay on the ground with severe tears all over her flesh, with blood matted hair and blood soaked shredded ranger's uniform, but the poison from their fangs and claws wouldn't let her die. But neither would the Holy Ghost, either. She managed to blurt out, "Oh Lord Jesus, I'm being torn *apart* inside. Please let me *die*. Let me pass, and *burn up* my body before it transforms." The pain in her flesh was only outdone by the pains in her soul that tried to escape what it couldn't escape and this repeated over and over and over. . . an indescribable hellish torment.

When Marta heard her prayer, she appeared kneeling beside Mandy and placed her hand upon her chest. The demon beasts all sprang at her but when they landed, it was upon bare ground because Marta and Mandy had disappeared. And reappeared in the empty Ethereal Corridor. Marta now shined with rainbow colors, and spoke to Mandy who was laying before the kneeling Marta on the Corridor's spiritual floor, "The Lord has heard your prayer but sent me to give you a choice."

Mandy couldn't believe it. *Is this an angel? But I'm still in the very same condition.* After coughing up blood twice and spitting it out, she said, perhaps a little *too* contrarily, "*Choice?* It doesn't seem like I have any left."

Marta could feel every bit of Mandy's suffering and her tears rolled down her cheeks. But Marta, having suffered so very much when *she* was mortal, that allowed her to look beyond Mandy's condition. "As soon as the Lord brought you to *be*, you will *always* have choice. *That* can *never* be taken from you. The Lord has beheld your service to Him, how you cared for Lady Stephanie, His anointed, and how you sacrificed yourself to save the others. I can end your suffering right now and escort you into the Kingdom of God where you will have eternal Peace."

Mandy looked into Marta's eyes, and when she did, it brought her focus beyond her torment. "That's my *choice?*" And Mandy painfully laughed at the absurdity.

"That's one of them. The other is that I take you, as you are now, to where the others have escaped to."

"As I am *now?*"

"Yes. I was allowed to come to you because of your prayer. Being up *here* is part of that answer. But now that we *are* up here, the Truce between Heaven and the Ethereal does not apply. But you *still* have a choice."

"But… but can't you heal me? How can I go to them like *this?*" And Mandy held out her torn arms indicating them and the rest of the wounds upon her whole body.

"Because that would be deemed *too much* interference."

And then a horrible rasping voice along with an oppressive presence behind Marta startled her. "Dinner time!" She never expected to meet anyone *here*, especially now, and *certainly* not a demon, and *not* one so huge. HrorrarrAggrang wasted no time and while Marta quickly stood to face him, he had already reached out his tail to grab Mandy. Whereupon, Mandy, who had loosed it the moment she heard the demon, swung her ax into his tail! She shouldn't have had the strength to do that but feeling that Marta was in danger, Mandy's true nature asserted itself even beyond the poison. After all, Mandy was a *Ranger!* And it didn't matter to her that she was in the Corridor.

An axe, or any Earthly weapon shouldn't have had any effect at all, but all of Mandy's weapons were blessed with special holy battle oil. The severe burning in his massive tail had Hrorrar-rAggrang quickly withdraw it up to his massive black eye where he shed tears of black oil upon his wound. But that gave Marta the time she needed. Remembering all that she had seen Lady Stephanie do, she gave no thought to the fact that she, Marta, was *not* a *faithwalker,* and she raised her right hand and a golden fireball with a burning bright blue center left her hand, struck the demon in his giant black eye, and blew up!

HrorrarrAggrang's surprise was evident, for he had been able to study Marta through the Father's orb that Karen had made. "You're *not* a *faithwalker,*" he blurted out as he disappeared but then reappeared a safer distance away. Clearly this meal wasn't going to be as easy as he had thought.

But the demon's statement shockingly brought Marta to realization. "Wow! He's right! But. . . Wow!"

Mandy had managed to pull her bow from her shoulder, and being shielded by Marta's golden glow, she fired an arrow without HrorrarrAggrang being aware until it struck him dead eye! The blessing sunk in along with the arrow so when HrorrarrAggrang's arm reflexively pulled the arrow out, the blessing didn't leave with it! Realizing the growing burning deep within his Great Eye, HrorrarrAggrang had to reach in with his now healed tail tip and fish around deep inside to pull it out. But Mandy had already fired several more arrows that struck his body.

Meanwhile, Marta got over her shock that she, without thinking, had just acted *exactly* like Lady Stephanie, and she raised her hand again and threw a giant, glowing cage around the demon! She hadn't really thought about doing *that* either, but it just seemed right!

HrorrarrAggrang really began to be irritated with all this. This cage was *ridiculous,* but first things *first.* He pulled out all the arrows and fished out the blessings that had contaminated him. Mandy was going to fire more arrows, but Marta said, "No need. Save your strength for your choice. Just watch."

HrorrarrAggrang cast away the last blessing then slammed his massive tail against the cage expecting to smash it to pieces but the glowing golden cage suddenly oscillated with rainbow colors and it wasn't damaged at all! Marta was in shock, again, because, though she had a feeling the cage would hold, she didn't really understand what she had automatically done! Then Yinauqua appeared beside her, also dressed in a mere full length brown peasant dress, with her long gray hair hanging in the traditional Appendaho three braids, but she glowed with many colors.

Yinauqua smiled pleasantly at HrorrarrAggrang, saying, "You're the one who tried to *eat* my husband! I'd recognize you anywhere, even in a cage!"

HrorrarrAggrang stopped struggling, pushed his embarrassment away, and peered at her. "I'm sorry, you're just not notable. It doesn't ring any bells. After all, I've eaten so many."

Yinauqua wagged her finger at him. "Tisk, tisk, I said *tried.*"

Now *that* drew sharper attention from the big ol' demon because there were *very* few that only fit into *that* category. *Actually, only one!* HrorrarrAggrang thought to himself, but he couldn't believe this mere *woman* had *any* relationship to *him.* She didn't even look that tasty, except she did display a bit of power with all those colors dancing about.

Mandy was bleeding all over the Corridor floor. Her dress was shredded and matted with blood and she knew she couldn't hold her head up to watch much longer. All of her wounds throbbed horribly. And she was running out of strength to fight the poison that was shredding her soul. Even the Holy Ghost inside her struggled to stay within her! But Mandy also perceived that Marta had help now, that a Ranger was no longer needed, so she laid her head back praying for the Lord to finally take her from her intense misery before it was too late. But Yinauqua turned to Mandy and raised her hand to her and multicolored sparks floated over and into Mandy, "The Lord Jesus has heard your prayer, but before He answers, you must make a choice!"

*A choice,* Mandy thought. She felt a bit strengthened by the blessing but not much. *What choice?* She thought with an absurd irony in her thoughtful tone.

Marta looked upon her, and said. "You'll see, dear Mandy. First we have to deal with our uninvited guest." And Marta turned back to HrorrarrAggrang and became stern. "You've *rudely* interrupted me." And Marta raised her open hand toward the demon then closed her fingers ever so slightly and the cage shrank a bit!

HrorrarrAggrang noted it but hardly believed what might actually happen to him. "You've *broken* the Truce. I have a *right* to consume *that* soul *and* body up here." And his tail tip pointed at Mandy. "You've *greatly* interfered by bringing her up *here* and now I *demand* my *rights!*" And he roared that last phrase and the Ethereal Corridor shook.

But Marta would have *none of that.* All her mortal life she'd been intimidated by those more powerful than her. Besides, she had been blessed to understand about all these things now. "The *Truce* has *not* been broken. I was sent by the Lord *Jesus* to answer her prayer." And when she spoke the Lord's name the whole Ethereal Corridor shook!

But HrorrarrAggrang would have none of it. He remembered the Lord when he had been up in Heaven. He wasn't impressed then, and *less so* now, *especially* since he *knew* his plan was going to succeed. "I'm speaking about this *cage.* You are interfering with my lawful *right to dine!*" And when he spoke that last phrase, the Corridor shook *again!* Then HrorrarrAggrang grabbed the cage with his tail tip and pulled violently but his tail tip fell off and wriggled on the silver Corridor floor outside the cage!

Yinauqua strolled up, smiled, and picked it up. A hole opened in the cage and she handed it back. "No hard feelings!" She said quite politely.

HrorrarrAggrang accepted her offering. He *had to.* After all, this was a *part* of him. "Thank you," the great ol' demon said. "*Who* was your husband?"

"Is," is all Yinauqua said.

Something about this woman's *dry* sense of humor stirred deeply in HrorrarrAggrang. It was the *exact* sense of humor that only one man had. "You *couldn't* be *Mafferan's* wife. I'd expect him to have someone far more worthy of consumption." And *that* was about the biggest insult any demon could utter and Yinauqua knew it.

"Before we let you out, one way or the other," And HrorrarrAggrang took immediate note of Yinauqua's *meaning,* while Yinauqua looked back at Marta and Marta closed her fingers a bit more, "I just want to ask you a question." And the cage shrunk *again.* It wasn't pressing up against the ol' demon yet, but he had to wrap his great tail around his neck a few times.

Mandy weakly called out, "Hey guys, ahh, could you speed this up just a bit."

Everyone looked at Mandy who seemed to be fading away. But all three said, "In a *moment!*" though with different tones and different meanings! It was clear, though, this mere *mortal* would just have to *wait* on her destiny. HrorrarrAggrang added, "*Patience* is shining blackness."

But Mandy answered back, "That's *virtue,* you *reprobate!*" Mandy suddenly had an extra fire burning within her she'd never felt before.

But HrorrarrAggrang answered back calmly, instructively, "That's *exactly* what I meant! You'll seeeee!"

Yinauqua began tapping her foot impatiently, and HrorrarrAggrang said, "What question?"

"I was innocently strolling by when I happened to look into the Corridor and saw these two *children* and then *you* popped in. How did you even know they were here so *very* fast?"

"Simple. I've been cultivating *that* one for some time. I saw that other child pop in and out so I knew to come here."

But HrorrarrAggrang had *no* idea who or *what* he was dealing with, *until* Yinauqua changed her appearance to her Heavenly one. Now she wore her Appendaho dress of deep burgundy embroidered with neon blue Appendaho design over her heart and around her waist. The shining spirit of the neon blue stung the demon a bit. HrorrarrAggrang remembered studying her and her husband and that Mafferan had gone through great lengths at times to avoid her. HrorrarrAggrang had originally thought it was Mafferan's weakness that made him do that but now he beheld a strange power he didn't understand *at all!* He instinctively closed his glistening Great Eye!

Yinauqua's face shined brilliantly gold but her rich brown *eyes* shined with such a brilliant blue light that her natural eye color was hard to discern. Then she *squinted* at the demon, saying, "That's only *partly* true! You *weren't* surprised *at all* when you popped in on them. But not only that, you seemed *very* familiar with Marta in particular. *Why?*"

HrorrarrAggrang, Marta, and Mandy were all amazed. Even Marta hadn't seen *this!* Not that she spent much time with Yinauqua, but still . . . what *was* that power? When he finally opened his Great Eye, he was abashed at what he said- the actual *truth!* "My Father and I have been watching Marta and others for some time now, *particularly* because they influence King Vaughn's and Queen Stephanie's outcomes so much. *She* is responsible for King Vaughn's escape from *hell!*" And he pointed his tail tip at Marta.

Marta couldn't help herself, and said, "Oh, not really. We just prayed a bit."

Mandy was *completely* astounded.

But Yinauqua wasn't going to be distracted *now*. This was the *whole* point of her being here! "*How?*" And though the one word question was simple, her complex *meaning* slammed into the demon's huge bulbous head.

And HrorrarrAggrang blurted out, "Queen Karen made us an orb. We can see into Heaven with it! It's . . ." HrorrarrAggrang strained to hide what he was about to say but simply couldn't resist Yinauqua's power to force the *truth* from him, "able to see *everywhere* into Heaven with the orb's full power to discern and influence!" And HrorrarrAggrang couldn't believe what he just divulged. *If the Father ever finds* this *out, he'll consume me for* sure.

What the ol' demon didn't know was that Mafferan had popped into the Father's secret, darkest room a bit ago, and, "Good to see you again, ol' chap!"

The Father couldn't believe it. *No one* entered here without at least knocking, and certainly no one *invaded* here! Just then there was a knocking sound!

"Sorry ol' chap. That was a bit delayed." But the message from Mafferan was *clear.* He could actually *read* even the Father's very thoughts!

The Father did something he hadn't done since he was in Heaven, he threw up a barrier so *definitely* no one could enter his mind. That's how he was able to make war in Heaven for so long. He was able even to let them *think* they read his mind even though they only saw what he wanted them to see. He hadn't had fun with those tricks in quite a while so he decided to employ them again.

But Mafferan wasn't interested in his mind any further and that greatly saddened the ol' demon. "You might be wondering why I'm here!"

The Father became irritated with such simplicity so he just merely gathered his very massive tail around his neck and tapped his tail tip against his massive arm and waited.

Mafferan waved his hand and the Father's original orb appeared over in a corner of the Father's room. "Sorry ol' chap. There's so much interference in here." As if Mafferan didn't mean for it to materialize in the corner but he walked over to it.

The Father couldn't help but leave his new orb and float over to *his* original one. *This* was the orb that *Vaughn* used to hold the whole Ethereal hostage, and if Vaughn didn't reset *something* every year, the *entire* Ethereal orb system would *crash!* So he *had to* float over to it. Mafferan opened up several programs, and various screens of the orb's inner workings popped up. "I wanted to ask you a very *serious* question because it is in *both* our best interests to solve this lil' problem."

The Father was busy studying the programs. Some of it related *exactly* to Vaughn's blackmail program. The Father immediately asked, "*What* question?"

"Well, you see, the boy has been way too busy to bother, what with your antichrist giving him all that trouble, and, well, I being an orb expert who's even *way* beyond his means, I was a bit embarrassed to even bother him. So I thought, well, the only other orb expert that even comes *close* to my abilities is you!"

The Father ignored the obvious insult that Mafferan was actually a better orbist than him. He had *no* idea what Mafferan's game was. *But* the fact that part of Vaughn's program was actually opened to *him* was too good to be true so the Father studied what was there while insisting, "What *question?*"

Mafferan said, "Oh, right. Well, it seems the boy's *very* ingenious program has a bit of a bug. It, ahh, might not function *quite* as intended!"

And the Father could tell Mafferan was actually telling the truth! This *was* serious! They could lose all their orbs except for the Father's, but more importantly, a mishap like this could lead to all-out war. But a war *without* their orbs would be a *great* disadvantage. "What do you need help with. You realize showing me all this is to your direct disadvantage?"

"Oh, not so. Even if you understand *perfectly* the whole thing, Vaughn *still* has to validate it all every year or . . . well, you know what happens."

But the Father wasn't so sure about *that,* but he wasn't going to tell Mafferan that. "I see. Well, show me the problem. We'll work on it together."

At the same time, back in the Ethereal Corridor, Yinauqua said, "Now *that's* the *whole* truth!" She then smiled very demurely at HrorrarrAggrang and asked him seriously, "Am I worthy to be consumed now?"

She wasn't even using her power on HrorrarrAggrang when she asked, but he nodded, "Completely!"

Yinauqua smiled tenderly this time. She looked *very* sympathetic which made HrorrarrAggrang *very* uneasy. And Yinauqua said, "Materialize the Father's new orb up here!"

HrorrarrAggrang couldn't believe what he just heard. Neither could any of the others, but Mandy, being a Ranger with a military mind realized that *everything* leading up to this point had to have been planned! This extremely complex development *couldn't* have just happened by *accident*. Mandy suddenly felt a deep urge to hang on to life a bit longer.

When Yinauqua saw that the demon hesitated, she asked him, "Are you feeling alright? Marta, loosen the cage a bit, dear. I think this ol' demon needs more air!"

HrorrarrAggrang didn't like the absurdity. There was no *air* in the Ethereal Corridor, and besides, demons didn't *breathe,* but for that matter, *no one* needed to breathe up here.

Yinauqua said sweetly, "Fine. Don't worry your pretty lil' tail about it. I'll just let it slip that you told me all *that* and the Father. . ."

HrorrarrAggrang cut her off. "If I do that, the Father will know *instantly!*"

But Yinauqua smiled, and said, "Trust me," then she paused to let that phrase sink in, then said, "You have *no* choice!"

It was true! Now HrorrarrAggrang *distinctly* sensed Mafferan's hand prints all over this diabolical scheme, but Yinauqua said, "Actually, *this one* is all mine! But my husband trusts me completely." And then she turned very dark and stern, so much so *everyone* up there felt uncomfortable, so suddenly the Father's new orb appeared beside Yinauqua!

Yinauqua reached *deep* into the orb for a bit then her hands flew around like lightning upon its surface and then she smiled again, and said, "OK. All done. You can send it back now!"

HrorrarrAggrang stared in stunned silence with not even a ripple to his continuously rippling spiritual hide! Even his shimmering went dull! But Yinauqua simply said, "The longer you hesitate, the more chance your *Father* will find out."

In the next instant, the orb vanished.

Mafferan looked deeply into the Father's Great Glistening deepest hugest Black Eye. "Well, ol' chap. I think that about fixes *everything*. Status que restored. Nice working with you. You know where to find me if you need me. You'll have to send someone other than Grinchback, though. He's, well, no more, if he ever was a demon in the first place!" And Mafferan vanished.

The Father felt uneasy but didn't know where to start exploring that. "This was *too* easy. But I couldn't resist. True, that *was* Vaughn's *whole* program but *also* true that there's nothing I can do about it." He floated back to his new orb and proceeded to study Heaven even more deeply.

Yinauqua said, "Marta, you can let him loose now. We have an understanding."

Marta hesitated but trusted Yinauqua so the cage dissolved. HrorrarrAggrang considered immediately consuming them all. *That* wouldn't be hard, now, but he *also* knew Yinauqua could read his mind and that she would escape, which meant it was too dangerous to harm the others, so he vanished. He knew he would just have to allow a bit of time to go by. The more time, the more plausible would be his denial if the truth ever did come out.

Yinauqua took Marta's cheeks in her hands like a dear child and kissed Marta on the forehead, and said, "The reason you are able to be like Lady Stephanie, who *is* my dear daughter, is because you have loved her so *very* deeply that even up here you became one with her! And in that oneness, you have also become in *many* ways *just like her!*" And Yinauqua disappeared!

Marta had tears rolling down her cheeks. *Everyone* in Heaven knew that Lady Stephanie was her hero. Mandy cried too, for she loved Stephanie so deeply, as well, and somehow could imagine the truth Yinauqua just spoke. But all *that* went way past Mandy's love and abilities. She hadn't even been holy for that long, and clearly Marta was an angel.

But Marta laughed. "I'm no angel. I'm really not hardly worthy to even be up in Heaven! I killed my mother!" And she looked deeply into Mandy then.

Mandy was dumbfounded but had to look back as deeply into Marta's eyes and part of Marta's life experience transferred right into Mandy's heart and mind! Mandy immediately started weeping bitterly because *nothing* she had *ever* suffered came even close to what Marta went through. And Marta was shocked again because she *knew* this mind transfer was also something Lady Stephanie had done.

Marta said, "Now for your choice. You are definitely ready to go home to Heaven, well, Paradise."

But Mandy knew there was more and she brought herself out of her weeping state to focus on the present. After all, Rangers *always* focus on the *present*. That was one of her first lessons. So she steeled herself. "That's one side of the choice. What's the *other*, again?"

"I can send you to where Lynnara and the others went but there is no guarantee as to your future Mandy. The antichrist rises quickly now and he will destroy and overcome *many* holy people. There are *no* guarantees. *But* if you pass away now, in the Corridor, I will be able when you pass to separate you from the poison. And since HrorrarrAggrang is no longer here to contend with me, I won't have any trouble at all to free you. You should come *home,* Mandy!"

But Mandy looked deeply into Mata's eyes, but this time she showed her the love Mandy had for the girls and Carla and Stephanie and Vaughn. And Marta said, "If I send you back to the girls you will *still* be in the condition you are in now. And once out of my presence, your suffering will multiply exponentially. Come home Mandy!"

Mandy began to weep again. She couldn't help it. "There has to be a way I can be healed."

"Lynnara has dealt with this poison before in Lady Stephanie. She couldn't heal her then, and even though she's now far more adept, she can't heal you now, either. Only King Vaughn's staff was able to free Stephanie and you don't have access to that. In fact, you *can't* have access to it, for if Lynnara somehow summoned it, Vaughn would discover everything and Carla's warning will come to pass."

"But Carla never told us what would happen,"

And Marta said, "Then *that* tells you everything you need to know! The battles now waging are within a hair's breadth of going one way or the other. If King Vaughn or Lady Stephanie have to deal with what you all are dealing with, *everyone* will lose miserably! It's simply too much. Come *home,* Mandy!"

Mandy wept even more bitterly. It was no small thing to ignore that *Marta* was telling her to come home, *especially* now that Mandy knew so deeply Marta's character. Still feeling the poison in her, Mandy wanted nothing more than to go *home* to Heaven, or Paradise. And even the Holy Ghost gave her the OK to go. But. . . Mandy wasn't a Ranger for *nothing*. It wasn't her God given calling for *NOTHING!* She remembered when she first met Lady Stephanie. Mandy was roaring drunk. A *slut.* And Stephanie popped right in front of her and Mandy ran her over. At that memory, Mandy began to laugh uncontrollably!

Marta looked at Mandy quizzically. This certainly wasn't what she expected. As a master teacher, she always prided herself on anticipating the responses to her lessons. This wasn't what she thought Mandy would do.

When Mandy saw Marta watching her, trying to figure it out, Mandy shared the story and Marta burst out laughing, too, but she still didn't understand why Mandy should be thinking of that.

Mandy said, "Stephanie had been watching over me even before I met her and she was *determined* to save me from myself! Even though I *hated* her meddling, was *insanely* jealous and *even* betrayed her for a while, she made sure, *even* while going through her own *terrible* suffering, that I would be saved. Those girls *need* me, I don't care *what* you say! I don't care if you say there's no way for me to be healed. There *has to* be a way. And if it means that I suffer a while, even a long while, I don't care. Just *please.* At least give me the strength to bear up under this poison and suffering so I can help them!"

Marta began to cry. She'd always loved Stephanie the most, but now she saw why Stephanie went through such great pains for *this* one. Marta's heart burned inside of her and she held out her hand and a bottle of the golden Oil of Peace appeared there. "Give this to Lynnara." And when she handed the bottle into Mandy's hand, Mandy disappeared.

Marta went to her knees in the Corridor and wept and prayed for them all, She had thought she was teaching Mandy, but Mandy's heart taught her, so with that new understanding of love, Marta prayed in earnest. Then she moved herself into the part of the Corridor where the girls and now Mandy were, and Marta waved her hand and a wooden chair appeared and she sat down to watch over them.

CHAPTER 5

# We Only Have One Life

*Yinauqua returned to find her husband preparing his famous fruit salad. No one knew how he could enhance their flavors and blend them so perfectly well but still each fruit be so distinct. Yinauqua's mouth began to water as she came behind Mafferan at the kitchen counter and hugged him from behind.*

*Mafferan, still slicing more fruit, said, "So, I take it we'll have no more spying up here?"*

*Yinauqua laughed, but paused, which Mafferan picked up on immediately, so she said, "Welll. . ."*

*That response only heightened Mafferan's anxiety because he knew his wife, that she could sometimes be too clever. "Pray tell, dear, what exactly did you do to the orb? I mean, can we talk freely here or not?"*

*Yinauqua laughed again. "I did nothing!"*

*Now Mafferan put the knife down and turned fully around to face his wife. "What? Then why did we go through all that to accomplish nothing?"*

*Yinauqua was really enjoying this. She rarely even exceeded her husband's intellect.* "Dear, I had reached my arm very deep into Karen's orb for some time and then I manipulated quite many things on the orbs peripheral control panels." *And she smiled slyly,* knowing *that the contradiction would only create more anxiety in her husband.* But he needs this from time to time to keep him sharp.

*Mafferan peered deeply into his wife but just couldn't pull out of her mind what was really going on, but he knew well that women* always *have that ability to shield themselves like that so he went to a new strategy. He pleaded with his eyes.*

*Now* that *always tugged at Yinauqua's heart, so she said,* "Even though I manipulated the orb quite a bit, I did exactly nothing!"

*Mafferan saw she told him the truth and Yinauqua noted the complex look on his face. She wanted to preserve that expression in her memory, one of the few times the great wise Mafferan was stumped. . . by his wife. But she decided she'd tormented him enough and confessed,* "Dear, if I really did throw the orb off, then they'd eventually catch up on it, and then they would go through all sorts of calculations to figure out the truth. But then they might actually stumble upon the real truth and we'd be at a great disadvantage."

*Mafferan calmed himself as much as possible, then monitored his tone closely.* "But if you did nothing, they already have the truth."

*And* this *is the point of reflection where Yinauqua was waiting for her dear husband to arrive at. She pinched his cheek like he was a baby then merely said,* "But they won't trust it."

*And she walked away, walked out of their circular home, and down the many colored stone street to visit Noah's wife.*

*Mafferan was amazed, and thought to himself,* And they'll be forever trying to figure out the truth where it's not! *And his heart burned with an extra love for his dear wife.*

Mandy was laying on another forest floor but this one was quite different. This one was dry with the sweet smell of corn and hay fields wafting in the gentle breeze and there was *no sense* of imminent danger. In fact, there was no sense of danger at all. It was a still, cloudless night, though, and instead of thick, heavy clouds and no moon, there was a full one which brightly lit the little clearing where she rested. *Why here?* She wondered, then tried to turn her head to look around but she suddenly noticed the severe pains all through her soul and body and she gasped and curled up in sheer torment.

*I'm a Ranger,* she told herself and forced her head to turn even though her neck muscle was ripped open. *What?* A round shelter covered in mostly yellow raincoat pieces was about fifteen feet away. *It can't be! It's much bigger than Stephanie described.* True. When Lynnara had arrived she knew it would be too small so she had bowed her head and enlarged it! It now stood fifteen feet in diameter, six foot high, with a shallow domed roof but all raincoats!

Severe waves of pain and now nausea wracked Mandy, and she felt like she would pass out, so she wailed, *"Lynnaaaarrraa…"*

Everyone heard the bloodcurdling scream. Lynnara instantly popped into the Ethereal Corridor, then seeing Mandy immediately popped beside her and knelt down. But she instantly sensed the severe amount of poison in her and gasped and tried to catch her breath. She *knew* what this meant. Moments later Lana and Rebecca ran out and fell on their knees to each side of Lynnara. Sam and Shara came, too, but kept a bit of distance not wanting to interfere.

Lana said, "Let's all try to pray for her and she went to put her hands on Mandy but Lynnara, eyes wide, grabbed her arm.

"You can't touch her! It's too much poison!"

Rebecca cried out for her mentor, "Lord Jesus, *pleeeease*."

And all three girls' hands began to glow. A sweet giggle resounded all around them and they all recognized little Michael's spirit! The glow in their hands was from his blessing before they left and the giggle was meant to express only now! The girls looked at each other then all in one placed their hands upon Mandy. The poison immediately raced to them to infect them, too, but was soundly rebuffed, but then the glow left the girls' hands and entered Mandy!

The poison attacked the glow and the glow fought back and Mandy began to thrash wildly as the two powers swirled inside her. Without thinking, the girls all leapt onto Mandy and did their best to hold her down to keep her from hurting herself further. Her blood began to smear all over them. The poison tried to run around the glow to get to the girls but the glow was faster and protected them all. And the battle raged on!

A glowing golden dome with blue highlights appeared over them, just in case! Lynnara had learnt well from Lady Stephanie. Shara and Sam stood outside of it in amazement. And the battle raged on through the night. When Lynnara sensed Rebecca and Lana were weakening, she used her *faithwalking* power to strengthen them. Even so, this was too much for an eight-year-old and two seven-year-olds.

"Oh Lord Jesus," Lynnara cried through her exhaustion as Mandy thrashed with even more force because her torment seemed to be increasing.

The battle between little Michael's blessing and the poison, even though it raged for hours, had made no headway, and the girls could barely restrain Mandy any longer. But if they didn't restrain her, she would wildly thrash herself to death without knowing what she was doing because it was the poison that drove her to kill herself. The glow could chase it around and keep it from converting her but not from doing herself harm. *That* was Lynnara's job.

Lana let go of Mandy and closed her eyes. It was time to look elsewhere for help, but without her eight-year-old strength, her two best friends wouldn't last long. Suddenly, Lana wasn't there in the forest. She was up in the Corridor Lady Stephanie had described to her. But this was a vision. There, a beautiful young woman with rainbow colors wept and placed a bottle of holy oil in Mandy's hand and then Mandy disappeared.

Lana came back to herself. She immediately grabbed Mandy's arm and looked in her hand but nothing there, and neither in the other. She began thrashing through the leaves around Mandy, but nothing. Lana screamed so loud it seemed to part the air around them. "Lord JESUS!" And a wind rose and began to swirl. The girls dove upon Mandy to shield her with their last bit of strength to protect her from the flying debris. Twigs, branches, and small stones pelted them. But moments later there was nothing but calm. Lana quickly looked around.

The ground had been swept clean but about ten feet away toward the shelter there was a glow and Lana ran towards it. She swept the bottle up into her hand and without stopping she opened it and ran over to Rebecca. Pouring a small amount into her hand, for she had seen how Lady Stephanie and King Vaughn had used such preciousness, she placed her hand upon Rebecca's head. Then she went to Lynnara and did the same. And then she capped the bottle and rubbed the residue on her own head.

When Lana finally had time to notice, she realized the oil was so powerful, it put her into a daze. Lady Stephanie had anointed her with such oil once before, right before she and her Mom were baptized. But *this* oil was even far more powerful. Strength surged in them and they resumed their positions over Mandy, praying now more deeply than ever. Mandy began to howl like a demon dog, then like a demon cat. Lynnara looked over to Lana, and gasped out, "Give me the oil."

Lana pulled it from her secret ranger dress pocket and Lynnara grabbed the bottle then opened it. She remembered what her third and bestest Mommy ever had done to Fred her demon father, but she couldn't pray *that* prayer. "Lord Jesus, free our sister from this *evil,*" and Lynnara poured the entire contents onto Mandy from her head down to her legs and it immediately sunk into her. Mandy roared so loud it deafened everyone and a force exploded around the girls and threw them all a good ways away. Then Mandy burst into flames all over!

Marta had been weeping the whole time, from the start of when the girls began to pray for Mandy. She wanted so badly to go to them, to help, but Mafferan had explained to her the cost of interfering. But when Marta saw all *this* transpire, she began to pound upon the Corridor's silver floor wailing the Lord's name, "*Jesus, Jesus Jesus. . .*" Like Stephanie when the Appendaho were being slaughtered, Marta didn't have to be looking at what transpired below. Her inner vision was connected to it and she saw it all. She not only saw it, but felt *everything,* everything about Mandy and the girls.

The Corridor began thundering when Marta's fists pounded upon it. "*Jesus, Jesus, Jesus. . .*" Demons and Heavenly beings alike couldn't help but turn their attention there. But Marta was oblivious to everything except the girls and Mandy. She focused so deeply upon them that it began to seem like she was right there with them.

Lynnara, Lana, and Rebecca's mouths dropped open but not because of the great thunder. Shara and Sam quaked with fear and shook terribly but managed to keep watching. Marta, like Stephanie when she first popped in on Lynnara's previous family because of her deeply empathetic grief, Marta had materialized in their midst pounding now on the forest floor and calling the Lord's name.

Lynnara remembered when Stephanie had popped in on them just like *that!* But *this* time she wasn't going to let whoever this was go. Last time she faked sleep. *This* time she sprang up and dove upon Marta, begging, "*Please*, help our sister. Help her *now!*"

Marta was dumbfounded but she remembered when this exact same thing happened to Lady Stephanie. "I . . ." She didn't know what to do, as she sat up and looked at the girls then over to Mandy still popping and bursting in flames and thrashing and crying out various sounds between herself and the demonic forces.

Lynnara remembered how Stephanie had apologized and said she wasn't supposed to be there, so she said to Marta, "I know you're not supposed to be here, but . . ." And she paused because she looked so deeply into Marta now and saw the incredible love she had. She was so much like Stephanie. And Lynnara said, "You go back up just like you never came down! I understand!"

If Lynnara had said *anything* other than *that*, Marta just might have. Instead, Marta threw her arms around Lynnara and squeezed her so tightly it was like they were both in another world. She now experienced what Lady Stephanie had experienced when she rescued Lynnara from Jargono's fire and they hugged for the first time, knowing the depths of Lynnara's wonderful soul. Then Marta got up and ran over to Mandy and dove upon her, the flames engulfing her, too!

Between the Oil of Peace, Michael's blessing, and what started out to be just a well-intentioned hug but now evolved into Marta's new considerable *faithwalking* power fully intent on battling the poison, too, the corruption began to swirl out of Mandy and into the air. Once there, Lynnara raised her little hand and beams of silver light struck the demon essence and turned it into ash.

When the flames died down, the girls ran over and Marta eased herself off Mandy and knelt on the ground. Mandy had been healed and even her uniform looked brand new but it seemed like she was asleep! Lynnara said, "Oh, oh! You weren't supposed to do that, were you?"

Lana put her hand upon Marta's shoulder to comfort her and Marta had immediate tears because of the feelings passing into her from Lana's touch. It was one thing to empathize and feel everything *that* way, but to actually *experience* it like *this*, well, there were no words. Lana said, "Something bad is gonna happen to you because you helped us when you shoudna'."

Marta stood up and straightened her brown peasant dress, and said, "I know, but I just couldn't help myself. I love you all so much."

Rebecca, Lynnara, and Lana all slammed into her with strong hugs and prayers. And then larger arms, and Mandy laid her head upon Marta's shoulder. The inundation of all their feelings all at once left Marta reeling as each of their consciousnesses flooded her. Whether it was just Marta's newfound faithwalking abilities or simply because she was now a heavenly being, she didn't know, but she fully embraced all their emotion and returned her own deep love to them.

Finally, Marta said, "OK. I have to go."

But before she did, Lana said, "You daughter came to be a very good woman and *she* had a daughter and two sons. *That* daughter is my *Mommy*!"

The truth of Lana's words slammed into Marta, their eyes meeting with growing knowledge. Through that connection Marta could see Lana was indeed her very own blood. Bawling, Marta collapsed to her knees as her past tribulations flooded her, and to see that all she suffered through bore such wonderful fruit. All three girls patted, stroked, and hugged her. Somehow, Marta knew this all was supposed to happen just like it did and that she was supposed to be blessed with just such a precious gift.

Even though she'd been in Heaven a good while, she never found out what happened to her daughter that she fought so hard to save. At only fourteen years old, she had to give the newborn infant away to a good Christian family right before Marta was executed for murdering her mother to protect her daughter.

Marta finally stood up, wiped her tears away, and looked into Lana's eyes, and Lana said, "You're my Great Granma."

Marta said, "You're my Great Granddaughter. I'm very proud of you."

Lana said, "I'm holy now. After a while, we're gonna spend a *lot* of time together *forever*. And my Mommy, too. She's holy, too. She's your Granddaughter."

Marta smiled at them all, and Mandy said, "You saved my very life, my very soul. I don't know what to say."

Marta just smiled with tears running down her cheeks again, but something suddenly came to Marta, an experience she'd *never* had before. It was *definitely* faithwalking, but she hadn't seen the like from Lady Stephanie before! Marta looked at Lynnara then placed her hand to the side of her head, whereupon Lynnara, whose eyes widened, nodded in understanding. Marta said, "Are you *sure* you can return it *here* when you need to?"

Lynnara nodded again. "I think so, because you just showed me how you're gonna do it. So I think I can."

Marta raised her hands and the shelter and everyone disappeared! And reappeared at what smelled like back down South! Marta said, "Lynnara, you *know* where you're at. Show them. Then, when you know it's the right time, return back with *everything* and *everyone!*" And Marta vanished!

In the Corridor Marta strolled at an average *faithwalking* speed. *Whatever happens to me, it was all worth it.* But that was *more* than a whimsical thought, as pain shot through her back and she was thrown down onto the Corridor floor and then she felt squeezed all around with hideousness. A demon she'd never seen before had wrapped her up in his coil. "You've broken the Truce. The *balance* will be *satisfied* when I *consume* you."

Marta looked deeply into this demon's Great drooling Black Eye whom she didn't even know. Through her pain and torment she remembered Lady Stephanie being in this same position but Marta had something else in mind to restore the balance. "OK. Go ahead!"

The demon was actually quite surprised. He had been ready to cast black oil all over her at the first sign of resistance. He had expected this to be a prolonged glorious fight. *But no matter. A meal is a meal.* And his Great Black Eye opened wide and sucked in Marta's soul and body whole!

And Marta found herself chained to a wall just like King Vaughn had been, but a special force field she created emanating just above her skin level kept her from feeling any pain now at all. Her wrists glowed with oscillating colors and the shackles crumbled and she stepped free. The beasts and other demons who had been ready to mock and torment her fled from her brightly glowing presence. She walked up to a pulsating object, and said, "This looks demonly important." And she grabbed it with her brightly glowing hands and began to yank it around.

Moments later the demon's Great Black Eye vomited her out. Standing before this sizable foe, she smiled sweetly just like Yinauqua. "I told you that you could eat me. I didn't say I would digest." Then Marta grew stern. "You got to *eat* me so the *balance* is restored. *Now,* leave *now* or I'm going to eat *you!*"

The demon's not so great Eye grew as wide as possible. He'd never heard of *humans* eating demons, but he'd *never* heard nor seen *anything* like *this* human. So he vanished.

Mafferan popped beside Marta. "Well, we all wish you wouldn't do anything like *that* again, please?

Marta went to one knee like she'd seen Mafferan do, "Forgive me, my lord. I should *never* have allowed myself to pop onto Earth like that. I interfered. I accept my punishment,"

Mafferan lifted her chin with a finger then laughed hard! "No, no, I wasn't talking about *that. That* was supposed to happen! Why do you think the Lord Jesus picked *you* for the job? Well, for *many* reasons but *that's* certainly one of them! No, no. I was talking about you letting a *demon* consume you!

In fact, all of us lost track of you. And when you popped back out, everyone had to give me my best fruit back!"

Marta stood up and shook her head. "Wait a minute. You *bet* on me?"

"To *win!* Of course I did." And Mafferan threw his arm around Marta just like she was his very own daughter as they strolled down the Corridor. For her part, having never experienced a father, she relished in his affection. Something about it seemed to mend something in her she wasn't even aware of, but she felt a new wholeness she'd never experienced before. And being up in Heaven, one would think everyone there was instantaneously whole. But now Marta realized that, for some things, there are no substitutes on either side of life.

So many new experiences flooded Marta. Now *seeing* that her terrible mortal struggles produced so much goodness that she had *no* idea of until now, that she had *real* family on Earth now. And now experiencing Mafferan like the father she never had. She reached her arm around Mafferan and clung to him with a precious love she'd never experienced before. Without thinking, she said, "The Lord's mercy and love are amazing! I never knew afterlife would be like *this!*"

Mafferan smiled, looked down at her while they walked, and said, "Oh, you ain't seen nothin' yet kid!"

Then Marta suddenly remembered how Yinauqua took her cheeks in her hands. At the time, she hadn't thought about it because of Yinauqua explaining why Marta was now a *faithwalker.* But as they strolled, she could still feel Yinauqua's motherly touch and her hand went to her cheek and tears came into her eyes. Such touch was foreign to Marta, but it also seemed to be mending her. Marta looked silently up at Mafferan and he looked into her soft, rich blue-green eyes.

"Yes Marta, we would absolutely love to have you as our daughter! There be many here who made it but none of their parents nor fore-parents for many generations returned to the Lord."

Marta said, "I didn't even know you could do that in Heaven."

Mafferan nodded then looked down again as they strolled. "It's something that occurs naturally dear child. The creation of man, woman, and child mirror Almighty God in his forms and relationships of the Father, the Son, and the Holy Ghost, a perfect complementary unity which *defines* the very essence of reality. So, at some point, to fulfill reality for us, we *must* also have up in Heaven a father, a mother, and children!"

# CHAPTER 6

# Finally, the *Faithwalkers* Come of Age

*Naamah wrinkled her brow at the sound of knocking at her back door. She had been busy decanting her special mixed fruit wine for Noah. Even up here, it was greatly appreciated, though it had little to no effect on a Heavenly constitution. Seven unique Heavenly fruits went in, one beaming golden liquid with a pink blush eventually came out. She wiped her hands on her apron and went across the kitchen to the door, wondering, Why would anyone use the back door? And knock. No one ever knocks except . . . But it wasn't Mafferan! It was Yinauqua, the first time she'd ever visited. Flustered, Naamah took off her apron, hung it on a hook beside the door, smoothed her long white hair, and said, "What a surprise. Please Come in."*

*Yinauqua bowed her head then hugged her foremother. "After all you went through with Noah, you look marvelous!" The twinkle in Yinauqua's eyes said so much more. She looked past Naamah to a rather large, clear, swan shaped pitcher with* a beautifully glowing liquid inside. "It looks so beautiful, I'd almost want to try it myself. Noah never lost his taste for it, huh?"

Naamah shook her head. "Not in the least. Did you know, he planted the vineyards, but it was me who made the wine? I mean, think about it. That all started before the flood. A hundred-and-twenty years he preached the world would be destroyed. I knew when he got home, he needed something to relax with!"

For some reason Yinauqua burst out laughing. She never knew any of this but looking into Naamah's eyes, she knew it all to be true. And Naamah knew Yinauqua knew and laughter rolled from her, too. She took Yinauqua's arm and led her into the circular living room with scant old wooden furniture. "I'm sorry it's not lavish like everyone else but the boat left a lasting impression upon us." She pulled two old rickety wooden chairs opposite each other and they sat down face to face. Naamah further said, "Ok. You came to the back door. I suppose the knocking is just idiosyncratic to you and Mafferan." In other words, this was going to be of the most troubling nature.

Yinauqua nodded. "The demons always watch the front door. And Mafferan protected your home from invasion when he last visited."

Now Naamah straightened and she tingled all over. She knew Mafferan had been charged by the Lord to keep secrets, but it was now apparent that his wife shared in them. And she was now sitting right across from her. But why would she want to talk to me? I'm really a nobody in history. I mean, no one even hardly knows my name.

*"Naamah," Yinauqua emphasized, "Without you, I am sure Noah couldn't have made it. The foundation stone under a house is not seen but we know the support it gives, even if many don't appreciate it. But I know Noah does. Likewise, my dear husband, the famous King Mafferan, does as well. We need to talk deeply. I need your advice!"*

When Judge Samuel and Colonel Asa materialized, they had no idea where they were. A beautiful, ornate, oval, mahogany dining room table with carvings around its perimeter and matching chairs occupied the center of an immaculate dining room. Matching hutches lined the spacious room, their glass doors allowing view of fragile porcelain tableware. Delicate glassware occupied the upper shelves. But what stood out was a giant computer screen mounted on the wall opposite to the head of the table.

Vaughn smiled, bowed to them, and said, "Welcome to our home. *This* used to be Jargono's castle before he bequeathed it to us. But my Lady Stephanie has redecorated most of it. This table set, however, we both agreed to keep, because there are so many good and profound memories surrounding it."

Stephanie smiled, and said, "I'm sorry for just plucking you off the stage like that, but..." And she hesitated and looked over to her husband.

Vaughn nodded that he understood, reached out his hand and his staff appeared in it. He looked back over to his wife and Stephanie nodded then raised her hands and the whole room glowed greenish golden. Vaughn raised his staff and its head glowed silver then that brilliance became part of the protective barrier Stephanie had erected. Just then, James came through the kitchen door dressed in his smart butler uniform. He bowed his head to them all then indicated they should take seats. Proceeding over to a hutch, he placed enough drinking glasses between his fingers, but Vaughn said, "Get one for you, too, James. You've *earned* it!"

Looking rather startled and embarrassed, which meant his stoic face ever so slightly grimaced, he nodded in compliance then distributed the glasses. Vaughn had to point to a seat for him next to himself because James had *no* intention of joining them at the table. It just wasn't proper.

After retuning with a beautiful bottle of peach-colored wine, filling the glasses, and saying, "*This* is one of our finest, made by the former King Jargono, himself. I hope you appreciate it." Then James straightened his uniform and rigidly took his seat next to Vaughn, who sat at the table head.

Stephanie, to Vaughn's immediate left, looked deeply into his eyes then nodded to him, and Vaughn said, "Colonel Asa, Judge Samuel, James. . ."

James immediately interrupted, "Sire, I mean, well, you're *still* the King to me, but, well, Sir Vaughn, I don't deserve my name to be mentioned in the same breath as our esteemed guests."

But Vaugh shook his head, "You are *not* just a butler, James. I have *always* regarded you as my *closest* advisor. Let me explain." Of course James wanted to deny it but he couldn't interrupt again because Vaughn continued to speak. "James, I am *sure* you watched the proceedings," and he nodded he had, "and that you said to yourself, 'I told them so,' and you would be *exactly* correct."

Stephanie leaned toward James and now spoke. "Dear James, to *you* first, we do sincerely apologize. We knew all along you were correct, from the time we embarked to teach democracy and push for unity two years ago!"

James wasn't exactly *sure* of their meaning but he sensed its depth and that they had hidden something all this time from him. Judge Samuel and the Colonel peered intently at all of them.

Vaughn picked up from his wife's lead, bowed his head slightly while saying, "My apologies to you, Asa, my dearest friend *first*, and also my commander." And Vaughn stood up and crisply saluted and Asa stood and returned the gesture in like manner. Vaughn continued after being seated again, and with another head bow, he said. "And my apologies to you Judge Samuel."

Stephanie sat up straighter, and said, "It's not that we deceived you."

"It's just that, well," and Vaughn looked down and hesitated.

Stephanie tugged her dress to pull out any wrinkles, then said, "We couldn't tell you the whole plan even from the very start because our enemy would have found out and immediately reacted."

Vaughn peered deeply into Colonel Asa's eyes while saying, "And we were in *no way* able to answer such an attack! Believe me, I assessed *everything*. I have *never* ceased being your Captain!"

All eyes were wide as the Holy Spirit gently filled the room with a foreshadowing of the meaning to come. Stephanie hung her head and when she looked back up at them her eyes glowed golden. "Vaughn and I had lengthy, *deep* discussions about this."

Vaughn looked down again, saying, "We kicked around many scenarios."

And looking straight at everyone, Stephanie said, "But we always came back to what we've *already* done."

And they both paused, which heightened everyone's anxiety until James surreptitiously cleared his throat, his not so subtle way to urge one of them to speak because they shouldn't treat *these* guests like that.

Vaughn and Stephanie looked at each other again, and Stephanie nodded to him, whereupon his stare into everyone intensified. "My dear friends. We knew from the start this democracy thing wouldn't work! Nor the unification!"

Stunned, they all sat frozen. *No wonder Vaughn's gaze is so piercing*, they thought. The Colonel began shaking his head, then the Judge, but neither could put into words what they were feeling and sensing.

Stephanie folded her hands upon the table, *definitely* imploring them, then she spoke up in a very Queenly fashion. "We did a lot more than just study the former United States Constitution. We studied their political history all the way back even for fifty years prior to The Great Religious War! That's more than a hundred-and-fifty years of *scrutinization!*"

Vaughn leaned back in his chair, leaned on his right arm, and began rubbing his chin, *definitely* a more regal posture, then continued. "The truth is, that War was probably a Godsend even though it killed so very many! Because had the political events continued on track as they had been proceeding in the United States, there would have been *no* Second Civil War! The far left. . ."

"Which even back *then* were the minions of the Beast that we are *now* dealing with."

"Would have *completely* taken over the United States in such a way there would have been *no* Second Civil War!" And Vaughn looked over to Stephanie in disgust for what he knew she was going to describe, but this part was *clearly* the *faithwalker's* breadbasket.

Stephanie turned dark and everyone felt her anger and readjusted themselves in their seats, and Stephanie's stare turned sharp. "The *Beast* had even back then managed to place many of his people into political positions of power. The far left pushed this *perverse* gender bending *crap* even back then. Those groups of protestors we now see, much more up here in the North but they're also down South, with their *funny* colors and their *perversion* demanding their *rights,* well, back before the Great Religious War, they had managed to take most positions of power or their sympathizers did. They controlled all of education, social services, media, the federal government, most large businesses, and had iron control through what used to be Canada and Europe." Stephanie looked to Vaughn, but Vaughn knew Stephanie wanted to continue so he nodded back to his dear wife.

And she nodded back, "Alright." Then she leveled her gaze back into everyone, and raised an eyebrow, saying, "The only places they *didn't* control were rural and still a *weak* majority in the southern states. But the *Christians* back then were *terribly* feckless. You can't imagine. It was *they,* through their weakness and *ineptitude,* who allowed the Beast to take over the Northeast and West Coasts and *all* major cities. And they tuned all those places into a *godless criminal and perversion haven!*" And the whole room shook and black rays beamed from Lady Stephanie! "Sorry. Sometimes I *still* forget and lose control a bit."

Vaughn decided to give her time to cool down, so he leaned forward, folded his hands on the table, and continued. "They had studied deeply their Christian enemy and found ways to introduce a lethal propaganda into all their entertainment, policies, and news. Christians, their values, *even natural family structure,*" and the room shook again but this time the black rays came from Vaughn, "Sorry. Even natural family structure was *demonized* and *that* perversion was taught as *normal* in their schools, *even* elementary school! You see, when I was, well, let's just say I had to spend some time down under and I had a *lot* of time to study history and other things. So I actually had access to *a lot* of detail."

Stephanie *had to* interrupt, and jumped in. "I couldn't *believe it* when Vaughn was finally allowed to tell me. I was *sick* for a while just thinking about it. You see, the *Christians* were so weak that *even* down South in all their schools this perversion was taught!" When Stephanie saw that neither Asa nor Samuel's *mind* could understand, she bluntly said, "Men having sex with men. Women with women like what was described in the first chapter of Romans!"

And Vaughn couldn't help but continue, his eyes once again turning black and piercing. "But *worse!* In Europe they decriminalized sex with animals. And on our West Coast in what used to be called California, *they brought back the ancient false gods* of the *heathen* before them. *Those* people *sacrificed* children to those gods!"

There was a dead stillness in the room. Asa and Samuel had completely forgotten about the original discussion and what this all had to do with it. They looked at each other visibly shaken, which was saying *a lot* from real men of this caliber. Asa said, "Please proceed. Somehow, all *this* has got something very important to do with *now.*"

Stephanie spoke up. "The *Christians* were so *weak* that they couldn't even get most of their children to follow their ways. *Plus* they allowed themselves to foolishly believe they couldn't have more than like one or two children!"

Samuel ran has hand through what seemed to be instantly graying hair, and said, "This is *hard* to hear, but I think I see where this is going. The elderly were all conservative and still barely holding things together, but once *they* died off, the votes wouldn't be there, and the South would fall."

Vaughn said, "They called them the red states, and *yes,* the demons had planned for them *all* to fall, but the Muslims who started The Great Religious War messed up their plans by destroying all of the large cities which gave the rural and small town Christians more say. Plus, the War seemed to have sparked a deeper revival of their faith."

Stephanie said, "*That* allowed the South to be what it is today! It gave Vaughn and I a place. . . to escape to!" And Stephanie's chest heaved for a moment then she wiped tears from her eyes and all were moved by her, for they had heard of all their harrowing exploits.

After a pause, Vaughn said, "What does all *that* have to do with today? A *whole lot!* Because, here up North, the demons have clandestinely introduced those same strategies and even down South to some degree they squeezed them in. Criminality, *drugs,* whoredom, lasciviousness, and *utter perversion.* Back before the Great Religious War, they *even* had created over *one-hundred* genders! And men that said they were *women* and *vice versa.* And they're even bringing *that* back here, *now!*" Vaughn had to stop before his anger brought down the whole castle!

Stephanie raised her eyebrows, and continued. "You all know I, well, pop around at times. Well, I'm able to pop around and watch things without *anyone* knowing I'm watching. The North is in *terrible* shape. Outwardly, they seem like they love us. And they *do* love the much better economy. But secretly they make fun of us. Frankly, they *love* their immorality. It was *so* horrendous observing all this that for the last year, I couldn't even bring myself to spy much at all, because I felt I knew where all this was eventually going!"

Vaughn leveled his gaze into them again, saying, "It just wouldn't take much for them to vote against me! I've been knowing that from the start. I mean, *we grew up here!*"

The others were beside themselves with confusion. They all wanted to ask, Then *why* did you abdicate and hand everything over? But they couldn't bring themselves to say it out loud.

Vaughn turned to James in all seriousness. "There's a reason *you* are my trusted first advisor. If I had held onto the Kingship but the Beast wanted to bring us down, what would he have done?"

James turned a bit red because sitting in the company of the esteemed Colonel Asa and *the* Supreme Judge of the South, he didn't feel worthy to speak past them, but something from the Holy Ghost itself prompted him to answer. "Well, clearly, the Beast would have fomented insurrection through cleverly planned conflicts, including assassinations in key places, sabotaged economic progress, and encouraged a perverse but highly propagandized underground and other such tactics."

Stephanie looked over to the Colonel and the Supreme Judge. "And what would have *had to be* our response?"

Judge Samuel stared at his folded hands upon the table not liking the images in his mind. "You two would have had to put the rebellion down."

Colonel Asa continued, "But the enemy would have planned for that, so he would have escalated until you two would have had to *directly* intervene with your personal abilities."

And Vaughn turned back to James, "And what effect would *that* have had?"

James was shaking his head in dismay, forgetting that such personal displays weren't becoming of his station, but he met Vaughn's eyes, and said, "They would have used your direct involvement to attack you as oppressors. They would have caused the people to *fight* with their *whole* lives to overthrow such unfair rulers! But to be honest, in *truth,* they *know* you are nothing of the sort, that you are truly compassionate. And so they *don't* fear you as they did Jargono and Queen Karen. *Them* they feared and would have *never* entertained for long *any* thought of rebellion."

Vaughn folded his hands on the table and looked squarely at them all, his gaze still holding the presence of a true King. "*Then* what does the Antichrist do?"

Judge Samuel, with a sudden deep insight, shook his head, then met Vaughn's gaze, "He pops onto the scene as the reliever of oppression, the *savior* they all long for."

Asa continued, "Then there's full scale civil war, *but,* as you pointed out, we were in no way prepared, especially having just fought the demon war and then all our efforts going into rebuilding. *But,* if they can take control through *elections,* then there's no need to waste their resources on a war that they can win through peace."

Vaughn leaned back in his chair, folded his arms across his chest, and nodded. "You are correct, Sir." Then Vaughn continued, holding them all in his intelligent gaze. "So, for the past two years, while my Lady and I have fervently 'preached' democracy and unification, and *all* our general unprotected conversations have been about how *well* everything is going, we *both* secretly convinced all the small military and judge stations to arm themselves to the teeth with special weapons! My apologies to you both and to your administrative staffs and officers, but if we had notified *any* of them, then our plans would have been discovered."

Stephanie hung her head in embarrassment, but then looked at them with soft eyes, "Vaughn and I learned a valuable lesson from studying the demons, and *that* was that the demons don't waste time with underlings unless it's for their greater purpose."

And Vaughn, still leaning back with arms crossed, said, "Which means, since the *demons* are predominately responsible for even our mortal enemies strategies, that meant none of them would be paying attention to the smaller stations. They would only be watching command and their immediate subordinates!"

Stephanie beamed with golden light. "All of those small stations, having all created secret armories, simply can't hold any more weapons!"

And Vaughn added, "And since we are *still* very much a bunch of small towns, as opposed to grand cities with million populations in need of huge military complexes, well, we're pretty much battle ready now! It's one of the reasons we slow-walked repopulating the refurbished mega-cities *down South!*"

James looked at Lady Stephanie and Vaughn and wiped tears from his eyes, something they didn't expect to ever see. "Forgive me."

But they both shook their heads, saying, "For what?"

"For thinking far less of you than I should have. So, I assume you will continue to play this charade out? That's what I would do. It gives you more time to study your enemy further."

Stephanie nodded, and said, "Yes, but not only that. We still have much preparation to do to ensure the safety of our people. Potential military victory is far different than preserving our people. That's what we're *truly* fighting for. I only wish that the Christians *before* the Great Religious War would have had sense like this, but they were so *prescriptively* enamored by loving their enemies that they neglected to adequately protect their own. Sadly, they just didn't. Believe it or not, I really *do* think that the terrible wars that ensued, The Great Religious War *and* the Second Civil War were to actually give the Christians time, to give them a chance at more of a future, so they could become. . . what they are becoming now!" And Stephanie couldn't help sobbing, because with all her might she had fought for them all, and everyone at that table knew that she fought for them at the cost of great pain and suffering to herself. But for the last two years, Vaughn and Stephanie had lived up North and they had *no* idea these two wonderful souls had never ceased fighting for them, never ceased loving them deeply!

Vaughn reached over and took his wife's hand and held it, and when she looked up at him, he said, "You will *always* be my Queen." And she nodded, trying hard to keep from outright bawling. Vaughn looked back upon the rest with his kingly gaze, again. "Colonel Asa, my original spy network is *still* very much in force. I have *much* to share with you! When the time comes, we can with one quick swoop take out pretty much all the infiltrators down South!"

Just then, clamoring and sing-song little girl voices were heard, and in strolled Lynnara, Lana, and Rebecca! Lynnara said, "Hey, we're all *really* hungry."

Stephanie studied them. Something was *different,* but she couldn't put her finger on it. She could tell all the girls looked famished but wondered why that would be as the very *best* food was at the Holy Mountain. Obviously Lynnara had mastered transporting everyone at even these great distances, which also gave Stephanie trepidation. She stared at all three girls but they *all* had the same *innocent* smiles. Stephanie squinted at them, but Lynnara immediately ran over and climbed onto Vaughn's lap.

Rebecca went over to Asa and climbed onto his lap, looked up into his eyes, and said, "I *love* being a Ranger!" He couldn't help but throw his arms around her and kiss the top of her head.

Lana came over to Samuel and took his hand in both of hers then looked up into his eyes and lingered there for a while. For his part, Samuel indulged her. And Lana said, "You're a *very* good man. But you *need to* come the rest of the way to Jesus! You think it'll interfere with you being Supreme Judge, but it won't. It'll make you even better." Then Lana stared even deeper into him, her deep gray eyes piercing his soul. "You're gonna *need* to be better!" Then she looked at everyone else. "We *all* do!

Stephanie stared at Lana, sensing a far deeper reach to her meaning but couldn't fathom an eight-year-old being there. When she tried to discern Lana more deeply, something prevented her! *Is it just that she's a child, or something* else?

# And When the Transgressors are Come to the Full

*The old chairs creaked with every subtle shift in posture, which, due to their uncomfortableness, was often. One would think that up in Heaven, no one would want anything to be disquieting but Noah and Naamah were far more, how should one describe it, odd than anyone else. But the harsh creaking began to seriously annoy Yinauqua so she peered deeply into Naamah's eyes. Now Naamah knew all too well about Yinauqua's gift of truth seeking. Everyone up here did, which caused most everyone to avoid her! Because, even though they were up in Heaven, holy, and all true, well, that didn't mean they didn't have secrets.*

*But Naamah was also quite unique. She was honest beyond measure, and the only secret she had was, in fact, why they kept their home so, well, uncomfortable. Naamah simply smiled and opened her eyes wide so there would be no impediment to Yinauqua's search. Moments later, Yinauqua blushed deeply, and said, "I'm sorry. I didn't know. I should be leaving!"*

But as she rose, Naamah took Yinauqua's hand and pulled her back into her seat. "It's OK. I see you're deeply troubled and not merely sight-seeing! You have no idea how it is to be us! Even up here! The first millennia was horrible! Everyone coming by wanting to know what it was all like, not because they wanted to console us or even learn something, but just simple curiosity! Of all the emotions you'd think they could have relating to the total end of the world and only we survived, you'd think folks up here would be, well, a little more mature! But," Naamah sighed deeply, "I guess we all have eternity to work on that!"

Yinauqua leaned back and her chair gave an extreme protest at the extra pressure. She looked even deeper into Naamah and a tear came into both their eyes as common understanding now grew. Yinauqua brushed them away but Naamah let them flow. Yinauqua said, "But this is exactly why I've come to you, and I see that what's happening now down there has affected you far more than anyone would surmise."

Naamah pulled her chair even closer and took Yinauqua's hands. Now she regretted making her home so uncomfortable for visitors because she wanted Yinauqua to stay. And neither Noah, nor Naamah made friends easily. After all, you never knew when the next calamity might just wipe everything away, and just because Heaven was perfect, well, you never knew, because everyone was still free up here. But her heart suddenly went out to Yinauqua in ways that she never expected. Another gift Naamah had, that she hadn't employed since being down there, was an unmatched empathy! She was the one who kept *urging Noah to be patient, to preach harder, to have hope! She was also the one who pressed upon Noah to at least open the door to the ark and take the babies, but, alas, the angel had taken away the key.*

*Now Naamah could feel Yinauqua's heart breaking because of what was happening down there, and to think that Yinauqua was now going through worse than what she had, suddenly woke Naamah's heart in ways she had no longer thought possible. At least Noah and she got to experience the rebuilding of life on Earth. But now was the final end and Satan would wring out every last drop of goodness possible. Noah and she were never harmed but that wouldn't be the case for those on the front lines down there. And they had already gone through so much. Noah and she never had to fight Satan because everything had been condemned by God already and God placed clear, untouchable protection over them. But, now, the holy people down there would fight for every last shred of goodness they could defend until the bitter end, even placing themselves in harm's way. Naamah squeezed Yinauqua's hands. "What can I do for you?"*

*Yinauqua steeled herself, leveled her eyes into Naamah, and said, "How do you know when you've crossed the line? How do you know when your love gets so deep that it steps outside the balance of the other six Spirits of God? How do you know when your love is no longer of Wisdom, no longer of Understanding, no longer of Peace, no longer of even Truth, no longer of Justice, and instead of always uplifting Life, it turns against Life?"*

*Naamah's eyes grew wide with memories, how she begged Noah to open the ark and take the babies, but also with the current understanding now flooding into her, and for some time she sat silently staring into Yinauqua, feeling her inner most turmoil. "What have you done, and what are you going to do?"*

Mandy sat on a simple dark brown wooden chair at a simple dark brown wooden table in front of the children. Lynnara, besides creating basic beds, shelves, and a bathroom, had apparently enlarged Stephanie's makeshift circular shelter quite a bit, spacious enough to pace around if need be, and Mandy certainly felt like jumping out of her seat. She shook her head at Sam and Shara, and said, "I can't do this! I can't keep calling a *girl* by a *boy's* name, and a *boy* by a *girl's* name. You're no longer *Shara.* You're *Shane.* And you're no longer *Sam.* You're *Samantha.*"

Far from being upset, the two looked at each other and practiced saying their new names back and forth and then calling each other by those names. Their faces both lit up and their eyes danced in joy as they said to Mandy, "We *love* them." And Samantha said, "*Finally,* I feel like a *real* girl."

Mandy had spent hours with the children, who nonstop described everything they knew about their homes and what they had seen on their way up north. Mandy couldn't believe the depravity and the brutalness, but the one thing that bothered her more than *anything* was that Samantha and Shane had met others who were also trying to escape, but to minimize the chance they would all get caught, they had made sure to all pick different routes up north, Mandy now understood why Marta had moved the shelter *down here* as she studied an old, stained map that Shane had pulled from his pocket.

Mandy pointed at a place on the map. Calculating from the map's legend, she said, "This road here is only three miles to the east." Then she looked up at the children and they knew her thoughts. Mandy said, "Would only take us one hour, maybe two, depending on the terrain, to hike over there."

Shane looked at Samantha and they spoke in their native tongue so that Mandy couldn't understand. Clearly Samantha wanted to try but Shane had reservations. Samantha said to Mandy, "We don't mean to sound ungrateful. We're not selfish, either. But . . ." She looked at Shane.

"Look. You should be dead! If it wasn't for some *angel* saving you, you *would be* dead. And *we* haven't known freedom."

Samantha said, "Until now. What my brother is trying to ask is how can you help anyone when it took everyone else to barely save us?"

It was a question that kept plaguing Mandy. *But* Mandy was a Ranger. Simply put, Rangers do what Rangers do. "You all stay here. I'm just going to hike over there and from this side of the fence try to scout it out."

Samantha and Shane both shook their heads and stood up with Mandy. They all *knew* what Mandy would do and had determined to go with her. Mandy did wish at least Lynnara was here but she also knew that the girls had to maintain the illusion and *that* required they stay away for a while and spend time with Stephanie and Vaughn.

An hour-and-a-half later Mandy pulled out the map and saw they were exactly opposite where the children indicated. She showed them the map and they nodded. There was an old abandoned road that went right under the electric fence and disappeared into the woods but it still had noticeable remnants of concrete. Grass and forest weeds grew through many cracks and old leaves and dirt were strewn about it, however, previous winds and rains had managed to keep a decent amount of it clear.

The kids weren't trying to hide themselves because they were on their *own* side of the fence, now, though their lack of fear probably came more from all they had recently seen, feeling somehow protected even now. That sense of fearlessness suddenly shattered when they heard voices call from the other side. Then three children, two possibly girls and one possibly boy sprinted out of the woods and up the road. Shane hollered back at them putting his hands up to signify they should hold up. Samantha told Mandy, "Shane told them not to touch the fence 'cause it's electric. They didn't know."

The two boys who looked and acted like girls seemed about thirteen years old but the girl who looked and acted like a boy was only about eight. They all looked alike with dark brown eyes, black hair, and fear. Then there was more chatter, and Shane told Mandy. "Demon dogs patrol the fence line. They'll be back soon!" When Mandy asked what *soon* meant, there was more chatter, and then Shane said, "They're not good at time but they've seen them come and go maybe ten times since they've been here. They've been afraid to try and cross the fence because the dogs might come by any second. Sometimes there's two, sometimes only one because one doubles back sometimes sooner than usual."

Mandy shook her head. "Tell them to go back and hide where they were and I'll get them out. But they're gonna have to do *exactly* as I say, *when* I say."

And Samantha explained it to them and after they nodded, they ran back. Not long after that, two black demon dogs strolled by and began sniffing the ground where the kids had been. Then they began following their trail. Mandy pulled two arrows from her quiver and eased her bow off of her shoulder but just then both dogs ears perked up, they ruffed once each, and then took off sprinting up the old road and disappeared into the woods.

Mandy leapt up, took her backpack off, then replaced her weapons, then took a thin black rope from a compartment, and walked over to a nearby tall cypress tree. She smiled at Samantha, winked at Shane then disappeared between the thick evergreen fronds of the low branches. Then the children noticed other branches successively higher were shaking a bit. Every once in a while they thought they made out part of Mandy's uniform but since it was camouflage, they weren't entirely sure. But when they saw an arrow fly out from almost halfway up the tree with the rope attached then strike another tree on the other side of the fence, they smiled, though still not certain what this would do. Mandy tied off the special carbon fiber twine, peered up at the incline of the rope that sloped downward at about forty degrees towards her, and climbed back down.

The children ran up to her and grabbed each of her arms in excitement. Their eyes were bright jewels of hope. Mandy said, "Wave them here again, then tell them to climb that tree, tie the rope off *tight,* take their belts and sling it over the rope, hold on to each belt end for dear life, and slide down the rope one at a time and I'll be up that tree to catch them. And tell them to be *quiet.* No *screaming* when coming across! And then Mandy turned aside and went back up the cypress!

Samantha and Shane looked doubtful but then again, what else could they do, so they called the three children. One problem was that the girl didn't have a belt so Shane took his off and carefully passed it through the fence. One thing the other children *did* notice sharply was Samantha and Shane's appearance and they couldn't help but comment. Samantha told them she'd explain once they were safe, and the children ran to the tree and began to climb.

Mandy could see when the twine began to shake and she braced herself with her back against the trunk. The next thing she saw was one of the boys speeding towards her. She had practiced this many times in Ranger Training but all of her compatriots were larger and didn't zip down the rope nearly as fast. When the child slammed into Mandy, he almost knocked her breath away but her arms wrapped around him and held him tightly until she recovered. She motioned him down the tree but when she looked up again the other boy was already speeding towards her. The child had stuck his legs straight out for extra momentum and couldn't see Mandy in the thick branches.

Mandy didn't have any choice. As the child's legs came at her feetfirst, she backhand swatted them away with her left arm and the child's left shoulder slammed into Mandy's chest without her being able to brace herself. Not only did the impact drive the air from her lungs, it almost felt like her heart stopped and she couldn't catch her breath. Her legs began to buckle and everything started to spin.

Mandy came to herself sitting on a branch of the tree, her legs straddling it, and the boy holding onto her vest with his left hand and the belt that he had originally looped around the rope with his right! He was still turned sideways because, apparently, right after he collided and saw Mandy collapse, he grabbed her and wouldn't let go. But he had no good place to put his feet, and, anyway, he couldn't let go of Mandy lest she fall! He was saying something to Mandy she couldn't understand.

Mandy pulled something out of her breast vest pocket and placed it in her ear. Then she reached into her pocket again and turned a small knob on a small electronic device. Moments later, she could understand the child's speech. This translator was secret equipment that had been given to King Vaughn by his secret service. Apparently, they had been able to marry the device to their central computer back at the castle and it could instantly translate any known language. But since Vaughn was now a *faithwalker,* able to understand meaning, he no longer needed it and gave it to Mandy as a thank you for how she had stood by Stephanie no matter what. She never thought she'd need it.

The child was becoming frantic. He was saying the girl was sure to come down the line any moment and he couldn't hold on much longer, either. Mandy reached up to grab a branch and pain shot through her chest but she pulled herself back up, wrapped her arms around him and with great effort held his weight till she could ease his feet down onto the branch. And he was right because the girl was coming fast!

Mandy knew she just couldn't take another hit even if the girl was much smaller, and, besides, there was no time to do anything else! She spun the boy around, braced her back against the trunk and his back against her, grabbed his arms and pulled them open, and cried, "Catch her!"

Even though the boy didn't understand the words, her meaning was clear. When the girl slammed into them, he wrapped his arms around her. The impact made the boy grunt and then the force went through him into Mandy and she grunted as well, but fortunately much of it had been dissipated. After moments of catching everyone's breath and realizing this *actually* worked, Mandy indicated they should climb down.

The children were down a while before Mandy made it back. The pain in her chest made her wonder if her sternum was broken. She *really* missed Lynnara now. Samantha ran over to Mandy seeing she was obviously not well. Mandy said, "We need to head back." But voices and laughing in the distance from the other side of the fence had them all duck down behind the tree. Fortunately, the moist ground muffled a lot of sound. No leaves would crunch, no branches snap.

Mandy's ranger sense kicked in again. Pain or no pain didn't matter. Only what needed to be done mattered, and she pulled the children behind her and motioned them to stay very low. Two, slender, obviously grown men strolled up the old road but they looked like, well, they looked like demons because of their bizarre and garish makeup. Mandy turned a knob on her device to pick up their conversation and motioned to the children to be quiet because they were eager to translate for her. She pointed to her earpiece and that it would be alright.

The men were dressed in feminine uniforms which had certain colorful patches. Somehow, by their demeanor, in spite of their abominable appearance, Mandy knew these weren't just foot soldiers but officers. One pointed up the road in their direction, saying, "Believe it or not, right through *here!* And there are roads just like this one all across the border that are remarkably in good enough shape to bring a whole army across!"

The other soldier, obviously his inferior, said, "But why would our rulers think we have a chance to beat the United for Christ?"

The superior laughed. "I tell you a secret. You haven't seen what *our* King has prepared, weapons like no other, and training like no other. But even more importantly, the United for *Christ* doesn't even consider us. Look at this fence. That's *it.* That's what they think of us!"

"But that makes no sense. Even *we* defend our borders even though no one would hardly think we have *anything* to steal."

The superior laughed hard again and looked upward in glee. Mandy had knocked two arrows at once and held one arrow a bit spaced from the other and had turned her bow horizontal. This, she had also practiced. She waited to see if the officer had seen the rope above as he looked into his subordinate's eyes, "Because to the *gringos* we are *third world* still. *Even* after the plague *this* has *not* changed. They see us as *no threat at all.* But I tell you *this.* Before the Great Religious War, we had totally infiltrated the whole of the United States of America! We had *millions* of our soldiers just waiting to take over all their major cities. We had already *utterly* decimated them with all the illegal drugs they loved. We were so close to taking over!"

"What happened?"

"Well, the *plague* happened. And the Great Religious War happened. Most of our secret soldiers were wiped out in the large cities, and when we heard what the gringos did to the terrorist Muslim countries, we all agreed we didn't want any part of *that.* And we had *no* future after that until King Jargono showed us his holy light. *This* time we are going to *win.*"

The men strolled right up to the fence and the superior actually stuck out his index finger and *touched* it. He didn't even flinch when he got zapped. Then he laughed hard, again, saying, "A *fence.* This is all the respect we get. A *fence.*"

The other supposed-to-be-man said, "When do you think we attack? I *heard* King Jargono is running for *their President!*" And he rolled out laughing, doubling over.

"Well, that's just it. It's best to wait till he wins the election, and he already has *that* in the bag. But he knows the United for Christ won't stick to unification, that they'll make a *third* civil war. *That's* where *we* come in. While the United are all facing the North, their backs will be to *us,* and we just cut their little fence here, wipe out the handful of Rangers that patrol this border, and then take over. Their military will be so entangled up at their northern border, they won't be able to effectively respond to us down here even if they wanted to. And *then* we conquer *everything* south of their lines. Once their forces are sandwiched between us and the North, they'll have to give up. And *that's* when the fun starts."

The other officer licked his lips. "I can't wait to get hold of some gringo pussy. I'm *tired* of what we have down here and how they act like *men.* "

"Well, King Jargono promised all the officers we could have as much as we can stand, that we get to line up all their men so they can watch us enjoy their women *and* children.

The inferior officer said, "I can't wait. But what happens if somehow our plans down here are discovered. You know, those damned Rangers are actually some of the best secret service in the world."

"King Jargono's orders are clear on that, too. *If* we're discovered, and I *highly* doubt that because we're *third world.* No one *respects* us. But *if* we're discovered, we're supposed to attack right away. *That's* why everything is ready *now.* Just in case. And Jargono has his contingent plan for up North if that happens."

Then the superior scrunched his brow like he was remembering something, and *then* he looked straight up at the rope, and he looked at it go into the tree on *his* side of the fence, and then he followed it back till he was facing the fence again and Mandy let her two arrows fly and each hit dead center into the hearts of the supposed-to-be-men. They stumbled backwards, their eyes widened, they looked over to each other, and slumped to the ground. The dogs that were next to them circled their masters once, and when they turned to look across the fence, two arrows struck each one in the chest and they collapsed dead.

Mandy sighed. She had no choice, especially after they saw the rope. But how long would it be before *this* was discovered. Mandy paced back and forth mumbling to herself, ignoring the stabbing pain in her chest. The children understood the terribleness of what the soldiers had said but they had a deep sense that Mandy understood it way more than they did, so they waited in silence.

"Think Mandy, *Think!*" she scolded herself as she talked out loud. "If I tell Vaughn . . . I *can't* tell *any* of them. What about Carla? But how would I even get back to the Holy Mountain? Besides, knowing Carla, she *already* knows, maybe *even* knew all this was going to happen! Then what am I supposed to *do?* Dear Jesus, what do I *do?* If I can't tell anyone, then what good is knowing all *this?*" Mandy cried out in utter despair and frustration, and went to her knees and bowed herself to the ground. She fancied maybe Marta would show up again, but what could *she* even do?

The children came around and put their hands on their savior's head and shoulders until Mandy sat up and looked into the Heavens. "Why did you pick *me*, Carla?" That wasn't a complaint. It was a search for understanding. Last time her older sister Carla had entrusted the future of the whole world to Rebecca, just a little child. Now it seemed as though it was all on Mandy's shoulders. And for some reason, the Holy Ghost inside her was silent! "Why are you silent?" she asked aloud but the children just shrugged their shoulders. When Mandy saw it, she said, "No, no. Not you. Just talking to a special part of myself. Let's go back."

As they walked back to their shelter, something flashed in Mandy's mind. Vaughn had made a special book part of all the Ranger's and military's training. The Art of Fighting. And Rule One stated, Better to die fighting, being what you are, than lose the battle from within. Mandy said to herself, *Well, I* really *know the meaning of* that *one.*

Rule Two. With time, there are always possibilities, so never throw it away or rush to battle when time is open. "But I have no time, now. If those bodies are discovered, then there's no more time." Mandy stopped, then looked at the children. She became stern. "Listen to me. You all go back to the shelter. There's enough food and water and I'm *sure* at some point, the other girls will be back. I have something I *have to do.* Right *now!* If I don't get back before the others come, well . . . just tell them all that you know. Tell them. . . tell them I've gone in search of a black beard! Tell them that, OK? Now *go!*"

And Mandy left them there and began to run through the woods, faster and faster. "No time," she kept mumbling. "No time."

Rule Three. Procrastination is a choice. "None here," Mandy whispered as she ran and her chest pain increased.

Rule Ten. When gaining a slight advantage over a superior force, quickness is your best ally. "Well, dear Jesus, I'm trying. Help me to make it, *please.*" And onward she ran through the woods paying no attention to the briars swiping at her, until she finally came to a road and fell to her knees and vomited at the road's edge. Wiping away the sourness and spitting, Mandy got angry. Then she checked her map and began running up the road.

Rule Twelve. When faced with immanent defeat, seek to postpone the end; time always holds the possibilities of the unknown. "Ain't *that* the truth," Mandy forced out between huffing and puffing.

"It's not in the main rules but in their commentary. What was it?" Mandy saw a vehicle far up the road driving towards her and she collapsed to her knees in the center of it. "In the Art of Fighting, it specifically said *somewhere* that when facing a losing battle, one must change directions to change the situation."

When the four wheel Jeep pulled up, and the Rangers inside saw Mandy's uniform, they lifted her up and put her in the front passenger seat while the other Ranger stood on the outstep and hung on by the window. Mandy, still gasping, said one word. "Blackbeard!" And she passed out.

The other Rangers, the driver with short black hair and the other blond, whirled around and floored it back to the office. No one becomes a Ranger lightly. And while the men were none too fond of *any* woman being a Ranger, the few that *did* make it were due the utmost respect. How *this* young lady knew *Blackbeard,* of all the *incorrigible* people to know, was a complete mystery. And how she knew he'd be *down here* when they'd all only been here a week, was also a mystery, but *obviously* she had given *everything* she had to get this far. The driver said to the man on the outside, "She's a real looker, isn't she?"

It was true that seventeen-year-old Mandy, with her long, braided, reddish brown hair, physically fit form, and yet *obviously* a very feminine form was hard to pull your eyes away from, but *that* wasn't what either man really meant when they considered her. Even while unconscious, Mandy had a presence about her that commanded respect, and a righteous seriousness that drove the men's hearts to pound. Not since Lady Stephanie had showed up had they seen *any* woman like *this.*

# CHAPTER 8

# Heart to Heart

*Yinauqua pulled her three, long, reddish gray braids behind her, but instead of answering Naamah's question, she asked one. "What was it like knowing so much weight was on your husband's shoulders?"*

*Naamah sighed, looked down remembering, then met Yinauqua's eyes. She didn't fear Yinauqua's gift at all. She had longed for a serious friend to be one with. "Well, not only that, but I added to that weight! I mean, besides the fact that Noah had us and the three children to worry about. I knew that if he faltered even in the least, the terrible evil all around us would crush us all. Yet, I didn't do what I did for him out of fear for us. I mean, there he was facing the whole entire world alone." Steel suddenly flashed in Naamah's eyes. The abrupt change and the contrast surprised Yinauqua.*

*Naamah continued. "I'd be damned if I didn't give him the full love and support he deserved! I mean, there is no way in hell I wouldn't be the best I could be for him. So, instead of being fearful of his calling, of his duty, I encouraged him. 'Did you preach hard enough today?' I asked him. 'Did you really reach out with all the love and sincerity possible or did you just go through the motions?' For one-hundred-and-twenty years I kept finding different ways to encourage him and even inspire him."*

*Yinauqua wiped tears from her eyes again. There weren't many people here that could make her feel like a child. Naamah squeezed her hands tightly and gave them a tug so that Yinauqua looked up into her eyes. Now Naamah's gift came into play. It wasn't just empathy. She was able to call to any heart to open and share by appealing to the best in souls and Yinauqua felt it deeply and nodded.*

*"For the longest time I knew my husband had secrets from me. But I also knew he always told me the truth and that his love, even down there, as up here, is true for me and our Lord. But now, it's not him that has secrets, but me! Did you know that when our dear Lady Stephanie and Sir Vaughn were going through the most terrible suffering that I was going to break our protocol and go down and fight for them?"*

*Naamah's eyes widened because she saw this was true and she leaned back in her chair and it shrieked. She lingered within Yinauqua's heart and knew the utter depths of her love. Her eyes went distant and she shook her head, speaking softly. "I did not."*

*Yinauqua said, "For the first time ever, Mafferan held me with his power against my will and prevented me!"*

*Naamah collected her long gray hair that was before her, shook it out, and placed it all behind her. She shook her head again remembering the stories of Yinauqua's and Mafferan's youth. Keepers of the Tree of Life, she thought to herself, then looked into Yinauqua's eyes. "Not exactly." When she saw Yinauqua wanted her to continue, she said, "Your husband knew and knows your whole heart. And your whole heart wanted him to do for you what you couldn't, at that time, do for yourself."*

*Naamah knew many souls up here but none had ever touched her as deeply as now. "Now that you have secrets from him, you cannot rely on him to pull you out of the fire. You must be careful Yinauqua. Your love is not just known up here, but in the Ethereal, also."*

*"I'm counting on it!" Yinauqua said with an indecipherable look in her face.*

The Father had followed her all the way to Naamah's house and then kept trying to adjust the orb to penetrate through some kind of interference. "She used the *back* door, HrorrarrAggrang."

"Yes. She knows we watch the front but has *no idea* we can place tracers on *anyone.*" HrorrarrAggrang squinted suddenly at the orb, but then went back to normal. However, the Father was particularly sensitive to telltale signs of, well, *anything.*

"*What?*" the Father said with a tone that expected, without delay, an answer.

"Just a passing thought. Not worth bothering your Blackness over." The Father gave HrorrarrAggrang a look that said, *I'll be the judge of that,* so HrorrarrAggrang said, "It's just, for a moment, *just* for a micro-moment I thought I saw the orb flicker. That's all."

The Father did some quick orb manipulations and then went to the orb's internal GPS. He then split the screen and pulled up the orb's history record. Of course, the GPS was always the same, that the orb resided right where it has always been since *former* Queen Karen had brought it. But the Father remembered that Mafferan had engaged him for quite a while and that this orb had been unattended to. The Father had never shaken away the feeling that there was more to Mafferan's visit than what he claimed. Now, maybe, that was just the Father's own projection from what *he* would have done, given the opportunity, *or,* Mafferan was indeed *that deceptive!*

And there it was *again,* but *this* time the Father saw it, too. A micro-second flicker. He squinted his Greatest Black Eye at HrorrarrAggrang, "We have a problem. I don't think we can trust what we see in here, *at least* when using it to see *up there!*"

HrorrarrAggrang took front and center orb position and the Father floated above him to watch. HrorrarrAggrang split his tail into so many fine pieces that moved so quickly that everything seemed to be hazy around the orb. But *then* he stopped. The GPS *and* the history had been broken down into micro-second lines for that *particular* second in question. HrorrarrAggrang now slowly scrolled through each line until. . .

HrorrarrAggrang and the Father met Greatest Eye to Great Eye. There was a single micro-second record *missing,* but the GPS still recorded the same position. *That* meant that *someone else* had popped into the Father's most secret room *unaccounted for* and tampered! And it was at the *exact* time when Mafferan and the Father were supposed to be fixing Vaughn's master orb so everything in the Ethereal wouldn't crash. The persistent micro-second flashes were part of an alarm that obviously had been *almost* totally disabled!

HrorrarrAggrang *clicked* on the line for the missing record and the whole orb went blank. The Father squinted at him but HrorrarrAggrang held up his massive arm for the Father to wait a moment. HrorrarrAggrang split his tail, again, and after the haze vanished, the *micro-second* had been broken down into one-hundred parts. "*That's* the finest the orb can go." He told the Father.

HrorrarrAggrang began to slowly scroll through each line until. . . several of the lines recorded a *glowing* arm reaching inside of it! But all the rest of the lines were blank. The Father squinted angrily, saying, "Who's *that?*"

HrorrarrAggrang saved the image then fed it into their new identify program which had *everyone ever* from above, below and on Earth recorded in it. Moments later the image of Yinauqua popped up! HrorrarrAggrang said, "That's. . ."

But the Father interrupted. "I *know* who *that* is. Mafferan's *wife.* So we can't trust what we see up *there.* But it would be a severe infraction of the Truce if she tampered with anything else." The Father turned even blacker, which HrorrarrAggrang hadn't thought possible. "Yinauqua," was all he said, and the Father's secret room shook.

Sometimes it was best to change directions. When the Father entered into such moods he became unpredictable so HrorrarrAggrang felt it best to proceed to grayer pastures. "I don't see any way out this time. There will be no plagues, no terrorists, *nothing* to interrupt our plans."

The Father said, "Are we *clear* on our goal? This is *not* to be any quick destruction like before. We want *all* the *holy* people captured and held and the Christians, too. Now the *holy* people are our main target but we can kill two birds together. The *holy* people are all about protecting the ones they love and *that* would be, of course, family members, but broadly, all the Christians they're trying to get to be holy. We use *their* suffering to break the holy people. We make the Christians suffer in unimaginable ways until the love the holy people have for them can't take any more. And *then* when the *holy* people can't take any more suffering, *that's* when that *miscreant* Yinauqua won't be able to help herself and I *personally,* will be waiting. I want *that one* for myself, HrorrarrAggrang. Do you understand?"

HrorrarrAggrang bowed his bulbous head low before the Father. "Yes, your Blackness. *Perfectly.*"

"Be ready, because when Yinauqua breaks the truce, we enter *directly* back into Heaven at the *same* time our underlings enter Earth. They *can't* defend two fronts, *especially* with our Christ in charge there. But also, the power we've accumulated since we left Heaven is *considerable.* This battle won't be *anything* like our previous Heavenly skirmish. And Mafferan will come down to defend his *wife,* and then *others* to defend them, leaving Heaven wide open. But when Mafferan knows Heaven is invaded, he'll *leave* his wife to go up, and *that's* when I come back down and *consume* her!

And with *that* power, I'll go back up and consume him *next,* so they *both* can be together! See my compassion, HrorrarrAggrang?

ᴄᴏ

After the Jeep parked, the driver shook Mandy a bit and she opened her eyes. She rubbed her chest but it surprisingly no longer hurt. "I'm Max, *Ranger.*" And he held out his hand.

Mandy firmly took it. "Mandy, *Ranger.*"

"I'm John, *Ranger.*" the blond man said when he stuck his hand through the open window.

Mandy shook it firmly, too. "Blackbeard?"

John nodded then opened the passenger door. "How'd you know he was here? We've only been here a week, ourselves. Since unification, we no longer had a border to protect and they've always been short down here, so we picked the whole team up and found us a good place to squat. Frankly, we hadn't even notified our superiors yet!"

Max came around to stand next to John and ran his hand over his short black hair waiting for an answer, as well. One of the things Rangers are taught is to *mis*trust. But Mandy eased herself out of the Jeep and immediately pushed past both of them, who were surprised at her strength. "Dear Jesus," and she went down on her knees. "Thank you." And she bowed her head low to the ground. Because in truth, she had gotten the two borders confused! Didn't realize that *this* Southern Border *wasn't* the Southern border between the North and South *before* unification. "Dear *Jesus,* you made this happen!" And Mandy stood up and marched away from the men and up to a stone building with an old white door, whereupon she leapt up, screamed, and kicked the door in!

The men's mouth's dropped open and a man with a scruffy big black beard, eyes wide open pushed back from his old desk that was piled with papers, and said, "It was *unlocked.* You're gonna *pay* for that!" But in truth, his eyes told a much different story. Asleep, Mandy looked beautiful. But *awake,* in *person,* and all riled up, well, it was hard for *any* man to resist going down to their knees!

Mandy said, "I'm on *official* business." She turned to the men behind her. "Thanks for the ride and keeping your hands to yourself! Now *leave!* And *shut* the door!"

Blackbeard collected himself and straightened his posture, wiped the fawning look from his eyes. "Now *hold on* a minute. We don't know you from *shit.* Now, you *are* a pretty *shit,* but *that* don't give you any rights *here.* Throw her out!"

Mandy leapt high and whirled, and caught Max across the face with a back roundhouse which drove him out the door and onto his back! She then spun low and actually swept John's feet out from under him and he face planted. She rolled to sit on top of him then drew both simitars and drove the points into the old wooden floor with each blade a hairs breadth from each ear then stared at Blackbeard, her medium brown eyes boring into his very soul. "I don't have time for this. *None of us do!*"

Blackbeard nodded, unable to voice the respect he had for what he just witnessed. He motioned with his hand, and said, "Out, and shut the door." Clearly, if Mandy had wanted them all dead, she could have done that within a single minute and

Blackbeard knew it. He motioned to Mandy to take a seat in front of the desk where an old wooden chair still remained in place.

But Mandy became sullen and seductive, as she used to act before Lady Stephanie redeemed her. She walked past the chair, threw her arm around Blackbeard's shoulders, and placed her mouth beside his ear. He could smell the young lady's vibrance as she whispered, "This is unbelievably confidential. If you can't keep the secret, I *will* kill you! Can you keep a secret? Ranger's *Word?*"

Blackbeard knew she meant every word, and said, "Yes. Ranger's Word. But *who the hell are you?*"

"Lady Stephanie rescued my sorry ass and we're now *sisters!* And I won't just take that thing and *wrap it around your neck,* I'll *fry it, and eat it for breakfast!*"

And with *that,* Blackbeard *knew* without any doubt at *all* that Mandy was *indeed* who she said she was. His hand went to his neck and rubbed it, remembering Stephanie's similar words to him when she came looking for her husband. "Take a seat, young lady, and tell me all you need me to do. You *are* Lady Stephanie's sister! No doubt about *that!* And he suddenly roared in laughter, slamming his hands down on the desk multiple times and beaming with delight.

After Mandy got done explaining everything and even played the translated recording, she said, "Larson married my sister Carla, whom he and Vaughn and I helped rescue from corrupt priests' sexual slavery." Blackbeard rejoiced at his best friend's fortune then became dour over the rest. But Mandy wasn't done. "Carla had a vision that Vaughn would rescue her before he did! Blackbeard, when I ran into the room, Carla was *naked, chained,* but she looked at me and all she could say was, 'I know him! God showed me he would come.'"

Blackbeard rubbed his head several times as some kind of tingling kept itching him. "I don't know what to say."

But Mandy wasn't just telling him this to make small talk. "Blackbeard. Vaughn rescued Larson's daughter Rebecca from the minefield, and later, *that* child alone saved the whole future of the world because Carla alone had the vision that she could do it and she kept that through terrible strains."

Now the itching became so intense that Blackbeard had to say, "You're giving me goose bumps I don't even understand."

But Mandy got up from her chair, smiled warmly, then whispered in his ear. "But your heart *does!* Carla told me that in no uncertain terms can I let *anyone* know I'm down here and what's going on. She said if Stephanie or Vaughn finds out, we will *all* lose miserably." Mandy couldn't help it and she sniffed back tears. "Oh, what the *hell.* I'm not really tough like Lady Stephanie. I've already broken what Carla told me *not* to do, but I *seriously* don't know what else there is. It may *already* be too late."

Blackbeard swept papers aside on his desk then motioned her to sit there so Mandy could be close. He looked up at her, studying her person while tugging on his beard. *Clearly,* God, and he wasn't one to give God much thought because there was plenty to be concerned about in *this* life, but God meant for this young lady to be *here* right now, and he had to do everything in his power to help her. "Ranger Mandy. It's true you're no Lady Stephanie. *No one* could be her. But in your *own right,* you are marvelous, a sight to behold for bravery, strength, *and* wisdom! And look how young you are. *But,* if I'm to help you, all of us, you have to trust me. To do what needs to be done, I need those two rangers out there, and two more. I'll swear them all to Ranger's Word, but I can vouch for them all with my very life. Is that good enough for you?"

Mandy began to bawl. She'd never had such responsibilities before, nothing even *close.* Or maybe it was the compliments that undid her, having never thought of herself that way, but she also *hated* that she was crying now. "I'm sorry. I don't know what's come over me."

Blackbeard shook his head. "You are *exhausted.* That much is *clear.* He held up his phone, and said, "John and Max are even vouching for you *right now!* They texted me they found you having *run* through the woods for God knows how far and you *collapsed* in the middle of the road and all you could do was call my name and pass out. *Then* you come in here and boldly, singlehandedly kick the asses of my two best rangers. If I had a medal, I'd *pin it on you right now!* You go ahead and cry. You *deserve* it! But I need an answer *now.* "

"Yes. Do all you think is supposed to be done." And with that weight now shared with others, Mandy sunk down and began to pass out again but Blackbeard steadied her and hollered through the closed door. "Max, John, get in here *now.* "

The door burst open and when they saw Mandy slumped down, they lifted her up and placed her on a cot up against the far wall to their left. Blackbeard said, "The woman needs to eat. Get Franco and Jerry to meet us at G6 like *yesterday.* Use code only. Priority Alpha Zeta! I'll fill you all in on the rest later. And raise your hands. Rangers Word for all of you. *NO ONE* is to know *anything* about *any* of this. Oh, and tell Jerry to bring the fence hopper!"

They raised their hands and swore devoutly. All the hairs on their body prickled because Alpha Zeta was a code they'd *never* heard before. It was the end of the world code. John said, "I'll get her taken care of." Max was already contacting the other rangers.

༒

James was sitting at his desk in his office when surprised to see the little red light flashing on his computer console, indicating that one of the secret translators had been activated and that a considerable recording had been forwarded to the main computer. But he was completely overcome by the time he finished listening. Now James was also not one to rush into *anything,* even something as dire as *this.* The question was, "What is Mandy doing down *there?*" He had met both Mandy and Carla many times and heard the stories from Lynnara who absolutely delighted in sitting on his lap and telling him *everything* she knew about *everything.* That included Carla and Mandy. Speaking out loud to himself to better follow his thoughts, he said, "Carla foresees, so *she* must have sent Mandy. *Both* young ladies are holy, not deceived easily, if at all. Why hasn't Mandy called directly here?"

Part of James felt that for some reason Vaughn and Stephanie aren't supposed to know. Especially with all they have to deal with. "But it isn't right to take away their ability to choose what to do in this situation. They're really *still* our leaders." The Holy Ghost in him was silent! So James determined to contact them now. He went to rub his special ring, one that Lady Stephanie had made for him in case he needed her immediately *except* the doorbell rang! Torn between what he desperately needed to do *now* and his official butler duties, he surmised he had to answer the door. Maybe it was Mandy or someone else with news. But also, when he reached for the ring he had a queasy feeling about it.

James stood up, pulled his black vest tight, and went to answer the castle door. He pulled the large iron bolt aside then grabbed the ornate bronze handle and swung the door open. As soon as he did, Carla's dark brown eyes locked onto his, and she said, "If you summon Stephanie or Vaughn or anyone else, we are all doomed!"

James was flabbergasted, even for a middle-aged holy man. His butler skills saved him. "Carla, do come in. Lady Stephanie and Sir Vaughn are not home, but just I."

Smoothing her brown peasant dress, she smiled and walked in then took the course James directed for her as he shut the door. Once in the dining room, James was about to fetch food but Carla said, "James, please sit down. I know *you know* what is happening."

He paused, still half-turned toward the kitchen. His butler sense led him to the kitchen but everything else told him to sit, and he slowly tuned, but instead of sitting across from Carla, he pulled up a chair to her right side, and twisted it to face her, though she was sitting properly with her hands folded on the table. Without looking at James, Carla said, "This isn't easy."

He reached over and placed his hand over hers, praying for her, then said, "We live in perilous times, dear Lady Carla."

Carla sighed then twisted her chair to face him. "We have no win, James. None at all. All we have is the lesser of terrible choices."

James looked into her deep brown eyes for a long time. Carla didn't look away. She was only nineteen years old, about to turn twenty, almost a year older than Lady Stephanie, but the strain in her demeanor gave Carla the look of an ancient one. James looked down, then up, and he asked her, "Do you have visions of what *will* be or what *might be?*"

Carla sighed again. "It's far more complex than that. At first, when I simply saw that Sir Vaughn would rescue me. *Only* that vision. And he did. Then, the Lord showed me *everything* dear Stephanie was going through." Carla paused and wiped tears from her eyes. "I don't know how she managed it. I *really* don't. I could barely keep myself together just knowing, and it wasn't even happening to me. But at that time, my visions also began to vary. Because I prayed for a solution and the Lord began to show me different scenarios, all true, *if* a certain decision or thing happened. It became *very* complex." She paused then and looked deeply into his eyes, searching for something. "James. It's. . . hard sometimes to keep reality separated from all the other possibilities that would have also been reality. All my feelings get tangled, sometimes."

"And you don't tell your husband these things."

Carla smiled. "I can't do that to Larson, nor Rebecca. They have their own battles to fight."

James squeezed her hands tightly. "Then you've come to the right place at the *right* time. Did you know little Princess Lynnara tells me *everything* about *everything*?" And the way James said it with Lynnara's inflections suddenly made her burst out into uncontrollable laughter. So James repeated it with extra emphasis. "*Everything* about eeeverrryyythhiing."

And that was *too* much and Carla laughed so hard she could barely maintain her seat. James just smiled and waited, his deep blue eyes sparkling. After a bit, Carla said, "Oh dear, my *sides* hurt."

"Well, you needed that, Lady Carla. The Lord has given you a *terrible* gift, meaning that it has otherworldly responsibilities. I cannot fathom it."

Carla thought about that for a while, then said, "I think we *all* have been given the maximum we can handle."

James leveled serious eyes into Carla now. "Lady Carla, I am used to listening. King Jargono, bless his memory, confided most deeply to me and I always gave him my honest opinion. He *knew* that. You can confide in me."

So Carla sat for hours and explained all that she was shown, all her feelings, and what she saw as the best choices available. And James sat very still. All this far exceeded *anything* he went through with King Jargono and King Vaughn and Lady

Stephanie. Exceeded all of it put together! James said, "I wish I had a quick answer for you. This is a lot to digest and I think it's given me an ulcer already."

His eyes twinkled with a special humor and love and Carla leaned over and kissed his cheek. "James, I knew you were dear, but I never knew *how* dear."

And James expression suddenly took on a sharpness. "You didn't foresee *this?*" Carla shook her head, and James said, "Then we have *already* changed the future from *all* that you have just described! Because *your* feelings have changed immeasurably!"

Carla wasn't so sure about that, but she was also sure there was more to what James was describing than she understood. James said, "A moment." And he left the dining room but went away from the kitchen door and to his study. When he returned, he held out a quite feminine ring in his palm. "Lady Stephanie had many of these made for me. They are all connected to *this* one." He took Carla's right hand and placed it over her middle finger whereupon the gold ring sized itself perfectly and the ruby in it shined a red light then dissipated. "If you need me, rub the ring and I will know. Then I'll get Lady Stephanie or Miss Lynnara to take me to you."

Carla smiled. She was familiar with such rings, as she and Mandy, and Jean, and Lana, and Rebecca all had them but connected to Lady Stephanie and King Vaughn's rings. Still, Carla was touched beyond measure that she could so quickly contact James. "Thank you so much. For some reason, you've just given me hope, though from what I only know now, I don't know why."

James pinched her cheek as if she were a little girl, then said, "Now, food, then sleep. By the way, how *did* you get here? I thought you were camped out with Prince Michael at the Holy Mountain."

"Oh," Carla said, blushing. "That was a bit of a task. *First,* I had Jean tell Stephanie that Michael needed to see her and Lynnara, and, well, he *always* needs to see *everyone.* That's just the type of boy he is. But I *knew* Stephanie would be too busy so she just sent her daughter. So once Lynnara popped in, I told her to check on Michael, then deposit me at your front door, that there was no time to lose. After *that,* well, I really don't know what the child did."

After a scrumptious meal of crispy duck, grilled asparagus in garlic sauce, and a chocolate mousse for desert, James said, "Your favorite room is all ready for you, Lady Carla." And he started to turn to leave but Carla called him back.

"James, would it be alright if I stayed?"

James was abashed she would even ask. "Of course. How long, so that I know what to prepare?"

Carla looked into James's eyes with an unexpected depth and seriousness. "Here to stay to the bitter end!"

Chills ran across James's arms, which is odd for a holy person. "But dear Carla, what about Prince Michael, and what about the fact that you've been through *enough* in your life? You're holy, and you deserve to be at the Holy Mountain, not facing, well, *whatever* evil will come our way."

Carla wiped tears from her eyes but steadied herself. "Little Michael is a handful, but Jean has complete mastery over him, and there are plenty of other holy people there as well, not to mention that Arlupo can't help but to keep visiting the child. *Apparently,* he's learned *somehow* to invite her himself, so she can get past all the protection Vaughn and Stephanie placed over the mountain!"

James kept silently staring into Carla's eyes, expecting the rest of the answer, and when she saw James wasn't to be dissuaded, she sighed, then said, "My gifts are too precious to sit this out from afar. Everyone *needs* me, they just don't know it, yet. Besides, Mandy is here, and Stephanie, and Vaughn, *you,* so how can I abandon *any* of you? And of course, Larson and Rebecca and the other girls."

James sighed, saying, "You're so *very* precious. But you haven't seen nor felt what I have as Master Vaughn viewed the *Beast* thorough *that* screen right there. *Please* Carla. *Everyone* wants *you,* of all people, to be safe through the end. You have *no* idea what you might suffer if you stay here."

But Carla simply smiled, and casually said, "But I do! Good night, my dear James. I love you so much.

CHAPTER 9
# Who *is* Like Unto the Beast?

*"Come in Lord Mafferan," Moses spoke just as Mafferan was about to knock! The fact the he called him Lord was unsettling. Though Moses was quite a bit later in history than Mafferan, Mafferan never could help feeling like Moses was his elder.*

*Mafferan touched the mezuzah on the door post then opened and gently closed. The perfectly square living room walls had beautiful woven tapestries of red, blue, and gold geometric designs, yet different from the Appendaho though none the less just as holy in meaning. An ornate, square, ebony table rested in the middle of the room, and wicker chairs, like the kind you'd still find down there amongst desert people, surrounded the table in a circle. Moses' orb set on a golden pedestal and he humbly stretched out his arm for Mafferan to take a seat. After Mafferan sat, Moses took a seat that left two empty seats between them, whereupon Mafferan faithwalked himself over to sit next to the lawgiver.*

Moses' was dressed in a simple brown robe, and with eyes twinkling, said, "You could have simply got up and walked. Here, more to your liking," and Moses waived his hand and Mafferan's chair turned into a thronelike comfort chair with carved chestnut lions for the arms, royal colored seat padding and back, with a wooden lamb by his right ear and a lion by his left.

Mafferan had no idea Moses was a faithwalker but his surprise competed with how uncomfortable he felt sitting in such luxury while Moses was still in the desert, so Mafferan turned the chair as before. But before Mafferan could speak, Moses answered his thoughts. "I didn't know either, until my anger got the better of me and I smote the rock the second time and it still brought forth water, even though the Lord had told me to speak to it. I'll tell you, that realization was quite humbling!"

"Humbling," Mafferan said in awe and shook his head at all he was learning, for he knew Moses had already been declared by the Lord to be the most humble natural man ever. "My Lord Moses, I am but a child in your presence."

Moses knew Mafferan meant it, but said, "Nonsense. You are my elder. What can I do for you."

But Mafferan truly felt like a child and shook his head trying to remember if he ever had that feeling before, even when down there. "Yes. What more can you do for me. A question."

Moses nodded. "That doesn't sound difficult."

Mafferan folded his hands on his lap and bowed his head searching deeply in spirit. With head still bowed, he asked, "I know you went through unspeakable hardship, but what was the most difficult?"

For Moses, that wasn't hard to answer, but why Mafferan asked, eluded him. "When my people had yet again provoked the Lord, but this time even the Lord's patience had run out and He said unto me, 'Moses, step aside that I might destroy this people in an instant and I will make of thee a great nation.'"

Mafferan nodded, and said, "I thought so!" And he remained silent, which surprised Moses all the more.

"Why do you ask, Lord Mafferan?"

Mafferan sighed deeply. "You put in all that effort into your people, took their continual reproaches, but what really angered you was that the Lord, also, put in in His own effort and they were totally disregarding it. You wanted them destroyed!"

Moses leaned forward and his focus bore deeply into Mafferan. "You are correct!"

Mafferan met Moses eyes but his spiritual tears clouded his vision, and he said, "But at that same time, you also felt the souls of all your people and how they would feel plunged into eternal damnation and that feeling competed with your anger."

Moses held his gaze to Mafferan, folded his hands as his arms rested on his thighs, and waited for Mafferan to continue.

"How did that feeling win out over the others?"

Moses cocked his head in curiosity, "Others? More than just anger?"

Mafferan nodded. "Yes. Because you defied the Lord's directive when he told you what to do. That had to be even harder. And both your anger and not wanting to defy the Lord competed against what you ultimately decided. How did you do that?"

*Moses leaned back and beheld a man that rivaled him in humility. As long as Moses had been upstairs, no one had come to ask him that question. Most had come to basically sight-see. Which was OK, too, but that question defined Moses whole life! "All that you just described is true." Then Moses bowed his head and tears dropped upon his robe. Then he continued. "I remember it as clearly, more clearly now, than when it actually happened!" And he paused.*

*Mafferan could feel Moses inner struggles and became embarrassed. Embarrassed that he had caused these feelings in, of all men, Moses, and that Mafferan felt in no way worthy to behold them, but Moses looked up again, and said, "The Tree of Life isn't just in its physical location, but is ever present everywhere. It called to you, Mafferan, keeper of the Tree of Life, to ask me that question!"*

*Mafferan couldn't stand it any longer, and he slid off the wicker chair and bowed himself to Moses, saying, "I bow not unto you as God, but unto the depth of goodness he has placed in you that far exceeds any in me."*

*And Moses stood up, leaned down, and touched Mafferan's shoulder and they disappeared, and reappeared in the Lord's special room with such bright golden glow that it almost obscured their spiritual vision. And the Lord spoke to Moses, saying, "Give this man knowledge."*

*And Moses said, "All that you described about me, Mafferan, was true. But when I felt all my people's souls in hell, felt their torment, their regret, the love in me couldn't help but cry out and nothing else seemed to matter. When I fell on my face before the*

*Lord to plead for the people, it wasn't with the spirit of rebellion! The Lord had spoken to me through his Justice, but I responded to His Spirit of Justice with His Spirit of Love. But not just love for the people, for they had greatly offended, but also with my love for the Lord, that if He destroyed them all, then the heathen would mock God for not being able to deliver the people he had promised to save, that the heathen would say he brought out my people to destroy them, not to save them. And I felt with all my heart that this would not glorify our Lord, even though destroying them at that moment was and felt very right."*

*Mafferan was still on his knees with head bowed, but he straightened up now to look at Moses. "I know you have been watching closely your son down there. And I know these same conditions as we just discussed will come upon him, as they came upon you. And upon my daughter, as well. But these times are different, and it is not clear to me how to guide them."*

Lynnara felt she'd been away far too long but there was nothing she could do. Everywhere she went, her third and bestest Mommy kept *popping in on her!* She went to Rebecca's and Stephanie popped in. Then Lynnara popped over to see Carla but while she was *in the ethereal corridor* traveling there, Stephanie popped right into the corridor *exactly* where she was. "How are you, Lynnara?" she would ask each time. *Finally,* after the *sixth* time, when Stephanie caught her outside at Lana's, Lynnara said, "Mommy, why you keep following me? Don't you trust me? You know I can take care of myself! I mean, I'm a *faithwalker,* too."

But Stephanie just eyed Lynnara *very* closely until it made her squirm a little bit. Lynnara knew no deception would work on her Mommy, but she *also* knew how to keep her Mommy out of the part of her mind that dealt with *down South*. She *had to*.

Stephanie knelt down on the grass in front of Lana's door and threw her arms open, and Lynnara delightfully dove in for a much needed hug. She could feel her Mommy's strength pour into her and comfort her all around and she squeezed her Mommy as tight as she could. Because what Lynnara was doing down *South* was *all* for her Mommy but she didn't know it. Well, all for her Mommy and the whole world.

Stephanie, while on her knees in her brown peasant dress leaned back and took Lynnara by the shoulders and leveled her eyes into her daughter. Lynnara could feel her Mommy in her mind and heart and she put her little hands on Stephanie's cheeks. "I love you Mommy, more than you know!"

Stephanie squinted at her again. She had asked Lynnara several times what she was up to but each time Lynnara just told her what she was doing at the present. "Something is going on. I can *feel* it." And Stephanie pinched her cheek. "Well, whatever it is, Lynnara, you *know* if you need me or Daddy, we can be there for you just like *that*." And Stephanie snapped her fingers.

Lynnara nodded, and Lana came up to Stephanie and hugged her sister. "I miss you. You're so *busy* all the time. I don't like the new Jargono."

Stephanie was about to look deeply into Lana, because she *knew* that whatever Lynnara was up to, Lana was *sure* to be in on it, too, but when Lana spoke of Jargono, it refocused Stephanie. "I don't like him, either. It's *not* Jargono. He's the *Beast* I've been telling you about."

Lana and Lynnara's eyes grew wide and looked at each other. *Now* they began to understand Carla's warning that Mommy and Daddy had too much to do. Lynnara asked, "When are you going to fight him, Mommy?"

Now it was Stephanie that just smiled and whisked the question away, "Nothing to worry about, children. Sometimes it's not about fighting but about making the battlefield *first.* Do you understand *that?*"

Both girls shrugged their shoulders. Lynnara said, "Mommy, you *know* if you need me, I'm just," and she snapped her fingers like her Mommy, "that far away."

And Stephanie saw the deep seriousness, concern, and love Lynnara had for her, she could feel every bit of it. Stephanie reached out her arms and hugged them both. "Well, I feel better when you two are together. But I feel even better than *that* when Rebecca is with you. She's grown quite *practical,* you know? Where is she? How come you didn't bring her with you to Lana's?"

Lynnara said, "We're on our way over. With Carla being away, and Ranger Larson away, Rebecca said she had to clean up the house."

Stephanie looked at them oddly. "Where's Carla?"

Lynnara and Lana looked at each other and, realizing it was no secret, both said, "She went home to our castle!" And when they saw the look on Stephanie's face, Lynnara said, "I was on my way to see Michael when you popped in on me, Mommy. But when I was there, Carla asked me to pop her to our home. So I did."

Stephanie's face was a picture of deep thought and the children knew they didn't have to worry about her finding out their secret. "Well, children, I think I'll just pop home and see her." And she vanished. Lynnara gave a quick stare at Lana and Lana knew not to say anything, yet, because Stephanie was probably still watching them from the Corridor. The children began talking about and fussing over their hair until Lynnara said, "OK, she's gone. Let's go get Rebecca then get to work!"

Stephanie popped into the dining room at home dressed in her usual brown peasant dress but she kept her traditional, fiery-red, three Appendaho braids behind her. As she looked around, James sensed her presence immediately and came out from his study. "Lady Stephanie. Please have a seat and I'll get you some food. You *know* you don't eat enough."

Stephanie smiled, but said, "That's alright James. Where's Carla?"

Surprised, in a way, but not in another, James said, "She went to her room." And Stephanie left the dining room, went down the long stone hall and right when she was about to knock, Carla opened the door and they immediately fell into a deep hug.

They were more than just spiritual sisters. Ever since Stephanie met Carla in the military dining hall with that damned chain still around her ankle, they had immediately bonded within a special knowledge of deep suffering. And if it wasn't for Carla, Stephanie knew she, herself, never would have made it through the horrendous challenges she had faced. Yet, Carla knew, if it wasn't for Stephanie having befriended a rebellious, ungrateful Mandy, her blood sister, then neither Carla nor Mandy would have been saved.

"What are you doing here, Carla. Michael *needs* you." But that wasn't her real meaning, and Carla knew it.

Carla took Stephanie by the arms, saying, "Stephanie, I know you mean well, but you have to *stop* trying to spare me suffering and danger. We are *sisters,* as Mandy *loves* to say with such defiance against the whole world." And Carla had said that word *sisters* just like Mandy says it and Stephanie burst out laughing which engulfed Carla, too.

Stephanie said, "Every time she says it like that, she just makes me marvel. There's some kind of power in it that even *I* don't quite understand!"

Carla just shook her head. "I know what you mean. I feel it too. It always makes me think some miracle is right around the corner in defense of us, of our sisterhood. OK, come in, let's sit on the bed like we used to do and talk."

As Stephanie went into her room, she realized how much she'd missed these times together. But *still,* Stephanie had an uneasy feeling about Carla and the girls. When they sat down on the soft, magnificent quilt, Stephanie squared around to look deeply into Carla but before she even got a chance to enter her mind, Carla said, "The Lord Jesus won't let you or *anyone* do that!"

That shocked Stephanie, and she had a certain humility come over her, so she waited on Carla.

"Dear Stephanie, the Lord. . . gives me deep visions. As you well know. But they are *only* for me! And the work He gives me is *only* for me. So Jesus has made my mind and my heart impenetrable! Do you trust me, Stephanie?" And Carla's eyes bore deeply into *Stephanie's* heart!

Stephanie had sudden pains in her chest because she realized in some way that she *didn't*, or, at least that she knew Carla was withholding certain knowledge from her. But as she returned Carla's gaze with just Stephanie's natural heart and mind, Stephanie burst into tears because she loved Carla in such a special way. Stephanie *knew* the real goodness that *is* Carla. "I do, with all my being, I do. We are *sisters.*"

❧

They left the Jeep as close as they could but still had quite a hike. They all expected to be too late so were prepared for a battle, if need be. Mandy had quickly regained her strength and actually had to keep slowing down for the men to catch up. When she held up her hand for them all to stop, they ducked behind a wide oak tree, and there they stayed for about fifteen minutes just watching the dead bodies across the fence, waiting to see if it was a trap,

When they heard the other crew coming, John raced back to meet them. A bit later, Franco and Jerry came carrying the fence hopper. Blackbeard only pointed forward and everyone went into action. As Jerry, a wavy redhaired fellow and in the lead, got closer to the fence he stopped about five feet away and set the ladder feet into the soft ground, and Max began straightening the aluminum ladder to vertical. When it was sixty degrees toward the fence, Jerry immediately pulled a rope which extended a ladder section. Up it went, but at a certain point, Jerry pulled another rope and the extended section suddenly pivoted downward and slammed into the ground forming a perfect A over the fence. Jerry slammed his foot down on each of the spikes at the sides of the ladder feet to hold it to the ground then up he went straightway. At the peak, he deftly swung himself around and descended into enemy territory, after which he went straight to the tree where the rope was and climbed it. Franco had gone back for the Jeep.

Blackbeard went off to the left, then on one knee, took his rifle with scope and kept scanning from side to side. John did the same to the right. Max had also gone over the fence and was now searching the pockets of the enemy, pulling papers out, taking pictures with his phone, and then replacing them. Max was a burly guy with his black hair cut short in military style but he couldn't help from a shiver wracking through his body as he touched these profane dead bodies with their garish face makeup seemingly shouting at him. Even in death, they still possessed an abominable active presence.

Mandy still had no clue how any of what they were doing would avoid disaster, but everyone, without Blackbeard even explaining *anything,* seemed so purposeful, that success almost seemed imminent! Mandy saw the rope fall from the tree then Jerry climbed back down, Max took the enemy's pistols from their holsters, fired them across the fence multiple times then placed them in the enemy's hands. *Then* Jerry picked up one of the demon dogs, hoisted it over his shoulder and proceeded to climb back up the ladder and somehow managed with that heavy beast to swing back around and come down. He laid the dog down on their side of the fence some twenty feet in!

Max then climbed back over, and while Jerry held the ladder firm, Max planted his foot firmly on the lower rung, and with a great grunt, pulled the rope and the extended ladder portion rose from the ground, locked into place, and slid back down the ladder to its resting position. Mandy had never seen this done and her mouth was agape, her eyes wide. Blackbeard came over and threw his arm around her shoulders laughing at her reaction. What's the matter *little girl*, you're not used to seeing *real* men work?

Mandy looked into his twinkling dark brown eyes and just smiled. "It's very comforting, actually, but I still don't understand how all this helps."

"Just leave it to the *men*, little lady." And Blackbeard simply nodded to the rest.

Jerry went back into the woods, Max climbed the tree with the rope still attached on his side of the fence, and Blackbeard, still arm around Mandy, walked her a good bit away. After a while, the Jeep weaved its way carefully around trees and pulled in front of an old dead pine. Max had pulled the rope from the other side, then came down with it and loaded the ladder back on the Jeep. Then he climbed the old pine and tied the rope two-thirds the way up, but he didn't come down!

Jerry took the rope end Max had tossed and tied it to the Jeep's main frame. Blackbeard whispered in Mandy's ear,

"Timber!" And Franco made the Jeep lurch forward and Max threw his weight forward at the same time. The dead tree uprooted from the soft, damp forest ground, the Jeep veered left, Maxed leapt from the tree before it hit the fence and he rolled away. Mandy's mouth was agape, again, but her eyes were even wider than before.

The electric fence was now popping with sparks as the fallen tree had smashed a section of it tightly together. Max untied the rope, got in the Jeep with Jerry, but Franco grabbed a rake and as the Jeep slowly drove away, he covered up all the tracks including his own. Blackbeard let Mandy go, and took his phone, and mumbled. "I can't remember where that *damned* number is. They gave it to me in case of emergency but no one has *ever* used it. Never had need. But you know, you gotta have a number. Everything now rests on this little number, ahh, if I can find it."

Mandy's eyes were wide again, but she became aware of her little girl expression and closed her mouth, waiting. Blackbeard kept scrolling through his contacts, then went to his email, then back to his contacts. "Oh, I remember. I labeled it *Pain in the Ass,* not because of the number, but the damned *bureaucrat* that kept forcing me to do a thousand worthless things and the *last* thing was he gave me this number, just as an *aside!* Turns out, it's the *only* thing he did that's worth anything."

It seemed like the phone rang forever. Blackbeard had it on speaker. The man's voice that finally answered sounded rather mundane, even pleasant, with a unique accent! "Hello? Is this a wrong number?"

Blackbeard became instantly incredulous. "Fucking *wrong number?* Do you *know* what this line *is?* This is the *end of the fucking world* line. Who the *hell* are *you?* Does *that* sound like I have the damned wrong number?"

"One moment!"

And there they waited for close to twenty minutes until an equally disagreeable man answered with a similar unique accent. "Who the *fuck* is *this?*"

Blackbeard straightened, then smiled. "Well, *finally,* someone I can talk to. I'm the ranger at our southern border, your *northern* border. I'm sending you the coordinates right now. I *assume* you're speakin' from a cell able to receive this. You *got it?*"

A moment later, "Got it," the gruff voice spoke. "So why the fuck you callin'?"

Blackbeard let out a roaring laugh. "Well, I'll be honest seein' as we *obviously* see eye to eye, so to speak. We just had quite the strange occurrence on your side and our side da fence. Remember while back we had all those damned demons, dragons, and otherworldly creatures from hell runnin' around?"

There was a minute of silence then the voice calmed a bit. "That was mostly your problem. We only seen scant of it down here. You *know,* we're *third-world,* not *important* to you high-minded Northerners, so *not important* to your enemies neither."

Blackbeard squinted, muted the phone, and said to Mandy, "This guy's the real deal. He's sharp, savvy, and *dangerous.*" Then Blackbeard continued, "Well, we had a tree come down our side and smashed our fence. Went to investigate. Got *immediately* attacked by demon *damned dogs,* and while we were a killin' 'em, these human *demons* actually began firing guns at us across from your side da fence. Never seen human demons use guns before, but we had to take 'em out real quick. *Hey, we fuckin' did your job for ya.* You're supposed to keep *your* side da fence in *order!*"

There was a *long* pause of near to fifteen minutes, then the man came back on even calmer. "I sent this to the top, and our King wants to offer his sincere apologies. He'll convey his appreciation to your current but outgoing King. Folks are on their way. Be there in half hour. Let us know if you need help with repairs and we'll step up patrols." And he hung up!

Mandy looked at Blackbeard, and he said, "No. It's not over. They're sendin' their crack team to check everything out. We just wait here. You'll know what to do when the time comes."

Blackbeard turned to John. "How fast you think we can mine this whole damned border *at night* without any one the wiser, neither *them,*" and Blackbeard pointed to the South, "nor *them!*" And he pointed to the North.

John gave a low whistle, shook his head, then said, "We're gonna' have to swear a lot more Rangers to Ranger's Word."

Blackbeard looked at Mandy and she shook her head. This was just getting bigger and bigger, *almost* out of control. But then again, if *anyone* could pull this off, the Rangers could, so she nodded, and Blackbeard said, "You saw the boss! She said go ahead!"

John looked Heavenward, not a praying man, but he said, "Lord Jesus. Three weeks!"

Mandy said, "Get it *done. Get it done in two!*"

Both men staired at her then, because her tone took them completely by surprise, but the steel in her eyes convinced them. They all understood who Mandy really was, that she was the *sister* to Queen Stephanie, and that *surely* by spirit she measured up to every square inch of it.

Blackbeard said, "*Two* weeks Princess Mandy!"

"Two weeks," John said, and bowed his head to her.

Never had these men had such love for *any* woman other than Queen Stephanie, and they wondered how many more women might be like *this*!

Mandy was taken aback. She didn't even expect to say it like that. It just came out. *Princess? Am I a princess? Huh!*

# CHAPTER 10

# What Has Been, Will Be . . . But Worse

*Yinauqua and Mafferan both looked up from their golden orb into each other's eyes because someone was knocking on their door! Both were perplexed because no one ever knocked up in Heaven, well, except for them! Mafferan considered just hollering to come in but a peculiar feeling came over him that that would be entirely inappropriate, so they both went to answer with Yinauqua smoothing her brown peasant dress and Mafferan tugging on his tan tunic.*

*It's not often, in fact, never, that Mafferan or Yinauqua's mouths would drop open in surprise, but seeing him at their door had exactly that effect. Everyone knew him by name, and he is always recognizable by sight even if you'd never met him. He was that kind of the rarest of saints. Yet, he just didn't hang around anyone much, though rumors had it that he did spend considerable time with Moses, though, those were only unconfirmed rumors.*

*Mafferan went down to one knee, and Yinauqua, with her hand on her husband's shoulder, bowed low, both saying, "Out of respect for the very special goodness our Lord Jesus has made you to be."*

*But Elijah, in full black and white beard, with black robe tied at the waist with a simple twine rope, said with a smile, "Nonsense! We're all special." And there he stood in their doorway, still.*

*Until Mafferan and Yinauqua realized their rudeness, and apologized. "Forgive us Lord Elijah. Please come in."*

*And as they walked directly into the circular living room with the beautiful Appendaho tapestries on the circular walls and large, circular Appendaho handmade rug, all with holy Appendaho geometric designs in gold, royal reds, and royal blues, Mafferan was about to create a special royal chair for their guest when Elijah said, "You'll need to sit, but I'll stand!"*

It had been too long since Vaughn last sat at dinner with Harris and his family. This simple man, on the surface, merely dressed as the others in mere brown work pants and shirt, but Harris was Jewish, and therefore from among the thousands King Vaughn had rescued from the North. Harris, along with Ranger Larson, headed up the Jews now infamous secret service. Most of them were now, in fact, holy, which made them even more effective, able to shield themselves from evil in ways regular mortals could not.

Harris and Larson pushed their empty plates away and thanked Harris' wife for the wonderful turkey dinner, whereupon she smiled, gathered their four boys of four, six, and eight, and fourteen and left. Harris said, "I have something to show you all in my basement." And they got up, went through a narrow door, down steep narrow steps, and into a small empty room with an old, dry, faded, square wooden table with similar four chairs around it. A single, old electric bulb hung above the table by no more than the electric cord itself.

Vaughn reached out his hand and his staff appeared, then he raised it once, then smacked its foot down on the floor with a sharp protest from the concrete, and the whole room lit up with a silver glow, after which the men took their seats. This ritual was well known to them now.

Vaughn turned to Larson first. "Stephanie tells me Carla is at the castle now and plans to stay."

Larson's eyebrows went up. "How long?" But Vaughn just silently stared at him and Larson understood, saying, "Well, that's part of what makes me love her so very much. I could spend eternity just holding *that* woman in my arms!"

Vaughn said, "How long has it been since you two saw each other?"

Larson shrugged. "King Vaughn," for Vaughn would *always* be *their* King even after abdicating the Northern throne, "I don't think right now that we have time for me to figure that out."

Vaughn said, "Harris and I will handle what needs to be discussed now." And Vaughn, while sitting in his chair, smacked the foot of his staff down again and Larson disappeared!

Harris smiled. "I'm glad you did that. They haven't seen much of each other at all, and they *need* to. Besides, we can use him up North, now, anyway. It's a *lot* more difficult up there."

Vaughn's eyes twinkled, imagining Carla's surprise. "In truth, Stephanie told me to send him up. She *insisted!* And she's right. We men tend to keep putting our women on the backburner so we can *get things done.* But they *need* us, and truth be told, we need to be rejuvenated by them, too. Desperately!"

Harris nodded to the truth of that. He, himself, was equally guilty of neglect. Harris ran his hand over his short brown, wavy hair, saying, "It's just that we don't have enough time to get everything done that we *could* do."

Vaughn said, "Well, isn't that *always* true? Where do we stand, Harris?"

Thinking of all that *could* still be done, Harris sighed deeply, saying, "Doing it the way you wanted, takes a lot more time, but I understand that's really the *only* safe way. We even use the *underground,* believe it or not. Yea, it surfaced after you two became rulers, but then a new underground formed because, well, there's always a need for that. Anyway, our agents have spent *considerable* time in the bars, the shops, even the *grocery stores* just making idle conversations, planting the ideas. But *frankly,* it's a lot easier to motivate the undesirables down here to move up North than it is to motivate our people up there to come down here."

"What *percentage?*" Vaughn asked, his sharp brown, almost black eyes bore into Harris.

"For the undesirables, and that's *not* the many spies that won't leave because they've been *sent* to be here, I would say eighty to eighty-five percent have *already* left!"

Vaughn nodded appreciatively, but then asked the even more important question. "What about ours up North?"

Harris sighed again. "*Maybe* fifty percent. Up North they're also poorer so hard for them to just pick up and move. Of course, one word from *you,* and they'd probably *all* move the next day!"

But Vaughn shook his head. "One word from me like *that,* and we'll have another civil *war* the very next day. Stephanie, and even I, now, am able to watch people without them knowing. The Beast has been preparing the North for some time. It wouldn't take much at all for him to galvanize the people to rebel, at least up North. The northern people already feel that I and the conservative Christians think we're *superior* to them. They've even started their *own* Christianity that's *Beastlike* which only serves to further the danger. If I overtly try to make a division, *especially now,* they'll just call it quits even on the elections and simply try to *force* the kind of rule they want for the *whole* United States. They're at that point now, Harris. *Bold. In our faces!* And with the anti-Christ now *overtly* on the scene, they're just waiting for the go sign."

Harris nodded. "But they *won't* go as long as they feel they're gonna win the elections anyway."

"Correct." Vaughn hung his head in despair. "When things *do* flip, those poor conservative Christians are going to be *trapped.* There won't be *anything* I can do." And the deep pain Vaughn felt was evident. Harris could feel his heart breaking. Vaughn further said, "Fifty percent. That's a *lot* of families Harris. *Trapped. Tortured.* Put to the test. . . And I don't think they're ready. Up North is *not* like down South where we finally straightened out that *mess* of religious divisions. When we straightened it out down South, the ones that *didn't* want to correct themselves worked their way up North and created the same problems. But their *prescriptive* Christianity doesn't have the power of the Holy Ghost. *And,* it doesn't even have the power of the *right* prescription, which many down South who are not yet holy *do have* while they wait to be born again.

Harris said, "Up North is unique. Bands of roving Beast followers are randomly mocking, getting in the way of, and even *chasing* Christians around. Their children, too. Yet, the Northern Christians' response is to be *very* careful, to be *meek,* thinking *that's* what Jesus wants them to be. "

Vaughn shook his head. "They've been taught by their *feckless* leaders the *wrong* meaning of that word *meek.* It doesn't mean let yourself be abused. Doesn't mean you *cower* in the face of evil. *Harris,*" and the basement shook a bit, "I've watched these Christians hold family night at the library where they wanted to read their Bible and tell wholesome stories. These *funny* people with their *funny* colors and perversity get right up in their faces, *in the faces of their children* showing off their perversity as a *protest!*" And the basement shook again.

Harris shook his head. "I had no idea *that* was going on, but then again, with so much else to worry about, well, I just didn't know, but *clearly* that is part of a greater strategy. In the secret service world we call that 'grooming a population.' Getting them ready for a totally different kind of rule and life."

Vaughn said, "Do you know what these so-called Northern Christian leaders response to all this is?" Harris groaned in anticipation, and Vaughn said, "That's sad!" Harris' eyes went wide at the absurdity. And Vaughn said, "That's *it*, Harris. Can you *believe that?* Those perverts are shoving *poison* down the Christian kids throats *right in front of their parents,* and all they can do, all they can say is, it's *sad!* That's *not* what love your enemies means, to be so weak and *un*offensive. Jesus offended pretty much *everyone* at some point in time." Vaughn was infuriated and turned deep black but held his power in.

Harris shook his head, "They're a far cry from what Jesus said to be, If a town receive you not, stand in the middle of that town and basically tell them they're reprobates, the *scum* of the Earth and they're goin' to hell. *That's* the kind of love your enemies they *don't* understand! Standing up for the Truth no matter who feels whatever. And you know what? Those *prescriptive Christians* never ask how come no harm ever came to the holy people when they did that. They don't understand the power we have in the Holy Ghost and that it would be so *very* easy for us to *destroy* our enemies! *That's* where *meekness* comes in. They don't understand that when they turned the other cheek and the enemy smote them again, that it didn't harm them! As Jesus said, And *nothing* shall by any means hurt you! *That's* why they turned the other cheek! To *show* them they couldn't be harmed because Jesus is, in fact, our Lord! Such response then asks them a question, What have you gained by your evil? Now *that's* powerful love!"

Vaughn nodded and sighed. "*That's* the true meaning of *meek,* Harris. *That's* why Jesus told us to be harmless, because he gave us the power to *not be harmless!* In other words, we exercise *restraint, but* we don't allow them to get the better of us, *especially* to harm our children. We are *supposed to* protect the innocent, the weak, the elderly and such. But as far as we're concerned, if and when the Lord gives us over to be harmed and put to death for His glory and judgment, well, that's *His* choosing, not the *world's!* But mostly, now, He *doesn't* because the Season has *changed!* Love your enemies has now become *judge* your enemies through the Holy Ghost."

Harris nodded again, saying, "Cast not thy pearls before the swine lest they trample them under their feet then turn and rend you. *Clearly,* Jesus didn't want *any* of us harmed *nor* to cower, but what do you think would happen now if we, say, tried to show those Christians how to damn well stand up for themselves?"

Vaughn ran his hand through his dark brown, almost black wavey hair, saying, "I think the Beast doubles down and comes at them harder. The time for the Christians to stand up for themselves was when all that *crap* first began to happen. If they had stood up then, they would have backed the Beast off, made him reconsider, because he wouldn't have wanted a Northern Christian rebellion to gain strength against him. But *now?*" Vaughn just shook his head in contemplation, in searching out the possibilities.

Harris folded his hands upon the table, and prayed, "Lord Jesus, help these poor Christians, who, in spite of themselves, *still* love your name and cling to it in truth. Help them understand that if they don't *soon* leave the Beast's land and come South, they will go through tribulation the likes of which has never been known before!"

❧

Two hours later three Jeeps pulled up the old road and stopped just shy of the downed fence. Six burly military men got out, all wearing light brown uniforms, all black hair, and dark eyes, all in peak physical shape. These weren't funny looking people at all, but would fit well within any Ranger group, except the scowls and distrust on their faces identified them as the enemy. Their weapons remained on their backs and holstered but there was no doubt between Mandy, John, or Blackbeard that those weapons would be drawn faster than a sneeze if need be.

All the men began walking around inspecting everything, *everywhere*. One went far down to the left studying the ground and the other to the far right doing the same. One of them came up and kicked the demon dog on their side, then he shook his head. He looked directly up at Blackbeard recognizing his demeanor as the leader, and said, "This beast is almost as ugly as *you!*"

Blackbeard glowered at him, then reached down and grabbed the demon dog's carcass next to him then held him up. "This one's a fair resemblance to your *mother,* but I *still* said no!"

Both men glared at each other again then burst out laughing! Blackbeard said, "Come on over, friend. Take look 'round till your hearts content." And he waved them in, so three of the men used the fallen tree to scamper over the still live fence, while Blackbeard said, "I figured you wanted the scene undisturbed, so haven't touched it yet."

The man nodded and walked around for some time. One went way left, one went way right, while the other came back and stood there, and asked, "What happened?"

Blackbeard said, "This lil' lady was on patrol when it all happened."

Mandy eyed him, not showing any approval at all, even though the man was instantly awed that *she* was the one who caused all this. Part of him was immediately captivated by Mandy's beauty, of which he made note to himself to be *sure* and find *this one* when they invaded, but the other part of him couldn't fathom what Mandy did, so he eyed her suspiciously expecting an answer.

Mandy eyed him back. "This tree came down. Made a way for the demon dogs to go and come across the border. I get here and they go to attack me. I put them down quick. *Those two* showed up. Guns were fired. And I took them all out."

The man put his hand on his pistol. That was more than a threat, it was a signal to the others who all drew their weapons before Blackbeard and the others could blink. The man said, "You expect me to believe you downed *two* demon men with guns with a mere bow?"

Two men from the other side of the fence came right up to it and stood together about six feet apart, guns pointed at them. Mandy turned away from the man who insulted her, and walked away a bit, but as she walked, she became sultry again, the way her hips swayed and a certain tension in her body. *Everyone* was frozen in the moment and *that's* when Mandy whirled, and in one fluid motion her bow came off her shoulder, she knocked two arrows, and they buried themselves into the right thighs of the men across the fence. The force of the arrows, as well as the special blessing within them spun them around and landed them with their faces planted in the old road. And there they lay, moaning and in shock at the excruciating pain, more pain than they thought they should experience even from such powerful arrows.

Blackbeard raised an eyebrow at his impressed foe, who nodded in approval, and said, "Well. That was *convincing.* Do you want help with your *fence?*" He almost couldn't help from laughing when he said the word *fence* and Blackbeard didn't like the feeling he got from that.

But Mandy came back around, saying, "If we wanted your help, we'd *hire* you out of *pity*! Get the *hell* back where you belong!" Now, on *several* accounts Mandy knew this wasn't going to be received well, but she also had picked up on this bastard's thoughts of what he wanted to do to her when they invaded. Blackbeard tensed inside because he had felt they were in the clear *until* Mandy decided to do *this!* But Blackbeard did have sense enough to turn and walk away, as if to say, Ok, this is a *private* beef!

When the enemy saw Blackbeard's response, he felt free to react to Mandy *just between him and her.* "Listen you *young bitch.* You don't talk to a *grown man* that way, and *you* a *woman."* Then he pointed at his chest and thumped it. "And we don't *need* your fucking *pity.* And we'd *never* work for you fuckin' *gringos* anymore. We're. . ."

It was a good thing Mandy leapt in the air and kicked him square in the chest and knocked him on his ass, because the poor man had lost his temper so much that he was about to spill their secret plans! And Mandy knew it, *knew* he would, but also knew she'd cut him off before he did! But Blackbeard sighed because he *knew* Mandy could have simply knocked him out, but she *didn't*. Which meant Mandy wasn't done with him, yet!

"Mandy," Blackbeard said, but she simply shook her head with an ominous look that sent a chill even into Blackbeard. John came up and stood by him, whispering, "This oughta be interesting."

Mandy set down her bow, her quiver, took off her tool belt where her axe and knife were and then beckoned the man in a sultry voice, "Come on, if your *man* enough!"

The man threw his own tool belt down and the other still whole man from across the fence even came over to get a closer look, while licking their lips. Mandy began to tease and taunt the leader, laughing at him but he wasn't easily baited, and when Blackbeard saw *that* he knew this man was considerably high up in their order. He wished Mandy could hear his thoughts, *Mandy, you* don't *know what you're dealing with, here. Just stand down, even just apologize! There's greater things to consider here.*

To Blackbeard's surprise, thoughts appeared in his head from Mandy! *The* hell *I will. Do you* know *what this bastard has in mind for me, for* all *of us? I want them to* know *it ain't gonna be that easy!*

Blackbeard couldn't believe Mandy just communicated that way to him, just like Lady Stephanie, but in truth, this telepathy seemed to naturally develop in her during her training while seeking to anticipate her enemy's moves. She began to naturally enter their minds, but not only *that,* she could also plant in them a few thoughts as well. And things just grew from there!

The man walked slowly toward Mandy but she cartwheeled to the side so he changed direction, saying, "Ok lil' *bitch,* I didn't know you wanted to *dance* with me. I'll be your *dance* partner." And he vulgarly pumped his hips and his men burst out in raucous cheers.

But as he was pumping, Mandy spun around and threw two handfuls of grit she picked up from the road during her cartwheel. His reflexes were fast enough to keep it from his eyes and to throw his elbows in front of his face to block an expected aerial attack, but *not* fast enough to respond to Mandy's unexpected roll.

She rolled right up to his legs and kicked up square into his groin. And as he doubled over, Mandy, from on her back on the ground brought both her legs up against her chest then kicked up into his face with both feet as hard as she could and with a scream for emphasis.

He flew up and back onto his back and landed with a grunt. Then Mandy leapt up, whirled, and round-housed another enemy across the side of the head, then drove her elbow into the flank of the one who had been next to him, and when *he* doubled over, she brought her knee up into his face and he went down with face all bloody. The only other enemy left standing began to move toward Mandy but Blackbeard wagged his finger, "Nah, nah. I thought you guys were *tougher* than that! I mean, *three* men against *one* of our women. OK. But *not* four." And Blackbeard turned very dark, as well as John.

Mandy said. "If we *ever* go to war, I'll be sure and tell my superiors not to waste our *men* on you. Get the *fuck* off our land, and do your damned job on *your* side of the fence!"

The enemy didn't stick around, and between John, Blackbeard, and Mandy, they were able to cut up and remove the tree and set the fence back right just as evening fell. When it came time to part, Mandy had tears, "I don't know what to say. You have *no* idea."

And Blackbeard enveloped her in a massive, fatherly hug, patting her back. "If I *ever* had a daughter, I'd want her to be *you*. Hands down, *you*. You've got *grit* like no other." And John hugged her, too, and seconded the notion. Blackbeard said, "Two weeks, Princess Mandy, and the whole border will be *deeply* mined. What you *don't* know, but since you shared *your* secret, I'll share ours . . . Rangers Word?"

Now Mandy was intrigued. "Ranger's Word."

"King Vaughn and Queen Stephanie have armed *all* the smaller outposts to the teeth these last two years! They're no fools, though I really don't think they expected any attack from down *here*. Nevertheless, we're as ready as we could be! Mind you, the mines will only slow them down, but with time, we always have more possibilities."

Mandy began to bawl at the unexpected good news because, even though things were still dour, they were a *lot* brighter with this knowledge. All the way back to the shelter through the damp woods Mandy kept playing the unbelievable day's events back to herself. And she loved the fatherly treatment she got because both her parents had died when she was young. But when she went into the shelter, she stopped right in the doorway and couldn't believe what she saw. It wasn't just Shane and Samantha and the three she rescued, but *ten* more crowded in besides, and her mouth dropped open! "How?" was all she managed to say.

Shane came forward and took Mandy's hands and pulled her in the rest of the way, telling everyone, "This is *Mandy*, one of our saviors." Then Shane turned to Mandy, and said. "Once we saw what you did for us, we couldn't just sit here and do nothing. So we went to other places and figured how to save others! Don't worry. We hid what we did. We were *very* careful."

# CHAPTER 11

# Heroes in All Shapes and Sizes

*Elijah's presence filled their whole abode and his black robe and full black and white beard added to that effect demonstrably. Neither Yinauqua nor Mafferan had ever even spoken to him, but saw him a couple times at a distance. Mafferan had created a semi-comfortable Appendaho couch for him and his wife to sit upon while listening and Elijah wasted no time.*

*"Brother Moses and I are very different. And we had very different challenges. Moses was a law-giver, for the most part, and he even threw it around a bit." And Elijah paused, waiting for his audience to get the joke! When he saw they didn't, he said, "Moses threw the tablets?"*

*And Yinauqua and Mafferan looked at each other like children and shook their heads and rolled their eyes. They were expecting utter seriousness and never expected Elijah's sense of humor to be, well, a bit corny. They couldn't believe Elijah was like this! Mafferan said, "Well, I suppose that still falls within lawgiving. I suppose!"*

*And to that, Elijah gave a hearty belly laugh. "Yes, indeed. That's true." And after he calmed from appreciating Mafferan's humor, Elijah said, "Moses was a law giver, a plague caster, but I was a law enforcer!" And Elijah paused to let that difference sink in. Then he said, "Moses was a good deal earlier than I, and the children of Israel had many years to get used to, to acquaint themselves with the intricacies of God's law. But there comes a point when that law must needs be enforced. Do you understand why both Moses and I appeared on the Holy Mountain with our Lord Jesus for Peter, James, and John to see, but no others?"*

*Mafferan and his wife looked into each other's eyes again to see if they did, but, in truth, they hadn't thought about it, and were reluctant to offer or search out an explanation while still feeling dwarfed by Elijah.*

*Elijah sighed, and said, "Maybe I will sit down for a bit!" And he waved his hand and a matching chair appeared across from their couch! Mafferan and Yinauqua looked at each other again, even more astonished.*

*Elijah simply said, "Oh, I thought you two, of all the saints up here would have realized I'm a faithwalker, too. Come on now. Shut the Heavens so no rain? Open the Heavens for rain. Part the river and walk across dry? Healing? Dear children! You must get over being over-impressed by my presence. You are my equals!" And Elijah had sparks dancing around in his eyes that seemed to tease their very depths.*

*And there Elijah sat, waiting, but said, "I would love some of your famous fruit salad, though!" And Mafferan and*

Yinauqua shook their heads at themselves for how doubly rude they had been for not even offering their guest a drink. "While your dishing it up, you can think about your answer!"

But Mafferan and Yinauqua couldn't seem to multitask at that moment and they knew that question bore great importance to down there *right now.*

Elijah's demeanor suddenly changed to very serious, and he called into the kitchen, "Do you see how you feel right now? You haven't felt like that in a very long time. You can't think. Your feelings are jumbled, and there is no one greater than you up here for the task at hand! But that's exactly how they are going to feel down there! And you need to help them not be that way or they will fail!"

There's not supposed to be blushing in Heaven. Why would anyone be embarrassed, but both Yinauqua and Mafferan alone in the kitchen turned red, but they began to think, now, upon Elijah's question.

Elijah called into the kitchen, yet, again. "Each of you is made out of the Lord's goodness. There is never a good reason to doubt it, nor to hesitate on it, no matter what other circumstances surround you. If I had hesitated, Jezebel would have indeed had my head! There was much going on down there that was never recorded! That's why I ran so hard to the Holy Mountain before the Lord spoke to me! Why else do you think I rushed like that, even being a faithwalker? Don't doubt yourselves, faithwalkers!" And Elijah's presence particularly settled upon Yinauqua, though Mafferan was unaware of it!

Stephanie felt guilty as she popped into little Michael's semi-round, Appendaho room. It had been a whole day since she had last visited him, and that was simply *way* too long. Michael sensed his mother immediately and screeched with joy, jumping up and down in his crib from the nap he never took. Somehow, he always knew when his Mom would pop in, way before she did!

Stephanie swept him out of his crib and kissed him all over his face then mashed him into her bosom but little Michael fought the whole time to push back because all he wanted to do was his *favorite* thing to do, and *that* was to stare into his dear Mommy's special eyes. "OK, OK, what have you been doing?" Stephanie talked in baby talk to him and he screeched again in joy but then shrugged his shoulders which gave Stephanie great pause! That *shrug* was definitely a Lynnara shrug, and one that usually preceded *mischief.*

Stephanie eyed little Michael more closely and for the first time, *he averted her stare!* Stephanie took on a more serious tone. "Michael, what's going on?"

The toddler looked back at his Mommy, gave that *shrug* again, but this time he held up his little hands and they started to glow! Stephanie had never seen him do this. She could feel the deep blessing in his little hands which he then placed on his Mommy's cheeks. Stephanie couldn't help relish in it. "Ohhh, you're my little angel. But now it's *nappy* time *for real.* So you can grow *strong* like your Daddy."

And Michael starting calling out, "Daddy, Daddy. . . "

"I don't know where he is right now. But he'll be by. You *know* he will. Now beddy, Michael." And as soon as she laid him back down, he fell right to sleep, satisfied Mommy had shown up.

After softly leaving, Stephanie strolled up the stone path to the round stone cottage that joined to the nursery by a hallway, but Stephanie liked to come in the front door and see all the flowers along the way. Upon entering, Jean, in similar brown peasant dress, rushed out of the kitchen with strands of light brown hair escaping from various places. She rubbed her hands on her stained apron, whisked it off, and tossed it on a chair, then went into full embrace. "Stephanie. You've been *deeply* on my mind and heart recently. Are you OK?"

Stephanie shrugged and took Jean by the arms. "I guess. It's so good to see you, Jean."

But Jean sensed Stephanie's trepidation. "Fess up, kid!"

Stephanie sighed, then said, "I can't help feeling the girls, and even *Michel* are up to something. And I don't mean just childish adventures. I don't know. Lynnara's trying to cover it up. Lana and Rebecca, too, but . . . well, they're just acting. . . too *mature!*"

Jean grabbed Stephanie and pulled her into the kitchen and made her sit at the small round, white table. It's *then* Stephanie noticed the unbelievable aroma of chocolate chip cookies. "Oh God!" And Jean set the bowl before Stephanie then left to straighten herself up.

When Jean came back ten scant minutes later, the whole bowl was empty! Jean's eyes widened. "*Stephanie!* What's going on?"

But she just smiled and shrugged her shoulders. "Just hungry. Must be stress eating." Then after a pause, she said, "Jean, I'm serious about the girls, They're *up to* something."

So Jean sat down at the table and picked a crumb out of the bowl and ate it. "Hmm, they must have been good!"

That's when Stephanie realized Jean hadn't even had a single one. "Oh God, I'm so sorry. I don't know what got into me."

Jean took her by her hands and relished in holding them. "My dear daughter, you have to understand something. Those three girls aren't like they were thrown to the wind to raise themselves. You taught Lynnara *extremely* well, even *bonded* with her. And you raised Lana *better* than I ever could!" Stephanie was about to object but Jean hushed her. "*No!* It's true so don't argue! And Carla, Larson, *Vaughn,* and Mandy have raised Rebecca. Frankly, I don't see how *any* of them could have been better to her!"

"But Jean, they're still just *kids.*" And the worry in Stephanie's demeanor was obvious.

Jean leveled her eyes into her, then in a more challenging voice, she said, "Let's see, *Faithwalker.* You have the *Anti-Christ* to deal with. You have an *election* to *win.* You *still* have roving bands of gargoyles and an evil dragon here and there to *clean up.* You have *all kind* of people plotting against you. You are *still* baptizing souls. And, *Oh,"* and Jean threw the back of her hand to her forehead in mock faint, "a *husband* to *still* be wife to as well as mother to Michael. Are you *sure* you have time or should worry so much about those girls who have *proven* they can watch out for each other? By themselves, I agree, but *together?*" And Jean laughed.

Stephanie squinted at her. True, Jean had been holy for two years now, but she'd *never* asserted herself like *this* before. Actually, it was refreshing! And Stephanie took note of how the Holy Ghost kept growing and deepening her, *but* it sounded *almost* like she had rehearsed the answer.

Jean simply smiled, got up from the kitchen table, and said, "I think I'll make the cherry filled cookies you love so much."

Stephanie's eyes widened and she licked her lips, but then she sulked. "Darn! I have to be going." And she disappeared.

And reappeared back at the castle in the dining room where the ornate table she retained from Jargono seemed to be more comforting than usual. When James came out, before he even could ask, Stephanie said, "You know, I'd like some lamb and those wonderful rosemary potatoes you make, cooked with the lamb though, so they can absorb its wonderful flavor, and grilled asparagus with garlic, and that *wonderful* fluffy desert with the different tiny squares of flavor in it . . ." her eyes went up pondering, "*Oh,* and some cherry filled cookies!"

James eyebrows went up. And Vaughn, having sensed his wife's appearance at home, had immediately materialized behind her, and his eyebrows went up, too. He massaged Stephanie's muscles between her shoulders and neck and she purred. "You seem rather ravenous, my Queen." And he peeked around her shoulders and gave her an inquisitive look.

"Ehhh, just stress, probably."

Vaughn sighed. "Well, might as well add some more. Our *new* Jargono has scheduled a debate *this evening* on our favorite stage!"

Vaughn felt her muscles tense up, and she said, "Aren't we at least supposed to discuss this, and the way it'll be done?"

Vaughn shook his head. "He sent the thought into my head, and *that* was it! He knows we'll show up. We have to."

Vaughn sat down beside Stephanie in their usual places but this time when James brought out some bread, he didn't set the plates at the table heads but brought it directly to them at the table's side. But before Vaughn could retrieve the loaf from the bread basket to slice it, Stephanie grabbed the whole thing and began to chow down. Vaughn squinted at her but didn't comment. Instead, he asked, "What do you think?"

Stephanie sighed. "He picked *that* place because he *knows* it's where we fought so many battles against evil. By picking *there* he's like slapping us in the face with a white glove like a challenge to a dual to the death! Do you have pistols?" Stephanie asked wryly.

Vaughn nodded. "That was my feeling, too. How do you want to do this?"

Stephanie leveled her eyes into her husband. "This should be man to man. Besides, *you're* running for president. I'm only VP. You debate him and I'll support you. You worry about what to say and I'll watch out for everything else. If I need to, I'll send you thoughts."

Vaughn folded his hands on the table and stared at them and Stephanie sensed his foreboding. She placed her hand on his. "What's troubling you, my King?"

Vaughn could feel her love and affection pouring into him and he smiled softly but he kept staring at the table, sort of into nothingness. "He already knows what we're going to say, and I think he reads our minds faster than we sense his. That's *not* the way it's supposed to be, but it is. We're *lacking* somehow!"

Stephanie pulled on his hands and brought her head down to kiss them, then she put her hand to Vaughn's face and turned him further to look into her eyes. With a serious look, she asked, "Are you able to grow a beard?"

His eyebrows went up again, having not expected this. Then he scrunched his face in disapproval. "It's not military."

But Stephanie raised an eyebrow, saying, "But it *is* kingly." And while she kept holding his cheek, a full scraggly beard, dark brown, almost black, grew all over his face! And Stephanie said, "Trim this up as you like.

James came out right after that with bowls of green beans in a cream sauce. He almost dropped them when, at first, he didn't know who Vaughn was. Then he appraised him and asked, "Would you like me to trim it *proper* Sire? It's, well, a bit *wild!*"

Vaughn was about to say, no, but Stephanie said, "That's an *excellent* idea! And just as you were surprised, everyone else will be, too. That's a *good* way to start a debate for rule of the country!"

To *that* Vaughn nodded in appreciation. "I love you so much, but you ducked what I said earlier. Why?"

Now Stephanie looked down and James did a very unaccustomed action. He sat down at the table across from them and unbuttoned his black vest for comfort! "I'm getting older, fast!"

They both looked at him in surprise. But James said, "Pardon my breach of decorum, but for *this* I feel I sit more as your advisor than your butler. And as your *friend.*"

Both Vaughn and Stephanie bowed their heads to him and waited.

James sighed. "I remember when we first saw him growing in that glass bottle and *even then* he was aware of us and crashed our computer system. Ever since then, I have been praying on how to deal with this." James paused and they both nodded to him to continue.

James folded his hands on the table and his crystal clear blue eyes took on a fierce countenance. "Even from that brief encounter, it was clear to me what we were dealing with. But if we consider what that *thing* is made from, from each of *you,* from King Jargono and Queen Karen and infused with the Highest Counselor's essence and *probably* HrorrarrAggrang and Satan, too, well . . . There's never been *anything* like this in existence *ever!* For that matter, he is the *true* Anti-Christ."

This *truth* could no longer be avoided, but Stephanie and Vaughn realized that is *exactly* what they had *both* been doing. They had felt it would still be years before they had to deal with all this but got taken by surprise when the Anti-Christ showed up so soon. In retrospect, they knew the Holy Ghost had been nudging them to think about this but they just kept pushing it to the next thing that they needed to do, and the next, and the next. . .

Vaughn hung his head down, "I've been *grossly* irresponsible."

But Stephanie grabbed his folded hands again and pulled him around. "Let's focus on the present. What can we do *now,* in the next few hours before the debate?"

James cleared his throat and got their attention. "I'm not a faithwalker, and I haven't been holy that long compared to you two. *But* as an outside observer of all of you, perhaps I might make a suggestion?"

Stephanie's eyes teared up and Vaughn and James noticed she seemed to be a bit more emotional than usual. Stephanie said, "Dearest James, you are always so careful with us. *Please* tell us whatever you desire."

James nodded and caught them both in his intense stare. "When King Vaughn was in the belly of the demon and *you* and King Jargono sat at this *very* table, he challenged you to go deeper, to *advance* your abilities."

Stephanie's eyes went distant in memory and Vaughn gazed into his wife in surprise. James continued, "Jargono had you *practice* faithwalking skills you weren't aware of. Now, I believe the Anti-Christ is aware of all your skills *up to the point* when your essences were stolen from you to make him. But anything you develop *now* will take *him* by surprise!" And James got up, rebuttoned his black butler's vest, tugged it into straight perfection, nodded to them both, and left.

Vaughn and Stephanie were left alone staring at each other. Stephanie suddenly wondered why it was so quiet around the house because the girls usually made a bunch of chatter from *somewhere* in the castle but she just couldn't focus on that now.

Vaughn sighed, and asked, "How do *we* become faster, faster than the *Beast?*"

They sat silently for a whole hour, which didn't help the situation much because in a few more they would have to go to the debate, until Vaughn held out his hand and a deck of playing cards materialized. Neither of them had played cards since they were young kids and never had they played *any* card games together. A wave of irritation flooded Stephanie and she couldn't seem to call it back before it pushed her words forth. "*Vaughn!* We have such little time left, and *now* you want to play a stupid *game?*"

Vaughn eyed her silently. *Something is* definitely *different with her.*

And when Stephanie saw him eye her suspiciously, she couldn't help her next words, "Why are you looking at me like that? I'm telling you the *truth*. Don't be so *immature!*"

Vaughn tugged on his new beard, and immediately realized, *Hmm, I kinda like having a beard to tug on when I'm thinking. It's kinda like Mafferan.* But the mechanism by which his wife just misjudged him seemed important for their current situation. In a soft voice reminiscent of. . . *Something! I can't quite place when I last treated Stephanie this way, but I know I have.* "Do you really think I'm immature?"

Stephanie checked herself and turned red. "Oh God! I don't know what got into me. Of course not. I'm sorry."

Vaughn raised his eyebrows but careful not to shake his head lest Stephanie feel he disapproved of her. "What *caused* you to react the way you did?"

Stephanie shrugged her shoulders, but Vaughn needed to press the point. He swiveled his chair around to fully face his dear wife and she did the same. He took her hands in his. "Before our minds assess any situation, there's that period of time when information enters, and our mind takes hold of it, and *then* judges what's there. It seems to me that a mistake in judging could be fatal if we're off even the slightest, especially when we're dealing with such a challenging opponent as the Anti-Christ." And Vaughn paused to let it sink in.

Stephanie sighed. *Something is* definitely *different about me.* "I think, for some reason, I had a fear that you were running away into immaturity and *that* colored my judgment." She looked deeper into Vaughn now, then said, "But I don't see any of that in you. If *anything,* well, you just seem so manly, so *kingly…* Oh *Vaughn,* are we *really* doing the right thing in giving up our rule?"

Stephanie's grief suddenly overwhelmed her and Vaughn noted it again, but he focused on the task at hand. "To offset that kind of mistake, we need to be very instantaneously clear in ourselves." Then he opened the deck of cards! "But there's also something *else* we can do."

Vaughn shuffled the deck then looked at the top card. "Red or black?"

Stephanie was intrigued. *What does this have to do with what we're facing?* Stephanie guessed, "Black?" And scrunched up her nose in that cute expression that always made Vaughn laugh inside but he was extra careful not to laugh now, lest she take it the wrong way.

"Red," he said. "Come on *faithwalker.*" And Vaughn flipped another card.

Stephanie immediately looked into Vaughn's mind when he flipped the card then blurted out in triumph. "Red!"

And Vaughn nodded, then proceeded to flip card after card for which Stephanie consistently answered correctly *until* she got it wrong! Vaughn slowly shook his head then raised his eyebrows in question. "What happened?"

So Stephanie looked more deeply into him. "You *lied!*" But then she caught herself. "I'm sorry Vaughn. I didn't mean it like that. I meant, your mind said red when it was black!"

And Vaughn just continued to stare at her but when she only stared back, he said, "You remember when you fought your clone in the castle? You remember how you *won?*"

Harkening back, Stephanie chuckled. "I made him think I would repeat the same useless pattern but I *didn't* . . . Ahhh, that's what you just did to me!"

Yes, but *why?*"

Stephanie sighed deeply and flushed. Right now she wanted her husband so strongly that she was a bit surprised at how fast it came over her. She purred and squeezed his hands, "You know, I've *really* missed your point-making. It *always* just grabbed me so deeply *inside!*" And her eyes turned red hot with passion.

Vaughn blushed and Stephanie laughed. "I'm your *wife,* and you *still* blush." And she began to laugh so hard she had to be careful she didn't fall out of her chair. "It's so cute!"

Vaughn mock sighed at the word *cute* because Stephanie knew he hated to be called *cute*. But he also maintained his stare into her, waiting, and Stephanie realized she needed to focus.

"OK. So you're saying. . ."

"I'm not saying anything!"

And *that* also reminded Stephanie of how Vaughn was when they first met and it made her feel the same passion she had for him even way back then. "Oh Vaughn, I love you *so* much." But Vaughn kept his serious look.

"OK," Stephanie said again. "I think . . . I need to look deeper right away to see the real truth. I should be able to do that, right?"

"We both need to." And Vaughn began flipping cards again until no matter how he tried to trick her, she got them all right." Then Vaughn handed the cards to Stephanie and she repeated the process for him until he got them all right then he took the cards back.

"Now. Which suit?" And he flipped cards again. This proved to be harder because clubs and spades were black and hearts and diamonds were red. It required an even deeper, finer perception. And after *that,* Vaughn said, "*Now,* which card *exactly*!"

But James came out, and said, "I've given you all up to the very last moment. But now it's time for you to do your duty. God's speed to you both." Then James gave the slightest look of disapproval at Vaughn. And Stephanie burst out laughing.

"Here, my King. I know *exactly* what you want." And she touched Vaughn's beard and it went from scraggly to becoming perfectly trimmed into a square just like King Mafferan. Stephanie materialized a mirror in her hand and held it up, and Vaughn turned his head this way and that with extra emphasis until Stephanie burst out laughing again and dematerialized the mirror.

But as soon as they appeared on stage dressed for the occasion, a deep feeling of everything being off slammed into Vaughn. He looked at Stephanie, but she didn't seem to sense any of that as Vaughn stepped up to a broader podium and Stephanie came beside him to his left because there were two microphones. The imposter Jargono was another third of the way to their right so that the stage was split evenly between them. *That* positioning, in and of itself, was a takedown to Vaughn and Stephanie and they knew it immediately. Even though *former* Jargono was considered a great King, too, nothing compared to what King Vaughn and Queen Stephanie had accomplished for the country, but the positioning on the stage subliminally wiped all that out! They were all *equals*.

Vaughn searched to discover the *meaning* of everything feeling deeply off and an immediate connection between what he and Stephanie had just practiced came to his mind but before he could figure it out, Jargono began speaking. "I want to welcome my esteemed guests to this debate I just called and thank them for showing up so quickly." And he bowed to them.

Vaughn was now living microsecond by microsecond but he sensed the utter urgency of figuring this out *now. Before our minds assess any situation, there's that period of time when information enters, and our mind takes hold of it, and* then *judges what's there. It seems to me that a mistake in judging could be fatal if we're off even the slightest, especially when we're dealing with such a challenging opponent as the Anti-Christ.*

Vaughn knew Stephanie was about to bow in return to Jargono but Vaughn immediately telepathed *Don't bow. He wants that.* And right before Stephanie was about to automatically bow, she halted and instead of bowing she just smiled. Vaughn could tell she was in the process of responding verbally so he knew he still had precious microseconds to. . . *THINK! For God's sake THINK! There are levels to every situation, to every INSTANT!* Vaughn remembered Stephanie's words just a short time ago: *I need to look deeper* right away *to see the real truth. I should be able to do that, right?* And he had said, *We both need to.*

Stephanie said, "We extend our graciousness to you, whoever you are, and, nevertheless, intend to honor these elections to give the people their *choice.*" And Queen Stephanie turned to the crowd and bowed to *them.* And the crowd couldn't help but cheer, a crowd that filled the whole lawn, the street beyond, and the rooftops and windows, just like it was when Stephanie was yet pregnant with little Michael and she eventually won the United for Christ over to her.

*Good Stephanie. Very good,* Vaughn thought. *Now, what's behind my feeling of everything being deeply off?*

Jargono looked over to them but so briefly Vaughn wondered if the crowd would even be able to see such a microsecond glance. And it *wasn't* a friendly glance but filled with the utmost malice. *He* knows *I'm now in microseconds! He* knows *I've just become as fast as him! I need to be even* faster!

Jargono spoke to the crowd. "It's wonderful to see you all cheering for DEMOCRACY!"

And the crowd cheered even harder now and their emotions had realigned with Jargono. It was then that Stephanie realized, *I'm just reacting to the surface. What's* wrong *with me?* And her memory suddenly traveled way back to when she had healed the little girl in the playground and she had seen the gray arm reaching inside that mean little girl's head, and after she had asked the mean little girl what was wrong with her, the little girl immediately mocked back, "What's *wrong* with you, what's *wrong* with you?" But *this* time Stephanie saw a much deeper reality in that memory. There was also a faint blue glow around that mean little girl that she hadn't noticed before, but there it now was in her *faithwalking* memory. . . Shocked! *It's the same blue glow of the demon's orbs! They had her say that to me through their orb! Of course, but I never thought of it that way. No wonder she responded so oddly, so quickly! Because the orbs* enhance *their power, their reach, their intensity, even their accuracy!* And Stephanie, suddenly, from the inside out converted to being faster, because from the inside out she had immediately prayed to *be* faster! But she also immediately noticed something about the crowd in front of her. This time, most weren't from the South! These were *Northerners* who had been brought in! *Oh my God, help us! No wonder they cheer so hard for* him!

# CHAPTER 12

# This Little Light

*Elijah finished the bowl of scrumptious fruit salad and handed it back to Yinauqua, saying, "May I have another?" When he saw the surprise on Mafferan and his wife's faces, because the first bowl was so large, because his hosts didn't want to fail their guest again, Elijah said, "Well, ever since that angel woke me up twice and fed me twice, well, my eating habits haven't been the same!" And that twinkle in his eyes just seemed to continually dance inside them, also. They loved this man!*

*After the second bowl and Elijah licked it clean, he looked up, saying, "Sorry for my manners. You get that way from being fed by a raven for a few years. Now, back to business!" And that saying made them immediately tense, and noticing that, Elijah merely said, "Oh come on now. You've been through worse!"*

*They both knew Elijah expected an answer, and Mafferan said, "To be honest, Lord Elijah, we haven't come up with a respectable answer."*

*"Well, I practically gave you the first part of it!" And his hosts began to feel very small, whereupon Elijah suddenly pointed at*

*them and raised his voice, "THAT FEELING right THERE! That will cause you to FALL and them down there, too! When you feel that kind of ineptness, you can't access anything good that has all you need!"*

*And right there in front of Lord Elijah, both Yinauqua and Mafferan turned beet red which further embarrassed them until Elijah burst out laughing, and said, "My apologies. Time is short and you need quick answers. Block out now all the feelings and thoughts that interfere with the goodness our Lord Jesus made you to be!" And at his last word, be, the room shook and they felt clearly what they were and considered his question:* Do you understand why both Moses and I appeared on the Holy Mountain with our Lord Jesus for Peter, James, and John to see, *but no others?*

*Mafferan and Yinauqua's thoughts were in sync. The question has two parts, but to answer the second, we have to be right about the first, otherwise we'll draw the wrong conclusions for the second. Mafferan said, "Well, as you said, Moses was more of a law giver and you were definitely a law enforcer. When Moses cried to our Lord that the task of doing both was too much, He had Moses appoint seventy more elders to share in the burden where the Lord took of the Holy Spirit in Moses, and gave it also to the seventy. They became judges while Moses became a reference to solve the hardest questions. He clarified the Law, but the seventy gave the judgments that enforced the law,*

*Yinauqua said, "But you," she shook her head remembering how she had watched all this in real time from up in Heaven, "You slaughtered the hundreds of false prophets after they had failed your challenge. You burnt up armies sent after you. True,* there were many destroyed during Moses but *it was the Lord's direct work.*"

But Mafferan said, "But you *also had deep compassion, Deeper than anyone! You* raised the dead! *Through your word, people were healed and fed when there was no food nor healing." Then Mafferan looked deeply into his wife and she back to him until they agreed and she nodded for her husband to answer. Mafferan said. "Moses laid down the immutable standards which our Lord Jesus confirmed he had come to fulfill. But* Elijah, *well,* you *Sir, you showed forth that long after Moses, our God isn't just all* talk, *but that Jesus* will *fulfill through* action *His standards in due time.* But, *when the Lord Jesus came to Earth, it was to make us all a new heart, a new spirit that had the understanding and strength to keep us from failing when we were mortal, and even all up here.*"

Yinauqua said, "Every time Jesus *experienced human weakness, He added strength within* mortality *that didn't exist before through actually* experiencing *weakness and* responding *to it. Which is different from just looking down from on High. The same process also allowed him to bring new understanding into mortality from the inside out, not the weaker outside in, and* that *didn't exist before.*"

And Mafferan said, "*And when the Father withdrew from Jesus, that allowed Jesus to even deepen* faith *within mortality because Jesus* never *experienced abandonment before where He actually could not sense the Father* at all!"

Yinauqua continued, "*But when Jesus looked* inside *Himself, He saw the reality of goodness that the Father inspired in Him* from all that time *Jesus had self-reflected upon the Father, as it is written, The Father sheweth Me all things that He Himself doeth, and Jesus then said,* It is finished."

Mafferan said, *"Making that new heart and new spirit for us. That was what He had finished for us when Jesus felt abandoned as we mortals feel when dying. Jesus added new faith that hadn't been in mortality before, a sure knowledge of goodness in spite of feeling totally abandoned. He looked inside, saw the perfect goodness in Him that belonged to the Father, and so reconnected to the Father through that. Into thy hands I commend my spirit, Jesus said, and passed on in true faith, new faith, even for Him!"*

*Yinauqua looked deeply into her husband and he nodded to her, so she spoke up. "All three together, Moses, the Law giver, You Elijah, the Law enforcer, and Jesus being the loving unity that perfected all three together into one, well, that balanced perfectly the mercy of Love with Justice for everyone from the inside out. That completes a whole eternal unity."*

*Elijah nodded, then said, "Now for the second part. Why only Peter, James, and John? And why is that important now?"*


It had taken much longer than Lynnara had expected and she had to use all her abilities to keep her anxiety from her mother because if she sensed it, then surely Stephanie would have asked her what was going on, and *then* Lynnara knew her *bestest* Mommy *ever* would be so relentless that Lynnara would have to tell her not just the truth but the *whole* truth and *that* Carla had warned her would cause *everything* to fail.

But upon popping into the shelter with Lana and Rebecca, now all clothed again in their ranger uniforms, all their little mouths dropped open. Mandy was there pacing back and forth when they arrived.

As soon as Mandy sensed the others arrival, she whirled around and held her hand up, "OK. I have *a lot* to tell you." And the three girls just looked at each other, and Mandy held out her arm and ushered the girls to all sit at the table. But all the children from across the border had immediately begun chattering softly and Samantha and Shane were trying to explain to the newcomers about the other children simply *popping in.*

When Lynnara saw all the confusion, she looked up into Mandy's eyes, put her little hand on her hip, sighed, and plainly said, "This won't do!" Mandy took note that Lynnara looked and acted *exactly* like Stephanie did toward the girls.

Lynnara came up to the newcomers who had huddled in a circle up against the circular wall. Except for Shane and Samantha, their fear was palpable. Lynnara spoke in their native language telling them all to stand up and form a circle and join hands, then she disappeared then reappeared in the circle's center and looked up as if to Heaven, saying, "Lord Jesus, help me to help them understand. I'm not my Mommy or my Daddy, so I don't know how to do it for so many, but they need to all speak *our* language." And she stretched out her arms, her little hands open wide with her palms facing the children, and she closed her eyes concentrating on them all and slowly turned in a circle.

Mandy, Rebecca, and Lana, who were still standing by the table, were all looking at each other and back and forth to Lynnara. Lynnara had used her *faithwalking* ability before to give the first two refugees language, but this time she was doing something far more advanced, and she wasn't just asking for language. *This time,* she was praying in a fashion that they had all seen Lady Stephanie do, but Lynnara was combining her prayer with her *faithwalking* abilities, asking the Lord Jesus to guide her.

And the whole area of the circle lit up in golden light and the newcomers eyes went wide. Lynnara stopped turning, opened her eyes then waved her hand and curved bleachers arched along the curve of the wall with three levels, and she said in a very proper tone in her own language, "Please take your seats!"

All the children's eyes opened wide at understanding her speech, The tallest children sat on the lowest level and the shortest climbed up higher, and all couldn't fathom how they understood the language Lynnara now used. But Lynnara shook her head, as she counted the children. *FIFTEEN! Oh God, Mommy is gonna* kill *me. And it's getting crowded.* So Lynnara folded her hands and bowed her head, then began to glow in rainbow colors, then she suddenly clapped her hands sharply and the whole shelter expanded! The table was much larger, and there were twenty simple wooden chairs now, distributed around the table and around the circle of children, and rows of bunk beds! The shelter was a good twenty-five feet in diameter now, but all basically still the same as when a forlorn Stephanie had built it!

Mandy had goose bumps at how adept Lynnara was becoming. She'd never seen Stephanie just clap her hands like that and things happened. Lynnara had simply imagined what was needed and the clap was a *faithwalker* prayer request to let it be so. And it was so. All were in awe at her power but for Lynnara's part, she gave it no further thought, and began speaking.

"The Lord Jesus has shown me what to show you! Your *King* from where you came from is very bad. How do I know that?" Lynnara looked back at Mandy with an impish grin, then continued. "Before we popped in here, I took Lana and Rebecca into, well, a spiritual place where *faithwalkers* and those they bring can travel. But you can also see our world *here* from *there!*" And when Lynnara said *here,* she had pointed to the ground, when she said *there,* she pointed above. "Well, I know Mommy does this all the time. She watches me and *lots* of people without them knowing, so I did the same thing to her! Right before we came here! But I was careful so she didn't *know* we were watching, cause Mommy can sense those things. I can, too."

Mandy's eyes went wide and looked intensely at Rebecca and Lana but they just shrugged and looked down, but the *look* in their eyes confirmed Lynnara's account. Mandy shook her head but then remembered how she used to tiptoe and spy on Carla all the time when she was little.

Lynnara said, "I heard Mommy and my Daddy and James, he's our butler but he's really almost like a second Daddy, or, well, a Grandaddy 'cause he's a lot older than Mommy and

Daddy. And I heard them talkin' 'bout your evil King and how *bad* he is."

But at this point, a lot of the children were whispering, asking who Lynnara's Mommy and Daddy were, and Mandy knew it, so she stepped up beside Lynnara, and said, "King Vaughn and Queen Stephanie. They rule this country, and . . ." But she didn't have to say any more because all the children's eyes went wide, apparently somehow having heard who they are.

Shane spoke up, saying, "We've *all* heard stories about them. A few had escaped our land but actually *came back* to tell us about *them! All* the resistance knows about *them! That's* your Mommy and Daddy?"

Lynnara shrugged her shoulders, and said, "Well, my first Mommy got runned over 'cause I was bad. My second Mommy and Daddy, well, my second Mommy wanted to keep me but my second Daddy said it would be bad because we had an evil King back then, too, and he wanted to kill all the *strangers.* I was a stranger. So they gave me away to the evil King and Queen. He even tried to burn us all up! But Mommy, my *third* and *bestest* Mommy *ever,* she *faithwalked* and through the spiritual corridor she pulled me away and saved me. Well, then she died in the Dead Forest because the evil King tried to burn *us* up but Queen Stephanie, well, she wasn't Queen then, she *faithwalked* again to get us away but we ended up in the Forest where she died and demons tried to *eat us,* but I wouldn't let them and I saved Stephanie and she had given me *her* life but in the cave I gave her, *her life* back. *Anyway,* I asked Stephanie and Vaughn would they be my Mommy and my Daddy and they said yes if I would be their daughter, and I said yes. So there. *Anyway. . .*"

Lynnara was simply going to continue but all the children climbed down from their seats and bowed to Lynnara, saying, "Princess Lynnara, Princess Lynnara, we serve *you!* Only *you!*"

Lynnara, turning red, looked over to Mandy and Lana, but Lana stepped forward and said, "Princess Lynnara doesn't want you to bow to her, but only to the *true* God, Jesus."

And Lynnara said, "That's *right.*" And she waived her hand and suddenly all the children were back in their seats! *Again,* Mandy was shocked. It was clear Lynnara wasn't just doing things she'd learned from Stephanie, but she was becoming her *own* faithwalker.

Lynnara began to glow rainbow colors just like her Mommy, and said, "I'm not holy, yet, but I think that's just because I'm too young and I need to understand better, But I *do* love Jesus and only want to be what *He* wants me to be, 'cause he created us all to be good, and I don't wanna be *bad*. But my Mommy and Daddy, they're *both* holy and Jesus gives them *very* special things to do. But this is what they taught me.

"In the beginning there was nothing but God. *What* is God? That's *really* important 'cause the *what* makes the *who*. God is seven spirits in One." And Lynnara held up her little hands and as she called each, she raised a finger in counting. "Life, Love, Justice, Truth, Understanding, Wisdom, and Peace. But *how* God is, is *also* important."

Mandy came up and put her hand on Lynnara's back and Lynnara knew Mandy wanted to say something, so Lynnara said, "This is Mandy, my sister, and *she's* holy."

And Mandy said, "Is there anything more important to any of you than those seven?"

And the children truly thought a while about it, and then one by one, they all shook their heads no. Samantha said, "Those seven don't exist in our home," and she put her hand to her heart, "but in our hearts we *know* now those seven are *real*, We all *feel* it." And she tapped her chest over and over, and all the rest began doing the same in affirmation.

Mandy wiped tears from her eyes, beholding a miracle she never expected, but the children's appearances began to grate on her deeply so she whispered in Lynnara's ear, and Lynnara nodded.

Lynnara said to the children, "The seven Holy Spirits of God are what they are and always have been. But also *how* God is. In the beginning there was only God, no other. And He had a part of Himself that looks at Himself, just like He made us to have in us. And the more that part looked, the more that part loved what he looked at. And *that* part saw inside God all of us! All different special combinations of God's goodness. And he wanted to give us all our *own* life and not just be God's thoughts and feelings that come and go." And Lynnara waved her hands about then continued. "So God looked at that part of Himself, how it loved God *perfectly*, and how it would be even *better*, more good, if that part could create us, even make us live forever if we want to, so God said, Let there be Light.

And God made that part of Himself free. And then, all that Light wanted to do was make God's goodness grow, and so the Light created everything good, and all of us.

"But the Light and God his Father knew some would turn bad and *a lot of us* would get tricked by *evil,*" And all the children began nodding profusely, feeling so badly, and hating their appearances more and more because it was *obvious* that their saviors were all very feminine girls and Mandy, a feminine woman. "So that Light promised to find out for Himself what it was like to be just like us, just human beings with bodies, and pains and all that bad. So he had God make him born through a woman and she called him Jesus. And Jesus hurt like we hurt. And the Devil, he's the chief demon, an evil spirit, he came and did *everything* to try to make Jesus bad, but Jesus wouldn't give in. And *finally,* the Devil had bad people to put Jesus to death, they actually *nailed* his hands and feet to a cross. But Jesus had told them, you *can't* kill the person inside this body, because *I* am the Truth and Life and the way to love God *perfectly.* So I *prove* it to you by letting you kill my body but I'll rise the third day." And Lynnara looked up to Mandy to make sure she was doing it right, and Mandy had to wipe more tears from her eyes.

It's not that Mandy didn't know these things, or hadn't heard them before, *but* there was something extra special in Lynnara telling it like *this.* ""Keep going Lynnara. It's *good.*" And all the children, including a rapt Rebecca and Lana nodded.

"So Jesus died on the cross but only his body. But being *mortal,* he lived a *perfect* life, a *holy* life, which *meant,* that now the way to be perfect had been made in. . ." And she looked up to Mandy with question, saying, "*Mortality?*" And Mandy nodded, "*That* meant that he had made a way for *us* now to be perfect, too. He made us a *new* heart and a *new* spirit right out of himself having beaten all evil and death in *mortality* so that *we* can beat it now, too." And Lynnara got extra serious as she stared at the children, and asked, "Does that make *sense?*" Just like her Mommy asked her all the time.

And the children all spoke as one, "Yes, Princess Lynnara."

Lynnara smiled, and chirped, "So all ya gotta do now, is just keep askin' Jesus to help you figure out how to give your *whole* self back to Him so He can give us a new one, but you'll be the same person, only *much* better. I saw it happen to my sisters Carla and Mandy. They're even *better,* but *still* my sisters."

Lana asked the children, "Do you want to be free from all the hurt they've done to you?"

They all shouted yes in various ways. And Lynnara began glowing brightly, "Let's start with *this!*" And she clapped her hands again, but this time it thundered so loudly it shook everyone's insides, and when the thunder slowly subsided and disappeared, all the children had changed. The girls looked like real girls with long hair and had brown peasant dresses on, and the boys looked like real boys and had brown pants and shirts on.

And all the children jumped from their seats and began dancing and rejoicing, and Shane and Samantha worked with them all to take new names that fit them. But then Lynnara shrieked in pain and clenched her gut and doubled over, and she cried out bitterly, "*Mommy!*" but she wasn't crying out for herself, but for her Mother she loved more than *anything,* and the next moment Lynnara left *everyone* and disappeared! One thought kept coming to Lynnara within the microseconds of her travel, *I* told *Mommy if she needed me to just call.*

CHAPTER 13

# The Lord God Giveth
# and the Devil Stealeth

*Elijah walked up to their golden orb in the middle of their round living room. The orb set on a black iron pedestal that rested on a round oak table with Appendaho ornate carvings which seemed to flow with the oak grain. Below the table was a round Appendaho rug with similar but unique designs. The secret to such art was the meaning of balance. Every faithwalker needed to adhere to that fundamental law or reap untold horrible consequences. Elijah tugged on his black and white beard then waved his hand at the orb and it focused on Earth, on the United States in the south. He said to Mafferan and Yinauqua, "Unfortunately, this lesson isn't in time. And I'm not sure you two want to see this!"*

*Yinauqua looked at Mafferan but he immediately adjusted the orb to search for Stephanie and the view of the stage came into focus, but Mafferan immediately blurred it, which Yinauqua didn't understand. Her anxiety level kept growing exponentially.*

197

*Now that she had regained her focus, she could sense something dire with her daughter.*

*Mafferan turned to Elijah, saying, "Peter was not an educated man. He was direct, stern, and had a knowing for what he thought was right and trusted it implicitly. Our Lord had to work hard on him to understand he still had to give all of himself up and repent even though he was truly holy to the standard of the day."*

*Elijah studied Mafferan, thinking,* He's finally back to his own self again. But it's too late. *And Elijah looked deeper into him.* Hmm, it's faithwalking that even *I* don't understand! Hmmm . . . "True. So what!"

*Mafferan ignored the comment, saying, "John is easy. He had the best understanding of the new heart, new spirit that would be given and was and is given. He focused on love and so he was entrusted just like Daniel to revelations of the end times that we are now in, times that are dominated not by love but by justice."*

*Elijah grew stern. "Don't you find that odd, that the Lord entrusted John, not a fighter, to the end times Justice and not Peter?*

*Mafferan squinted at Elijah.* It is odd but why is this important, important enough for him to take time to stress it? *"No. That much Justice takes that much Love to balance it. Peter's strength was the deepest faith, the deepest willingness to go to any extent to glorify the Lord Jesus. That's why he was crucified with his heels upside down. He was still a fighter, just fought in a different way after his conversion."*

*Elijah looked deeply into Yinauqua, not Mafferan, and asked her, "What does this have to do with you?"*

Yinauqua, at first, looked like a deer caught in a bright light, but she quickly brushed that away. She could feel there was no time left for failure. She had to finally be honest about herself. "My love is some of the strongest here in Heaven. I know that. But I don't have what I need to balance it when everything presses on my love to act. That's why I need my husband to, well, restrain me, at times!"

It was a stark admission here in Heaven, to admit that even perfection must grow under certain circumstances. Elijah nodded, and said, "What happens to you and your love and those you love if your husband isn't there to restrain you?"

Yinauqua looked down, and answered, "I fail, my loved ones suffer even more. My love is out of balance and who knows what it becomes. But I can't seem to help it."

"You daughter down there, is just like you! And if that love is violated deep enough, it can even turn on the person doing all that loving!"

Yinauqua began to weep. "I know! Just like me." And she began rubbing her chest without even thinking about it.

Mafferan squinted at Elijah, and said, "But there's still more to this. Peter and John balance each other. Peter's practical, unwavering faith and sacrifice and John's revelation into everything not practical, into the utter devastation of all goodness on Earth along with a love that allowed John to actually be the only one of Jesus disciples to live out his full days on Earth. John didn't have to sacrifice anything of himself because his love for Jesus was so perfect!"

Elijah smiled, "And James?"

Yinauqua said, "He was quite unlike either of them. He was a reasoner. When he saw how faithful people began to become religious *as an end in itself* instead of holiness, he tried to work within their framework to bring them back. *Pure religion is* this. And he listed many things that all together describe what's close to holiness. James had an abundance of patience."

Mafferan's eyebrows rose with revelation. "Jesus didn't just represent the unity of Moses and you, he stood on the mountain with you and mediated between you two as you discussed these very times here! It's one thing to be a law giver and a law enforcer with the hope of creating a future for the world but quite a different thing when you are charged with rendering and enforcing final judgments on the world. You two needed the Lord Jesus in the flesh to draw the parameters for you perfectly, otherwise you couldn't function in the end!"

Elijah said, "Well, for how those who would be sent to Earth in our places needed to function. Such a thing begged to have this all thought out beforehand!" But then Elijah raised an eyebrow and squinted indicating Mafferan needed to think further.

And Mafferan nodded. "James was the one to establish the continuance of Peter and John's work by focusing the religious at least in the right direction because he knew all the holy people and their knowledge would disappear but the religion of Christianity would prevail. Then Paul came and greatly expanded it all, using all their framework all the while trying to make holiness clear."

But Elijah still waited for more, and Yinauqua said, "Moses, you, and Jesus. Peter, James, and John. Stephanie and Vaughn." And

*Yinauqua paused and looked at both her husband and Elijah, then said, "Who's the third? Who goes with Stephanie and Vaughn?"*

*Many came to their minds like Carla and Mandy, Harris, and other holy people but none of them felt like they were the third even as wonderful as they all were. They were all doing their part, but not the third's part. And in fact, the Holy Scripture doesn't even mention the third!*

*Elijah smiled at them both, thanked them for their excellent hospitality, and disappeared!*

A gentle warm breeze blew, the kind that was soothing with hints of sweet smells of late spring or early summer that generated an innate sense of hope for. . . something. The Jargono imposter laid down the rules as he spoke to the crowd. "There's no need for a moderator, we can simply challenge each other, test each other's mettle, and you all can be the judges."

Vaughn saw his thoughts before he put them into play and was able to immediately respond, "A while ago, my wife asked the *real* Jargono a question that he couldn't answer. *What* is power to you?"

Stephanie smoothed her holy dress and tried to collect herself because she felt love burning inside her for her husband, so proud of him that his answer came back perfectly, but Jargono smiled and responded without hesitation. "Power is worth nothing if the people are not truly satisfied. Of course, they often don't know like true leaders know about what is good for them, so true power is the willingness to do the best for people even if at times they think less of you."

It was such a true and endearing answer that even some of the real United for Christ's people gave serious thought to it. But the holy people scattered all around quickly brought them deeper understanding, which Stephanie also brought out. "That's a very convenient answer for a leader but we choose not to hide behind such dishonesty. Basically, you can say *any* situation where our citizens disagree needs to be dealt with by a leader willing to go against them for their own good. But in a *democracy*, it doesn't work that way. You're *not* a *King* any more. A *President* must deal with the will of the people expressed through both the Senate and the House as *co-equal* branches of government. And *often* the deadlock means *nothing* gets done. That's just the way it is in a *democracy*. It doesn't really sound like you're cut out for this job. You *still* just want to *rule* all by yourself. You don't even have a Vice president picked, yet."

And the crowd, who, though they were from the North, still very much had their own minds and they couldn't help but pay heed to Stephanie's argument. *She's right,* many said to themselves and others.

Vaughn saw that Stephanie was also sped up now. *We're keeping up with him, for now. But that's not good enough. And this damned feeling won't let me alone.*

Jargono said, "It's easy to twist my words and meaning. Let's talk policy. You *claim* you are *fair* rulers but you have oppressed *many* in your kingdom." And many in the crowd raised rainbow flags demanding open equality. Then others raised black flags demanding the old reparations they used to receive for when their ancestors left their home and everything they had in the South to fight for the North. Vaughn had made it very clear that *no one* would receive any more money like that, that they had to leave the past behind and start anew.

And another group raised yellow flags demanding their rights. These were men but looked like women, and women that looked like men.

And another group of very young adults demanded their rights to adult privileges.

And on and on and on, groups with unique huge flags raised them in protest against Vaughn and Stephanie so that before too long, it looked like the whole crowd belonged to some group with grievances. In truth, it was just a few people with very large flags that made it *seem* like all those people under the flags belonged to those flags. But those few kept hollering, making it *impossible* for Vaughn and Stephanie to speak and be heard unless they used their faithwalking powers, but both knew that if they did *that*, it would be twisted against them, saying they don't want a democracy but plan to rule by force.

Jargono raised his hand and called for silence and everyone instantly calmed and quieted. "If you elect me, *no one* will be left out. A country is only strongest when it's most needy are elevated and allowed to contribute. And you are *all* most needy! So in *my* government, you will *all* get to contribute and be rewarded generously."

When Stephanie and then Vaughn began to speak, hecklers quickly drowned them out, and they looked at each other, not knowing what to do. *Obviously* this was planned and wasn't *fair*, but. . . Vaughn was disgusted with himself. *It's been too long since I visited my Book of Wisdom. The Holy Ghost has more than sufficed me, but* that *book is worthy in its own right. If I'd had a discussion with it, I am* sure *it would have warned me of this and helped me come to a solution.*

But Stephanie merely shouted above the crowd, "*Shame on you! When you were starving after the demons war, who came to you who hadn't slept in days?* I did. And I made sure you were fed and cared for. Many of you were lame. *Who healed you? I did.*" And she pointed to one black-haired male protestor in the crowd, "You're not even from down here but I *know* you, You're from the North but when a gang beset you to abuse you, I stood between you and them and *dared* them to harm you. Then I warned them if I heard of any more trouble, they would be arrested. How quickly you forget?

"And *you,*" she pointed to a young blond lady holding a purple flag for which Stephanie forgot what *that* stood for, and she said, "You were about to be *raped.* I heard your cries and immediately popped in on you and burnt your attackers to a crisp! How quickly you forget?"

All of these things were true and the whole crowd knew it, they could tell.

Jargono cut in. "Well, with powers like *you* have, it's no skin off *your* teeth to do all these things but you *still* allowed all these poor people to be *oppressed!*

And the crowd started jeering at Stephanie. There weren't even any gray arms reaching in any of their heads, but Stephanie *definitely* saw that faint blue glow around Jargono. *Damn! He's so powerful and yet he's using the demon's orbs to help him, too.*

Vaughn spoke up now, but before anyone could heckle him, he said, "Anyone opens their mouths while I'm trying to speak, I'm coming off this platform just as a *man* and you and I can *talk* a while!"

Everyone silenced then. They all understood what kind of *talk* King Vaughn meant, and *none* of them wanted to face him even if he gave his word to just be a man and not use his powers. Stephanie had heat rush all through her. *Oh God, he's such a* man. *A good* man. *I love him so much.*

Vaughn stepped away from the podium and up to the front edge of the stage and Stephanie joined him. With just his natural voice, it carried just as clear as if he was using a microphone, he said, "*We* are the ones who gave up the powers of being King and Queen to give power to you all. This, so called Jargono, promises to give you power but anyone can promise you *anything* to get your vote. But *we* have proven by our *actions* that we are *real.*"

Jargono said, "And everyone *knows* my noble actions, as well. Did I not sacrifice my life to save yours? But I was meant for the greatness of helping *everyone else* to be great and so I was brought back to life to help even you all again."

And to *that* the crowd cheered deeply, saying, "He *did* save even them. He *deserves* to be President. We've had *enough* of the others. We *owe* it to Jargono."

Jargono said, "The truth is that I want *you,*" and he pointed to the crowd, "to have powers like me! Show them!"

And one fat man in the crowd suddenly levitated above them, and said, "Jargono taught me how to use my mind better."

Another, but a thin, older man with a bald head, had people move away from him then raised his hand and fire shot into the sky from his fingertips.

A red-haired young man told everyone to watch and turned invisible. And on and on and on it went, each showing a power and declaring Jargono had done it for them.

Vaughn finally said, "You call that power. Really? Can you *force* someone to love you? And what kind of *character* is *worthy* to be loved both by others but *also* to your own selves? *We* have taught you *that* and you *know* it. *That's* real power! And I have seen *all* your lives, whether from the North or South be *vastly* improved because you improved your own selves on the *inside!* And *we* are responsible for helping build that *American* culture of *dignity.*"

And of *all* the things that had been said and done this day, *that* rang the truest and most deeply in everyone's hearts. They *knew* this was true even if they didn't want to give King Vaughn and Queen Stephanie credit, even if they were jealous of them. For all couldn't help feeling a growing integrity in their own lives because of their example. They had been so very different from the old government and even from Jargono's rule. Granted, many were free to be evil, for sure, but it was still freedom. They sensed they might not get such freedom with this new Jargono though they weren't exactly sure why.

Vaughn saw Jargono turn the deepest black but only within a microsecond, yet his gut turned over.

Jargono smiled to the crowd, and said, "As I said before, I also have inspired you, and it was *I* who made *sure* you would have King Vaughn and Queen Stephanie. I even got rid of their enemies ahead of time!"

The crowd all nodded to the truth of *that,* and many had wondered if *they* would be next! In fact, the ones from the North knew they would *never* have accepted them as rulers had Jargono not done all he did to install them. And Jargono said, "Let's just wait for an undeniable sign from God."

Both Stephanie and Vaughn had the hairs on the backs of their necks stand up. Stephanie sensed Jargono was going to attack her in a microsecond. Part of her couldn't believe he would do that in front of everyone but then she realized he could do it so fast no one would even see it. She instinctively raised a shield around her whole body but with triple strength around her head. She used to constantly have her defenses up but it had been so long since she had fought an actual battle, and besides, she'd been feeling a little *off* lately.

Vaughn immediately knew Jargono was going to attack him and that no one would even see it. He immediately reached out his hand and called his staff which threw an impenetrable force field around him. Vaughn knew *he* was the real target because it was *he* who was running for President.

*Both* faithwalkers judged wrong. In a microsecond, Jargono appeared in front of Stephanie and reached his hand through the Spiritual Corridor parallel to inside her pelvis, bypassing her protection, and then rematerialized it, then *squeezed!* As searing pains doubled Stephanie over, he sweetly whispered in her ear. "There will be no more *generations* for you *EVER.*"

As Stephanie's legs gave out, she fell over backwards in a horrendous, gasping shriek right in front of the crowd and they all saw blood wetting her holy dress and oozing past her feet and running down the front of the stage. But to the crowd, Jargono was still at his platform and had been there the whole time. "Well," he said. "I asked for a sign but I really didn't want something like *that* to happen to my enemy. Someone call a doctor. Obviously, she can't heal herself!"

And she couldn't, partly because she just realized what she had known all along but denied because of all her other responsibilities. Stephanie had been pregnant again. The *had been* stabbed her heart as if a dagger had been plunged in and twisted, much more pain than she could handle. Along with the fact that somehow she had let *him* do that to her. But also, there was some kind of power, some kind of poison she didn't understand. It was like the black oil but *worse. And* she could feel the crowd disdaining her deeply, believing that God had condemned her and Vaughn with this *sign. Failure* resounded throughout all her being, failing to protect her precious innocent child, and failure to be the light that everyone needed, failing Vaughn, and her whole being crushed as if a whole mountain had been cast upon her.

Vaughn was kneeling by her side, his heart collapsing because he failed to protect his wife. They had been on top for so very long now, but also the nature of her injury he didn't understand at all, and Stephanie knew it. She also knew that before she died, the last thing she *had to do,* was tell Vaughn the truth. "Miscarriage. *He* did this to us! I'm so sorr…" And she passed out in the middle of the word, which to say it, finished crushing her soul.

Tremendous rage ripped through Vaughn but he fought to control it because he *also* knew Jargono *wanted* him to react this way. He laid his staff upon his wife expecting her to be healed but the staff was simply inert and no power came forth, and Vaughn didn't understand *at all.*

Yinauqua collapsed to her knees wailing and Mafferan knew there was *nothing* able to restrain her if she wanted to go, even though Mafferan knew it would be the wrong thing for her to do, that *this* also was set up by the Anti-Christ to tempt *his* wife also, but not only *that.* Mafferan knew that the Anti-Christ knew that if Yinauqua would go down to Earth, Mafferan would come too, because they knew Yinauqua by herself didn't have enough power to stand against *that one!* But if Mafferan went down there, *that* would also make things worse because the Anti-Christ would call them an evil invasion and would give him license to bring *his* forces to bear and *that* would put all humanity in a no win situation.

Yinauqua grabbed her husband and pulled herself to stand up. She raised her hands and her holy Maroon dress with neon blue Appendaho design appeared upon her. She looked into her husband's eyes and shook her head, "You *know* how badly I want to go down there *now?*"

And Mafferan changed into his Kingly garments of royal blue with gold bands at his sleeve edges and tunic hem. "I do, but you *know* I'm going with you."

But Yinauqua hugged him tightly, buried her head into his neck, and whispered a prayer in his ear, "Oh Jesus, where is the *third* person for *them?* It's not *us!* Oh *God, it's not us,*"

And *this* calamity Yinauqua had foreseen for some time! *That* knowledge had affected her quite deeply. She would always be a prophetess of God. But not until Elijah had come to their home, did she know *how* she would be able to resist her tremendous love overcoming her in such horrible circumstances. But now she had finally grown from the inside out a commitment to Understanding that she *knew* was real even if that Understanding was, yet, out of her reach. *Sometimes, all we can do is wait on the Lord.* And she wailed in her husband's arms and he held her tightly, shaking his head, not knowing what to do, nor, if in the next instant, he, himself, would go down. And Moses and Elijah materialized beside them and Moses placed his hand on Mafferan's shoulder and Elijah did the same to Yinauqua while these holy men looked into each other's eyes.

Tremendous thunder shook the orb and it brought all their attention to it.

Seven-year-old Lynnara appeared upon the stage but in a smaller version of her Mommy's holy dress, and her eyes blazed like the sun with a love like no other. This was her bestest Mommy *ever,* and her little heart had sworn a long time ago that she wouldn't lose *this* Mommy like she lost the other two. But *more* than that. Lynnara *knew* that Stephanie was like the very essence of *reality* itself, and her whole *being* was committed to love her. Silver sparks flew off of her as she knelt beside her Mommy and put her little hand on her shoulder but looked over at evil Jargono, and she pointed at him but then glared at the crowd. "*This* is a *very* bad man."

If *anyone* else would have said this, the crowd would have disregarded and mocked. A few even recognized Princess Lynnara, but to all, she was just a *child,* like a little angel. The crowd narrowed their eyes at Jargono as he laughed inside. He knew who this brat was, that she had a little power, and he said to the crowd, "Well, it's clear she loves her Mommy. Good girl!" he said with endearment but the edge of mockery was apparent to Lynnara.

She looked down at her unconscious Mommy then up at her Daddy, who was shocked at the power he could feel from her while Vaughn had surrounded them all with protection from his staff. But Lynnara stood up and walked outside of it toward Jargono, and he laughed. "Now child, it's OK if you want to hit me. I won't hold that against you." And many in the crowd couldn't help laughing. *Of course* the Princess would feel this way. But the sign was given just like King Jargono asked for. *Vaughn and Stephanie are evil,* the crowd was *sure* of it.

Lynnara said again, "You *are* a *very bad* man." And she clapped her hands and a glowing golden cage with silver sparks bursting from it appeared around Jargono and he couldn't help from laughing. But when he grabbed it to rip it apart, it cut into his fingers and wouldn't move at all. Immediately, he studied it *and* Lynnara deeply. She had the same power as her Mother which he knew full well, but there was also something odd with her that he didn't understand. And when he tried entering her mind, he couldn't! She was at least as fast as he was! Which he quickly realized was natural for most children to be faster than adults. But also, because her mind *was* a child's mind, it didn't work in ways he could understand and *part* of that was due to her being a child, but another part was. . . something else that evaded him.

Vaughn had been about to extend his protection out to encompass Lynnara but the Spirit withheld him as he watched in amazement but still trying to process what had happened to them. Lynnara's eyes blazed as she pointed to her Mommy, and she said to Jargono in a level voice, "You're going to *regret* this!" Then she raised her little hand with her palm out toward Jargono and a blazing golden fireball with silver sparks trailing behind raced toward Jargono so fast that it hit him and blew up before he had time to react. When the black smoke cleared, he was gone.

Lynnara knelt back down and put both hands upon her Mommy, but looked up at Daddy. "I have to take Mommy away. I'll take care of her. Don't worry Daddy. The bad man will be right back so you have to stay. I love you, too." And she leaned over Stephanie and kissed Vaughn on the cheek and they disappeared!

Part of Vaughn was in a daze, but the *other* part stood him up and turned him so black no one could see him anymore. And Jargono reappeared where he had been standing, saying, "Wow. That *kid* packs a *punch*." And he laughed as he dusted himself off.

Vaughn's staff began to crackle with energy and Jargono knew he couldn't fight with *that*, so he said, "Well, I guess we can cancel *elections.*"

But Vaughn said, "Why, are you afraid you'll *lose?*"

And everyone could sense Jargono *did* have some fear about him, not knowing it was the staff causing it. And Vaughn calmed and turned to the crowd. "Most of you have been brought in from the North. Have a safe trip *home.*"

When the country at large heard that most of the people there were from the *North*, it changed *all* the people's perceptions down South. They couldn't *believe* the depths of deception that had been foisted upon them. But many up North laughed when they heard it, saying, "Well, that's *politics.*"

Jargono soured on this whole debate thing, and said, "You know, I'm tired of being *nice*. Where is your *God* now? The world's *savior,* your precious *Queen* has just been *judged*. Oh, that's right. *You're* supposed to be some kind of *judge,* right? Go ahead, *judge me!*"

The hard part in this was that a part of Vaughn had *no* understanding of why this all was happening. *None of it* made sense. And *oddly,* he felt as if a gray or black arm was now reaching inside *his* head. *That* hadn't happened since he was filled with the Holy Ghost. And a deep feeling of nothingness suddenly inundated him, like *he* was nothing, *worthless.* Vaughn hadn't felt like *that* since he was a misfit child screeching and twisting himself in torment. And the dazed part of himself came back, saying within him, *How come you just got* beaten *by such evil? You* can't *win, You can't win because God has been a* lie *and you* know it *now. You* feel *the truth of that.*

And it was *true!* Vaughn could *definitely* feel like that part of himself was *indeed* telling the truth! All he felt was devastation and within that devastation *nothingness,* no goodness *at all.* But

Vaughn had been *here* before, when he was a child in torment and he cried out from his depths, *What am I? Why am I here? What is life?* And Vaughn remembered way back then that he realized life wasn't just life but it was Life with a capital L, and that Life *had to be* pure, pure *Goodness,* otherwise no reality would even exist *at all.* And *that* knowledge he had *proved* to himself way back then when he didn't know *anything* about *anything,*

But this empty feeling in him now told him, "You were *lying* to yourself the *whole time.* You *know* that now. What *life* do you have *now?* You just believed what you did because you *wanted* to."

Vaughn shook his head and laughed, saying to himself, *Not such a great life now.* But he also knew he wasn't lying to himself. He had fought too long and too hard for the *true* knowledge of Goodness, but *also,* frankly, he had proven it to himself beyond *any* doubt. And he also knew, *Ha! VERY tricky. Of course I wanted to believe it. Why would I* not *want to believe what's good? And wanting to believe doesn't make it* not *true. But* why *has this all happened?* Judge Vaughn said within himself but unto the Lord Jesus, as well, and he looked over to fake Jargono, saying, "When the Lord Jesus and I have judged you, *you* will know it," And he vanished.

And Lynnara materialized with her Mommy and placed her in a simple bed in the center of the shelter. Everyone saw the bed materialize moments before Lynnara arrived. As soon as Mandy saw Stephanie, she raced to her side heartbroken but Lynnara held out her hand and used her power to push her back. "You can't touch her yet."

All the other children gathered around whispering, *knowing* that this was *Queen Stephanie*. And they all began to greatly fear, because they had trusted she was their ultimate savior, and Lana knew their thoughts, and said, "Only the Lord Jesus is our savior. And to doubt goodness for *any* reason is *stupid!*"

And all the children saw *that* plainly and all fell to their knees begging forgiveness. Rebecca said, "Ask God, not us. Stand up and get out of the way, or do something useful!" And Rebecca went to her knees with Lana and whispered something in her ear before she began her prayers. Mandy reflected on Rebecca's words because they were *Mandy's*. She often told Rebecca to *always* do something useful, and Mandy went to her knees on the other side of Stephanie, then all the children behind them did the same.

Lynnara put both her hands upon Stephanie's pelvis and they burst into flames reminiscent of when they had poured the holy oil onto Mandy. Mandy looked up at Lynnara, wondering, *When did she become* this *powerful?* But Lana knew her thoughts, and said, "Lynnara and the Tree of Life are one, even though she's not even holy yet, but she is! *This* is who she is the whole time!" And Rebecca looked up from kneeling and nodded, and whispered in Lana's ear again, but this time Lana nodded, and whispered back in Rebecca's ear.

Mandy asked, "What happened Lynnara?"

Not wanting to waste time with long explanations, Lynnara leaned over Stephanie and touched Mandy's head, and everything she knew about it flooded Mandy, and Mandy said, "Dear Jesus, she was *pregnant?*"

And Lynnara nodded.

"The Anti-Christ did *what* to her?"

And Lynnara didn't answer because she knew she already showed it to Mandy, who suddenly turned *very* dark. Mandy had sworn a long time ago a sister *oath* to God about Carla and Stephanie, and it now burned hot in her so she stood up, saying to all the new comer children, "Let's *go*! Let's go do something *useful.*" And they all left with Mandy!

Vaughn had tracked his wife through their rings and materialized beside Lynnara. He looked around in puzzlement but was amazed at his daughter's flaming hands. Lynnara didn't look up, she was too deep in concentration, but said, "This place is the surprise Stephanie wanted to show you way back when you just met. This is the shelter she built. . .ahhh, well, when I first came it was a *lot* smaller. But I made *improvements,* because there's so many children now!"

Vaughn's amazement with Lynnara competed with this new information. He realized Stephanie had been *right* about Lynnara. She *was* up to something. Lynnara knew that it was finally time to tell Mommy and Daddy *everything* but she *had to* keep concentrating on Mommy because she was about to die, and Lynnara just felt that if Mommy died again, *This time she won't be back*, and it was unthinkable what would happen if the *faithwalker* died. So Lynnara did something *no one* had ever done. She looked up into her Daddy's eyes and simply said, "*Understand!*" And her eyes blazed, then Vaughn's eyes blazed, and he was slammed with the understanding of all Lynnara had been through.

Vaughn raised his staff and the whole shelter briefly glowed silver. Then he knelt down on one knee beside his daughter while leaning on his staff as Lynnara stood over her Mommy in deep concentration, flaming hands moving almost imperceptibly, searching, searching, searching. . . for something. Vaughn couldn't follow *anything* Lynnara was doing but played back in his memory when he first met her, when she had exuberantly asked if he would be her Daddy. Now Stephanie's life was literally in *her* little hands, Vaughn said, "You know how to contact me when she wakes up. I'm going to go do something useful."

Lynnara simply nodded, and Vaughn vanished.

The problem was that Stephanie wasn't just suffering from poison and physical trauma, though the Anti-Christ had *literally* crushed her private insides where babies grow. When the Anti-Christ had told her there would be *no more generations,* Stephanie suddenly realized her deep connection to the little person growing inside her person and there was instantaneous recognition of utter goodness, utter value in that little person which at the same time as understanding *that, that* person had been destroyed. Pregnancy is a private sacred knowledge to women, but sadly, so is the tragic loss of such little innocent life. And she couldn't reconcile her guilt.

So while little Lynnara battled an unknown poison, and tried to at least stop Mommy from bleeding inside, she *also* was trying to reach her heart and mind. "Dear *Jesus,*" she called out, "I can't do this myself. I'm just a child." And Yinauqua, dressed in her burgundy holy dress, appeared beside her.

"I'm here to answer your prayer, daughter!"

Lynnara was overjoyed. "Am *I* your daughter, too?" She asked, very much like a little girl.

"You are *now!*" Yinauqua said. "The Lord Jesus has sent me to answer your prayer." And Yinauqua's hands burst into flames, too, and she placed them in the center of Stephanie's chest while Lynnara concentrated on her pelvis. But even Yinauqua, with all her experience in suffering, couldn't seem to reach Stephanie's heart to reason with her.

Yinauqua called for her husband and he materialized, but just dressed in his usual tan tunic and brown pants. "Place your hands on her head," she said, and his hands burst into flames and he did so.

No one had known exactly the extent of the Anti-Christ's power and what he would be capable of, but the Lord's words now came to Mafferan's mind and he spoke them aloud, "Except those days be shortened, no flesh would survive! For if it was possible, he would even fool the very elect!"

The fact that it took all three of them to try and save Stephanie brought the full weight of the meaning of those words into all their hearts.

CHAPTER 14

# We Can Only
# Wonder Why

*The Father rarely danced but he bounced around the orb now, while several of his tendrils reached into its blue depths invading Stephanie's utter recesses. It had been a long time, "Too long," he spoke aloud, since they had been able to access her, but now, what their Christ did opened her up wide. "Such a miracle," the Father boasted.*

*HrorrarrAggrang said, "Even all three of them won't be able to overcome us using the orb."*

*The Father said, "And once we break her will completely, I'll suck her right into myself right through the orb!"*

*"It's just a matter of time. She can't overcome the pain, so the pain will overcome her. At last." HrorrarrAggrang spoke delightfully as he, too, reached into the orb with his arm, being careful to counter what the others were doing while the Father concentrated solely on his next meal.*

*"Just a matter of time, and I'll pull her right out from under them all!" And the Father laughed at such a victory against them all. Never had he imagined anything so sweet.*

Stephanie huddled in the corner of her little bedroom while her father bellowed at her and her mother just watched with her hand to her mouth. "You're *nothing*. You'll *never* grow up to be the right kind of woman,"

Somewhere in Stephanie's consciousness, she wasn't sure if this really happened to her or it was just a bad dream, but *now*, it was reality. She *felt* like that little child. She *is* that little helpless child with searing unspeakable pain crushing her heart making it harder and harder to breathe.

Yinauqua cried out, "Dear Jesus, I can't believe it. We're *losing* her!"

Lynnara turned black all over. "No, we're *not*!" And she disappeared!

And reappeared in the Father's darkest room!

The Father was *delighted,* and HrorrarrAggrang said, "Wonderful! A *snack!*"

The Father said, "You can have her, since I'm about to *consume* her *Mommy.*" And when the Father said *Mommy* it was with Lynnara's voice.

"No you're not!" she said in a matter-of-fact tone as she raised her little hand, and she cast a never before seen energy blast at HrorrarrAggrang. Part golden fireball with a blue center, but part ball lightening, the creation of which had never been done before. And it sped so fast even HrorrarrAggrang couldn't duck it, and when it hit, it didn't explode once, not even twice, but *thrice!* And HrorrarrAggrang literally blew to pieces and splatted all over the Father's deepest darkest most secret room.

The Father grew angry with the invasion, *shocked* such a mere child should have so much power. At first he wanted to summon Mafferan directly and charge him with breaking the truce, but *how* was this an infraction? It clearly wasn't. This was just a *naturally* occurring *abnormal* child.

The Father covered himself in Sacred Black Oil but Lynnara wasn't interested in him. She raised her hand and another energy blast sped toward the sacred orb! Lynnara *knew* they had been using it against her Mommy. In a microsecond, the Father knew how powerful that blast was. He'd just seen what it did to HrorrarrAggrang, his offspring. In a microsecond he imagined what it would be like to lose his only *very* precious orb. And in the next microsecond, he threw himself over the orb to protect it!

Lynnara hadn't expected *that,* but then again, she was just a child and expected she didn't know *a lot* of things. The blast hit the Father's back, blew up three times, and scattered much of him all over the walls of the room. But he was so massive there was still much of him left and his massive tail swept out with lightning speed to grab Lynnara. But she knew she couldn't win against *him* so she vanished and reappeared back at the shelter and resumed her position.

Yinauqua saw Lynnara crying and touched her head and she knew what Lynnara had done. With widening eyes, and a bursting heart, Yinauqua said, "That was *very* brave, my *wonderful* daughter."

When Mafferan heard his wife call Lynnara her *wonderful daughter,* with such deep meaning, he marveled at the child.

"You've *definitely* improved things. I think we'll be able to bring her around now."

But Yinauqua said, "It won't last." And she touched her husband's head to impart understanding. "That's why she's crying. She knows."

"I *failed*," Lynnara wept, not understanding why she felt so sure she would succeed but she actually *failed*. It was the very first time her faith had been challenged to its utter depths since she came to be what her third and bestest Mommy had made her to be, a *faithwalker*. Yet, the fire in her hands did not waver.

Yinauqua and Mafferan looked at each other then Yinauqua said, "Your Mommy has felt like that *many* times. Even I just did before *you* went below and, well, raised holy hell!"

Lynnara couldn't help scrunch her face up at the joke even though she didn't want to laugh right now. Tears still poured down her little cheeks. "Yea, I guess I did. I didn't really think about it. I just *did it.*" And she sniffed back tears.

Mafferan said, "Both your Mommies are like that!" And he had a mischievous smile which Yinauqua noted.

Lynnara looked at her, saying, "You're like that, *too?*"

Yinauqua nodded. "It took me a long time to be, well, less ruled by my strongest feelings, but yes."

Lynnara didn't understand. She *loved* her strongest feelings. She loved the power of it. Power not for herself, but for others. And Yinauqua answered her thoughts, "I understand that *very* well. So does your Mommy. In fact, it's how she rescued *you* from Jargono's fire! She didn't even know what *she* was doing, but she just felt it, and *did it!*"

And something about that burned inside Lynnara's heart and the flames from her hands began to hiss with more intense heat.

Stephanie grew angry and she suddenly stood up, screaming at her mother, "Why don't you *do* something?" *Now* Stephanie was *sure* this never happened, that it was a dream. But then she felt a familiar feeling. A power was attempting to manipulate her dream.

The Father was back at the orb. He didn't even have time to collect much of his essence where *a lot* was still splattered all over. *It's a good thing HrorrarrAggrang can't see what happened to me. I'll put him back together later. After I put myself together, and after I feast.*

The Father squinted his Greatest Eye. *That's not supposed to happen. She's* manipulating *her own dream!* Then he remembered Stephanie had done such things in the past and he doubled his efforts to regain control.

Stephanie's Father ran up to her and shoved his big fat finger in her face, "You will show some *respect* for your *mother!*"

But Stephanie boldly stood up to him, "Why *should I?* YOU NEVER DO!"

And he smacked her across the face and knocked her down and Stephanie jerked her head and her eyes opened. Mafferan said, "Welcome back."

And then all that happened to Stephanie came back to her and she weakly raised her hand to her mouth, "Oh God."

"We'll help you get through this," Yinauqua said.

"Mother," Stephanie said weakly, surprised they were both here. "Where am I?"

"Don't you recognize it?" Lynnara said with a broad smile, and Stephanie weakly looked around. Lynnara said, "It's your *shelter* you built! I just sorta made some improvements."

Then Stephanie recognized it, the yellow raincoat pieces for the circular wall, and she was immediately inundated with many memories. *This* is where she came when she suffered the most when she was a child. *This* is where she first found her person again after having been almost destroyed by Gary and his gang. *So many feelings churning on a tempest sea,* she remembered. *But this is so much worse.*

And her feelings of the loss of her unborn child savaged her, a gaping unfulfilled hole in her person along with her failing that child, and she felt herself losing consciousness again but Mafferan called her back. "Your daughter went into Hell for you!"

*That* snapped Stephanie more awake as she now focused on Lynnara. She weakly said, "You did *what?*"

Lynnara looked into her Mommy's eyes and her eyes glowed, and she said, "Understand!" and Stephanie was immediately brought up to speed on *everything.* She was also *shocked* at what Lynnara just did. Then she saw what Carla had done. "Oh my God!" and Stephanie looked upon Lynnara and now Rebecca and Lana who stood at her sides, knowing what they *also* had done. "I love you girls so much!"

And when Stephanie felt and said *that,* it gave Lynnara the extra help she needed for her work inside her Mommy and she shouted, "*I got it!*"

Everyone looked over to her and their mouths dropped open. Lynnara's hands were *inside* her Mommy but in the spiritual plane, and she said, *"Of course!* The *poison* is in the *Corridor!* I should have thought about that earlier!" And Lynnara grunted and leaned back and with her hands and half her arms looking transparent, she pulled out of Stephanie what looked to be a black, hairy serpent with giant fangs. As soon as it was pulled free, it turned on Lynnara to attack *her* but Mafferan shot a silver beam into it right into the Corridor and it turned to ash.

Lynnara went back to her Mommy and *now* she was able to *completely* stop her bleeding, and then to heal her, except . . . she looked up to Yinauqua, "I don't know how to do this part."

Yinauqua looked to her husband and he came over and put his hands on Lynnara's shoulders. "I'll help you."

In better times, Lynnara would have relished in Mafferan's wonderful holy touch but these weren't better times. And there was something preventing even both of them from restoring Stephanie fully back to normal. She was healed, but no longer able to have children, and Mafferan sighed, and Lynnara said, "It doesn't feel right," as she turned around and looked into Mafferan's eyes. She didn't understand.

But it was something from Stephanie that was preventing full healing. Her guilt for allowing her unborn child to be so brutally murdered. And Stephanie said, "I don't deserve to have any more children! Of all that I was supposed to defend. . ."

And Lynnara finally understood. "That's not *true* Mommy. You're the bestest Mommy *ever.*"

And then the Father, through the orb, slammed full force into Stephanie's consciousness and she passed out. Over and over again, Stephanie heard, "You're guilty, *guilty,* GUILTY, *GUILTY. . .* And she couldn't fight the truth of it.

As hard as the three tried to bring her back, they just couldn't overcome Stephanie's own will fighting against them. "Mommy, mommy, *mommy,"* Lynnara wept over her, "You're the *bestest* Mommie *ever!"* And she fell on her mother hugging her as tightly as possible.

And Yinauqua couldn't help weeping because she didn't know how to reach her daughter. But Lynnara, feeling her Mommy was about to pass away, threw an odd forcefield around her. It sizzled with energy just above the skin level. It crackled and popped and sparked silver bursts! Mafferan looked at Yinauqua and they both were astonished. "You're not leaving, Mommy!" Lynnara said. No one had *ever* seen *anything* like this!

And Vaughn materialized, whereupon Lynnara turned and looked up into his eyes and said, "Understand!" And he did.

King Vaughn, just dressed in basic browns, leaned upon his staff and wept. He *knew* his wife better than *anyone.* Yinauqua was weeping louder now and Mafferan even had tears. With all that power they all had, *no one,* not even Vaughn with his blessed special staff could overcome Stephanie's own will. She no longer felt she deserved to live because she simply could *not* get past the pain and guilt, and in fact, *continuously* she felt over and over the insult of the Anti-Christ's attack on her and her inability to prevent losing her child. And Vaughn knew *that* wasn't even coming from the orb.

Vaughn wiped tears from his eyes and sighed heavily like no other. He remembered pushing the huge boulder from the mouth of the cave but *this* was a *lot* harder. He sighed again *knowing* what was coming, and he said to Lynnara, "Let her go!"

But Lynnara whirled on him, her eyes blazing, "No!"

Vaughn said the second time, "Let her go, Lynnara."

But she screamed at him, "*NO!*" And she started to crackle with energy.

Vaughn grew stern, and said the *third* time, "Let her *go, Lynnara.*"

But Lynnara still refused, screaming, "No, NO, *NO.*" And she threw and extra force field around herself, too!

Yinauqua thought she had mastered herself, but she couldn't help it, and even Mafferan felt she was right, and Yinauqua said, "Vaughn, what does it hurt? With time, there are *always* possibilities."

And Mafferan even said, "You know she's right about that. Why don't you ask the Book of Wisdom?"

But right now even the Book of Wisdom seemed of no account because Vaughn knew the truth, that they had no win here anymore, and prolonging this was only degrading everyone's strength that they still needed.

Vaughn raised his staff and smacked it down hard on the ground and it thundered. All of Lynnara's energy fields collapsed and Stephanie immediately died and they all knew it. Lynnara ran at Vaughn and pounded her fists on his chest, screaming, "I *hate you,* I HATE YOU, *I HATE YOU.*" And the Father was delighted. Not just because Stephanie became one of his best meals, *ever.* But also at what was now transpiring,

And Vaughn said to Lynnara, as he vanished his staff and wrapped his arms around her, with tears running down his face, "I know, but *I* love you more now than even *ever* before." And he kissed the top of her head as Lynnara began to wail because she lost her *faithwalker* connection to her Mommy and she felt so lost like her guts had just been torn out.

And Yinauqua collapsed, unable to bear being conscious. And before Satan could grab *her*, Mafferan transported Yinauqua and himself back into Heaven,

Rebecca didn't understand *any* of this. But as a Ranger, Mandy had taught her that as long as you're still breathing, you *fight!* And even *after* you're not breathing, if evil is around, you *still* fight! And she didn't care that everyone else gave up. Her and Lynnara, and Lana *knew* Stephanie and God Jesus. There was *no* failing allowed!

Then she noticed Lana on her knees but when Rebecca touched her, she fell over. Vaughn and Rebecca looked more closely at her. Her eyes were closed but darting around. She was having a vision. But this *wasn't* a vision! And Rebecca knew now that Lana had taken Rebecca's whispering seriously.

Lana had moved in spirit passed having just visions but actually entered the *reality* her vision focused upon, just like Rebecca had suggested! When Stephanie had felt defeated before, when she was still pregnant with Michael, *none* of the adults could get through to her, but *they* did! "God be with you, Lana," Rebecca said, as she placed her hand on her best friend's chest and prayed all she could for her, rocking back and forth just like Vaughn did to her when he first found her.

And each rocking back and forth seemed to add a bit more intensity to her love.

Stephanie was chained to a black wall but she didn't care. Many demons and beasts were dancing around her, and many evil people Stephanie, herself, had sent to Hell, and they were all mocking her, and swiping at her so that her holy dress was torn and she bled. But she didn't care.

Lana growled strenuously as she broke past the terrible pain that tried to stop her from entering, and she squeezed herself through tangled vinelike things with thorns and yanked her single braid out from that mess, and she *forced* her way through some kind of black energy barrier, then she glowed with brilliant silver light as she walked into the pack of evil creatures and beings and *things,* and they all fled. And she ran then *leapt* at Stephanie and disappeared into her!

Guilty, *guilty, GUILTY* resounded all around and Stephanie as a little child of maybe five lay curled up on a deep black floor weeping, crying over and over, "I'm guilty, I'm *guilty.*"

Lana knelt down in front of her, and asked, "Do you deserve to be punished like *this?*"

And little Stephanie looked up from the floor with fire in her eyes, and said, "YES! I'm guilty."

"Is that the *worst* evil, *ever?*"

And little Stephanie looked up into Lana's soft green eyes, and asked, "Do I know you?"

"Not yet," Lana answered softly, "But you will. Is that the *worst* evil *ever?*" She asked again while she remembered how

Stephanie used to teach her how to deal with her father. Lana didn't know what she would have done without Stephanie.

Little Stephanie, her red hair splaying all over the deep black wretched floor thought the question was odd. *What does that have to do with me being guilty?* But she couldn't help but think about it because the truth called to her, and little Stephanie said, "I don't know."

And Lana placed her hand upon little Stephanie's head, and said, "I met my Mommy, well, my Great Gramma Mommy, and she's in Heaven now, but she watches over all of us."

And when Marta refocused her orb, she was able to actually see where Lana went in spirit, and when she heard what Lana said to little Stephanie, she burst out crying, *knowing* what Lana was about to do, and hoping it would be enough.

And Lana concentrated on Stephanie and shared what Marta, her Great GranMommy, had shared of *her* life with Lana. And after a bit, little Stephanie said, "She had a hard life. She deserves to be in Heaven. But I *don't!*"

Lana was surprised and defeat began to creep into her but she called out to Marta because she *knew* she was watching. "Mommy, it's not *enough*. Come Mommy, *please come!*"

And Marta's eyes grew wide. *Can I go? It was a prayer. I can answer prayer. I'm still charged with protecting them against the demon's cheating.* Then Marta grew angry and spoke aloud, "I don't give a *damn* if they say I'm allowed or *not!* Well, because all this is *evil* so how can I not be allowed? Then she realized, *Besides, they're not even on Earth any more. And the* truce *says* nothing *about Hell! But how do I get there?* And she remembered how Stephanie had gone into Hell to save Vaughn, and Marta disappeared, and reappeared beside Lana's spirit.

Lana immediately turned around and hugged her and Marta was overjoyed to once again hold her. Marta said, "I know what you want me to do, and I know why. I hope it's enough, We love her so *much*."

And Marta knelt down to be at eye level with little Stephanie who had sat up. One of the problems was that when Stephanie was still on Earth and she was pregnant, her hormones did what hormones do and affected her consciousness. And then the miscarriage created a hormone backlash and *that* affected her consciousness. *That* effect still existed in her consciousness now along with everything else.

Marta said, "Lana asked for me to visit you so you can answer her question."

Little Stephanie said, "What question? I'm guilty."

"Yes, I know, but is that the *worst* evil, *ever?*" And Marta put her hand upon little Stephanie's head and shared with little Stephanie Marta's *whole* miserable life while mortal.

Little Stephanie's eyes grew wide and then she threw herself to the floor, again, weeping, pounding the deep black floor with her little fists, and as she wept she began to grow up and weep even harder. When she became her full adult again, she sat up and looked into Marta's eyes, and said, "But you *saved your* child. I *killed* mine!"

But Marta said, "I actually *killed* my mother. You didn't *kill* your unborn child. You were just overcome. But in *truth,* you *saved your* child when practically everyone had abandoned you." And Marta called out, "Michael, come *here*!" And little Michael materialized beside Marta and Lana and threw his little glowing arms around Stephanie, burying himself into her bosom. This was the *second* time he had visited Hell! First he had to save his Daddy, and *now* his Mommy. *That* made sense. "I miss you, Mommy."

And Stephanie began to weep, feeling little Michael's love inundate her, and realizing all she had gone through to *save* his little life.

Michael pushed back to get a closer look at Mommy. He looked into her eyes and saw such pain he didn't understand. "I love you, Mommy." And he poured how much he valued his Mommy straight into her heart and she grabbed him so tightly and squeezed and rocked back and forth.

Then Marta and little Michael and Lana were standing in front of Stephanie chained to a deep black wall in Hell, and Stephanie said, "I don't belong here."

And Marta frowned, and said, "No, you don't."

And Lana, holding Marta's hand, shook her head vehemently, and said, "No, you *don't*"

And little Michael held out his arms to his Mommy.

Lady Stephanie looked at Marta and sensed she was a *faithwalker,* even a powerful one! *Well, look at* that! she thought. And Stephanie said to her, "Do *you* want to do it, or shall I?"

Marta smiled, "I'd love to. I'd be *honored.* I'll be the talk of all Heaven." And she burst out laughing for a while until Lana said, "*Mommy!*"

And Marta said, "Oh." and she raised her hand and silver beams shot from her fingers and the chains restraining Lady Stephanie all turned to ash and she floated down to stand in front of them. But Marta grew angry. Blood stained Stephanie's favorite holy dress, and it had been shredded. It was Marta's favorite dress, too. She frowned again, but this time the dress was made like the day Arlupo gave it to Stephie, and all the cuts and bruises all over Stephanie's body were healed, but the *faithwalker's* internal damage could not be healed.

"Thank you, but I'm *still* guilty. But that's not more important than the good we all have to do." But Stephanie was still reeling from all that Marta shared of her life and couldn't help but look deeply into her eyes in amazement. Stephanie had never even imagined going through what Marta had experienced. And, yet, here she was in *Hell* to save *her!*

Marta threw her arms around Stephanie and they hugged deeply, and Marta said, "If you only knew how much I *love* you, how much I *respect* you. In fact, your mother Yinauqua told me that because I love you so much, I became one with you and through that oneness *I* became a *faithwalker* like you!"

Stephanie was shocked and so deeply honored that she pulled away to look even more deeply into Marta's eyes, and then into Lana's, and then into little Michael's. Stephanie shook her head. "Well, I guess I must be worth *something* for all of you to come into *Hell* to save me. I would have thought Vaughn would be here, too! After all, I went to Hell to save him, but I'm sure he's busy with something even *more* important."

Lana said, "He would have but he knew he couldn't save you. *I* had to tell him to let you go! But through my mind because if I had said it out loud, Lynnara would have *killed* me. She put some kind of energy around you and wouldn't let you leave and Vaughn had to tell her *three times* to let you go. Then he had to smack his staff on the floor to stop Lynnara. *OH,* she was so *MAD!* She hit him!"

Stephanie's eyes went wide and her eyebrows went up. "Lynnara *hit* Vaughn?" Then she thought a moment then said, "With *what?*"

Lana nodded, saying, "A whole *bunch* of times. But just with her fists and said she *hated* him!"

Stephanie shook her head at how much love she felt from everyone, and at how deeply she had been overcome. Marta said, "One more thing before we literally get the Hell out of here." Marta placed her hand to Stephanie's cheek and her hand oscillated with many colors which moved into Lady Stephanie, And Marta said, "You'll know when it's time. By the way, you know you're in the belly of Satan, himself, right? *We're* only here in spirit,"

Stephanie said, "It's OK. It's about time I finally dealt with *him!*"

And Lana and Marta vanished, but Michael was still there! In fact, he *wasn't* spirit! But there inside Hell with soul *and* body! "Well, I guess we have to leave together, son."

And Stephanie walked around for a while, her glow making everything to flee, until she came to a massive pulsating bulge which she knew was vital. "Well Michael, my little *faithwalker!*

Have you ever made a fireball? Like this!" And Stephanie held out her hand and produced a small, golden fireball.

Little Michael held out his hand and a sizzling gold and silver fireball that was as big as he was hovered in front of him above his hand.

"Wow!" Stephanie said, now questioning the wisdom of teaching her son this. "Oh, well. Now, take it and *throw* it at *that* right there like *this.*" And Stephanie hurled the little fireball into the pulsating deep black vein.

The Father looked up for a moment experiencing slight indigestion. "Hmm, the faithwalker isn't digesting as well as I thought." But the Father was busy working on Lynnara whom he *finally* was able to provoke. While in Vaughn's arms, she kept saying she *hated* her Daddy over and over no matter how he tried to comfort her.

Excitement thrilled little Michael at the idea of *throwing* the fireball. He *loved* throwing things, all *kinds* of things, but *this?* So he threw it as hard as he could then used his little mind to, well, give it an extra *push!* The fireball raced to the vein and blew up with a loud thunder and all the various demons and creatures and humans scattered. Michael leapt up and down with joy then produced *three more* in rapid succession and threw those before Stephanie could say *anything!*

The Father wretched the first time, but when all three fireballs hit him, the Father did the unthinkable. He *vomited.* And out of his deepest, darkest, biggest black eye Lady Stephanie and little Michael floated out! And, holding his hand, they walked over to his orb, and Stephanie shook her head, as she saw Lynnara acting brattier than ever but Vaughn taking it all in stride.

The Father went to attack Lady Stephanie but she didn't even pay him any mind. Instead, she merely said, "What are you going to do? *Eat me?*"

And *that* halted the Father as he experienced something he never had before. Helplessness. Stephanie turned to face him with little Michael. "This is my *son,* Michael, The one you tried over and over and *over* again to *kill!*"

Little Michael waved his little hand at him and the Father couldn't help but wave a tail tip back! Stephanie said, "Show this big old devil what you just learned Michael."

And he created a *massive* fireball, as tall as his Mommy.

The Father's big black eye grew wide, but in the next instant, that fireball hit him straight in the eye along with three more! A lot of the Father blew apart with charred pieces splatting on his walls until he vanished. Stephanie looked at little Michael, saying, "Well, how *rude* to leave his guests all alone in his secret room with this *wonderful* illegal orb!" And Stephanie concentrated and called out, "Lynnara, you *bad* girl! Come down here a moment!"

Lynnara stopped crying, her eyes went wide, and she looked into her Daddy's eyes and climbed off his lap where Vaughn had been restraining her a bit. She smiled. Got an impish look in her eyes as she rubbed them dry, then said, "I'll be right back, Daddy!"

And she vanished, but reappeared beside Stephanie and was *shocked* to see little Michael who ran into her arms and they hugged tightly. Stephanie said, "OK. I *hear* you've been a *very* bad girl to Daddy!"

Lynnara's eyes went wide and her eyebrows raised. *Mommy knows EVERYTHING,* she thought.

And Stephanie said. "Well, as your *punishment,* I have a *chore* for you to do!"

Lynnara looked down, then up. *Chores aren't* that *bad,* she thought. And she looked up waiting.

"You see this orb right here? Well, the devil has been using it to make you and *everyone else* to be bad. What should we do with it?"

The Father rematerialized in his secret deepest darkest room and little Michael laughed and squealed because he'd grown very fond of playing with the devil, and he shot three more fireballs at Satan who managed to avoid the last two and he teleported himself to a different part of his room, much farther away. And Stephanie said, "OK, Michael. Let him watch what your sister is going to do."

And Lynnara looked over at the Father in pure delight and stuck out her tongue! The Father couldn't believe the insult, and from a mere *mortal* child. And then Lynnara raised her hand and shot a very compact red fireball into the orb and they all vanished.

The Father rushed to his orb to grab it before it blew up but didn't quite get ahold of it in time. It blew most of his arm off while it blew the orb into tiny melted pieces.

Stephanie, Michael, and Lynnara all appeared in the shelter right in front of Vaughn sitting now upon an elegant golden thrown with jewels embedded on it! He still wore his common browns, though. Lynnara said, "WOW!" and she climbed into his lap and hugged him. "I'm sorry Daddy. I *love* you."

Michael pushed at his sister to move over and he climbed up, too, then stood up on Vaughn's lap and kissed his cheek. Vaughn managed to look past them to Stephanie and raised a single eyebrow.

Stephanie smiled because she understood the *meaning* of the throne and his actions. "My *very* wise and strong *King*," and she knelt to him on one knee and bowed her head.

"Rise, my Queen," he said, as he put the children down and took her in his arms and kissed her deeply. Michael jumped up and down and Lynnara covered her eyes but peeped through her fingers.

Then Rebecca came over, and said, "I told Lana she *had to* do something because none of the adults were doing *anything!* And Rebecca hugged Lana.

Lana said, "I didn't know I could do that until Rebecca told me I could. So I did! I'm sorry, Lynnara, I couldn't tell you 'cause you'd be *so* mad to let Stephie go."

Lynnara came over and all the girls hugged together and little Michael wormed his way into the center of them all.

CHAPTER 15

# Seven-Headed Dragon

*HrorrarrAggrang, the highest demon, except, of course, for the Father, eyed him narrowly, but since he didn't even give HrorrarrAggrang a salutation upon entering his sacred chamber, HrorrarrAggrang finally spoke. "What are you doing here? You're supposed to be very busy up there."*

*The Anti-Christ ignored him but kept studying HrorrarrAggrang's orb, even touching it rather intimately, until HrorrarrAggrang squeezed himself between the orb and the human demon which had the Anti-Christ dematerialize before he was actually pushed away. But he rematerialized above the orb and continued his study.*

*HrorrarrAggrang had enough of this insolence and extended himself as if to consume him, and the Anti-Christ said, "Brother, I told our Father I would make him a new orb. I need to study yours first. As soon as connection was broken between his orb and I, I came home. Is this not my home, brother?"*

*HrorrarrAggrang had never been spoken to so congenially, yet, effectively. "You are going to make a new orb? You do know you are nothing but an experiment? We're attempting to make you a wife right now."*

*"I have no desire for that, and I've already destroyed all the rest of your cloning. There will be no more of that. I AM sufficient!"*

*HrorrarrAggrang couldn't believe what he heard but before he could say anything else boring, the Anti-Christ interrupted HrorrarrAggrang's thoughts, "All of your underlings are experiments that serve your purpose. But some overcome their masters and so enforce their purpose. And how do you know you are not also an experiment? But does it matter? You even tried to eat our Father. I am not so foolish as you. But consider this: I am made from demon powers and several faithwalker beings as well as from the best of human genius. But my arsenal now has power that neither any of you nor them above have ever seen. Would you like to challenge me now or later?*

*A booming voice shook the room and also HrorrarrAggrang but not the Anti-Christ who still floated above the orb. "Now children. There will be none of that between you two. You must work together to achieve my ends."*

It had been a *very* long while since Vaughn and Stephanie found themselves in bed together at home in their castle down south. This was the only place that really felt like home, because even the Holy Mountain, they knew, wasn't for them, not for their destiny. James and Carla had both moved down south into the castle to join them and that added to the homey feeling. As Stephanie puttered around the bedroom, her wavy red hair just hanging free and scattered across her back and shoulders, she noted that Vaughn was being extra charming and tender, but she just couldn't seem to respond to it very well.

As Vaughn removed his captain's black uniform and neatly folded it and placed it on a bedroom accent chair with fancy upholstery and curved wooden arms, Stephanie's eyes were naturally drawn to him but then she looked away. As he stripped naked, which had always been a delight to her, her eyes couldn't help to begin to stare but then she pulled herself away again.

Normally, Stephanie would have gleefully stripped down to being natural also, for they always rejoiced to sleep that way, but this time she went behind a changing screen and donned a simple black cotton nightgown, one more fit for an elderly woman, and then she climbed under the sheet and covers before Vaughn even turned around. When he finally turned towards her, Stephanie briefly noted that he was looking forward to being together, but she looked away as he approached. When he climbed in then immediately scooped her up in his arms, she tensed all over.

Vaughn let his breath out very slowly, and propped his head up with his hand while lying on his side. His other hand caressed Stephanie's cheek but also gently turned her head to face him, whereupon she teared up but she didn't exactly know why.

Vaughn said, "Do you know what the hardest thing I have ever gone through is?"

His deep brown eyes, almost black, were softer than she had ever seen, and the depth of his meaning exceeded where she was able to go, but Stephie said, "I don't know. When you stood before Satan down below and dared him to eat you? Or maybe. . . no, I'm sure it's when you allowed yourself to be eaten by the Highest Counselor."

But Vaughn slowly shook his head. "No. I knew the Father below wouldn't consume me. He was too smart and controlled to allow his temper to get the better of him. And I *knew* you would save me from Hell because I was *sure* of your love for me, and I knew that love would find a way, particularly the way that I *knew* existed!"

Stephanie teared up and started to sob at how dear Vaughn was being, at his total faith in her that she didn't any longer have in herself. Vaughn gently turned her head back to him to look her in the eyes. "The hardest thing I have *ever* gone through, only *much* harder for you, was not just what the Ant-Christ did to you and how I failed to protect you. . ."

But Stephanie interrupted. She hadn't even given *this* any thought. "Oh Vaughn. Don't blame yourself. There was *nothing* you could do. You haven't been a *faithwalker* that long. I was *born* to be what I am. *I failed.* Not you." And she broke down weeping.

But Vaughn shook his head that was still held up with his bent arm and hand. "*I* was given the staff of Moses to judge the whole world by. *I* was responsible to protect *especially* you."

Now Stephanie was greatly conflicted, but she didn't want to blame Vaughn. "Well, OK, but even Moses messed up *after* he had that staff, and *He* talked to God face to face. You're too hard on yourself." But as she finally looked deeper into Vaughn, she saw that he actually *wasn't* hard on himself! "Vaughn, why aren't *you* feeling guilty then?"

"Because if I don't accept that even *we* have limits, well, then, are *we* Almighty God? Even with the Holy Ghost in us, and being perfected, we will still be taught all things for *eternity.* Which means our perfection will eternally grow, which means we will always be limited by simply being a *being* and not God, who is omniscient, omnipotent, and omnipresent. And this is true for *every* creation of the Lord Jesus."

Stephanie had stopped crying and sighed and looked even deeper. "So what's the hardest?"

Vaughn wiped a tear from his eyes. "The hardest thing I have *ever* gone through, only *much* harder for you, was not just what the Ant-Christ did to you and how I failed to protect you. It was when I realized that he had so harmed you that you couldn't escape it here in your mortal life! You are a *woman.* And there is a *particular* sacred structure to *being* a woman in body *and* soul which as we know has the unique capacity to bring forth and nurture the *utmost* value, as Virgin Mary did, but also as you bore Michael, and *all* women who are able to bring children into the world and nurture them. And *that* means that when *that* structure is violently violated not just in body but in *soul,* too, and on top of that, when the new life it contains is destroyed, *that* causes insuperable pain and defeat like no other."

And Stephanie instantly bawled and wailed and Vaughn gathered her in his arms and held her and caressed her back and head for a long while until she calmed. Stephanie said,

"Lana told me that Rebecca told her to find a way to save me because the adults will fail like they did last time when I was pregnant with Michael. It was those *children* that brought me out of that place, Vaughn. No one else could have. So this time, Lana actually searched out a vision of a solution then found a way to enter that vision, *herself,* in real time!" Stephanie wiped her eyes and looked deeply into Vaughn and put her hand to his cheek. "Do you have any idea how unbelievable it is what she did? I *still* am in awe at that girl. You had good sense to listen to a mere child."

But Vaughn shook his head. "I already knew I had to let you go! I understand you better than you even understand yourself. But to contemplate letting you actually die, to go into *Hell* where I actually went, so I *know* what that's like. . . And to know that *only* there would you have a *chance* to be free . . ."

Stephanie looked deeply into Vaughn, again. She had picked up clearly what he meant by *chance.* "Wait Vaughn. You mean you weren't sure like you were the other times? You didn't *know* I would make it out?"

Vaughn stared into her eyes a while and teared up, then shook his head! "No!" And he wiped more tears from his eyes. "Because the damage done to your body *and* soul had been *so* extensive, I couldn't see to the end of it. So I couldn't see a solution, *particularly* past your pain. I only *hoped* that in the most miserable place in existence, that *there* the contrast would help you find a way out!"

The profoundness of his answer, of his love, descended upon Stephanie like nothing else before, and her heart pounded so hard in her chest it hurt. But she also sensed that there was even more! And she had to ask, "But why? Why would this be different from the other times that were so hard for you, like when Jargono had actually killed me? You didn't know then, either."

But Vaughn didn't hesitate. "When Jargono had killed you before, well, it just wasn't the same dynamic, nor was my understanding *anywhere* close to what it has become. But I *knew* you had a chance then because of the *way* you died. *This* time, though, well. . . that *chance* is totally different."

Stephanie's heart burned inside of her at the depth of that meaning. "Your true love for me sent me to Hell? To save me?"

"For the *chance* to be saved."

Stephanie said, "Actually, it wasn't Hell that did it! I felt I deserved to be there amongst all that evil!"

Vaughn looked at her quizzically with growing surprise and Stephanie let it build for a bit, then continued. "Apparently, Lana has a Great *Gramma Mommie* that watches over her from Heaven, and apparently she watches all of us, too. Apparently, she even became a *faithwalker* in Heaven because she loved *me* so much, she, well, she said she became one with *me*, and through that love became a *faithwalker.*"

Vaughn was hearing unbelievable things except he believed them, so he waited for Stephanie to continue.

"Great *Gramma Mommie* Marta had shared some of her life with Lana and Lana thought if she shared that with me, it would be enough to bring me to my senses. But it *wasn't.* So Lana *actually* called her Great Granma Mommie to come into *Hell* for me and *she did!* Can you *believe* that?"

Vaughn kept wiping tears from his eyes, then said, "Yes! *Absolutely.* Because you are that worthy to be loved."

Stephanie looked away. "I don't know," was all she could say. "Vaughn, *I* have the responsibility. *I* am *the* faithwalker. I *failed.*"

But Vaughn shook his head, and said, "*We.* As I told you, I have the Staff and was charged by God to wield it. This is a *WE* Stephanie. A WE. But what did Marta do?"

"Vaughn. . . she touched me like I do to people, and she shared her *whole* life with me." And Stephanie burst out weeping, and Vaughn held her for a while again, until, through her sobs, she spoke. "I thought. . . I had a pretty. . . *bad* life." Stephanie shook her head. "But I had. . . *Heaven.* . . compared to her! So *that* brought me out enough."

Vaughn tugged at his beard, and Stephanie began to laugh, so when he looked at her in question, she said, "You *like* your beard now!"

And Vaughn nodded, then said, "Can you share with me, what she shared with you?"

Stephanie thought for a bit because such things she considered as sacred. Marta's life now became part of *her* life but the question was whether she had the right to do that. But Marta's voice suddenly appeared in her head, "Please do! It would be an honor!"

And Stephanie could hardly believe it! And she said out loud, "An honor?" Whereupon Vaughn looked at her questioning, so Stephanie told him what just happened.

"But Vaughn, how could it be an *honor?* It's *horrible!* I *still* can't fathom it, how she continued on, how she is *now* what she is."

"I *might* know, but I *will* know after you share."

Stephanie shook her head for a bit as she reflected. "Oh Vaughn, are you *sure?*"

Vaughn said, "I defied our daughter, which is no easy task," and Stephanie burst out laughing at the truth of that, "and let you go to *Hell,* where you wanted to be. I think I *deserve* to know this burden!"

This kind of logic was *particularly* all Vaughn and Stephanie's heart pounded with love for him. "OK Vaughn." And she placed her hand to the side of his head then bowed her head down in concentration.

Vaughn turned so black he disappeared for quite a while but then finally came back to himself. But there wasn't even a tear and Stephanie didn't understand why. "What Vaughn?"

"Because I understand now *why* it's an *honor* for her life to be shared. *Evil* had *its* purpose in doing what it did to her, but Marta beat it all by deciding that once it happened to her, then *she* owned it! Which meant she could put *her* purpose to it. And *her* purpose to it was to rise above all that evil and now to use what happened to her to help others to be good!"

Stephanie is a *faithwalker,* which means she *knows* true meaning when she hears it, and *this* rang as deeply true as possible, and her eyes went distant and Vaughn rolled onto his back to rest.

Stephanie was alone in her thoughts. *If Marta could go through* all that *and overcome all that evil, I should be able to overcome. She even killed her mother. But she* deserved *it! My unborn child didn't deserve me failing him, or her. I don't even know if him or her.*

Vaughn sighed and rolled back to Stephanie and purposefully squeezed her and she could feel his desire but pulled away, but she also realized that it wasn't right for her to do so. Not like that. Vaughn said, "What the Anti-Christ did to *us* was worse than rape, because not only did he enter inside you against your will, but he *crushed* your fertility, and destroyed *our* child. But his *planned* destruction goes even much deeper that that!"

Stephanie didn't understand but began to be afraid, worried, and angry all at once. She looked at Vaughn, so he continued. "We truly love each other. We are *one.* One in spirit, mind, heart, soul, *and* flesh. Tamper with the oneness of *any* of those and you begin to destroy the oneness of the rest!"

Stephanie was floored at the understanding of the harm, but she protested, "But. . . but . . . the flesh is just flesh. The others are above *that.*"

Vaughn caught Stephanie in his stare and locked her there! And she knew it! But she also knew he was being a man. But she also began to fight against it, something she *never* did with Vaughn before nor *ever* wanted to, and he let her go! Vaughn said, "Whether you pulled away from my affection, or *just* fought against my mind, it's the *same!* Because it's *one* oneness." And Vaughn got out of bed, used his faithwalking ability to create for him an old man's white pajamas, then turned to Stephanie, and asked, "How do I look?"

Stephanie was surprised he *finally* was able to use his powers to dress himself. But . . . "Well, do you *mean* to look like an old man or was that just your faithwalking still misfiring on dressing yourself?"

"I meant to." And Vaughn left the room, left Stephanie alone, but as he was leaving, he reached his hand back and made his wife disappear!

And she reappeared in the shelter down near the border, in the very same bed where Lynnara had created it in the center of the shelter. Stephanie looked around dumbfounded, both at what Vaughn just did and that the shelter was empty. She looked at the bed where she had died and gone to Hell. She looked around at the shelter, at the furniture, but really, even the *feeling* of it being *her* shelter that she had built when she was a child, well, that *feeling* was remarkably all still there. Lynnara somehow had preserved it all when she made her improvements, and Stephanie laid down on the bed, rolled on her stomach, and began to bawl, just like she used to do here.

All her emotions rushed upon her quite suddenly, and she truly felt like she did when she was only fourteen years old. She remembered how she narrowly escaped being gang raped. Then she spoke aloud. "With all my power now, I couldn't keep myself from being raped *this time.*"

*Why did this happen to me* now, *but not back then? And why am I having so much trouble with this now?* Stephanie sat up and held out her hand and the Book of Wisdom that her ancient ancestors had gifted to Vaughn appeared resting on her palm.

She opened it to ask her questions but they had already been recorded!

Answer: You were more powerful when you were a child than you are now!

The answered floored Stephanie. She *almost* dropped the Book. She *knew* it didn't lie. And the Book read her heart and answered!

Answer: You were more powerful than the *level* of evil that assaulted you when you were a child. You held off your attackers just long enough for Vaughn to rescue you. And you have beaten all evil up until you didn't because *now* is the End Times.

"But. . . but. . . but, doesn't Goodness have an answer against *all* evil? The Holy Ghost was *meant* for that." Stephanie realized she was saying a lot of *buts* again. She hadn't done that for quite some time. And she realized it was because for quite some time she had never been challenged beyond her capacities.

Answer: *Dependent upon* your abilities to understand *yourself* and have faith in the goodness you are and *will* go after further *faithwalker*.

"The last time I was *really* challenged in a way to crush my spirit was when Karen was evil and forced me to Judge Mathew. My challenge with Michael was different. I would have *died* defending him."

Explanation: You didn't *doubt* yourself, nor your sacrifice, though it pained you beyond measure in *both* instances.

Stephanie said, "True."

Answer: The last time you doubted yourself like *this* is *never!* The closest would be when you took drugs and fucked whoever!

Stephanie's eyes went wide, both at the language and comparison. The Book *almost* seemed angry at her. "But how can that *be?* How could I *now* be even *worse* than when I did all that *terrible* stuff?" She wasn't asking the Book that question, but wondering aloud. But then she said to herself, "Oh, because I *killed* my unborn child. That's why.

**ADMONITION!**

But there was nothing after that word. And it was in bold! And the Book *never* did that before. "Are you angry at me? Why is this. . ." And before she could finish her question, the Book began to answer.

ADMONITION: The *faithwalker* has asked for rebuke.

"Rebuke? I did?"

ADMONITION: When someone has broken a sacred trust, Goodness becomes angry.

"I killed my child. I'm guilty."

ADMONITION: No. You are killing *yourself!*

The Book slid out of her hands and on to the floor and Stephanie stared blankly at nothing. But then the Book of its own accord began to glow golden, and its cover had become pure gold with no title at all, and it rose and opened.

Answer: You are destroying your husband along with yourself!

She would have dropped the book again but it was floating before her.

Answer: You are one. If you are worthy of death, if *you* are truly guilty, then as you die so does he because you are one. You have *always* been one, even before you were born!

"But what can I do?"

Answer: Nothing!

Now weeping forced its way through from depths unknown, from fibers in her being that were so primary, they were unthought of. Yea, from the very survival instinct that all have, even a bug, when it convulses with every effort to stay alive. Her heart pained her like never before and she fell off the bed and onto the earth and wailed. "There has to be *something. Please help me.* I don't want to hurt Vaughn."

The Book dropped on her head and Stephanie jerked up. The Book still glowed but was closed so she opened it.

Answer: True tears have been shed. The *faithwalker* has asked for *meaning.* Choose life, Life, and LIFE!

Stephanie sat up on her knees and her hand went to her heart as if to feel what was there. It didn't *feel* like life! When she had looked inside herself before when she was a child in this very shelter, she had felt life inside her, and from then on, always *life.* But *now!* "I asked what I can do and you said nothing. But it's not about what I can *do,* but about what I can *be!*

Answer: The *faithwalker* speaks truth.

Stephanie continued with both her hands, her finger tips touching her breastbone as if to feel deeply into her heart. I feel death inside me but you said *choose* life. I'm killing Vaughn with this death. How can I choose life when I killed my unborn child?

Answer: Nothing in your heart desired to *kill* your child. You were overcome. You are in the *End Times* and if you want to beat *this* evil, you have to rise to the occasion!

*My God, it's not just that I killed my child, it's that I was* beaten *by evil. That's* also *causing me this dead feeling.*

Answer: The faithwalker is *stubborn.* To rise above evil, to be stronger than it, and *unique* for each soul, you must experience certain depths *before* you can beat *all* evil! Marta is a *different* soul and to be able to do what *she* has done and now does, she had to overcome the evil attacking her. Can *you* overcome and *choose life, Life, and LIFE?*

"You're saying. . . I was unable to protect my unborn child.

Answer: You were unable because the forces that created the Anti-Christ had been planning for a *very* long time focused solely on *one* goal, on overcoming *you!* You and Vaughn have limited attention abilities because you are human beings and your abilities are all being used past their maximum. In other words, you are stretched beyond your means because this is the End Times.

"But. . . but . . . but there *has to* be a way for us to prevail."

Answer: Why?

"Why? Oh, I shouldn't be dumb like that and repeat your question. That's *stupid. Why.* . . why. Because . . . because Goodness *has to* have what's needed to overcome all evil. Right?

Answer: The *faithwalker* is regaining her *faith.* She is choosing life. Yes. But you have to be able to receive it. Choose life, Life, and LIFE. What is your favorite door?

"My favorite door? Oh, ahhh, Oh my God, I'm such an idiot. The one. . ." Stephanie stood up, dusted herself off, and climbed onto the bed and went on her knees. She looked over to the Book and using her faithwalking power made the book rise and settle before her. "My favorite door is the Open Door God gave me for my prayer to *choose* life, Life, and LIFE. The Holy Ghost, Jesus, and God the Father. A Door the Lord Jesus said he would *always* answer!

Answer: The *faithwalker* is restored.

And Stephanie sat back on the bed and began to weep again, but this time not in misery, but in thankfulness. Her fingertips found her breastbone again and she could feel life there, again. "Dear Jesus and God the Father, help me to forgive myself."

Marta, her hair in the three traditional Appendaho braids just like Stephanie used to wear, but dressed only in a brown peasant dress, appeared in the shelter, and went to her knees on the ground but propped herself up on the bed next to Stephanie and folded her hands. Her hair was in the Appendaho braids even though she was not from those people but she loved Stephanie so much, she emulated her. "I've been sent for your prayer, *Lady* Stephanie."

Stephanie, still in her old lady, black, nightgown, motioned her up on the bed and Marta bounded up, while Stephanie sat cross-legged, and Marta said, "Put your fingertips back where they were!" And Stephanie did so with both hands. "Search as deeply as you are able and find in yourself where you wanted to *kill* your unborn child, where you *understood clearly* that your actions or inactions would kill your unborn child."

Stephanie spent some time trying to find it. She *knew* it had to be there somewhere because she *felt it,* or at least the guilt. And the guilt meant *there had to be* some fault *somewhere.* But after a most serious search, Stephanie looked into Marta's soft green eyes, and said, "I can't find *anything.*"

And Marta replied, "Then in *that* matter, there is *nothing* to forgive! You made an unwise *assumption* that you should have been able to beat all evil and then faulted yourself for the *impossible* at *that* time. The Anti-Christ *knew* he could set this up in you!"

Stephanie turned dark. "He knew." She stated flatly.

Marta looked into Stephanie's depths, and said, "Yes. Now, what are *you* going to *do* about it?"

Stephanie put her anger aside because the answer wasn't there. Instead, she went to her knees on the bed again and began to pray. "Lord Jesus, I cannot even *begin* to describe the pain I still have, and the violation throughout my whole body, my whole *being,* and I am so *ashamed.* I don't feel worthy of *anything* from you. Help me. Vaughn said my sacredness as a woman has been violated. It *feels* like that." And Stephanie began to weep black tears. "Oh Jesus, Jesus, *Jesus…*"

When Marta saw *that,* she created a glass vial and unknown to Stephanie, Marta held out her hand and commanded her tears to float up and go into the vial. When Stephanie was done weeping, she began to pray again.

"Dear Lord Jesus, was my unborn child even old enough to have a place with you? With Michael, I have a deep connection, but my unborn child I never even knew if the child was a boy or girl, yet I briefly became aware of our *deep* connection. . . right before the child was *murdered*." And Stephanie began weeping again, but this time her tears of grief were golden.

Marta was weeping now, because at least she had *her* child. She couldn't fathom feeling connected to a child and then *not*, and not knowing *anything*. And Marta wept bitterly for Stephanie because her heart was breaking for her. And the Lord Jesus spoke inside Marta, saying, "Collect her tears again!"

Surprised, Marta sat up and created another vial. The first one, about a cup of black tears, was still floating in the air, but now she did the same for another, and after a while a whole cup was collected but the vial shined with golden light. And Stephanie was unaware, and Marta resumed her weeping again, not just for Stephanie and her unborn child and that whole situation, but also for Stephanie, her *hero,* to have the strength to not only resist all evil, but to *beat it*. When Marta was mortal, she never beat *any* evil, so she desperately wanted Stephanie to do so. "Shouldn't *we* have some victory on Earth while *mortal?*" Marta prayed deeply in her heart, her mouth moving to the words but not vocalizing because she didn't want to intrude upon Stephanie.

Unbeknownst to Stephanie, Marta had never felt right in Heaven until she began to watch *her* in her spare time. Every pain Stephanie felt, Marta felt. And when Stephanie went through her ordeal with little Michael, Marta was beside herself with grief, and all *that* inspired her to become the master teacher she was, and inspired the class she taught, and now to be a *faithwalker,* and to have been given her current assignment, but *especially* to finally be whole.

And then Stephanie prayed a *third* time. "Forgive me, Lord Jesus. Forgive me God the Father, for I have let myself be abused by evil and I couldn't resist. Forgive me for losing my faith, and *me*, of all the people on your Earth, have become *helpless.* Oh God, I *still* feel helpless. I don't know how to stand against such evil. But you have goodness that will stand no matter what. You *have to.* Forgive me and bless me with such goodness."

And when Stephanie sat up on her knees, she saw three vials floating in the air, and Marta wiped her tears from her eyes but was shocked because there was a *third* vial floating in the air, and it shined with rainbow colors. And the voice of the Lord sounded in the room from everywhere, but the voice was the voice of I AM. "The third vial is yours, Marta. Drink the golden vial!" And Marta drank the vial of golden tears from Stephanie and there was sweet life in them!

And the Lord spoke again, saying, "Lady Stephanie! Drink the rainbow vial of Marta's tears!" And Stephanie drank them and they were bitter and sweet.

And the Lord said, again, "The black vial is all the damage evil has done to you Lady Stephanie. What will you girls do with it?"

And both Marta and Stephanie raised their right hands and silver beams shot from their fingers and the vile turned to dust, and then the dust was disintegrated!

And the Lord said unto Stephanie, "Marta's tears have answered your prayer against evil! Go home to your husband and be one, and you *both* shall have power over all the enemy, and nothing by any means shall harm you, but wait now till my speaking is finished."

And the Lord's presence shined upon Marta, saying, "Because you have honored me like no other, both when you were mortal and gave birth to your child though everyone was forcing you to destroy it, but also honoring me when you killed your wicked mother and put that wretched evil out of my sight, and because you have wept for Lady Stephanie, my anointed, my chosen *faithwalker,* and in spirit you have become her beloved sister, the tears from Stephanie that you drank *is* the life of her unborn child! For when the child was murdered, Stephanie automatically reserved the child's life within hers and now grows within you! And I return you to mortality, to the Holy Mountain to bear Stephanie's child for her, and it shall be your child also, to raise in peace. When you materialize upon the Holy Mountain, you shall be mortal again, for I raise you from the dead to live out your days in peace!"

And the Lord's presence departed and Marta and Stephanie were both in shock as they stared at each other aching to be in each other's arms. And they both faithwalked to stand up together, and then hugged one another in a holy embrace, a sacred sister's embrace, a sacred mother's embrace. And then Mandy came into the shelter and beheld them glowing brightly, and Mandy recognized Marta right away and ran over to hug her, for Marta had saved her life when she wasn't even supposed to be there.

And all the children came in quietly, but many more newcomers came in as well. And the Lord's presence shined on them all again, including the new-comer children. "I am the Lord God of these my holy servants. They shall teach you my ways and you shall hear them."

And the children fell on their faces, and the new ones who were wrong in appearance were transformed to be correct before the Lord, both in body and garment!

And the Lord spoke directly to Mandy. "You *are* my holy servant, but also you have sworn and kept a true oath of sisterhood to Stephanie, my anointed and chosen. You and Carla and Stephanie, and now Marta are all sisters within your holy oath!" And a golden vial of holy oil appeared over Mandy's head and poured upon her. And the Lord said further to Mandy, "Because you have not coveted the powers of others, nor did that even cross your mind or heart, but have gone to the limits of all your mortal strength to save others from evil so they might honor me, I give to you the powers that you have not coveted, *faithwalker* Mandy!" And the Lord departed.

And Rebecca, Lana, and Lynnara squeezed into the tent, and Lynnara put her hand on her hip, and said, "This won't do. It's too small." And she raised her hands and the shelter expanded yet again! This time to thirty-five feet in diameter. And the Lord came again, this time speaking to the three girls. "Ranger Rebecca. Because you have been true, and more than a sister to Lana and Lynnara, but you have without *any* doubt given your life to protect them, receive my Holy Ghost and power!" And Rebecca shouted and danced, and sang, and then the Lord's presence shined on Lana.

"Lana, Marta's daughter, your bravery has come before me." And a vial of oil materialized over *her* head and poured upon her. "So you can travel wherever and whenever you desire, as well as bring others." And then the Lord's presence shined on Lynnara.

"Precious *faithwalker,* and also protector of the Tree of Life handed to you by my anointed Lady Stephanie, now daughter of Lady Stephanie and King Vaughn, your true love is unmatched. You have much to learn. Begin by receiving my Holy Ghost that you have *repeatedly* said you didn't have! And Lynnara spread her little arms wide and looking up into Heaven she slowly turned round and round embracing the Holy Ghost as it descended upon her, and looking up, she saw the Heavens open and angels singing over them all.

And Lynnara laughed, and said, "Mommie, I see *angels,* Can you *hear* them. They're so *beautiful.*"

And they *all* looked up and their vision was opened, and they all beheld Heaven and the angels and they all rejoiced together for some time. And after the Spirit of God had departed and they all commiserated for some time, Marta finally said to Stephanie, "It's time for me to go."

And Stephanie held out her hand and a ring appeared. "For you, my sister, and mother of my child. You're going to be mortal again, so this will prove very useful."

And Marta gladly put it on, honored by the gift and knowing *exactly* what it was because she had often seen them from Heaven. And she turned to Lana, and kissed the top of her head, and said, "To see and hear the Lord bless you so. . .

has fulfilled my deepest desires. I'm so proud of you, my holy daughter." And Marta left and went to the Holy Mountain and immediately became mortal and pregnant with a girl child.

Stephanie materialized in their bedroom where Vaughn was propped up by pillows in their four-post bed with a white pointed cap that had a fluffy tassel at the end and he was reading a book. *And,* he wore glasses! Stephanie immediately burst out laughing. "You look like an old man."

Vaughn answered in an old-man's voice, "Well, little *darling,* sometimes I *feel* like an old man."

Stephanie pulled off her old-lady black nightgown, tossed it in the air, and vaporized it! Naked, her eyes sparkling, she replied, "But I don't feel like an old woman. . . anymore." And she sauntered over to Vaughn's bed laughing and took his cap and put it on her own head. "What do you think?" But Vaughn wasn't looking at the cap and Stephanie slapped him on his chest, saying, "About the *cap.*"

"I'm not looking at the cap." But in actuality, Vaughn was peering deeply into her soul because *everything* about her had *changed.* And not just having her troubles resolved.

It actually had been a good while since they had been together because there was just way too much to do. As Stephanie lay with her head on her husband's chest, she said, "You know, when the Lord said that *Marta* would bear my child for me, I wasn't sad at all." And she leaned up to look in Vaughn's eyes with amazement. "I mean, being a woman and all, you might would think I'd be jealous or something. But *really,* knowing Marta now the way I do, I could *see* what the Lord was doing for her, and the way she loves me so deeply, and the absolute *horrible* life she had Vaughn. You *know* her life now, I mean, having our child is the absolute *perfect* thing for her!"

Vaughn began shining in rainbow colors but completely unaware of it and Stephanie burst out laughing at the sight. Vaughn looked at her in question but when she told him, he said, "No I'm not." Which made Stephanie laugh harder.

Vaughn said, "I completely agree with you. It's an honor to her beyond comprehension, making her loving soul rejoice in unbounded thankfulness. Frankly, I couldn't be more honored, too! But there's more!" And Stephanie eased back to look into his eyes and Vaughn had that wonderful point-making look again and Stephanie loved it. When she saw Vaughn was prolonging the suspense she poked him in his side.

"OK, you don't have to get *pokey*." And Stephanie scrunched her nose at him, and Vaughn said, "The Lord could have restored your fertility but he didn't. Why?"

In the back of Stephanie's mind the question had been there, *is* there, but held at bay because in no way was she going to doubt nor question the Lord's actions. But now Vaughn brought it right out into the light. Stephanie thought for a bit, but then shook her head. "I don't know, but I'm fine with that, because, *Vaughn,* I was in such *bad shape* and I didn't even know it. When the girls rescued me from *Hell,* I thought that was *it. Done.* But that wasn't true at *all.* I brought Hell with me *inside!"* And then Stephanie paused and looked deeply into him. "You *knew!* I mean, *you* sent me to my shelter." Stephanie tingled all over at the depths she now realized Vaughn had understood her and what she needed.

Vaughn caressed her head while he spoke. "In my gut I knew *that* was *exactly* where you needed to be. The Spirit hinted to me to send you there but the *meaning of it all* just felt completely right, so I did. But I didn't know all *that* would transpire. It's all truly marvelous. *Now,* what about my question?"

Stephanie sighed. "Why do we have to bother with it?"

"Because I either bring it up now and we address it, or the Anti-Christ will frame it. Which do you want first?"

And Stephanie recalled what the Lord said, Go home to your husband and be one, and you *both* shall have power over all the enemy, and nothing shall by any means harm you. And what Abraham had said to them a while ago, that they would never be apart any more. Stephanie realized now that their full strength absolutely depended on them *both* being one together. And she could see the word of the Lord now being fulfilled with Vaughn asking her *that* question.

"Alright. Maybe because I really did have some guilt and being infertile is my punishment. I accept that Vaughn. I deserve it."

But Vaughn shook his head, reached his hand up and his staff appeared in it in bed with him. "*You* are a stubborn woman." Vaughn said with a smile. "By this staff that Almighty God has given me to judge the world by, I swear to you that there is no fault in you in this matter or *anywhere.* The Lord God, Jesus, who made us a new heart and new spirit has *perfected* us even right here in this wicked Earth."

And Vaughn sent his staff back to rest so it vanished while Stephanie looked deeply into her beloved husband. "I don't know. This *faithwalker* is lacking meaning! Help me, my dear husband." And she cupped his cheek with her hand.

Vaughn responded by quoting scripture, a rare thing for him because he almost always simply spoke in true meaning. "But woe unto them that are with child and give suck in those days. For in those days shall be tribulation as was not since the beginning of the world, no, nor ever shall be." And chills ran all over Stephanie and she clung to her husband for more warmth.

Vaughn said, "The Lord's blessing was for both of us together. But if you were carrying a child. . ."

"It wouldn't just be both of us, in a way." And then Stephanie's eyes went distant, remembering the times she was pregnant, and even up until the time she wasn't. "You know, Vaughn . . . when a woman is pregnant, well, you wouldn't know, but *everything* is different. To tell you the truth, it's a little disorientating. Well, in subtle ways."

But Vaughn just raised an eyebrow at his wife which meant for her to think further.

"Well, I think, to *really* be successful against the Anti-Christ . . . *Vaughn,* when he attacked me I could *feel* him . . . you have *no* idea. I think to *beat* him we have to be *totally* committed and focused. I think. . . well, being pregnant made me vulnerable." And then Stephanie paused and began to turn dark, and she said to Vaughn, "You know? I think he *knew* that. He *knew* he could beat me because I was pregnant!"

Vaughn said, "When you're pregnant, part of your consciousness is automatically directed to nurturing the growing conscious person inside *your* person. It would be *impossible* for you to maintain the *full* concentration you need against *him.*"

But then Stephanie doubted. "But Vaughn, when I carried Michael, I did a *lot* of fighting, and he even helped me!"

Vaughn said, "I heard about that. But *still,* that's not fighting *this* level of evil, plus, Michael was grown enough to help you fight. You weren't far enough along for that, yet."

Stephanie grew *very* dark. "He knew. And he wasn't just trying to destroy me, but *you* through me. I'm *sorry* Vaughn. I treated you *horribly.*"

"Well," and Vaughn mock slapped himself, reminding Stephanie of when she hit him so long ago, "What are men for?" And he smiled his special smile.

But Stephanie leapt out of bed turning so dark Vaughn could hardly see her. "No! I need to *fix* this. I *owe* you that much, Vaughn, for all I put you through!" And Stephanie held out her hand and Vaughn's staff appeared in it along with her being dressed in her holy Appendaho dress and three braids. "I'll be right back!" And she disappeared right as Lynnara walked in.

And when Lynnara saw that *look* on her Mommy's face, Lynnara *knew* her bestest Mommy *ever* was back to normal, and she said, "Oh, oh! I *told* him he was gonna regret it!"

And Lady Stephanie appeared in HrorrarrAggrang's personal room and roaring thunder shook it and the orb and the new orb the Anti-Christ was building. She raised the staff and lightening streaked from the staff's head across the room and struck the new orb that was almost finished and it shattered into tiny melted pieces. "You'll have to begin again, and *maybe* I'll let you have it!"

In microseconds Lady Stephanie could see the Anti-Christ slowly raise his hand to cast something at her, but before he could, she raised the staff, and lightening hit him dead center and blew him across the room. While he was still smoking and tamping away little fires on his tan tunic, the *faithwalker* said, "This election, we're going to *beat you.*" And she vanished!

When Stephanie reappeared, it hardly seemed like she was gone at all, but when she told what happened, Lynnara was rolling on the bedroom floor in laughter, then saying, "Tell it *again,* Mommy." And then she stood up, said, "BOOM," and fell over laughing again, kicking her feet in the air.

Vaughn just smiled, then said, "Boom," and little Lynnara went into another bout of laughing even harder.

CHAPTER 16

# Girls Got to Have Fun

*HrorrarrAggrang hovered over the Anti-Christ while holding his tail-tip in his arm, and his tail-tapping grew louder by the moment. No one had ever tampered with any ethereal room. In fact, the Alpha prided themselves in the design: simplicity and unencumbrance. What's truly important is themselves, and of course the extension of themselves which is their personal orb. Nothing else mattered so the rooms were absolutely perfect. Four perfectly square walls in a perfectly square room with their orb floating in the center with adjustable height and nothing else. Perfect.*

*But the Anti-Christ, without explanation was busying himself in HrorrarrAggrang's room constructing various . . . I have no idea what he's doing. The Anti-Christ went over to the last corner and began materializing various parts, constructing . . . HrorrarrAggrang's tail-tapping grew even louder whereupon the Anti-Christ broke into song based on the beat of the tail. That was too much for the second-in-command Alpha.*

*"Excuse me. We don't sing in here. And, what are you doing to my sacred room?"*

*The Anti-Christ finished what looked like a small orb with a cone-shaped protuberance pointing to the room's center. Then he waved his hand and it disappeared, rather, it became camouflaged. He walked away from HrorrarrAggrang and pressed his back against the wall, then said, "I would do the same if I were you!"*

*"Excuse me, but this is my. . ."*

*The Anti-Christ waved his hand and Lady Stephanie, decked in her holy dress, suddenly appeared, and walked towards the orb without saying anything. Another irritating display of disrespect. Suddenly, beams of sharp black energy shot out from each of the four corners. They were so black they made the whole room seem gray! Stephanie had managed to erect a glowing forcefield of multicolored energies but the beams were so intense she went down to her knees and eventually was overcome. Her remains became a small, shiny, black crystal!*

*The Anti-Christ walked over, picked up the jewel, kissed it, and put it into his tunic pocket. Then he walked back to the wall and pressed against it, then waved his hand and the same thing, almost, repeated again! The Anti-Christ said to HrorrarrAggrang without looking at him, "I'm building the Father an even better orb and I won't have her interfere. After I'm done testing, I'll begin building. She'll arrogantly show up, and my necklace shall be complete! The power of it will be unimaginable! In fact, even these jewels, the products of our clones, have much power."*

Queen Stephanie and King Vaughn, upon Lynnara's *insistence,* sat in matching golden thrones in the center of

Stephanie's much upgraded shelter. But Vaughn refused to wear what his daughter told him and was in his usual brown work pants and shirt, though Stephanie complied and actually delighted in wearing her holy Appendaho dress. But the pressing issues now before them gave them a stern demeanor as Vaughn and Stephanie gazed over the crowd.

There were well over *one-hundred* new-comer children, all of whom now spoke English. They had all been healed and all their appearances matched the sex they were born to *be*. Except that, apparently, Lynnara had given them their choice on what clothes to wear, and having such freedom, they were adorned in various different colors and designs, though the girls still wore feminine clothes and the boys masculine clothes, and the three girls still maintained their ranger uniforms.

Lynnara had explained in detail to her parents how Mandy and the rest carefully rescued all the children, and now that all their abilities had been greatly upgraded, it allowed them to travel into enemy territory much deeper than just near the border fence. Nevertheless, Vaughn had called the meeting with urgency.

Looking rather uncomfortable, because he *hated* to sit in a throne, Vaughn sighed before beginning and Lynnara began to laugh, then announced, "Daddy *hates* thrones. That's *why* he sighed." And she laughed some more, and when Vaughn made a sour face, she laughed even harder and all the children joined in. Even Stephane, his precious *Queen*, couldn't help laughing.

Vaughn sighed again, which brought *another* round of laughter, and it made his heart ache for the joy of it. But the current contrast in these children's lives weighed heavily on him. "It's been only a single month since Mandy, Lynnara, Rebecca, and Lana, *without us knowing or approving . . .*"

Lynnara chimed in, calling out, "Carla!" And Carla, in her usual brown peasant dress, her long brown hair hanging freely behind her, materialized in front of the thrones, saying, "I take full responsibility. Jesus sent me the visions that the girls had to do what they did without you knowing!" And she curtsied!

Stephanie narrowed her eyes at Lynnara, thinking, *This was* too *smooth! That child* planned *this out! And Carla, too!* Whereupon, Lynnara proudly said, "We *did,* Mommie! But I think the plan *worked!* Don't you?" And Carla hung her head a bit and shook it, not anticipating Lynnara's immediate honesty as well as how easily she could read her mother's thoughts.

Now Vaughn had a chance to pay his Queen back for laughing at his throne anguish, "Well, don't you?" he said with his eyes twinkling in delight.

Stephanie sighed, and Lynnara laughed *again,* and said, "Mommie doesn't want to admit it, but she *has to!* 'Cause it's *true.*"

And all the children, who were standing lined up with the shortest in front and the tallest in back, started saying *together,* "It's true. It's true! King Vaughn, Queen Stephanie." And all the girls curtsied, and the boys bowed.

Stephanie narrowed her eyes again, thinking, *This is* all *planned out!*

And Lynnara was about to say something *again* but Rebecca, standing next to her, grabbed Lynnara's head and put her hand over her mouth.

Lana said, "It's really my fault 'cause I had the first vision. Well, I didn't know about Carla when I had it. But we were about to go even before Carla showed up, so it was my fault."

Vaughn cleared his throat, acting very kingly serious and everyone quieted. Stephanie became very stern, and all the children *knew* they were in trouble. Then Vaughn and Stephanie looked at each other and burst into laughter! Little Lynnara placed her hands on her hips and said, "*Mommie, Daddy,* you *planned* that out!" And they both nodded and smiled.

Vaughn said, "Now down to business. Take your seats!" And all the children scrambled to bleachers that ran halfway around against the circular wall opposite to the sleeping area with the tallest children at the lowest levels and the shortest at the top because the smallest children wanted to be up the highest.

Vaughn said, "We're overjoyed to see you free. But we had to save you *very* secretly because if our enemy found out, they would attack us right away and we don't want that yet. But you already know this." And all the children nodded.

Mandy had the shelter door flap open with one foot in and one foot out listening to both inside and out. Though she was now a *faithwalker* and her extra sense heightened immensely, she *still* employed her ranger's skills, as well. And she was only at the beginning of her *faithwalker* development, though she had the luxury of witnessing both Stephanie and Lynnara and even Jargono.

King Vaughn said, "I have reports that our enemy is growing very suspicious that they can't find you all. It's time for us to leave here!"

All the children looked at each other, then Shane, since he'd been there the longest and they had appointed him their spokesman, said, "But we *know* there are *at least* as many of us here still out *there*. We can't just leave them." And all the children nodded and verbalized agreement.

Queen Stephanie nodded, and said, "We understand deeply what you're feeling. We feel the same way. But in war, hard choices have to be made. Make no mistake, we *are* at war right now, it's just no regular weapons have been fired. You know yourselves even *I* was attacked and *badly* hurt. But the Lord Jesus restored me."

All the children nodded but sulked. Mandy spoke up, saying, "My Lady, Sire, may I speak?" And they nodded and she turned to the children. "I've been with you all this whole time and you've seen me fight for you. You know how I told you the story how hard I ran to try and keep the war from happening too soon."

And all the children nodded. In fact, they had made Mandy tell her story over and over again, *especially* when she kicked the door in and beat all those men. "Well, you know I'd give my life for you all." And they all nodded. "Now it's time for *everyone,*" and Mandy *particularly* looked down to the three *whispering* girls that stood next to her, "And I *do* mean *everyone.*" And Lana looked up at Mandy, and Lynnara and Rebecca began to listen more closely. "It's time for *everyone* to follow our King and Queen's orders. And the truth is, even after they lose this election, they will *still* be *our* King and Queen!" And Mandy looked back at Vaughn and Stephanie and smiled a mischievous grin because she knew they *hated* being King and Queen, but, in fact, it was true they would remain so.

But both Vaughn and Stephanie hadn't really thought about *that*. Vaughn had intended on going back to only Captain. Stephanie touched his arm, "My King, I know we haven't discussed this, and we both kinda wanted out from this royalty thing . . . but Mandy is right. Our people are expecting it. And anyway, once war starts in earnest, they're going to need us like that, I think."

Vaughn sighed again, but much more deeply. "Well, my Kingly decree is *this:* Lynnara, do you need help moving everything or can we trust you to move *everything,* leave no trace *at all.* This is very important because they will soon send spies across the fence to inspect *everything* trying to prove the children crossed over. If they *do,* we have war too soon."

Lynnara hesitated. She didn't want to leave. But she also understood and the Holy Ghost was showing her she had to listen. But when she looked over at the bleachers and saw all the dejected faces and how they looked to her to stick up for them. . . Lynnara sighed deeply, just like her Daddy. She wiped tears from her eyes. Her heart began to pain her like never before. She had experienced a lot of different pains but *nothing* like this. Lynnara looked up to Lana, and so did Rebecca, and Lana sighed deeply.

Lana turned to all the children. "It was me whom God showed that you were in trouble and I came to save you. But now we have to *go,* or many will die. "

Children whispered to Samantha and she to Shane, then he said, "But what if we leave and even without us, someone manages to escape?"

It was a question Vaughn and Stephanie had considered but had no answer to. But Mandy said, "That's why I and Lynnara and Rebecca and Lana are staying behind!"

Both Stephanie and Vaughn adjusted themselves in their thrones. Neither of them trusted Lynnara, even though she was holy now, because the goodness in her little heart was likely to act without wisdom just because she cared so much, and the Holy Ghost is a bit different with children than with adults. And if *anything,* being holy now made her feel even *more* independent, though it was comforting that the Holy Ghost abided in her. But for children, the Spirit of God was, well, lenient, in a way. *Adults* still had their responsibilities. Stephanie sent her thoughts to Vaughn, *"Well Mandy is close to being an adult,"*

Vaughn sent back a laugh. *"Look at us from fourteen years old till now!"*

*"But Mandy can't handle the Anti-Christ. I barely could."*

Vaughn sighed again. "No! You all move the shelter, *everyone, everything no matter how small.* No traces, and *no going back!"*

And that was it. Shane said to everyone, "We should be thankful for everything. It's *not* right we're sad. That's *ungrateful."* And he stared hard at everyone until they all acknowledged he was right.

Mandy looked down and kicked the Earth around a bit just inside the shelter. She looked up at Carla, now standing next to her, and whispered into Carla's ear. But Stephanie said, "*Mandy! You're as bad as the kids!*" And Mandy looked down, kicked the earth some more, and shrugged her shoulders. She *hated* to give up even an inch to evil. The words the Lord spoke to her came to heart and mind, *But also you have sworn and kept a true oath of sisterhood.* It seemed like that oath was calling her now to obey her sister's command. The Holy Ghost in her heart asked, *Are you as wise as they are? Will you doubt them?* But Mandy answered the Holy Ghost, *But we saved those kids, and Vaughn and Stephanie didn't even know.* And the Holy Ghost said, *Because I sent you and gave you what to do.* And Mandy was silent, still considering. The Holy Ghost wasn't giving her anything more on this matter and didn't *really* tell her what to do.

All the kids were now focused on Mandy. Even the three girls. Mandy suddenly became aware that *she* was the center of attention of a large group. She'd never experienced anything like *that* before, where *everyone* waited on *her* decision! *Lord Jesus, everyone's looking to* me! And the Lord replied within her, *So am I!*

Samantha climbed out of the bleachers and came to Mandy and hugged her. "I owe my *life* to you. When you jumped away from us to draw all the demon animals away so we could escape, my heart broke. I swore then I would always honor you. My sister is *still* out there, somewhere, trying to escape." And then she turned to all the children. "But I *know,*" and she tapped her heart strongly with her hand, "that we have to *go!* And listen to King Vaughn and Queen Stephanie!" And she turned and hugged Mandy again, and was about to go back but *all* the children had gotten up and lined up, and hugged Mandy, saying things like, "Thank you for saving us. But we have to go. Listen to your King and Queen." And Mandy began to sob because she knew she would listen.

Vaughn and Stephanie and the thrones vanished and Lynnara called to Mandy to stand with her in the center of the shelter. Lynnara chuckled, saying, "Follow my lead." And Lynnara extended her arms out from her sides and then Mandy did. Lynnara concentrated on everything that had to go and then where they were going to, which was back to where the shelter had been, and Mandy copied the child and they all vanished. A bit later, the three girls and Mandy came back.

Mandy said, "We have to erase *all* signs, including where everyone went potty." The three girls wrinkled their noses, but Mandy said, "Spread out." And after a while, Lynnara and the others came back showing they'd picked up buttons and other odd things and Lynnara sent them to the shelter. With a sense of finality, they were about to leave when quiet voices from *their* own side of the fence startled them so they hid behind a large leafy oak.

Mandy no longer needed her translator. The first thing she had worked on in her new *faithwalking* was language. The meaning was clear, now. A tall man in camouflage said to a shorter man, "Even if a few escape, what harm can they do. They're just kids."

But the shorter man who seemed in charge, said, "Who are *enlightened,* The others in the United for Christ won't understand and they'll be immediately *deeply* offended. Enough to warrant investigating us. That will lead to us losing our edge. I frankly think we should just attack now. It would be far better. In *fact,* one word from me and we *will* attack!"

Mandy whispered to the girls as Lynnara and Rebecca prepared for battle. "Follow *my* lead!" And Mandy walked out right in front of them with the three children behind her. "Attack *what?*" Mandy demanded.

The men immediately drew their pistols but before they were even aimed, Mandy had leapt in the air, kicked the tall man in the face to her right, pulled her right hip knife with her left hand and drove it into the short man's thigh at her left as she landed! It struck bone and he went down in a shriek. Rebecca had her bow drawn on the tall man, saying, "Don't get up. Don't *move.*" When he doubted a mere child could even shoot him, Rebecca said, "Do you feel *lucky?*" It was an odd question, but part of Ranger Training was to watch *very* old movies by an actor called Clint Eastwood, and Rebecca used to go around to *everyone* asking in her Clint impersonation, *Do you feel lucky!* Now she was overjoyed she actually got to use it for real. For his part, Rebecca's impersonation worked and he held still!

Mandy sat atop the shorter man whose gun was still in his hand, and she said, "I *dare* you to try and use it!"

The man actually thought about it. Even though his country reversed the roles of *most* men and women, *he* had to be 'normal' for his job and he *hated* to be bested by this. . . really *hot* feminine woman! He *really* wanted to kill her, then maybe abuse her body afterward.

Mandy reached back while still facing him and *yanked* her knife from his leg then in a smooth swing held it to his throat. "Either *use* the gun or throw it away." And when he hesitated, she yelled, "*NOW!*" Whereupon, without thinking and against a great part of his will, he tossed it away. And with knife still at his throat, she said, "What *attack?*"

Mandy knew these men were deadly professionals and extremely sharp and the girls knew it, too. The evil look in their eyes said as much and it made Lynnara's skin crawl. She wanted to consume them in a massive fireball and she'd *never* felt like *that* before. Lana didn't even understand what Mandy was doing and couldn't figure out how this was going to work out, but she had no visions, either.

The shorter man kept silent though, but Rebecca, remembering *many* movie scenes said, "I'll shoot *this* one!" And she *did!* In the thigh. But before the tall man could pick his pistol off the ground next to him, Rebecca had another arrow already knocked and pointed at him. "Then the *other* leg!"

And the tall man said, "What the *hell.* It makes no difference *now.* Attack *you.* Yea, *that's right.* We're taking our country back!"

The shorter man shook his head, saying, "Go ahead, kill him, or *I* will!"

Mandy burst out laughing! "You two are so *funny.* That deserves you your freedom!" she said as she got off the man. "Sorry I stabbed you, but that's always my first reaction! So funny. Attack us. Take our country."

Lana played along. "If all your men fight like you, and you get beat by a *girl.* . ." And she rolled on the forest floor laughing.

Lynnara asked, "What's *third world* country? That's what *you* are. Third world. What's that?"

Mandy said, "It means they're backwards. Stupid. Unable to be like *us.*" Mandy turned back to the short man who limped over, picked up his weapon, and holstered it. Then Mandy said, "One moment." And she took her phone and dialed up Blackbeard's special number. "*Hey* you guys. This is Ranger Mandy. We met a while ago when a tree came down on our fence and some demon dogs and demon men were around. Well, I and my little. . . " and Mandy burst out laughing, "I and my little junior Rangers came across a couple of your guys inspecting the fence on *our* side, and, well, before I knew it, I took 'em both down and me and the kids sorta held them for a while before we realized the misunderstanding."

"One moment," the operator said.

And Mandy looked back at them, and said, "I don't know who trained you with those stupid ideas, but *seriously,* if you come across *that* fence, we're *obligated* to attack you. You're just lucky I have a soft spot."

But Rebecca *still* had her arrow aimed at the tall man and Mandy had to order her, "Junior Ranger, stand *down!*" Then Mandy thanked them! "You know, I couldn't have *imagined* better training for the kids than what you guys just did. That's what you were doing, wasn't it? You *knew* we were hiding behind *that* tree and put on a *show* for us. I'm really *sorry* I attacked you before I realized." And she held out her hand and the short man shook it!

Mandy said, "Sit down you two and I'll patch you up!" So they leaned up against an oak tree and Mandy fished first aid from her small pack at her left hip.

Then a man answered the phone in a gruff voice, "What the *hell* did you do to my men?"

Mandy laughed, then said, "Hold on. I'm bandaging up your soldiers. My junior ranger will explain." And Mandy handed the phone to Lana.

Lana went into lengthy descriptions of all the action that took place but left out what the men had said. Because she was a child, the burly sounding man didn't feel he could be rude or interrupt. When Lana *finally* finished all her story, the man said, "Can you put your Mommie back on the phone."

But Lana said, "Oh, she's not my Mommie." And she went into a lengthy explanation about Stephanie and how Stephanie became her *sister.* Finally, Mandy took the phone.

By this time the man was truly suffering, perhaps more than his injured men and he merely said, "We'll send someone to get them."

An hour later, through which the girls tortured their enemies with stories about dolls and how they all used to play together and how they all train together now to be Rangers, a couple Jeeps showed up on the other side of the fence, and Mandy called across, "Hold on. It's *electric.*" And she pulled her phone, did things they couldn't see, and then said, "OK, you can squeeze through. However *they* got through before, I'm *sure* they couldn't do *that* again."

So they brought stretchers and put the men between the horizontal fence cables and left. Lynnara said to Mandy, "But now they're gonna *tell*."

But Mandy said, "Nah, they won't. It's bad *enough* they got beaten by poor lil' me. But if they say they got caught divulging secrets, they're *dead,* and they know it. He really coulda just called and began the war, but I took that away from him now. He can't lie about finding something that *clearly* wasn't there nor can he plant any false evidence because it won't square with those that picked them up!

Then Lana and Lynnara began to imitate the enemy and Rebecca did her favorite line again, "Do you feel *lucky*?" And they collapsed in laughter rolling in the dried leaves that had piled up over the years. Mandy sighed deeply with relief. *That's twice. Let's not make it three.*

An explosion practically knocked everyone senseless. Had it not been for Lynnara erecting a quick shield, they'd all have been dead, but the shield wasn't strong enough to keep them all from being addled and thrown to the ground. Rebecca was lying face down and motionless about ten feet to everyone's left. Lana had managed to pop about twenty feet away just after the blast, but Lynnara was flat on her back trying to focus, and Mandy had been blown further behind her.

A red-haired woman with short haircut like a man, dressed in purple pants and tee-shirt, materialized about five feet in front of Lynnara. Mandy sat up, and said, "Stephanie?" but she still wasn't in her right mind.

Lana popped closer, but not *too* close, and said, "That's *not* Stephanie."

The clone raised her palm at Lynnara who was just beginning to gather her wits, "Bye bye, *brat.*"

At hearing *that,* Mandy's Ranger focus immediately snapped her fully back to reality and she raised her hand without thinking and cast a glowing red fireball, her first! It hit dead center and blew the Stephanie clone about fifteen feet away, but she stood up quickly, saying, "Now *where* did you learn *that?* You're not a faithwalker."

Lynnara stood up now, and turned *black*, saying, "And neither are *you*. Do you feel *lucky?*" And Lynnara clapped her hands and a blistering golden fireball with a blue center raced toward the imposter. She erected a quick shield but was surprised to see how fast Lynnara's attack was. It blew her another fifteen feet away but she bounced up with anger, reached out her hands and grabbed both Mandy and Lynnara with her force and slammed them into each other, and they fell down dazed again.

The clone immediately popped next to Lynnara and hauled her up by her throat. With legs kicking, she tried popping away but couldn't. She tried what her Mommie explained to her, to *walk around* her enemy's attack but she couldn't seem to do that either. The clone laughed. "I know *everything* you know."

Lana watched helplessly as the Holy Ghost forbade her to get involved. Lynnara got angry and shook her head. "No you *don't.*" And she hauled off and punched her right in the nose! Even though Lynnara was only seven-years-old, almost eight, she packed a pretty good wallop and the clone dropped her and backed off, taking time to heal herself from the terrible stinging.

Mandy cast another fireball but the clone just laughed and swatted it away as if nothing.

Lana said, "I can take you all away. She can't block *me*." And the clone looked over to Lana and shot a racing black lightning bolt at her, but she popped away halfway closer to her friends. But Lynnara said, "We can't go. If we do, Mommie and Daddy will find out."

And the clone laughed. "Just as I told them. You all are on your *own*. Your *Mommie* would never have let you come down *here*. I'm going to enjoy killing you."

Lynnara clapped her hands again, but this time nothing happened, which upset her. She'd never *ever* felt this powerless. And Mandy waved her arm and tried to hurl the clone away from Lynnara but nothing happened, so she dematerialized, but then popped right behind her intending to break her neck. But as soon as Mandy rematerialized, a blast drove Mandy backward. Only her defensive shield, which is one of the things she actually *had* practiced a lot, saved her from dying.

While Mandy was still dazed, the clone used her force to draw Lynnara back into her hand and she slowly tightened her grip choking Lynnara to death. She kicked, she flailed her arms, but couldn't break free, and she *hated* feeling fear trying to creep into her. *That's why she's taking her time! She* wants *me to be afraid of her.* So Lynnara went limp and began looking only into the deep love she had for God, But the clone shook her and broke her concentration. "Nah, nah, I know about *that*, too!" And she laughed and began squeezing slowly again,"

Mandy was still dazed and could hardly move, but shouted, "Lynnara," as she felt her being overcome and there was nothing Mandy could do. But an arrow suddenly shot through the sides of the clone's neck and her eyes went wide. She dropped Lynnara and turned to see Rebecca on her knees who just fired yet another arrow that hit the Stephanie clone dead in the forehead. Yet she still stood there staring, and Rebecca said, "My *best friend* asked you a question. Do you feel *lucky?*" And Rebecca shot her again through the heart and she fell over finally dead.

Lana popped next to Lynnara and had her in a hug, then Rebecca joined in and Mandy slowly came over. Lana said, "That was *too* close. We're just kids, ya know?"

Lynnara nodded, remembering what the Lord had said to her that she had a *lot* to learn. But then Lynnara remembered something and *then* grew stern. She used her power to pull everyone behind her, and, sure enough, rising from the dead clone was a dark spirit intent on attacking them. Silver beams raced from her fingers and the spirit screeched then turned to ash.

But then Lynnara reached her arms straight over her head and acted like she grabbed something, and then she pulled hard, and *another* Stephanie look-a-like crashed to the ground wearing the same ugly clothing. "She was *spying* on us the whole time from the corridor."

Rebecca knocked an arrow, and Lynnara prepared an even stronger fireball but the clone sat up and held up her hands and begged, "Don't kill me. *Please* don't kill me. I'm just an understudy and I *hated* her. Take me with you. I can help!"

Lynnara said, "You look *just like* the other one."

Rebecca pointed an arrow at her but the clone said, "*Please.* I don't even know how to use my powers yet."

Lynnara felt she was telling the truth. Rebecca lowered her bow a bit, but Lana, who had popped behind the new Stephanie clone, reached in her secret pocket and pulled out a bottle of light oil. She put a small amount in her palm then flicked it onto the clone's head and she immediately burst into flames!

The clone used her faithwalking power to try and put the flames out. She popped away into the corridor but the flames didn't go out even though there was no air up there. She came back and rolled on the ground trying to smother the flames but to no avail. The flames consumed her *and* the evil spirit.

Lana shook her head and said to everyone. "She was *lying!*" Then Lynnara said, "I think. . . I think *she* was the boss and the first one was the understudy!" All their eyebrows went up, but Mandy said, "That makes sense. She ordered the first one to confront us while she watched and learned."

All the children sighed and looked up to Mandy, saying, "Now what?"

And Mandy pulled out her phone again! "Hello? Is this the same person as last time? I want to warn you of more demons! Yes. We're the same people as before. We were just *attacked* by two *very* strange demonic people with *powers!* That's how we know they were demons. Yes. Powers. What happened? Well, we killed them, of course. So there's no more worry, but I just thought you should know because you're our neighbor. You're welcome. You're certainly welcome to come view the bodies, too. Parden me? That won't be necessary? OK. "

Lana shook her head. "Do you think they *believed* you? That *thing* we just killed. She said she told them we were alone. So they *know* what we were doing. What's that mean, Mandy?" Lynnara and Rebecca nodded in agreement, wanting to know, too.

But Mandy was speechless for a while, just shaking her head. "I don't know. Part of me wants to go spy on *them,* but I *really* don't think I'm anywhere near powerful enough yet to do that."

Rebecca narrowed her eyes at Mandy. "You're a *faithwalker* now." Then Rebecca gave it some more thought. "Can you make me invisible?" Now all the girls looked at Rebecca in surprise. "I mean, not just so I can't be seen. I mean, so *no one* knows I'm there even *if* I can't be seen?"

And *that* got Mandy to thinking, but as she thought about invisibility, it began increasing her abilities to perceive, because if she was going to make someone *that* invisible, well, she'd *have to* be able to sense that deeply. And sense, she did!

Mandy took her bow from her shoulder, knocked an arrow, then acted as if she was following a bird through the air, and then, as the girls tried to follow her, she fired. But there was no bird at all, The arrow went up a ways but then suddenly disappeared. Then a body materialized in the sky and fell at their feet dead with Mandy's arrow in her heart! It was, yet, *another* clone of Stephanie! Rebecca shook her head, saying, "She *wasn't* invisible!"

Mandy said, "I just suddenly felt we were being spied on from the corridor, and I, well, I shot my arrow up *there!*"

Rebecca looked at Mandy again, waiting. Mandy placed her hand on Rebecca's head and she disappeared! A moment later, Rebecca asked, "Can anyone see me? Can you sense me?"

Lynnara shook her head and so did everyone else. Rebecca said, "Mandy, Lynnara, and I should go spy. But I'll stay a ways away from you in the Corridor. So if anyone comes up to mess with you, I'll kill them! But Lana needs to go back to tell Stephanie and Vaughn *everything.*"

Everyone looked to Lana to see what she saw. Lana looked into Mandy's eyes. "I think Rebecca's right but we're just kids. What do *you* think?"

As a Ranger, Mandy was all in, but… "You know, we've been outthought every step of the way. Let's go back and run it by our King and Queen first?" And to that everyone agreed and vanished.

# CHAPTER 17

# They Start Young

*Mafferan looked at Yinauqua as she waved her hand and their orb turned off, then she looked up into her beloved husband's eyes. "Well, do you think Moses and Elijah's efforts have really helped?"*

*Mafferan squinted at her, then said, "You never really know until the time comes. They're at a distinct disadvantage because the Anti-Christ has orbs to help him continuously but Vaughn's orb can no longer be trusted to look below. Besides, the demons spend all their time with their orbs but Vaughn can barely spend any."*

*Yinauqua's eyes teared up but she kept control. "Do you think Stephanie will fall for his trap? They know if the Anti-Christ finishes that orb, it'll make it near impossible for them to win."*

*Mafferan looked down for a while. "I don't know. In many ways both of them have moved beyond us, so I don't know. The Holy Ghost is with them deeply, and the Lord has upgraded them all. But I don't know. The Anti-Christ? That level of hard-hitting deception? I don't know. But we have to be ready when the time comes."*

*Yinauqua placed her head on her husband's shoulder and wrapped her arms around him and he enveloped her, as well. In many ways they simply felt mortal again. Perhaps that was because the time was drawing near when both the old Heaven and old Earth would pass away. Or perhaps they had become so deeply involved in mortal pains, that it became more real to them than Heavenly reality.*

Stephanie and Vaughn sat together at the side of their dining room table in their usual garments. James sat at Vaughn's right side, but not quite at the table's head. Lana sat at Stephanie's left similarly, while Rebecca enjoyed the head of the table next to Lana, and Lynnara sat next to James at the other table head. Mandy sat across from Stephanie and Vaughn. Since Lana had been chosen as their spokesman, she and Stephanie had twisted their chairs to listen closely to each other. It very much reminded Stephanie of how they used to be together when Stephanie first came to live with Lana and Jean.

Stephanie shook her head. "Lana, I don't think *any* of you should be going back and *certainly* not to spy deep into enemy territory, Corridor or not."

But Lana replied, "But *really,* we couldn't tell Rebecca was there at all. Mandy could even make us *all* inviable."

But Vaughn said, "When you do something like that with more than one, the chances increase *greatly* that one or more of your thoughts will touch an enemy and they'll perceive it." Stephanie nodded in agreement.

But the girls weren't giving up that easily. Rebecca said, "That's what I kinda thought. That's why I said just make *me* invisible, But *not* like that clone Mandy shot who wasn't *really* invisible. If they sense a thought from me, they'll think it comes from what they can see. But not me. And I can protect everyone!"

James said, "You're only considering what you *know*. It's what you *don't* that will kill you. And what you *don't* know is, one: can their *orbs* see you? And *two,* what does it mean that they *already* knew you rescued a lot of children? Why haven't they attacked? We had it on good understanding that they were going to attack if they were found out. What changed?"

Stephanie squeezed Vaughn's arm and he turned to look into his wife's eyes. "That just makes it even *more* important I go down there and make sure that orb *never* gets built. If the old ones can't detect, say, invisibility, chances are the new one will. But we can see if *your* orb can detect Rebecca. Remember, *that* orb used to belong to *their* Father."

Vaughn sighed deeply because he'd already expressed grave trepidation over Stephanie going down below again. Now James chimed in. "My Lady, you went down below and *attacked* them, *hurt* them in their *own* domain. They're not taking that lightly. We can safely assume they've planned for your return something you don't expect. This *Anti-Christ* has already proven he's beyond even a High Counselor, maybe even Satan himself."

Lynnara tugged on James sleeve and when he turned to her she got up on her knees then whispered in his ear. His eyebrows went up. He rubbed his face looking truly shocked. Then he turned, saying, "Sire, the Princess wants me to share something with you." And he cupped his hand to Vaughn's ear. In turn, Vaughn's eyebrows went up, his eyes went wide, and he turned to his wife and whispered in her ear.

But Stephanie's mouth went flat, and peeked around everyone to catch Lynnara's eyes, "You just don't give up, do you?" It wasn't exactly an endearing tone, but Lynnara just gave her soft daughter-pleading eyes.

Rebecca slid off her chair quietly, climbed under the table without anyone noticing, and then tugged on Mandy's ranger skirt. Mandy reached her hand under the table then went back to closely listening to everyone. When Stephanie was done with her lecture to Lynnara, Mandy said, "We're at a disadvantage because our enemy knows more than we do. My honest opinion is that you so pissed them off down below with your election challenge, well, the Anti-Christ decided it's more important to humiliate you in the elections than just attack, which he feels he can do at any time anyway. His goal is to make us suffer in the worst possible ways, so now he has a better way than just attacking us right away!"

Stephanie mumbled, "Great." And the tension in the room increased greatly at Mandy's very believable Ranger assessment, but then Stephanie yelped and jumped up ready to fight. But the sound of giggling calmed her, yet made her angry at the same time. Stephanie looked around the room but couldn't sense where Rebecca was now. She had reached around Stephanie's chair and grabbed her sides with both hands.

Lana asked Stephanie, "Can you sense her?" But everyone knew no one could because everyone tried. Rebecca popped her head back up visible again beside Mandy and giggled some more.

Vaughn made a mock scolding face and Rebecca laughed in delight. "Give the Queen and I some time to discuss it privately."

And that was it. It wasn't a command but it might as well have been. But Stephanie said, "I'm not so sure the Anti-Christ knows *we* know about the children, about the truth in South and Central America. They might think you all have the children hidden away from them *and* us, and *that's* why they haven't attacked. They probably deduced the same reasons why Carla told you to keep it a secret in the first place."

Everyone nodded to the truth of that, also, and not knowing just made Mandy's case stronger, but also Stephanie's desire to destroy the new orb again. Stephanie said, "Call a debate next week, and when the Anti-Christ shows up, I won't be there with you Vaughn. I'll go down below. It won't take me but a moment to destroy the orb, then I'll pop on stage with you."

But James said, "My Lady, pardon my intrusion *again,* but if Vaughn is preoccupied with the debate and you get in trouble, he won't be able to rescue you. And the Anti-Christ is *sure* to keep him there."

But Stephanie said, "If *he's* not there, I can *certainly* handle anything else."

Rebecca went over and took Lana's hand and they disappeared and Lynnara right after them. Mandy said, "Stephanie, remember when you had all the Rangers help train you? I watched you, and, well, it was *unbelievable*. Do you think you could do that for me?"

Stephanie looked to Vaughn and he nodded and then Stephanie looked to Mandy and they disappeared. Vaughn sighed *very* deeply and James leaned over and put his hand on his shoulder and squeezed. "You have *a lot* to deal with, Sire. I have to say, King Jargono could not have dealt with what *you* are now facing. He was always used to being on top, unchallenged. But *you* and Lady Stephanie have clawed your ways up from the bottom, which is why your enemy has trouble beating you. At the moment of your dire need, you all do the *unexpected!* Because you have an unfailing fortitude."

Vaughn shook his head then turned in his seat to face James. "You know, I don't think that at *this level of evil* clawing ourselves up from the bottom matters that much anymore! If we hit bottom *again,* as Stephanie just did, we won't be able to make it back!"

James blue eyes sharpened and the Holy Ghost in him prompted him with additional understanding to go with the feelings he now had. "Vaughn." And he paused to let it sink in that he simply called him by his first name but with a very deep love. This was incredibly *personal* for James and he wanted Vaughn to know it. "I wasn't always a single butler. At one time in my younger life, I had the love of my life. She was a *marvelous* woman with a wonderful feminine instinct that always seemed to know when I needed a certain support to help me face the dire challenges of the day. But there came a time when she wanted to nurture a certain group of hard-up folks and I told her I didn't think that was such a good idea.

But she poo pooed my instinct in favor of her natural feminine instinct and when I came home I found her with her throat cut and our few valuables gone. I *should have* done what you did with *your* wife, both when you killed her gang and later Gary, and the incredibly *hard* decision you made even against Princess Lynnara's protests, when you let Stephanie pass away. I should have been a *man!* I should have made the *hard* decision come hell or high water and kept my wife safe even against her anger or displeasure. Because as a *man*, our true masculinity urges us to step up at times and put our foot down where no woman can go. They simply don't have *that* level nor kind of judgment. You've done wonderfully, so far, but don't think you have to capitulate now for *fairness* sake. In other words, *don't* make my mistake *ever!* The *ultimate* responsibility is on *your* shoulders. And God has even given to *you,* first and foremost, a staff to lean on when you need it!" And James stood up, bowed his head to Vaughn, squeezed his shoulder again, and said, "I love you as my very own son, and I rejoice that God has given me *you*." And James went to bed.

Vaughn sat there a while, alone, feeling all that James had said, then he disappeared and went to visit Harris, who remarkably, had already set a plate at their modest round wooden dinner table. As soon as he stood in their midst, "King *Vaughn,*" Bradly, his youngest son of five years old shouted. "Daddy said the Spirit said you'd be here!"

Vaughn's eyebrows rose and he noted he'd been doing that a lot lately. He rubbed the boy's curly red hair then turned to Dania, Harris' wife, her wavy dark brown hair pulled back in a single pony tail. "It's been too long since we've all been together like this."

Dania said, "Take your seat at the table head *King* Vaughn." And she had a loving but mischievous smile because everyone knew Vaughn *hated* to be called King. For that matter, Bradly and his older brother and sister were laughing, too."

Vaughn's heart pained him as he beheld his best friend's family. He couldn't imagine *any* of them suffering what shortly would come to pass, and the weight of those premonitions kept him silent through the meal as the children and Dania told Vaughn all the local news from the town where Vaughn and his people had settled after they'd escaped the North. Even though Vaughn and Stephanie had moved back down here, they had no time for smalltown particulars, so this time, now, Vaughn considered as time well spent.

After a long while, quite surprisingly, Vaughn suddenly spoke, asking, "Harris, what do you think about slowly moving all our people to the Holy Land?"

They were all stunned. Bradly gave a "Woooow!"

Dania looked deeply into her husband. They both had received the Holy Ghost over a year ago along with many more but many more had yet to receive Him. Many were still seeking, but all were serious. Harris said, "To the Holy Mountain? Not all of us would be able to reside there. And you said the inhabitants outside the protection are quite hostile."

Dania said, "Vaughn, why are you asking?"

Daniel, his brown wavy hair sprawling in all directions and their oldest at fourteen, said, "King Vaughn has that *look.*

There's bad trouble coming. He wants to save us again." Daniel was eleven when Vaughn had guided them all through the dark woods where the evil spirits attacked them, where Vaughn had read Queen Stephanie's glowing letter and saved them all. All those memories and *many* more of Vaughn and Stephanie teaching them in their holy temple and how they fought evil men and evil monsters played in Daniel's heart and mind.

Dania leveled her eyes into Vaughn, "But if trouble comes, you're going to *need* us. Because I *know* you won't desert these people, even if they're not *us*. You know why?"

Vaughn beheld this woman. Most of his conversations were with Harris and only niceties exchanged with his wife. Now he saw why Harris loved her so much. Vaughn raised a single eyebrow at her, and she responded, "Because you're *us*, but you also belong to everyone else, too! And they belong to you. And *that's* why you saved Rebecca in the first place, before you even knew you were us and we were you. Jews. Because your heart is very special. You'll fight here until you and Stephanie can't. Because you two belong to everyone and they to you."

Vaughn folded his hands on the table and stared at them and there was silence. He hadn't put that into words in his thoughts. Not like *that*. But it was true, and Harris and his whole family knew it was true. Oddly, Daniel spoke up and broke the silence. "I think what Mom is saying is that we're not abandoning you! None of us are. We won't go, We won't leave you."

And even Bradly shook his five-year-old head, no, saying, "Because we love you, and Queen Stephanie, too."

Vaughn looked at Harris, and said, "New holy mothers having their first child will go with their husbands. Will they do that?"

Harris said, "I'll see to it they know the offer, but I think, as before when your wife set this up, that they will. But that's not why you're here." Harris looked at his wife and she rounded up the children for bed, but Daniel objected.

"I wanna stay. I'm *fourteen.*"

Harris was about to object, but Vaughn said, "I was fourteen when I knocked out the big bully who tried to turn me into a perversion. He was this big." And Vaughn raised his hand over his head. "And this wide!" And he stretched out his hands. "And I was about your size." And he turned to Daniel.

Daniel's eyes widened, "Wow. How'd you *do* that?"

"I didn't know it then, but in retrospect I see that God was with me even when I didn't know it. God is with *you* now. That's why you want to stay." And Harris eased off staring at his son. "You have a good boy there."

Harris said, "We haven't been able to penetrate their domain. The ones I send, even holy, they don't return. That's never happened before. When we sent men into Jargono's North, most of them came back. You know, I was one of them."

"Barely," Vaughn said, and he turned to Daniel. "I was there when your father barely made it across the fence. I carried him on my back for fifty miles, running. And Stephanie and all of us prayed for him till Stephanie figured out what they'd done and cured him weeks later."

"I didn't know all that but I remember Dad was gonna die 'cause that was only two years ago."

Vaughn looked around the room to see if the protection he had placed was still in force, then he told Harris and Daniel all about the Southern Continent, the children, and the perversion they had twisted everyone into being. Then Vaughn said, "Maybe that's why your spies never returned. There's no way they could fit in." Then Vaughn turned stern. "No one else can know what I just told you all, because if it's discovered *I* know, it's likely this Jargono clone will immediately attack us before we have our defenses fully in place and before we can get all our people out from the North. By the way, none of our satellites are able to enter their airspace, either."

Harris ran his hand through his wavy brown hair and shook his head. "We need intelligence but we're definitely at a loss here."

Daniel said, "Then send us!" And Vaughn and Harris both were about to explain how foolish that is, but Daniel continued. "You dress us and transform us to be like them and sneak us across and we'll infiltrate. They won't suspect us 'cause we're *kids*,"

Vaughn shook his head strongly. It seemed Lynnara's secret idea wasn't just hers but seemed to have a life of its own. Vaughn rubbed his face hard. Harris wasn't too far behind but he saw his eldest son like he never saw him before. Yet, before Vaughn had rescued Harris and his people, life was *very* hard for them. Daniel was old enough to remember it, so he was tougher than one would expect in spite of a relatively good life for the past two years.

Harris looked deeply into his son, "You'd need trained. That would be *hard* training. You got friends you can trust who would want this? You could *die* doing this."

Vaughn said, "Or worse."

Daniel straightened. "My friends and I *hate* the way things are now! You may think it's a good life but we're bored as Hell with school and doing basically *nothing*. At least when we were up North, we helped our families live. We had *meaning!* Now we just go to boring school and *play*. And *that's* boring, too, because we're used to actually *doing* something that actually counts! Up North we hunted, we gathered, we helped Mom and Dad put food on the table and trade and a lot of things, that, well, compared to what we have now it wasn't that much back then but *it was!*"

Vaughn sighed. "Stephanie's gonna *kill* me." Vaughn rubbed his ring and concentrated on Mandy and Lynnara. In the next instant Lynnara, Lana, Rebecca, and Mandy appeared ready to fight, all still in their Ranger uniforms. But Vaughn motioned them all to take seats, which they did so quietly, sensing this was Kingly business and they were somehow obviously part of it. Vaughn nodded to Harris so he explained everything they had been discussing.

Then Harris said, "And my son Daniel here, came up with an idea."

And Daniel explained what he thought they could do, whereupon, Lynnara said, "*Daddy*, that was *my* idea."

And Vaughn said, "I know, but I didn't share it. Daniel thought of it all on his own."

Lana said, "That's because the Lord wants it done."

Rebecca said, "You'll need trained. So will your friends."

And Mandy said, "Let me have two weeks with them. While I'm being trained how to fight like Lady Stephanie, I'll have the Rangers train all of you, too."

Then Lynnara said, "Then I think we need another week to have all our new friends train them how to act down there. This'll work Daddy."

Vaughn sighed deeply again then shook his head with foreboding, but he rubbed his ring, anyway, and Stephanie appeared ready to fight. But when she saw everyone, she immediately got angry, thinking Lynnara was up to no good. But Lynnara said to her Mommy, "Understand!" And everything that transpired popped into Stephanie's mind and she sat down in silence, a bit shell-shocked.

Everyone waited in silence for a while, and then Stephanie prayed, "Lord Jesus, if this plan is from you, show us a sign." And immediately Daniel began to glow and everyone looked upon him.

Daniel said, "What?" Because he didn't know he was glowing.

Harris said. "You're glowing, my son. The Lord God chose *you* as the sign that we should do this!"

And Daniel bowed his head on his folded hands that he now rested on the table. "God of our fore-fathers Abraham, Isaac, and Jacob. Lord Jesus at twelve you went into the temple *alone* and confronted rulers. But we're. . . going into Hell on Earth. Help us."

And the Lord spoke within the room as a man speaks to a friend but His voice was everywhere the voice of Being, "Choose the friends in your heart and I will be with you all as I was with your forefathers in their young age!"

It so surprised Daniel both in feeling and experiencing that he slid from his chair and bowed low on the floor. He had never heard the voice of the Lord before though he had felt his Spirit at times. All he could say was, "Lord Jesus help us that we fail not."

And the Lord spoke again to him, "I will not give you my Holy Ghost nor your friends while you are in your enemy's land for they would detect it, but I will be with you and with your friends. While you train, my servant Trevor shall also join you. He shall instruct you on what difficulties you will have impersonating evil. Lynnara, Rebecca, Lana, and Mandy cannot go for they would surely die."

It wasn't what the girls wanted to hear and they all looked at each other, then at Daniel who sat back in his chair in awe. Mandy said, "Well then, *our* job is to train you so *you* don't die." And the other girls nodded.

# CHAPTER 18

# The Lord is My Shepherd

*Yinauqua, with her red and gray hair in her three traditional Appendaho braids, dressed in her holy dress of burgundy and gold Appendaho embroidery, popped into Marta's cottage, into her new circular living room that was still scant of furniture. For her part, Marta was overjoyed to invite her and smoothed her brown peasant dress in an attempt at composure. It was wonderful living on the Holy Mountain, and the people were wonderful, and she never knew being mortal would feel like this! But she missed her old, well, new, well, Heavenly life, too, and all her Heavenly friends. Still, there could be no honor like the honor she now felt in carrying Stephanie's child, now her child also. And when everyone on the Mountain found all this out, they were all in awe of her, having the deepest respect for Lady Stephanie, but now, also, for Marta, as well. Never had Marta experienced anything like this the last time she was mortal.*

*Yinauqua waved her hand and a glowing blue orb appeared in the center of Marta's living room supported by an ornate iron stand resting on a mahogany table engraved with Appendaho* animal glyphs around its perimeter. When Marta saw it, she gasped and her hands went to her heart. "Oh my God, how I've missed our orbs, but this one is so beautiful."

Yinauqua smiled tenderly, "Well, it's yours!"

Marta couldn't believe it. She'd never had her own personal orb, but only used common orbs in common places like where she taught. And no one on the Holy Mountain had one. "Oh, I don't deserve anything like this, and certainly not my own personal orb. I'm too young!"

But Yinauqua shook her head, saying, "First of all, you can argue that with the Lord! He told us to make it for you! Second of all, well, you're going to need it!" Yinauqua pointed into Marta's orb and as Marta beheld for a bit, she put her hands to her mouth in utter dismay. None of this was foreseen nor expected. Yinauqua said, "Well, since you requested to stay on mission, it looks like your responsibilities have now expanded. The Lord has also given you to watch over all those children going deep into the enemy's land!"

Marta was dumbfounded. "But. . .but. . . but how can I watch over all of them? And what can I do in the Anti-Christ's land? If I interfere directly. . . I don't know." Marta wasn't given to this kind of fretting, but she felt entirely inadequate.

Yinauqua said, "Maybe she can help!"

As Marta looked through the orb, she recoiled. Then she reached her hand into the orb, selected the person, brought up her file, and used her faithwalking power to absorb all her history to date. Marta almost fainted and Yinauqua wrapped her arm around her while Marta's head lolled back and forth.

*When her strength finally returned with embarrassment, she said, "I'm so sorry. . . but, well. . . I sensed it but had to be sure. You have no idea!"*

*Yinauqua wasn't familiar with this soul but after seeing what happened to Marta, she decided not to look further! All she knew was that the Lord Jesus had nudged her to recommend the woman! "Tell me, " Yinauqua said.*

*But Marta began to simply transfer all the knowledge, but Yinauqua caught Marta's hand before it reached her head. "Just tell me!"*

*Marta swallowed, then looked deeply into Yinauqua's eyes. "You know all I've been through. Well. . ." Marta sobbed. "Well," and she sobbed again. "That woman makes what I've been through look like Heaven!"*

*Now Yinauqua's head reeled. "The Lord had me recommend her to you!"*

*Marta pointed into the live orb, saying, "That woman was one of the few that Vaughn judged and spared from the demon villages he and the Lord destroyed! She gave birth to a human demon and was pregnant with a second when Vaughn spared her, rather, I should say, the Staff of Moses spared her!"*

*Yinauqua was shaking her head. She remembered now but chose to forget about it in favor of all the other more important things she needed to attend. But now it seemed the Lord was throwing into her face what she didn't want to look at before.*

*Marta said, "And Trevor is deeply in love with her. Frankly, she's not holy and I really don't know if she can be."*

*For some reason Yinauqua asked, "What's her name?"*

*And Marta said, "Silvia," When Marta saw Yinauqua's eyes go distant, Marta said, "What?"*

*"The name simply means a forest. But the personality associated with it is that of a big sister. And a forest is something that contains much resource as well as comfort. She might be just the right one to help!"*

Lady Stephanie and King Vaughn, only in their common clothing, held hands while leaning on the castle balcony watching Mandy, Daniel, and his three friends in the courtyard below being trained by Larson and other Rangers. After only one week, Mandy was doing flips, twists, spins, ducks, all while casting multiple forms of energies at dummies, and fending off the ranger's serious attacks with various weapons, some of which were formidable hybrid blasters imbued with spiritual energies. All the while, Mandy maintained a defensive shield all around her.

Stephanie shook her head while watching, saying, "You know, she's *much* more adept than I am! And after only one week!"

Vaughn, still watching with amazement, said, "Well. . . she's *younger* than you." And he said it with a straight face.

"What's *that* supposed to mean, *old man?* Am *I* an old woman? Mandy's only two years younger."

Vaughn smiled his special broad smile and winked. "Mandy has a Ranger's heart. Always has. I remember when you were in the depths of Matthew's torments lying on your bed just mumbling to yourself. Mandy grabbed me and spun me around and *ordered* me, saying, 'Why are you just standing there? *Do something!* I'll take care of her!'"

Stephanie thought about it. "Wow! She did? I didn't know."

"Sure did, and you should have seen the fire of fight in her heart, the utter love to protect you. She was *born* a Ranger. But you were born a *faithwalker.* Different gifts, but *somehow* you used your faithwalking to *transform* yourself into a fighter, too. But I don't think that can match what Mandy naturally has!"

Stephanie nodded. "What about you? You fight better than me, too. And it's not just because you're a man, is it?"

Vaughn nodded that he heard his wife, but having never given it thought before like this, he looked inward. "For me, actually, yes I do think it's partly because I'm a man. When I slaughtered the army that killed your people, I used my bare hands to smash their faces, rip their guts out, and more. I don't think *any* woman has *that* much ferocity and judgment in them because it's simply not in femininity and God never meant that to be in their hands nor heart. But *also,* I think it's history!"

Stephanie's eyebrows went up, but then Abraham's blessing to know Jewish ancient history came to the fore and visions of ancient Israelites slaying all kinds of manifestations of evil creatures and evil men flooded her mind and heart. "Wow! So you've inherited all *that?*"

And she sent the knowledge to Vaughn through her eyes meeting his, and he nodded! "Especially once I received the Staff of the Lord, but I *know* it was all with me all along. In fact, it's even how I was able to knock Gary out the very first time." And Vaughn spit in disgust over the balcony, remembering how vile Gary was and thinking merely breaking his neck was too good for him.

Stephanie nodded, seeing the truth in it, but then began shaking her head at her past, that in one way was so overwhelming for her at the time, but now in comparison to the evil she had faced since and facing now, well, Gary seemed of no account.

Stephanie said, "Daniel and his friends are really doing well. Looks like they've inherited, too!"

Vaughn nodded, and said, "And I've prayed for them to wake to it all, as well."

James came up behind, saying, "Pardon my intrusion, but our Jargono clone has declined your request for any more debates. He said, 'Frankly, there's no more need, as the last debate was quite sufficient to prove to the people who should be their ruler.'"

Stephanie said, "I can't believe it." But Vaughn just nodded and tugged at his beard, narrowing his eyes. Stephanie grabbed his arm. "Vaughn, we *still* have to destroy that *orb*. Maybe we should go together? *Together,* nothing can overcome us."

But Vaughn kept up his beard tugging. "Certainly nothing on Earth. But to go down *there*. . . I'm not so sure. We're really not supposed to be there, but we've taken many liberties." When Vaughn saw his wife in deep concentration, he took her by the arm with a particular husbandly, Kingly force, saying, "Stephanie, *promise* me you won't go down there without me, nor without *telling* me first and giving us further time to consider it *together!* I think we've *both* had enough of hiding from each other and going on our own!"

The feel of his grip was like no other she had felt before. Deeply loving, deeply protective, but with a particular authority as well. She automatically respected and appreciated the first two, but the last one. . . Stephanie looked deeper into herself to understand this new feeling. His authority seemed to bring out a definite response from her femininity! A certain automatic yielding, but *not* as a slave or as being oppressed, but as being part of a greater whole, and her *true part* was to yield to his unquestionable masculine authority, but not just *yield*, but *support* it. Vaughn was a true man, and with a *definite* noble warrior's history that flowed in his blood just like oxygen! How could true femininity *not* embrace *that*? She would *never* be *masculine. That* wasn't in her nature. "Alright, Vaughn," And Vaughn knew she meant it.

"My *King,* "And Stephanie curtsied to him but with a *very* mischievous smile and batting eyelashes. Vaughn just shook his head and turned back to watching everyone train and Stephanie put her hand over his folded hands that were propped on the balcony. It was comforting to hold such a man.

James, who had been leaning on the other side of *King* Vaughn on the balcony reached into his vest pocket and pulled out his phone. "Excuse me. Can you say that *again?*" After a long pause, he said, "And you say, 'Right outside the castle? *Hundreds?*" And there was another long pause, and James said, "Excuse me, in the *daytime?*"

His eyebrows went up and turned to face his King and Queen who had already turned to watch him. "My Lady, you might *not* want to go there. *Apparently,* we have *protestors* right outside the gate trying to enter the castle. And, well, some of them are in various states of, well, *undress.*"

Stephanie turned dark, and said, "James, you *know* where I've come from. I *doubt* very much anything could embarrass *me.*"

Vaughn simply put a comforting hand to his Queen's back in a very dignified Kingly fashion and they walked down to the gate, while James kept protesting that maybe they should first espy from the wall.

There were a dozen burly castle guards dressed in black uniform, a special wing of the military, standing at the foot of the drawbridge where every so often a group of protestors in multicolored various garbs would rush them and all were promptly, easily repelled. Some were kicked away, *slapped* away, picked up and *thrown into others* away. And then they would regroup. There were also many brightly colored signs with slogans and perverse pictures. But when they saw the actual King and Queen appear in the gateway, they all broke into chants.

"We're queer, we're *here,* we're *in your face!*"

"Trans rights are *human rights.* Trans rights are *human* rights.

"No justice, no *peace.* No *justice,* no PEACE!"

"We're *queer,* we're *here,* we're coming for your *children!*"

And *then* Stephanie saw certain *naked* men on a platform on wheels being rolled up to the gate and the aroused men put their, well, their members into the mouths or buttocks of other aroused men. On a bed on the platform, other women buried their faces between the legs of other women and Stephanie turned red and turned her back and stepped away! She recalled the demon villages her and Vaughn had destroyed and some of *them* had done similar actions but as part of their *worship* to their demon gods. But *this* wasn't any kind of worship to what they thought was a higher power who demanded it. *This* was pure debauchery of the *worst* kind. But then the Holy Ghost spoke within her, saying, 'No. There can *always* be *worse!'* And Stephanie mumbled out loud, "Worse?"

James came up to Stephanie, and said, "My Lady, *please,* Let me escort you back inside. Let King Vaughn deal with this."

But Stephanie turned very dark and a cloud of darkness formed around her which had *never* happened before. When the crowd saw *that,* they all began chanting, "Kill us! *Kill us!* KILL US! We'll *DIE* for our *FREEDOM!"*

Vaughn burst out laughing! *Hard* laughing to the point he bent over holding his gut. The incongruity of his laughing compared to the utter wrath Stephanie was about to unleash, well, it frankly ruined her desire to wipe them all out without mercy, and the dark cloud fizzled.

The crowd was at first perplexed at the King's reaction. He didn't seem to be upset *at all.* And when they looked to the Queen and saw her wrath was gone, they began to chant, "We *won't* be ashamed. We *WON'T* BE ASHAMED." And they pushed the platform as close as they could get it before the guards beat the pushers away and pushed it back.

Vaughn stood up wiping his tears away. He looked back at his wife and winked! Then he turned back to the crowd and his voice carried so they all could hear. "Have you come here just to make a spectacle or to talk and accomplish something productive?"

The question gave them pause but then they resorted to their chanting again. "We're HERE, we're QUEER, we're IN YOUR FACE!"

Vaughn raised his hand for silence and they slowly complied, and he said, "I pass a new law right now. Right *now*, I'm *still* your King. There will be *no more* public nudity, and *certainly* no public displays of sexual practice. This is to protect children and ensure societal *sensibilities.*" He pointed to the various public displays, then said, "NOW!" And he looked over to the guards, and then fifty well-armed troops in battle grays came onto the drawbridge.

Certain obvious leaders of the protestors began milling around talking to people and clothing was brought and then the sexual displays ceased and some of the signs were lowered. Stephanie looked upon Vaughn, at his *unbelievable* control, and held her peace.

Vaughn said, "Clear that platform and I will meet right there in public with your three top leaders in one hour!" And he turned and left, and put his hand to his Queen's back in a very dignified Kingly fashion.

James said as they walked deeper into the castle, "Sire, I have *no* idea what you're up to but I have to say that is the *greatest* display of restraint I have *ever* seen."

Vaughn said, "Well, there was no way I could have stopped my Queen from giving the enemy what they wanted, so I laughed at the absurdity of the whole damned thing!"

Stephanie looked over at her husband and her mouth dropped open but didn't know what to say, but she began to reconsider everything that just happened. *They did seem to want to provoke us,* even *to kill them. They're like those mindless programmed dragons we fought, but some of* them *I actually got to begin thinking for themselves. Except. . . these people were actually* born *human beings, have their* own *minds and hearts. And they want to be this way!* Stephanie began to turn dark again.

They found themselves in the square courtyard where the training was still intensely continuing. Many people and children were watching from the walkways above and around the courtyard. Vaughn pointed to them, saying, "*This* is *our* reality. *This* is our goal. I will engage the Beast's minions on *my* terms, *not* on theirs! And I will *judge them* when the Lord and *I* see fit!" And he walked away from them! James' eyes widened but Stephanie's mouth dropped open *again.* Something was *definitely* different with Vaughn now. He didn't exactly give her an order but it *felt* like it. James turned to his Lady, and said, "Queen Stephanie, your husband is a King beyond my wildest imagination."

Stephanie looked into James' sincere, holy eyes. Part of her was being poked from *somewhere* to rebel, and for the first time Stephanie realized this *feeling* had been plaquing her recently every time Vaughn and her had possible disagreements, a feeling similar to what she used to experience before she was holy. She refocused on James, and said, "The Anti-Christ has finished his orb!" Then she tried driving away the feeling but it would go then come right back. *This is really annoying. Last time this happened, Vaughn and I both joined as one and sent a fireball into the Ethereal. But I don't think that will work now.*

The Holy Ghost asked her, 'What's your favorite door?" And Stephanie shook her head at her foolishness, and prayed, "Lord Jesus drive this evil presence away from me and *keep it* away."

It immediately ceased but Stephanie had no idea *exactly* why except that her prayer was answered. *Or the Anti-Christ stopped attacking me before the prayer went into effect! But then how would that affect the prayer?* She shook her head at the complexity then decided to spend the time before Vaughn's *appointment with perversion* by practicing with Mandy.

Strolling into the courtyard, she noticed the girls and Daniel and his friends were gathered together listening to someone, but as she got closer, she recognized Trevor towering over them, wearing browns just like Vaughn. Trevor had definite presence to him now, a far cry from the drug-addicted, self-destroyed, tormented, weak person of his past. Sensing her, he came out from the crowd with a woman, her short blond hair only to her ears, and adorned only in a brown, frayed at the knees, peasant dress. Trevor went to one knee and took Stephanie's hand, saying, "Lady Stephanie, it's so good to see you again." And he bowed his head then took and kissed her hand in reverence! "You have *no idea* what you have done for me. You should have killed me. Instead, you forgave me and saved my soul." When he sensed Stephanie about to object, he said, "I know, I know very well *Jesus* saved me *but* he placed my fate in *your hands* and *you* opened the door that was shut to me. It took a *very* special soul to be able to *freely* do that and to even go against Vaughn." Trevor shook his head remembering how Vaughn was about to kill him when Stephanie jumped in between them, grabbing Vaughn's arm as he swung to kill Trevor. "This is Silvia. You briefly met her at the village."

Stephanie paused, having been first inundated with memories of her struggle with Vaughn to save Trevor who had just tried to poison them, but now also being introduced to the very woman whom she couldn't bring herself to forgive when the Lord sent her and Vaughn to destroy the demon villages. It was an odd confluence of feelings.

Silvia, her hair now actually blond, once all the slovenly grime was gone, went down on her knees with Trevor at her side, bowed her head to the ground, and said, "My Lady, kill me now! You should have back then! You have the right! I don't deserve to live, to even *exist.*" And she meant it, still feeling all the depravity in her soul from all she'd done with demons and bearing their offspring, and Stephanie perceived the depths of her torments.

The children had all gathered around them now and were transfixed. Lynnara's eyes went wide, knowing this was adult stuff that went *way* beyond her understanding. *This is something Mommy* never *told me about!* And she tried to pull from her Mommy's mind all that happened but was blocked. Lana's eyes went distant then she gasped and put her hand to her heart and tears welled up as she studied Stephanie. Rebecca came between them and took their hands, bowed her head, then silently prayed. She knew her best friends' souls as well as her own. She knew Stephanie's, as well. Daniel and his friends stood quietly looking from Stephanie, to Trevor, to Sylvia, to the girls and then back again.

And there Stephanie stood, and also noticed that annoying presence was back, a bit different this time, but recognizable. *Lord Jesus,* she sighed in her heart, *there's so much happening to me all at once.*

Daniel looked into Stephanie's rich brown eyes. and said, "Trevor was explaining to us how hard it was for him to go back to the demon villages after you forgave him and the Lord filled him with his Holy Spirit. He said you and Vaughn had a *fight!* Cause you didn't want him to go but Vaughn said a man has to do what a man has to do."

Stephanie now focused on Daniel and the memories he conjured, then her eyes sharpened. "Vaughn was right, and I. . . well, I wasn't as wise as he was. If I had let my compassion rule at that time, we never would have known till too late about the human demon hoards." And Stephanie looked upon Sylvia, still on her knees and now shaking, because, though Trevor was holy and she had been able to tolerate his presence, the power emanating from Lady Stephanie was considerably stronger.

Daniel said, "Trevor explained how you put the poison black oil back into him to hide God's presence from the enemy but that it would be different for us because we're not holy. He was explaining how it would feel to have evil constantly attacking us and how we had to actually *hide* fighting it yet *still* fight it! How when the enemy would scrutinize us, he'd sense some goodness in us but we had to convince the enemy we were too weak to pay it mind."

Stephanie became absorbed in the internal images Daniel was depicting. Silvia, still bowed, spoke softly, her voice quivering. "When I realized how *evil* everything was but that I no longer wanted any parts of it, it changed me and I *knew* it. And I thought all the demons and the evil people around me could see very clearly that I'd changed. But they couldn't. Just because *I* could see it, didn't mean they could. They were just used to me being a whore, and that's what I was to them. Just give them what they're used to seeing!"

Stephanie mumbled aloud, "Goodness can see and understand *everything*. But evil can't understand goodness, and it doesn't even understand itself." And Stephanie began to sniff, her heart paining her, remembering Arlupo, who taught her that wisdom seemingly so long ago. And Stephanie longed to see her best friend again, because she very much now felt as she did so long ago when she needed Arlupo to comfort her, to advise her.

Daniel said, "Wow! That's really deep, Lady Stephanie."

Stephanie refocused, but looked down at Sylvia, saying, "My best friend who went to her death to save me taught me that."

And Sylvia looked up into Stephanie's eyes and saw her tears, and said, "It be a blessing to have such a friend who gave you such memories, my Lady. Would that we all had such tears!" And she bowed her head, again, but distinctly in prayer. *What meager good can this, my wretched soul do, in spite of me being lost and bound for eternal torment? Give me* good *to do that my conscience suffer less whilst I'm here.* Trevor had given Silvia a Holy Bible a while ago, and she had taken a fancy to the old English words that in some way offered comfort.

And Stephanie heard her prayer and Lynnara stared deeply into her third and bestest Mommy *ever.* Stephanie reached her hand down and lifted Silvia's chin so that their eyes met again. Stephanie said, "Not that long ago, believe it or not, I was actually in Hell, and I felt I *deserved* to be there."

Daniel and his friends and Trevor were shocked, and looked to one another. Sylvia shook her head trying to drive such *impossible* images away. "That *can't* be true, my Lady."

Stephanie said, "But it is. Worse than being a wretch and bearing demon offspring is being a God-given *faithwalker* and *allowing* your very own holy, innocent child to be *murdered* right inside of you!"

And everyone was speechless as Stephanie waved her hand and a kind of vision opened in the air above them for all to see, to see what happened to her, to see her in Hell, and to see her thoughts and feelings. But Silvia spoke up adamantly, "No, *no.* That's not *true.* You were *overpowered,* my *Queen.* Do not *feel* that way or you give them *power* over you!"

But Stephanie said, "I understand that *now.* What about *you?*" And as they looked deeper into each other, Stephanie showed Silvia how even the evil pleasure she had reveled in was a result of her being tricked and overpowered, and how *that* was *not* a part of her soul, *now,* nor when *she* was born into the world!

But Silvia wailed, "But it *is.* I feel it *all the time.* It *never* leaves me, I don't deserve to live, but I *can* be of help. Send *me* with the children! I'm used to what they will endure."

Stephanie held out her hand and the Lord's Staff of Judgment and Life appeared in it, and she held it with its foot on the ground beside her. Daniel, and his friends went to single knees, feeling the power of God all around them and in the staff. Sylvia recognized it, also, for it had delivered her from her demon offspring. Stephanie said, "This once passed over you in judgement and spared your *existence*." And Stephanie raised the staff then brought the foot of it down on the ground right in front of Sylvia and it thundered all around them and Sylvia shook greatly while Daniel and his friends bowed low to the ground.

Stephanie said, "Choose! Choose between being a true help for goodness sake or to continue to wallow in your past evil. If you can take hold of *this* staff, your deepest prayers will be answered!

With the staff being but inches away from her bowed head, it felt as if she would die. The staff actually *felt like death* to her. That her very existence was dissolving just from its proximity, so she *knew* if it was even *possible* for her to just merely *touch* it, let alone *take hold* of it, she would go out of existence.

"Very well," Stephanie said, and she began to withdraw the staff but the next thing Sylvia knew, she sat up on one knee and sprang upon the staff wrapping her arms around it, clutching it to her breast. Her wail reminded Stephanie of her own cry right after the Anti-Christ had murdered her unborn child. Both were the cries over utterly lost life.

It thundered again and the ground shook. Mandy and the Rangers, who had come over, went to single knees, and bowed their heads. And Stephanie let go of the staff, while Silvia cried, "Forgive me. *Kill me! Let me go out of existence!*"

And the staff shined so brightly no one could see into this Light. And the Lord spoke from above but everywhere, saying, "Your former self is put to death. Arise from the dead and teach these children what they need to know."

And Sylvia found herself standing, holding the Staff of God in her very own hands. It didn't seem real that she was holding it, so she looked into Stephanie's eyes for help to wake up. Stephanie smiled and held out her hand and asked with a voice like Lynnara, "Are you going to give it back?"

The girls broke out laughing, but Sylvia realized this wasn't a dream, that she *actually* held *the* Staff. And she said, "God is real. Jesus is *real.* Thank you." And she handed the staff back to Stephanie and she sent it away to rest and it vanished. Then Lynnara rose up and hugged Sylvia and the other girls followed suit. For the first time in her life, Sylvia felt. . . well, she felt the clear presences of these children, their affection and love, and she marveled at the newness. The Lord hadn't given her his Holy Ghost, but she felt the Lord's presence now dwelling with her.

Trevor took her by her hands, saying, "Like Daniel and his friends, Jesus won't give you the Holy Ghost now, but when you return with the children, you all will receive it."

Sylvia looked upon Daniel and his friends and they came and went to one knee, saying, "Teach us, teacher Sylvia."

Marta rubbed her chest as she peered through her orb at Stephanie and the rest. *Again* the Anti-Christ tried to walk around her orb's protection of them, trying to see past her interference with his orb's sight. It was a constant battle that Marta began to relish in, and then suddenly the Anti-Christ's orb turned off! In the next moment, Marta heard Vaughn calling to her, so she went outside but didn't see him. Yet she heard his voice again and followed the sound until she reached the very perimeter of the holy protection cast around the holy village. And there Vaughn stood looking, well, dorky as only Vaughn could.

Vaughn said, "Well? You gonna let me in or *not?*"

Marta hadn't been mortal that long and she wasn't used to feeling fuzzy-headed. She said, "That's *ridiculous.* Just. . ." She was about to say, Just pop in, but the babe in her womb seemed to summersault in protest. She grabbed her stomach, "Oh!" Then looked at Vaughn and was about to finish saying what she intended when Michael, dressed in yellow jammies with blue bunnies popped next to Marta and took her hand.

Marta looked down into his shining eyes and Michael pointed to Vaughn, and said, "That's *not* Daddy!" And the haze that fogged Marta's mind cleared. When she looked up at Vaughn, she narrowed her eyes at him, then waved her hand, saying, *"Reveal!"*

And Vaughn transformed into the Anti-Christ, whereupon he said, "*You're* not supposed to be on *Earth. And* there are *no* orbs supposed to be on *Earth.*"

Marta was about to reply but before this fake Jargono could react, little Michael raised his little hand, saying, "Go away." The Anti-Christ burst into flames like he was a match-stick and he disappeared!

Marta looked into little Michael's rich brown eyes, and said, "Wow! That was *too* close."

Little Michael said, "No to talk to *bad* man!" And he smiled his special broad smile.

Then Marta looked into Michael's eyes again, saying, "Except these days be shortened, *no* flesh will survive because if it were possible, the Anti-Christ would even go into Heaven and fool the angels! Now I understand that. Wow!"

Little Michael nodded, saying, "That *wasn't* Daddy."

CHAPTER 19

# Justice

*Arlupo called to Marta, and Marta said, "If you are the real Arlupo, Stephanie's best friend, come in!"*

*And Arlupo, her long black hair hanging freely, dressed in her holy Appendaho dress of light blue with pink embroidery along the hems of the sleeves, neck, and bottom, popped beside Marta, who stood looking into her orb, watching the Anti-Christ and his orb.*

*Arlupo said, "Does everyone know to be on their guard now?" Marta simply nodded as she concentrated, reached her hand into her orb, and using both the orb's power and her faithwalking, she created a glowing mesh in the Corridor and prevented all of the Anti-Christ's attempts to use that route.*

*Then she said to Arlupo, "When your Mother Yinauqua told me my responsibilities had increased, I had no idea I would be orb bound! I kinda thought. . ."*

*"That you'd be fighting great big battles or something like we watched Stephanie do?"*

*Marta did something else in the orb that Arlupo didn't understand, then said, "Yea. I guess so.*

Arlupo put her hand on Marta's shoulder. "There is literally no one able to do what you are doing now! Your orb is very special, specifically designed for you and your tasks! Only someone with your particular constitution and abilities along with this orb is able to go up against the Anti-Christ from here on Earth! And Earth is the only place from where this can be done!"

Marta shook her head, did something else in the orb, then said, "I don't understand. We have orbs in Heaven. . ."

Arlupo said, "They're not combat orbs!"

Now Marta paused and looked into Arlupo's shining rich brown eyes. "Combat orbs? I didn't know there was such a thing."

Arlupo said, "There is now!"

Then Marta noticed Arlupo was hiding something behind her, so she raised an eyebrow and tried to peek around. The warmth of Arlupo's smile sank into Marta and reminded her of how Arlupo used to look at Stephanie when she was on Earth.

Arlupo turned deadly serious, and said, "That was a very close call you had there. Most all of you would have been dead before you could have done anything! You are the only faithwalker here!"

Chills ran over Marta, and her heart suddenly pained as she realized her responsibilities and the consequences of failing. And then she recalled what he did to Stephanie and her hand went to her belly and bile came up in her throat. She knew for certain the Anti-Christ would have done the same thing to her. It would have been the first thing he did if Marta would have foolishly let him in. Marta's anger rose now, and she turned very dark because there was no way she would let any more *harm come to this child. "I'm not used to being mortal again, and it's strange to be so vulnerable given the Lord has blessed me with so much power, I mean, being a faithwalker, and all."*

*Arlupo said, "None of Vaughn's or Stephanie's plans, nor any of our people's efforts will prosper if you can't keep that evil orb from them. And just so you know, he brings it to Earth, too! Because the connection is more direct."*

*Marta looked up at Arlupo with new understanding. "Oh, so that's why my orb has to be on Earth. In order to be fast enough, direct enough?" Arlupo nodded, but she was still holding something with one hand behind her back! Marta said, "Arlupo, what. . ."*

*Arlupo hugged Marta with her free hand and kissed her cheek, then said, "If you only knew how much I love you! All that I hold dear is in your hands! And I understand your heart and bravery. So I brought you a gift." And Arlupo set a plain brown bag down on the pedestal table next to the orb. "Now send me back." And as Arlupo was vanishing, she said, "You're one of us."*

*Marta scrunched up her nose wondering what that meant then noticed the Anti-Christ had gotten to Stephanie again. He kept avoiding her prayers by changing what he was doing, so what one prayer worked against, didn't work against the change. It was almost too difficult for Marta to follow because the very nature of the evil orb's energies kept changing. It was that constantly changing energy that kept attracting just enough of Stephanie's attention that she opened her awareness to it. But not usually enough awareness to directly deal with it.*

*Then the evil had freedom to work in the background of her consciousness. Marta also noticed the Anti-Christ was trying to reach her, as well!* "And how did he fog my mind? I mean, the protection here won't allow any evil."

Arlupo's voice sounded in the room. "Unless enough of your attention is attracted to give the evil permission to enter! Look at your gift!"

Marta put her orb on automatic, to react as it had been reacting to evil. *That should give me a few minutes.* She reached into the bag, felt something soft, pulled it out, and gasped. Her heart pounded. *It was a real Appendaho holy dress. And the power in it shot up her arm!* "WOW!" *But this one was odd. It was deep black velvet but with golden embroidery, the same as Lady Stephanie's around the neck, hems, and waist. But it had an expandable design for when her pregnancy grew larger.*

Marta pulled off her brown peasant dress and donned the gift and her head spun for a moment as power she had never felt before inundated her. Arlupo said, "That is a rare Appendaho battle dress, only worn by our ancient faithwalker priestesses when we were in great peril. That particular dress has only been worn twice before! By Yinauqua, our first mother, and by the wife of the man in your holy Bible called Job! When she and her husband went through great tribulation, she wore that dress for a whole two years until she was tricked by her grief to take it off. And once off, she succumbed to temptation and told her husband to curse God and die!"

Marta said, "I'm not taking this off. Not until the very end when the Lord Himself makes all things new."

*And Arlupo said, "That would be wise, my sister. You carry my beloved friend's child, and now you wear her dress! It shall help protect you from the Anti-Christ and his tricks!"*

*Marta was dumbfounded. "But Stephanie needs it more than me."*

*But Arlupo called down. "But she needs you more than the dress!"*

*Marta was dumbfounded, again, whispering, "Lady Stephanie needs me more than the dress! She needs me!" And Marta went back to her orb work with fervor.*

*Little Michael somehow had gotten away from his baby sitter again and popped beside Marta and promptly hugged her leg. He loved the soft feel of her new dress but also the tremendous power within it. He squealed in delight and Marta's hand went absently to the boys head and her fingers gently caressed through his wavy red hair as she concentrated into the orb and used her other hand to work it.*

And when *exactly* one hour had passed, Vaughn popped directly onto the platform, dressed in a black robe with seven Hebrew words embroidered around the collar, each word a particular metallic color. One obviously homosexual man, one obviously homosexual woman, one supposed to be man but looked like a woman, and one supposed to be woman that looked like a man stood waiting. They all wore rainbow-colored shirts and odd pants. All their hair was died in rainbow colors and they even had rainbow colored contact lenses! In *that* way, they all looked alike, they were all *equal!*

For Vaughn's part, each color of the seven Hebrew words was twined together as embroidery at the hems of his sleeves and robe bottom, but the presence of his colors conflicted greatly with that of his adversaries who looked completely garish.

Vaughn folded his hands behind his back and stepped to the front of the platform facing the protestors and needed no microphone. Someone in the crowd shouted an obscenity and threw a rotten tomato at him, and others threw eggs. They all ended up whizzing by him and striking his various opponents whereupon the obnoxious behavior ceased. Vaughn said, "I'm here as your *King*, to hear your grievances as my loyal subjects! And to seek a solution!"

Everyone hushed. *No one* expected anything like *this*. Someone began to shout, "We're QUEER, we're HERE, we're IN YOUR FACE."

But Vaughn said, "Obviously! But that tells me *nothing* of what you *really* want or feel or think. Am I wasting my time? I'll leave." And he began to fade out and vanish but the four on stage with him shouted for him to remain so he came back.

The tall, lanky, homosexual man said, "We want equal rights."

To which Vaughn said, "Everyone gets one vote and they're all equal. Yours as well as mine. We're *equal*."

But the fat, homosexual woman said, "We want the same opportunity as everyone else. In jobs, homes, *everything*."

Vaughn crossed his arms over his chest and his robe sleeves, which belled out, hung down. "You want *me* to *order* people what to do with their own property? Do I get the *same* privilege with what *you* own? *My* decision?"

The fat woman looked to her partners and the woman that wanted to be a man tried puffing her chest out like a man, and boisterously said, "Not *you*. But whoever wins the elections."

Vaughn leaned forward a bit to her, "Well, Miss. . ."

"*Sir,*" she corrected.

"What's your name?"

"*George.*"

"Well, *Miss* George. . ."

"*MR,*" she shouted.

Vaughn narrowed his eyes a bit and began to turn dark. "Do you want to order *me* and others how to speak? Do I get the *same* equal right to order *you?*"

Again there was pause. And the man that wanted to be a woman said with an affectation, "The neeeew government will haaave laaaws that *everyone* will follow. It's the *laaaaw,* we'll follow. *Youuu* taught us that." And the others all nodded.

"I *never* said there would be laws limiting speech. In *fact,* I taught you all everyone would have *freedom* of speech. Isn't that right *Miss* George. What's your *first* name?"

She became exasperated. "*George* is my *first* name."

"Oh," Vaughn said. "Well, *Miss* George . . ."

"We're QUEER. We're HERE. WE ARE IN YOUR FACE." And Miss George ran right up into Vaughn face and shouted it!

Vaughn spoke quietly, "The *next* time *anyone* runs towards me and gets within six feet, I'll consider that a hostile action and *react* accordingly. You can back up now, or I'll consider your *proximity* to be hostile and *react* accordingly." And power began to build around Vaughn and they all felt it and Miss George backed up.

The homosexual man said, "But we have trouble finding good jobs, good housing, good *everything* because people don't like us."

Vaughn said, "You want *me* to make them like *you?* Do you *like* me?"

The homosexual man ogled Vaughn, "As a matter of faaact, I dooo!" And the crowd roared in laughter screaming vulgar things the man should do to Vaughn, but Vaughn grimaced in disgust.

Lady Stephanie, still merely garbed in her brown common peasant dress, watched from a balcony with James, and said, "I can't *believe* Vaughn's composure. I'm sorry James, but if they'd treated *me* like that. . ."

"I feel the same way, my Lady, but there's only *one* Vaughn. But I wouldn't be too quick to assume his direction. And I wouldn't be too quick to assume that if *you* were down there, you *wouldn't* do the *same* thing. Look what you just did with Sylvia!"

Stephanie shook her head. "Those people *down there* belong to the *Beast*. There is *no* forgiveness for *them*." And Stephanie turned dark and the sky above began to fill with dark clouds and thunder growling like a hungry animal. The people down below began to squirm and chant their slogans again.

Vaugh said, "Let me ask you all a question. Because there are a *lot* of you, and only *one* of me, *and* you're all seeming to lust after me, so if I came down amongst you, what would you *all* do?"

And the crowd roared in laughter begging Vaughn to come down and saying more vulgar things they'd do. "But I'm not like you. I have *no* desire for that."

"You're HOMOPHOBIC, You're HOMOPHOBIC," the crowd began to chant, and Vaughn saw they had planned for this, or were being guided. Stephanie would be able to see if any gray arms or whatever were reaching into their heads, but he hadn't developed that faithwalking sense yet.

Vaughn raised his hand for silence and smiled, and strangely, they all complied. "Thank you for the respect! I'm not homophobic. I'm not afraid nor scared of you *at all.* In fact, when I was younger, many men tried to brutalize me like that and I fought to near death against it. I *would have* died if it weren't for my beloved Queen who is at *this* moment feeling rather protective of her husband, as you can see from the sky! But I'm *not* being homophobic, being scared, afraid of you. I am *repulsed* by you. My feelings are naturally towards the *complementary* sex. I don't call women my *opposite* sex because in *truth,* the man and woman together form a *complementary unity.* If we were *opposites,* we would be trying to destroy one another because *opposites* are antagonistic. However, *complements* can make children together because they *are* a complementary unity that supports life, not destroying it.

The homosexual man said, "You have to understand something. I'll be honest with you. *We all* feel the *exact* same way about you and *all* straight people. I could *never* even *imagine* being with a woman. *That* disgusts me."

And the crowd began to cheer in agreement and chanting again, "We're QUEER. We're HERE. WE'RE IN YOUR FACE. Trans rights are HUMAN RIGHTS. We want RESPECT!"

Vaughn held his hand up and got silence. "What do you mean by respect?"

"We want LAWS protecting us. Guaranteeing fair employment, housing, and social justice."

Vaughn folded his hands behind his back again. "You want me to respect *queer* people?"

"*Racist! Homophobe, BIGOT. . .*"

Vaughn held his hand up to speak and it took a while for them to allow it. Then he said, "I told you, I *don't* fear you. *And,* you are *not* a race. And I only called you what you have been calling yourselves. *Queer.*"

The lesbian said, "But your *meaning* is *different.* We want ACCEPTANCE!"

And the crowd began chanting, "ACCEPTANCE, ACCEPTANCE, WE WANT ACCEPTANCE."

Vaughn waited, then said, "What does acceptance look like for you? *Besides* housing and jobs, what *is* social justice?"

The woman wanting to be a man puffed up again. "Call us what we *tell you* to call us, for one thing. I'm a HIM not a her and a MR not a *Miss.* And we have a *RIGHT TO LOVE WHO WE WANT.*"

Vaughn said, "But that's a *lie.* You're *not* a man, nor a MR, not even a HIM. Lying is against our values. And it's also *not* love to behave the way you do with each other."

The crowd became furious and began to chant again but a huge thunder shook everyone's insides and they hushed. Vaughn said, "Sorry, my *Queen* must have lost a bit of control. Look, masculinity and femininity are *complements* to each other, mutually supporting life together. But when you destroy those qualities by being with the *same* sex, you are engaging in *mutual* self-destruction. And just because you really enjoy the same lies together, that enjoyment isn't the joy of life, but of perversion. *Perversion* is when you *deform* the natural ways of life into *no life.*"

Someone shouted, "I was *born* this way! You can't judge us for how we were *born.* We're *innocent.*" But only some in the crowd joined in with that.

Vaughn said, "Well, OK! What do we call it when someone is *born* with an abnormality? You *know* homosexuality is *abnormal, You, yourselves, all* have mothers and fathers who mated together. By *that,* being born with inclinations that *contradict* your very existence is *abnormal.* What do you call it when you are born abnormal?"

No one answered. They couldn't even think it through! So Vaughn answered for them. "You are born with a *birth defect!*"

The truth of it slammed into the crowd. They wanted to chant some more but didn't feel the chants would be adequate. Someone said, "*You're* defective, because you don't *LOVE! God* said LOVE everyone. Even your ENEMIES."

Vaughn darkened. "Let's be honest. *If* you're born with a birth defect, who's *proud* of that? No sane person is. They work hard to *overcome* their defect, do everything they can to come to be as close to normal as possible, because *normal* is the standard of *life,* of *goodness."*

The crowd began to chant, *"We're good, YOU'RE EVIL! WE'RE GOOD. . ."*

Vaughn and Stephanie let this go on for a while until they calmed themselves, and Vaughn said, "Let's be honest. You want to be hired over straight folks, right?"

The crowd chanted, "No JUSTICE no PEACE. We DESERVE to be hired FIRST! Because you've HATED us."

Vaughn said, "OK! I have a solution for that! But first let's get this *all* out in the open first."

James looked at Stephanie, and asked, "Did Vaughn discuss *this* with you?"

Stephanie shook her head, transfixed upon her beloved. She didn't know where he was going, but sensed a fundamental change was coming, something from Justice that she hadn't perceived, so she held her peace and the sky calmed.

Vaughn said, "You want first pick at housing." And the crowd chanted their slogan again about justice and peace. "You want laws *assuring* you are respected by *everyone."* Same chanting. "Let's just say you had your very *own* cities that *you* ruled. And straight folks are walking down the street and they *obviously* feel uncomfortable by your presence and the way you act. What would you do?"

The homosexual man said, "Well, we have to teach everyone *not* to be that way, to be *fair.* It starts when they're children."

Vaughn said, "Alright. So you would teach children *against* the natural revulsion against you?"

The homosexual said, "Of course, because *we* are just as natural. Actually, it's *more* natural to be homosexual than heterosexual. There's a *lot* of research to back that up. But your society *teaches* children *against* homosexuality which is more *normal* than heterosexuality."

Vaughn said, "But what if, say, there is an *abnormal* child who is *born* heterosexual. What do you do with him or her?"

The lesbian said, "Well, to be *honest,* since we're talking about *honesty.* Most of us *choose* this life because it's *better.* And for *those* children, in fact *all* children, all we have to do is just *show* them how pleasurable it is to be us! Then they'll *love* it!"

And the crowd cheered and chanted, "You'll *LOVE IT. YOU'LL LOVE IT!*"

The sky quickly grew dark again and Vaughn waited, then said, "Adults have a lot of power over children. You say adults *force* children to be straight so you'd *force* them to be homosexual for their own good. How would you show them, *children, your* truth?"

The homosexual man said, "Looook. Let'sss be *honessst.* Children are *sexual* beings from *birth.* I meeean, they're *born* sucking. And they *love* mouth pleasure. That's why *everything* goes into their mouths. We would just expose children to what's *natural.* And they can experience whatever pleasures they want to try. They have *rights* you know. But many parents keep their rights away from them. It's time to correct that."

Vaughn said, "OK. I get you! One last thing. If you get everything you want, and some guy is walking down the street and you get a bad vibe from him like he doesn't want homosexual attentions, what's the *fair* way to treat him?"

They all chimed in at once until the dominant woman who wanted to be a man won the aggression, and *Miss* George said, "Well, he's *obviously* a hater. And if he wanted to keep living around *us* then he'd have to *prove* he could get over it."

"How could he do that?"

They all laughed, and *Miss* George said, "He'd have to have sex with a homosexual man."

But the man that wanted to be a woman said, "Or, have sex with me or someone like me. That wouldn't be as bad for him, because we're really women."

Vaughn said to *him*, "So, if you made an advance to a man like that and they turned you down, what should happen to have Justice and Peace?"

The man that wanted to be a woman said, "Easy. He's a hater. Doesn't deserve respect. Maybe we just help him by *proving* it to him. He'll end up liking it in the *end*." And they all laughed and the crowd laughed raucously.

Vaughn said, "OK. I have a solution. Even though your sense of justice makes sense to you, and even though in the *future* you may be able to win the whole world over, that's simply not possible right now. The homosexuals, and other *perverts* aren't safe around normal folks. And judging from *your* feeling and understanding you just described, if straight folk are caught in areas you control now, then *they're* not safe to be what they are. We have completed *many* restorations of the old cites and they're now like brand new. There's been quite a lot of investment, hard work by me, my Queen, and many others to bring them back. I give to all of you, *all of your kind,* New York City, San Francisco, Los Angeles, Philadelphia, Chicago, all the major cities in the North except for Pittsburgh in Western Pennsylvania because Western Pennsylvania is mostly conservative in values. I give you the *best* that the United States has to offer. No straight people are allowed in those places, and any there now *must* come out. They're *yours* now. And I will amend our transfer of power so that no matter *who* wins the elections, this decree will stand! Is that satisfactory to you?"

Everyone was stunned but the four on stage asked the crowd and they all agreed this was *wonderful.* But Vaughn said, "One more thing. Straight people might be *terribly* jealous of all that you have just received and they just get *stuck* with their *boring* small towns and country living. I make another decree to go along with the first. They *both* have to be observed or *none* at all, There can be *no* homosexuals *anywhere* except in their cities. I won't be responsible for the harm that comes to you if you aren't where you now belong."

The crowd murmured for a good while until Vaughn said, "OK. I get it. The deal is off. I've failed, but I tried. I'll have to order that *all* of you be destroyed right now! We are at war, and I'm *not* on *your* side. And I'm going to play to *win!*" Vaughn called out to his military waiting just inside the castle, "Come out and kill them *all!* And order all straight people across the country to kill them all!"

The four on the platform ran up to Vaughn, and said, "Wait, wait! We accept your terms!" And the crowd cried out, "We ACCEPT. We ACCEPT!"

And Vaughn called out to the military who *weren't* homosexual *at all,* "Stand down. Apparently, we have a deal!" And Vaughn turned around to walk into the castle but then turned back, and said, "You all *know* I am also appointed as a supreme Judge down South and that I will be maintaining that position even if I lose the election for President. And that the Judges from the South are *now* your Supreme Court Judges, and *all* your judges. As a *Judge,* look for me to visit you all in your cities, and my wife, too, who has also been made a *Judge.*"

And Vaughn walked off and the crowd shook their heads not understanding the odd feelings they were getting. Nevertheless, they couldn't *believe* their good fortune. Many even considered actually voting for Vaughn but many others overruled that feeling because they *knew* Jargono would be *far* better,

Vaughn appeared beside his wife and James on the balcony just as they were about to leave. They couldn't stomach the celebration, but Vaughn said, "What did you think?"

James said, "Well, the loss is great because of all you put into the cities and the real Jargono before you. But truth be told, most of the conservatives can't stand the big cities, so, really, it's no great loss to us."

Stephanie took Vaughn by the arm, "Vaughn, what did you *really* mean, we would visit them?"

Vaughn darkened. "At the time appointed by the Lord Jesus, we will *visit* them! As we *visited* the demon villages!"

James rubbed his head, trying to push away the goose-bumps. "Sire, that may be *difficult* with the looming war."

Vaughn laughed, "No more so than when we were at war before and we had to destroy those demon towns!"

James said, "But you *convinced* Jargono to help you. You won't have that help this time. *And,* there will be *many* who claim they're perverse just so they can live in such luxury."

Vaughn said, "Well, I hope they don't mind being *forced* to be perverted. And I hope they enjoy their *short* lives there! But with everyone moving around, this will help to further get our people to safety *before* the war breaks out! "

Lynnara popped up to the balcony with Lana while Rebecca was still helping the other Rangers finish up. Lynnara said, "It's time to take Daniel and his friends and Sylvia to the shelter so our new kids can finish training them."

Lana said, "Between those kids and Sylvia, I *really* think they'll be OK."

Stephanie said, "I'll be right back. Don't go *until* I get back." And the way her Mommy said it, Lynnara knew to listen without deviation.

Stephanie popped into Marta's living room and was stunned. She felt the power from the dress but was equally taken by its beauty.

Marta ran into her arms and they held each other in sacred sisterly embrace with Stephanie also immediately feeling everything about her child inside Marta. The babe leapt in her womb and Marta understood all the communications between them. Marta said, "Your best friend Arlupo gave me this." Then she stepped back modeling the dress and explained it while Stephanie had tears. Stephanie hadn't known anything like that existed, and with such a *dear* history.

But Stephanie said, "It's *yours* to keep, no matter what! We're *sisters*. We're *one.*"

Now Marta had tears, and she hadn't thought it possible, but she loved Stephanie even more than before.

Stephanie said, "Marta, the girls are about to take Daniel and his friends to the shelter."

Marta pointed to her split screen orb where two parts were on the castle, the girls and Daniel, and one part on the Anti-Christ, and *another* on his orb, and yet *another* down below! She said, "I know!"

Stephanie's head swooned. On a previous visit to see Michael, Marta had briefly shown her the orb, but since Vaughn had his own orb now, it didn't impact Stephanie the way it first impressed Marta. But now seeing all that Marta was doing, Stephanie said, "Marta, there's *no way* I could follow all that at once."

Marta said, "I know, but the *real* Vaughn came by and shared Mafferan's orb blessing with me! I can do even more than this if I have to."

Stephanie said, "You'll cloak the children when they travel so *he* can't find them?"

Marta said, "He doesn't know *anything* about them *now*, and he won't *ever!*"

"What did you mean by the *real* Vaughn."

Marta touched the side of Stephanie's head and imparted what happened and Stephanie turned dark, but said, "Has Lana told you what will happen to Vaughn and me, yet?"

Marta nodded and had immediate tears. "That's going to be so *hard* for me, I don't know if I can take it!"

And they hugged for a long time and it was like the babe inside Marta was pressing her little hand against Marta's tummy trying to touch Stephanie's tummy.

CHAPTER 20

# Fair Play or Not

*Mafferan popped into Jargono's old castle up North, into the living room that the fake Jargono had converted to his liking. There were dark paintings of demonic battles with demons victorious over their prey hanging on all the walls. Only a massive ebony table with a black iron stand and a large greenish blue orb occupied the center of the large rectangular room. Mafferan said, "A bit scant on decoration."*

*The Anti-Christ ignored him, busying himself with the orb, still trying to penetrate through Marta's blockade. "It won't help them. This is just to pass the time for me."*

*Mafferan walked up right beside him and glowed a bit but it had no effect on the Jargono clone. The clone said, "Your glow feels rather nice. Refreshing, actually. I can absorb your power and make it my own. Would you like to spar now, or later?"*

*Mafferan eyed him then studied his orb. "Quite a marvelous piece of work you did here. Nothing like it."*

*The Anti-Christ said, "Except the orb you gave to the mystery woman carrying Stephanie's child!" When Mafferan didn't even flinch, he said, "I sensed the child's presence in her. I had to* recognize it since we had rather intimate contact." The clone looked right into Mafferan's eyes, and said, "You're a distant relative! I can feel that, too. In a way, I'm also your offspring!"

Mafferan tugged at his beard. "You have your own interests at heart. Not the Ethereal. Not the Father below. Your own."

"Boring! Of course I do. That's the way the Ethereal works."

"But your Father knows this, too. Be careful, old chap. There's always more than meets the Eyeeee!" And Mafferan said it like the Highest Counselor used to say it and the Anti-Christ knew it, and knew what had happened to him.

"Boring," was his uninterested response.

"You know your fate already. You know the prophecy concerning you. Yet, you know you have a free will because of the form you are in. Then you know your fate is, yet, still in your own hands. You're made out of powerful parts of good people. Even now they rebel against your demon side. But your demon side doesn't want prophecy to be fulfilled either. So change it! Take another path!"

The Anti-Christ said, "Oh, I intend to. I'll be seeing you and your lovely wife soon!"

Mafferan waved his hand, and said, "Reveal!"

And the Anti-Christ became a large seven-headed dragon with a name on each head. The first was Death, the second was Hate, the third was Confusion, the fourth was Deceit, the fifth was Injustice, the sixth was Chaos, and the seventh was a word from the Ethereal meaning, I AM My Own Truth.

Mafferan said, "Hmm, pick a head to lose, old chap." And Mafferan vanished.

*But the Anti-Christ said in return, "No matter! And his deadly wound was healed."*

*But Mafferan's voiced came back at him, "You only know what's recorded, but I know the things not written down! Pick a head!"*

*The Anti-Christ frowned in disgust at Mafferan's foolishness. "You know better than that. I'm no stupid Christian who knows nothing but the paper and ink, and they don't even know that well. I have access to all recorded history through the orb"*

*But Mafferan said, "That's what I said! Pick a head!"*

*"Boring." Was all the Anti-Christ said. Mafferan understood that of all the things that could be said to him, saying he was boring, which means his contribution is worthless, which means he is worthless because worthless produces worthless, well, it could have rightfully been infuriating except this is exactly what Mafferan expected.*

The wonderful breakfast that James made went practically unnoticed as they ate silently together in their usual positions at the side of the oblong dining table in their castle in the South. Stephanie wore her brown peasant dress and Vaughn wore the standard brown that most common folks wear but the brown seemed duller than usual. The wonderful stuffed pancakes had blueberries and grilled bananas inside. The maple syrup was freshly homegrown, deep brown, and rich with a hint of rum, but it all went down unappreciated.

Stephanie shook her head, looking at her plate, saying, "Something's not right. I feel so. . . bla!"

Vaughn nodded in agreement. "This is an odd feeling for *us*. Quite disconcerting, but I really don't know what to do about it right now. It's like I don't even want to put in the effort... for *anything.*"

Stephanie nodded in agreement. For that matter, James seemed to be preoccupied and hadn't graced them with his usual morning wit. But he now came in and announced, "Sire, my Lady, *Harris* is *here* to see you!"

It was unusual for Harris to come, himself, to the castle, though in truth, he didn't live that far away, now that Vaughn and Stephanie had moved their permanent residence to the South and more or less abandoned Jargono's old Castle. James brought Harris, in his usual brown clothing, to the dining room then bowed his head slightly and off he went.

Stephanie and Vaughn invited him to sit at the table head, and he uncomfortably took the position more aptly meant for a King or Queen. And there he sat, his dark brown eyes staring at his folded hands, with all of them being silent with that same dry feeling. So Vaughn and Stephanie informed Harris that they'd just finished breakfast and that Lynnara had left, as usual, to find her friends and travel to the shelter where they were finishing training Daniel, Harris' son, and his friends. Vaughn told Harris Lynnara's story of how Sylvia put them through quite a bit of hardship by making them imagine deeply what being like their enemy really is- the feelings, the nuances, especially the fear. But then Mandy would scold them when she sensed they lost their bearings to the act! But then Sylvia would scold them when their defiance was even the slightest bit noticeable. At one point, the boys were practically in tears, but then the newcomers explained how they found strength they weren't supposed to have and how they hid it. When they did *that*, what both Sylvia and Mandy were telling them clicked into place. And when they roleplayed different scenarios created by the newcomers, Daniel and friends got excellent reviews.

The hardest to deal with was when one of them would be beaten or mistreated. The others had to practice a complex reaction of obviously wanting to protect their friends but showing great fear and submissiveness to counter it. *That* they had to practice *many* times until the feelings they all sensed were just right. Vaughn said, "Today's the last day of training and then Mandy smuggles the children *into* enemy land. What do ya think?"

Harris ran his hand through his brown wavy hair which had gray at the temples now. That was *his* son about to. . . about to do what even he couldn't. Harris was the mastermind behind King Vaughn's whole secret service. He'd went up against Jargono, Judge Mathew, and been tested in many ways he never spoke about, but *never* was his most precious love on the line like it was now. Dania and Harris were holy, true, and his wife fully supported their son and his friends' mission and her husband's willingness to offer him up, but if Daniel died, or worse. . . There were no words to describe what followed for them because though they knew the promise of a life hereafter, that didn't lessen the love that was supposed to be lived for *this* one. Moreover, Jesus said in *that* day, really in the End of Days, the love of many should wax *cold* and *no one* wanted that. Plus, our fates are never known till *that* day, the Day of Judgment.

Harris looked into his King's piercing eyes. It was *Harris* who first began to chant, Long Live King Vaughn back in the deep forest up North where they were trying to escape from Jargono. Because no one had *ever* sacrificed all that they had for him and his people to have even just a mere *chance* at life, but Vaughn and Stephanie did *exactly* that. Harris wiped the wetness from his eyes and put his hand to his heart, and said, "Long Live King Vaughn and Queen Stephanie." And he held his level stare into Vaughn's eyes, then said, "*That's* what Dania and I think about sending the children into enemy land."

Vaughn took in a deep breath then let it out slowly. "I meant, what's your *professional* opinion!"

Without blinking or flinching, Harris said, "From what you described, and the tabs I've been keeping on them, myself, no one has *ever* been prepared better than them. And though young, I'd put them up against any seasoned man!"

Vaughn narrowed his eyes into his, "Harris, they don't know *anything* like seasoned men. You *know* that."

"They know *better!*" Vaughn's eyebrow went up, and Harris responded. "You were *sixteen* when you saved us all," and Vaughn was about to tell Harris that Daniel is only *fourteen*, but Harris knew it and cut Vaughn off, saying, "but Stephanie was *fifteen* when she went up against Jargono when he was evil. *And* you went up against him. And you both won against a man like no other. Because you put God *first!* My son and his friends are of the same mind and heart."

Stephanie, sitting next to Vaughn at the side of their table leaned forward toward Harris, her rich brown eyes softening even further. "What's troubling you, my friend? You didn't come here to discuss what you always do at home when we visit, nor even about your son and the other children."

Harris looked down at his folded hands, again, and he seemed to pray for a bit. Then he looked up and caught both their eyes. "Our ambassadors have been recalled."

Vaughn said, "Which ones and why?"

"All of them. Two supposed reasons. One, because we are now the *United* States again. And Two, because there were also elections all over the world and the new rulers have banished them."

Stephanie's look sharpened, and said, "What's the *real* reason?"

Harris said, "Each new ruler of each country had a different name but each one is the *same* man! Our enemy! The Anti-Christ."

Vaughn leaned forward and sneered. "How the *hell* did he pull *that* off and *without* us knowing?"

Haris sighed. "It's my fault. I didn't pay as much attention *out there* as *in here*. But what they did was control very closely what went on in the capitals where our ambassadors lived and worked. The other countries aren't like ours. They're closed and tightly ruled ever since the plague changed *everything*. As far as being the same man, these countries' people don't pay that close attention to what happens in the next city block, let alone in a whole different country. And the rulers probably, no, *definitely* knew but were probably bought off and told that *all* the countries would be brought together into one *great* country to rival us. And that's probably what the Anti-Christ is telling them all right now."

Vaughn sighed. "What's he telling *our* people that we don't know but you do?"

Harris sighed even deeper than Vaughn. "To the Northerners, he's telling them that the old conservatives here are dying off and there's not enough of us left to keep them from their *glory*, from what his rule promises. So they're quite emboldened. To the Southerners he's telling them two different things. To the old fashioned Christians, he's encouraging them to keep doing what they've always done. He knows that's totally ineffective now. To the younger Christians, he's telling them it's a new age and they need to adapt. Both are told to keep loving their enemies, but to the old Christians that means to pray for them, treat them well, bless them, but *don't* confront them or make them feel *uncomfortable* because that's not kind. To the younger ones, it means to *accept* their enemy's perversions, just love them for who they are."

Stephanie said, "We've been so busy trying to protect everyone, we had *no* idea it was like *this*. For *us,* we still remember the feelings, the unity we all had together when we all fought the demons together. And the few times I popped in on other people, *that* was the feeling they shared with me. But I guess that makes sense that I would call that to their heart and mind at the time. I just assumed it was still the *predominant* feeling throughout their lives."

Harris said, "Well, if we can't *protect* them, then what's the point of knowing? Our holy people are constantly on the ground challenging all this, but it's uphill for sure, always has been. But also, we're no longer adding many new holy people at all. Few requests to be baptized now. And most who go under the water now, do *not* receive the Holy Ghost right away. They're waiting, seeking further how to actually do it. And since we've had peace for a while, the general people aren't galvanized like they were when they were fighting to just stay alive. You've made everything comfortable again."

When Harris saw them both hang their heads, he emphasized, "Look, don't beat yourselves up. You two gave great speeches *many* times, but speeches are like movies or ball games that people watch and enjoy and then move on. *But* regardless of all that, the South will vote for you *without question*. Frankly, they love you two. And *that* means they'll support you when we split from the North again."

Vaughn and Stephanie sighed deeply, their heads swimming in so many directions. Harris said, "I'm sorry. I know you two have too much to deal with. I didn't want to add to that when I knew nothing could be done more than what we holy people are already doing. But you *are* our rulers and you have a right to know *everything*." And Harris stood up and bowed to them both and showed himself out because he could see their grief and knew they needed to be alone.

Stephanie dried her eyes and turned her chair to face Vaughn. "I need to *really* do something I haven't done in a long time." Vaughn's eyebrows went up, and Stephanie said, "I used to visit many different places and people, *really* taking time watching from the Corridor. It seems I've lost touch with *everything* by being too quick and I *need* to get it back, to actually *feel* what's *really* going on."

But Vaughn studied on what his wife said, looking into the beyond, then said, "I remember you telling me what you *used* to do back up North. I was so moved by it! Never told you how much, but it's *deeply*. Ultimately, it's what brought us our wonderful daughter! You know, I think I'll try what you're going to do, too!"

So Stephanie smiled with deep appreciation then stood up, ran her hands down the length of her body and she was garbed in her holy dress, her hair now in her three traditional Appendaho braids. Surprisingly, Vaughn materialized his black robe and they both vanished.

# CHAPTER 21

# Reality That's hard to Swallow

*All the Alpha gathered together in the Father's deepest, darkest Ethereal room and it was blacker than they had ever not seen before. At least it felt blacker. But this meeting hadn't been called by the Father, but by the Anti-Christ in their Father's name. There was much speculation and clamor in the room when the Anti-Christ appeared in their very midst glowing a kind of dingy gold. Many of the Alpha had an instantaneous reaction to the glow and began to attack whereupon the Anti-Christ changed into a seven-headed dragon and each head consumed a demon! When the rest saw that, they all settled down.*

*"Now that we all share a common understanding, we need to get down to business."*

*Business? Everyone thought.* No one ever talks about business. We're Alpha. We have our own business. *They all thought.*

*"And that's why you all have been* failing *miserably. I'm here to change that." Forms suddenly appeared in every Alpha arm! "I expect you all to fill out the forms. When you finish*

*they will disintegrate and send the information to me. Please understand that your orbs must backup all claims you make. Falsifying information will not be tolerated." One of his dragon heads belched then smiled.*

*One of the lesser known Alpha but still of respectable size raised his tail and the Anti-Christ called on him. "How shall we address you? Also, these forms have considerable length and are asking for us to account for every single tenth of a second for each entire Ethereal night. To fill these out properly means we'll have to cease all other operations. That would effectively remove us from our Earthly duties for quite some time."*

*The Anti-Christ turned back into his human form, and said, "Alpha King of the Earth is what I AM." And when he said that the whole Ethereal shook, not just the Father's room. All the Alpha were dismayed and began to wonder if their experiment had gone* awry. We should all just attack him at once and be done with all this. *Was the common thought but none spoke it out loud.*

*The Anti-Christ smiled at them all, then said, "I expect the forms to be completed within three Ethereal nights. The Earth certainly won't miss you in that duration, but you can have your underlings take your places until the forms are finished. I will be meeting with all underlings next, to encourage and offer my assistance during this troublesome time in the Ethereal."*

Troublesome time? *Was the common thought.* These are our underlings. He has no *right* to interfere with our plans for them.

*The Anti-Christ smiled deeply again, then said, "I'm forming the Underling Union! From now on, underlings shall have Underling Rights. We're tired of always living in fear of you!"*

*Great Eyes bulged. The level of anger became palpable. What is the Father thinking? Many wondered.*

*The Anti-Christ said, "You all are dismissed. Please hurry, as the Underlings are waiting at the door!*

*Though none of them dared raise objection, they couldn't help but feel that they were being replaced. A sense of dying tradition permeated all Alpha. Though they weren't from the original tribe, they had still been around for what seemed like Alpha Eternity. Yet, now, they all felt doomed, worthless. They even lost their appetite to consume each other.*

*Then one of the Alpha asked, "Has anyone seen HrorrarrAggrang?*

Vaughn peered down from the Corridor wondering exactly why the Holy Ghost led him *here*. He thought for a moment and his robe vanished, replaced by common browns. When no one was looking, he popped right onto a barstool right in the middle of the long bar counter. The lighting was typical, the aroma's expected, and the inhabitants were all in various stages of sobriety, and *no one* even noticed Vaughn just popped in out of nowhere. That was a good summation of the understanding level of the men and women here, but perhaps even everywhere.

A moment later, a tall but bulky man with black hair slammed his hand down on the counter and raised his voice at the man next to him, saying, "*Shit!* What's it matter? King or President. They still rule and we do our best to walk around it, just like any other obstacle, like right here, us all getn' *drunk* in what *used* to be the United for *Christ.* But now it's in the open that *used to be* underground."And he bellowed out a laugh, then said, "Because our *Queen* saw somethin' *noble* in us. *Shit!* You feel noble?"

And Vaughn said, "I do!"

Whereupon the hulking man spun around on his stool to see some stranger *inserting* himself into a *private* conversation. "Hey, who asked *your* opinion?" And he did a quick size up of Vaughn, saw he was much smaller than him, and added, *"Punk."*

Vaughn folded his hands on his lap and looked down, then back up at them and the man laughed, thinking that was a *sissy* expression. "That's right. You *better* look down, *boy!"*

This man aged about thirty and Vaughn barely looked twenty, which was his real age. Vaughn tugged at his dark brown, almost black beard then lifted his eyes and stared into the man's depths. *This* was one of *many* citizens he fought for and would die for. In a level tone, Vaughn asked, "How *exactly* does feeling noble feel?"

The man's eyes crossed a bit. He backed his head away, and said, *"Hell,* how should *I* know?"

Vaughn said, "Well, because if you *don't know,* then maybe you actually *do* have some value in your sorry state that you don't even know about, but our Queen sees it, and loves you for it."

A blond man, also about thirty, on the other side of the black-haired man leaned on the counter to view Vaughn from around his friend, and said, "Actually, I been knowin' his sorry ass long time. Durin' the demon war we jus' had, he fuckin' saw these little kids rounded up by those gargoyle. They were a scarin' the kids up before they were gonna eat 'em and the kids knew it. *Hell,* just *one* o' those beasts, it took *ten* of us to kill and we were only five left. But *this dumb son-of-a-bitch,* he looks at us, and says, 'To *Hell* with *all* you!' and he whips out these two blessed sabers he loved, and. . ."

The man interrupted, "Well, they *say* they were blessed by some fancy oil or somethin' but *Hell,* all I cared 'bout is was they sharp."

The blond man continued, "Anyway, he yells this crazy battle cry and runs right into the midst of 'em. There were *three* gargoyles, and those damn suckers were *fast,* too. And he starts swinging those swords. We had blessed knives and axes. Don't know how to use swords. But *Hell,* if he was gonna die, then we would, *too. "*

The black-haired man was clearly remembering it all, and he looked down for a moment, then into Vaughn's eyes, and said, "I ain't never been much. Not bright, not steady 'nuff for a good woman, but, well, *Hell,* I don't know. Somethin' just came over me when I saw those little boys and girls cryin.' I can *still* see their faces. and, well, I don't know. *They* had value I didn't. So I figured I'd do my best. That's all."

The blond man said, "No, that's *not* all. *None* o' those kids had parents any more. Gargoyles killed 'em *all* right in front of their children. And after we *actually* killed those demons, well, Joe, here, says, 'We gotta find someone care for 'em. But no one around there was able, so *he* takes 'em all with him and demands each of us give up part of our rations to feed 'em. Know where those kids are now?" Vaughn shook his head, and the man says, "At *his* home! He been taken care of 'em *all* since then. Works himself practically to death with all these odd jobs he takes."

Vaugh leveled his eyes into the man, saying, "We're gonna need many more *men* just like *you.*"

And the man laughed, and said, "I was jus' 'bout to *drop* your sorry *smug* ass. Now you're sayin' this *shit.*"

Vaughn held out his hand and his staff appeared in it, then he stood up and his black robe garbed him. Both men practically fell off their seats, but before they could say anything, Vaughn took his staff and tapped the head of it on each of the men's shoulders. The burly black-haired man started to swoon and would have fallen off the barstool had his friend not steadied him, but even he felt an indescribable power that made him lightheaded.

Vaughn said, "It *is* blessed oil. And this *is* the Staff of Almighty God. The Staff of Life and Judgment. The blessings you have now received are *real.* You'll see in time." Vaughn held out his hand and a card appeared in it. "This is how to reach James, my chief advisor. Tell him what just happened and that *I* said for you to tell *him* to put you to good use."

The man looked down and shook his head. "I can't leave those kids. I'm all they got."

Vaughn said, "Not anymore." And Vaughn concentrated and rubbed his ring and Lynnara, her brown curls bouncing but still in her little ranger uniform she loved so much, appeared right in the bar! This was the *second* time she'd been in a bar. The first was when her third and bestest Mommy *ever* took her to one and they accidently popped in on a couple having sex.

Lynnara looked around, frowned, then into her Daddy's eyes, and *Vaughn* said, "Understand!"

And Lynnara's eyes widened, both because her *Daddy* had mastered *her* skill at giving understanding, but *also* the *meaning* Vaughn sent her was profound. She turned to the men and they both, now, went down on one knee recognizing her. *Everyone* knew Princess Lynnara because of how she stood up against the fake Jargono. The TV's broadcast it over and over for days. And they bowed their heads, saying. "It's an honor to be in your presence, lil' Princess."

Lynnara smiled then looked at her Daddy and he nodded. Lynnara said, "You don't have to bow to me. Take me to your home and I'll help you. You'll see. Then do what my Daddy said to do. Do you like castles?"

The men sat back on their stools and looked deeply at Vaughn now. The black-haired man said, "Beggin' your pardon, Sire. Really, I don't deserve your kindness. Forgive me bein' rude like that. I didn't know. Don't know why, but I jus' didn't"

Vaughn said, "Because I didn't want you to know. I wanted to see the *real* man the Lord Jesus sent me to see. Go in Peace." And Vaughn vanished.

‿

Stephanie, dressed in her holy dress and her three traditional Appendaho braids, peered from the Corridor at a bunch of children trying to play in a dilapidated playground. The pavement was all cracked, filled with holes and upended pieces, and it very much reminded her of the one at her old school but this one was only about a hundred miles south of the southern town where they had settled. She wondered, *I thought we had fixed everything up. Why is this still so run down?* Apparently, restoration wasn't nearly as complete as she had assumed.

One of the little girls, about five-years-old with blue eyes and blond pigtails at the sides of her head said, "I am Lady *Stephanie* and I *command* you to be gone."

A girl, about seven, in flowing black hair cringed, rolled on the broken up playground, and screamed, "I'm gone, I'm *gone.*"

Then a little boy, about eight, with short black hair grabbed the blond girl, and said, "I'm going to *destroy* you." And he wrapped his arms around her.

But then a red-haired boy about six-years-old, and carrying a stick as tall as him, said, "*I* have the Staff from God. I'll save you Stephanie!"

Stephanie began wiping tears from her eyes. She had *no* idea they were thought about like *this.* When the kids finished their game, the oldest child pulled out some trading cards from his pants pocket for the others to look at, and when Stephanie, from within the Corridor came close, she saw that some of the cards had pictures of *her* on them! And there was Vaughn and others she didn't know. The cards had writing and numbers on them, But the thing that struck Stephanie the most was how the children so seriously took to examining the cards.

Other kids pulled cards from their pockets, and then they sat down on the playground to play the card game. The blond girl, though, had no cards and just watched, her sadness obvious. Stephanie looked more closely at her and saw that her dress was a dingy pink and ragged. The red-haired boy suddenly looked up at her, then looked through his deck, then gave the blond girl a card and she immediately brightened. "Lady *Stephanie,*" she said, looking up at the boy.

For a moment, Stephanie thought the little girl could see her in the Corridor, but when she looked closer, Stephanie saw that the child referred to the card she was given. The child held it to her heart like it was a precious treasure.

An older group of boys came up ranging from eleven to thirteen, and a black haired skinny kid with typical blue jeans and obviously the gang leader, grabbed the cards from one of the younger kids. When the others in the gang saw *that* they did the same thing to the other kids. But the little blond girl, clutching her Stephanie card to her chest was defiant. "It's *mine.* He *gave it to me.*"

But the leader came over and a brown-haired boy about eleven grabbed her from behind. The leader grabbed the child's hand, pried it open and took the card then ripped it up in front of the little girl.

Stephanie looked closely to see if there were any gray arms reaching into their heads but surprisingly, there were *none!* These kids were just being evil all on their own! But in the next instant, the gang left and the other kids, some crying, some cursing, went into the school. Except for the little blond girl who still sat on the playground bawling her heart out. She had loved her Stephanie card.

Stephanie looked around and saw that all the kids were gone to class, and she materialized sitting in front of the girl, and said, "Are you going in to school?"

The child looked up into Stephanie's rich brown eyes and became transfixed. Then she looked at Stephanie's holy dress and her eyes became wide. The next thing Stephine knew, the little girl had sprung onto her and climbed into her lap, hugging Stephanie!

Stephanie wrapped her arms around her and began rocking. *This so reminds me of me a long time ago.* She kissed the girl on top of her head, and Stephanie said, "You know who I am?"

The little girl nodded while her head was buried in Stephanie's bosom, and the child said, "I told them you were *real,* but *they* said you weren't. That it was just a game. But others said you were kinda real, that you had been on TV. So others said you were just a *story* on TV. But *I* said, NO, you're *real.* They took my card." And she started crying again.

Stephanie lifted the child out of her lap and stood her up and with her thumbs wiped the child's tears away. "What's your name?" Stephanie asked.

With her little blue eyes riveted into Stephanie, she said, "Beth."

"Well Beth, those mean kids don't care about your tears. They actually *enjoy* them. So don't cry about it anymore. OK?"

The little girl nodded and then a bell rang from the school. Then she said, "I be in trouble now. 'Cause I'm *late.*"

Stephanie stood up and took the little girl's hand and they began walking to the school, and Stephanie said, "Wanna do show and tell?"

The little girl looked up at Stephanie, and said, "I got nothin' and I dunno if teacher let us."

Stephanie winked at the child. "You got *me!* And I'm *Queen!*"

The child's eyes grew wide, then she broke from Stephanie leaving her behind to run into the school, shouting, "I got Lady Stephanie. I *got* Lady *Stephanie. Show and tell.*"

But at the door a woman in gray hair and typical brown peasant dress grabbed her by the arm, saying, "You're *late.* Go *home!*"

The little child stood defiantly, saying, "I *got* Lady *Stephanie.*"

The woman sneered at her, saying, "You don't even have a proper dress. *Get out!* Your parents will be notified."

Clearly, this was a woman who had been in the school system a *long* time and either she never received nor cared for Lady Stephanie's educational reforms that *clearly* described how children should and should *not* be treated. The little girl's dress transformed into a miniature of Stephanie's holy dress right before the old lady's eyes and she let go of the child and practically collapsed, breathing hard.

But when Queen Stephanie instantly appeared next to the girl and took the child's hand, The old lady *did* collapse to the floor. Stephanie said, "I'm here for Show and Tell for *this* child. I'm her excuse for being late. Is that good enough?"

The old lady managed to stand and bow, saying, "Yes, my Lady. Her class is. . ."

"*I'll* show her!" And the little girl tugged Stephanie's hand, leading her to class.

Stephanie opened the door and went in first then the child who *immediately* announced, "I got *Queen* Stephanie for show and tell!"

All the children's eyes went wide, thinking, *Is it true? Is she really?*

The teacher, in a standard brown peasant dress, brown hair in a pony tail, about thirty-years-old, said, "Oh, ahhh, we're not having show and tell right now!" There was a touch of defiance in her tone. All the children looked from the teacher to their Queen and back again.

Stephanie smiled, read the teacher's mind and heart, then said, "Why did you move to the South if you hate Christians so much?"

The woman turned red and she no longer looked into Stephanie's eyes. She struggled to try and hide her thoughts because someone told her Stephanie could read minds. She never believed that but *now?*

A blond boy, dressed in brown shirt and pants, about twelve in this mixed age class, called out, "She told us not to tell *anyone* or we'd be punished." And other kids chimed in, saying, "She did. She *did.* We couldn't even tell our *parents.*"

Stephanie narrowed her eyes at the teacher, saying, "That's *not at all* resembling the educational directives I *ordered.*"

The teacher suddenly grew bold, saying, "Your time here is over! You're just a *formality!*"

Another student called out, a girl of eleven in red wavey hair like Stephanie but actually wearing a long pink dress. "This *bitch* and all her *friends* all tell us the *same* thing and that we'd better listen to *them* or they'll even have our *parents* arrested!"

The floor began to rumble a bit as Stephanie's aura turned from gold to black. This woman was *definitely* hiding something that escaped Stephanie's first mind reading. She turned to the students, and said, "Hello class."

And they all chanted, "Queen Stephanie, *Queen* Stephanie!" And they all got down on one knee and bowed their heads.

"What *else* should I know, children?"

A blond girl, about twelve, said, "We used to have *great* Christian teachers but they all left."

"That's *very* odd," Stephanie said, looking back at the still defiant teacher who suddenly decided to take back her class and came beside Stephanie, saying, "Show and Tell is *over!* Get back to *work!*"

Stephanie said, "You fired!"

But the teacher laughed. "You *can't* fire me. *NO* authority any more per your *constitution* which you all have *already* said you would observe."

That much was true, but Stephanie did something a little bit unqueenly. She hauled off and hit the woman with her fist right in the jaw and down she went! The class was in an uproar, cheering, immediately acting out what they just saw, and saying things like, "Wow!" "Hit her again!" "Bitch *deserves it,* "

The teacher was shocked but Stephanie said, "What are ya gonna do, *arrest me?*"

The teacher was so enraged, she lost control, and sneering deeply, she said, "We've been teaching your *precious* little children for two years now. You have *no* country. No *home* anymore *anywhere!*"

Stephanie shook her head because she saw truth in what she said. *How could we have been so* very *blind?* "You've taken over the schools without us knowing."

She began to laugh. "We're all looking forward to seeing you hung up on that cross, except *this time* it'll be *real.*" And she stood up defiantly and smoothed her dress.

Stephanie narrowed her eyes at her, and said, "It was *real* back then!" Then Stephanie reached out her hand and the woman was pulled by the *faithwalker* to stand right in front of her and Stephanie put her hand to her head, saying, "Reveal!"

Then *all* of the woman's thoughts and feelings flooded into Lady Stephanie. Like a reflex, the woman was hurled away soaring *over* the class and went through a glass window, and disappeared when she fell. All the children's mouths dropped open. Then Stephanie turned towards the class. "I need help. Who is willing?" And they all began to chant, "Queen Stephanie, *Queen* Stephanie."

"You kids know each other and kids from other schools, too. By order of the Queen who is *yet,* still in power, All schools are now *closed.* Closed until we do a full review of *all* educational staff. Parents are directed to inform their local congressman of *all* their complaints after you kids tell them *all* that's been happening. I'm putting an *end* to this right *now!*"

The kids pulled out their phones and began calling people, and Stephanie knew it wouldn't take long before the whole country knew. This was better than any announcement on the TV. Stephanie walked away from the class to a corner and took her phone and called Harris and told him what happened.

"Lady Stephanie. I had *no* idea, I'm so sorry. No one *ever* thought to actually *check* on the *children*. We just assumed everything would be in good hands. Now I see the enemy has targeted them both deeply *and* broadly and *certainly* outmaneuvered us."

"Harris… Vaughn told me you're pretty confident you have all their spies marked out. Are you *still* sure?"

"Yes, Lady Stephanie."

"Vaughn also said you're able in one single day to take them *all* out. Are you still *sure* of that?"

"Yes."

"Then do it *now!* We're in a lot worse shape than I ever dreamed of."

"Done, Lady Stephanie. I'll also let the military know to be ready."

Stephanie turned to the class. "I *really* need all your help. The *enemy* has taken over our schools and I need *you* to help me *stop it.* Organize yourselves. Make a list of all the schools in your area and confirm with other kids that they are *closed.* Pass this along to kids in other districts, and they pass it on from there until every single school is *closed* in the *whole* country!"

Then Stephanie watched the kids spring into action and relished in how important they all now felt. After just a bit, all their phones beeped, and Stephanie said, "Every one of you now has a recording of all that happened here! Courtesy of James, my wonderful advisor, and Carla and Marta, my *sisters!*" For Stephanie had telepathically told Marta to make the recording with her orb, who then told Carla through her orb who was very receptive, who then immediately told James the computer system had received Marta's recording! Then James sent it out to all the kids! That fast!

All the kids were *shocked.* They never knew Queen Stephanie had *sisters.* Then they checked their phones, and were saying, "Wow!" Then they sent the video to all their contacts.

Stephanie turned to Beth, who had gone up to a child who had a phone to see the video, and Stephanie said, "Look at all the *good* we just did *together.*" And the child ran into Stephanie with a big hug. And when the other kids saw *that,* they all ran forward to hug her, too. Stephanie was in utter tears because she felt the sweet preciousness of all the children at the same time feeling what great harm they had been enduring. *Lord Jesus. Help us. Give us a way to* win.

༎

Vaughn sped through the Corridor until stopping at the next general area the Holy Ghost led him to, but this time it was way back up North. When he realized it, he sighed, but knowledge instantly flooded him that he had achieved better than he'd expected. *Eighty-seven percent of all my supporters have migrated South.* Still, the thirteen percent gnawed in his stomach. And the rest of the people up North, well, they weren't exactly likable anymore. The question before Vaughn now was, when he popped out of the Corridor when he arrived at his exact destination, which kind of person would he find?

Dressed in his black robe and calling his Staff to hand again, he leaned on it, wondering about the thirteen percent, until the Staff, itself, suddenly burst in energy and surrounded him with an energy field. Moments later, gold and black energy blasts pommeled the barrier and it lit up in various beautiful colors but Vaughn was at peace within and leaned on his Staff, waiting.

It took a while because the Anti-Christ wanted Vaughn to speak first but seeing that wasn't going to happen, he appeared before him in his usual tan tunic and brown shirt and pants looking very much like Jargono even down to the way he wore his straight black hair combed to his left side.

Vaughn lifted his dark brown, almost black eyes to peer into his but was surprised to see that his eyes were actually like Vaughn's. Vaughn said, "Hmm," and nodded in understanding.

But that wasn't really directed at the fake Jargono clone and the Anti-Christ knew it. Vaughn turned away and began to seek where *exactly* he should go next, but, without intending to, the Anti-Christ said, "Without that staff, you'd be dead."

Without turning around to directly face him, Vaughn said, "Without *my* genes, you wouldn't have *my* eyes. The Lord *Jesus* gave me *His* Staff because He *is* Wisdom. He gave me His Holy Ghost because He *is* Love. But I *know* what you are."

"Then you *know* I'm the one that will put you to death. Unless we could meet somewhere in the middle."

Vaughn nodded again but *still* didn't turn to face him. "Good and evil are mutually exclusive. *Opposites.* There can be no compromise."

The clone smiled and spoke with compassion. "How's your *wife* doing? Has she gotten over losing your child, yet?"

Vaughn turned to face him. "It's written that Jesus said the Holy Ghost will teach *us* all things, even *whatsoever* Jesus has said unto us. That's a *whole lot more* than what's written down. If I were you, I'd be worrying about *all that* that you *don't* know." And Vaughn's smile was as menacing as any Alpha could be when extended over its prey but the Anti-Christ just smiled without even flinching, and said, "I have my own personal orb that surpasses even yours. It even reveals history the other orbs can't reach. I know *everything.*"

Vaughn laughed. "Like I said, the Holy Ghost teaches us *all.* And *that* is a *lot* more than what's recorded in the Bible or *even* in *any* orb! And *whatsoever* Jesus said means *everything* He has said anywhere, anytime from the beginning in *secret* or not! Compared to *that,* you know nothing! I'm no Christian because they're prescriptive. I'm *holy,* as the Lord God said to be. But even my Christians will have victory over you because they *now* hold to the *right* prescription, having purged themselves of the *poison* you had inserted into Christianity for over two-thousand years!"

The Anti-Christ laughed, saying, "You have *no* idea how I'm going to make them suffer. Their souls *can't* withstand that. And before I crush *you,* you're going to see me crush *them.* See how well you do with *that!* You *never* know until you *face it. Experience* has a way of changing *everything.*"

Vaughn nodded, and said, "You can't even win a fair election, and you think you can win over faithful souls. Pitiful."

But the Anti-Christ laughed, yet *again,* saying, "Who said anything about *fair?* It's about winning and crushing your enemies." And he vanished.

Vaughn sighed then disappeared and reappeared in the Corridor where the Lord bid him next. He didn't want to simply travel in the Corridor where the Anti-Christ could follow him so he chose to pop from one Corridor place to another. But then he wondered, *How did I do that? Because when we pop from one place on Earth to another, we use the Corridor!* It was a mystery and he made note to discuss it with Stephanie to see what she thought. But then Vaughn wondered how the Anti-Christ found him in the Corridor in the first place.

Vaughn looked down upon a farm town that looked almost deserted. Once upon a time, judging from the population sign at the main street heading in, this town had seven-thousand people. Now, maybe only hundreds. Vaughn knew part of that was due to his clandestine encouragement to leave. But part of it was due to younger folks leaving smaller towns for larger ones. But part of it was *also* due to the increasingly hostile culture up North against common decency.

Vaughn materialized in front of a café without his robe and staff, dressed in common browns, and he eased himself in. A young lady with smiling bright blue eyes and long braided red hair with a white apron over a long brown peasant dress met him, and said, "I'm Jenny. Would you like the counter or booth? I prefer the booth, myself, but that's when I'm *with* someone. Do you have someone coming?"

Vaughn smiled at her natural sweetness that simply bubbled over and brought instant delight, and said, "Counter would be just fine, dear."

"Oh, well, I'm sorry you're alone. You shouldn't be!" her warm, sincere expression wasn't hitting on Vaughn, but was simply honest.

Vaughn held up his left hand and she saw his very unusual wedding ring. "Wow! That's such a *beautiful* ring. I've never seen *anything* like it."

A *very* old man in very faded browns came out a door behind the counter, and said in a cracking but kind voice, "Jenny, you fixn' starve that young man to *death,* or you gonna take his order? Sorry young man, she's a talker, but she *means* well."

Vaughn smiled deeply, his heart pounding inside for these dear sweet souls. "I enjoy your grand-daughter's presence."

And he laughed as hard as a really old man could laugh, then said, "Sonny, *that's* my *great*-grandaughter!"

Vaughn's eyebrows went up. "May I ask, how old *are* ya?"

Jenny smiled, and said, "Pa Pa is hundred-ten. Be hundred-'levin next month."

And the old man said, "Live and God spare, but I hope to leave here soon."

Jenny frowned, and scolded him. "Pa Pa don't *speak* that way."

The old man came around the counter and sat down next to Vaughn, sayin' "You mind? I can't stand too long since I hit hundred and *nine.*" Vaughn smiled with appreciation and shook his head, and the old man said, "I'm chainin' her to this dyin' town. I don't want that. She shoulda lef' last year and moved South with the rest of 'em. But she won't leave me and I jus' can't travel."

Vaughn's heart pained him but just then three, young, seedy characters dressed in dingy browns pushed the door open with a clang then sat down at the counter around Vaughn and the old man. Jenny went up to the young men across the counter from her with the very same sweetness as she did to Vaughn, saying, "What can I get you gentleman?"

The one who sat next to the old man had oily black long hair, a long nose, and a cringe-worthy demeanor and grabbed her arm, smiling lustfully. "Let's start with *you.*"

And the old man, who was sitting on the swivel stool right up against that man turned dark, saying, "Now see here. . ."

But the vagabond swung around on him and pushed the old man backwards off the stool but Vaughn caught him and set him back straight. The blond man next to Vaughn poked something hard into Vaughn's side, saying "I don't care I kill you now *or* later."

Jenny yanked free then rushed to the cash register and it dinged open and she grabbed what she could and threw it on the counter. "Take it and *go.*"

Sadly, it wasn't much past fifteen dol and they all laughed. The blond man with the gun still shoved in Vaughn's side, said, "Hell, honey, you're gonna have to make up the difference."

The old man said, "Why you ruin your lives like this? Keepers won't stop till they track you down."

They all laughed again, and the blond guy said, "Haven't been *keepers* in any of these towns for a year. That why we make out so *good.* Don't worry, Honey. I'll be *second.*"

Vaughn, still just facing across the counter looking at Jenny, said, "You know, the King and Queen, when they hear about this, and they *will,* they'll hunt you down *themselves.* "

But they all started laughing. The third young man who had set down next to the black-haired guy, a fat boy with pock marks on his cheeks and short dirty brown hair, said, "They don' know nothin' what goes on. We been at this a while. And you know *what?*" Vaughn shook his head, and the young hooligan boisterously said, "'When the next king or whatever comes, they won't know nothin' neither 'cause we not important. So no value to them, they won't pay us any mind at all."

The black haired gangster leapt over the counter and grabbed Jenny around the waist and began trying to pull her to the back but *she* grabbed a pan off the griddle and slammed his head and down he went, out cold! Then she whirled back around with a roundhouse swing and leveled young Mr. pock mark across the counter and *he* slumped to the floor.

Then she turned to the man with the gun, saying sweetly, "Now aren't you all just rays of sunshine!" And Vaughn burst out laughing at her expression.

The laughing bothered the blond boy more than her frying pan and he shoved the gun harder into Vaughn's side, saying, "Shut it."

But he shouldn't have taken his eyes off of Jenny because she was already two for two. The cast iron frying pan zinged right past Vaughn's head, the handle and pan rotating in the *perfect* spin and hit the man across the side of his head and knocked him off the stool. His gun *wasn't* a gun but just a piece of pipe and Vaughn turned on his stool gazing down at him. But Jenny had grabbed a butcher knife from a holder, swung herself over the counter and had it at the man's throat, then said very sweetly, "You think you're the *first* idiots to come in here? *That's* my *Pa Pa* and *that's* my customer. How *dare* you come in here like this." And when he looked away from her, she pressed the knife harder at his throat, saying, now with anger, "Don't be *rude. Look at me when I'm talkin' to you!"*

The young man did as ordered, and Jenny continued, "Yea. No keepers. I been knowin' that. Let me tell you, the *garbage* still gets collected 'round here. And you won't be the first that I shove in my dumpster out back! And you know what?" He shook his head, his eyes widening with the fear she might actually cut his throat. "I've put near *ten* young men just like *you* out there and the garbage man, well, he sweet on me, and he dumps you all turds with no questions asked!"

And as he began to beg for his life, she did, in fact, cut his throat! Then she went over to the fat boy and cut his, too! And *then* she swung herself over the counter, grabbed a pitcher of ice water and tossed it in the face of the oily guy and he sputtered awake.

Jenny says sweetly to *him,* "Your partners in crime are *dead,* and I wanted you awake to see it comin'!" And she lunged at him and drove the blade through his heart!

Vaughn's eyes were wide. This *wasn't* at *all* what he'd expected and Jenny and the old man knew it. The old man said, "My children, and *their* children were all killed in the demon war. *That* girl is the only one who survived and she *swore* come Hell or high water, she was gonna protect me,"

Jenny came over very sweet and apologetic, saying, "I'm so sorry for all this. Let me get you whatever you want. No charge. But just give me a moment to *take out the trash.* And she grabbed the man she stabbed in the heart and began to drag him out the door behind the counter.

Vaughn held out his hand and his Staff appeared along with his robe. The old man began nodding, saying, "I thought there was somethin' really special 'bout you."

Vaughn said, "Allow me." And he went and touched the foot of his staff to each corpse and they and the blood all turned to dust. Then Vaughn made the Staff disappear, and said, "Gotta broom? I'll help!"

Jenny was in awe, "Are you. . ."

"King Vaughn, at your service Miss Jenny, ahh, but I see you didn't need my help. And no, I'll pay you for the meal. A hamburger medium and fries and sweet tea."

Jenny bowed and began sweeping up the dust but Vaughn came around the counter and took the broom. I'm on a tight schedule. How about you cook and I sweep. Dust pan?"

Jenny was flummoxed. "What kind of King *are* you. No disrespect intended, King Vaughn." And she curtsied.

"None taken, Sweetheart. And well, I'm just me." And while Jenny began preparing the food and Vaughn swept up the trash, Vaughn said, "Have you ever considered migrating South?"

Jenny shook her head. "Pa Pa can't manage the travel. Besides, this store was created by him! I can't see abandoning it."

Vaughn said, "What if *I* move you and your Pa Pa *and* the store?"

Jenny shook her head. "It's a really old building. It won't stand the move."

Vaughn sighed and leveled his eyes into hers, "*Jenny,* I'm King so I'm privy to *many* things that the people aren't. Neither you nor your Pa Pa will survive here. What's coming will be worse than *anything* the world has *ever* seen,"

Jenny began to tear up and she turned away and wiped her eyes, then said, "Oh darn it. You've made me cry."

Vaughn came to stand by her and took her shoulders and twisted her to face him. "I'm King. And I'm more worried about a different kind of tears." Vaughn called his Staff again, smiled at Jenny, then said, "By order of the King, I hereby order you, Pa Pa, and this whole store to move *South!*" And at his last word, Vaughn slammed his Staff down on the floor and it was as if the whole place and everyone in it turned transparent for a moment. Brief nausea swept through the young lady and old man. And Vaughn just smiled broadly.

Jenny smiled sweetly, saying, "Well, I guess that settles *that.*" But she was joking as Vaughn went and sat on the counter stool to eat a delicious hamburger while Jenny busied herself with tasks. Then she said, "I'll be right back, I have some stuff in the back to toss away. A bit later she came back but her eyes were wide as could be. "I. . . you. . . You weren't kidding!"

Vaughn shook his head, "Nope. You're now in the town where I and my people settled when we first came to the South. You'll find the people here are quite to your liking. And I always imagined a store *just like yours* filling this abandoned lot." Vaughn rubbed his ring and seconds later Mandy appeared in full Ranger uniform with her bow drawn. As she looked around for the threat, Vaughn said, "This is Jenny and Pa Pa, and *he's* a hundred-levin. Jenny wants you to train her as a Ranger and I approve. She already has considerable kill skills with a frying pan!" And Vaughn looked deeply into Mandy, and said, "Understand!"

Mandy teetered a bit, then said, "Wow! So you've mastered your *daughter's* skill." The tease in her smile did not go unnoticed.

Vaughn asked, "How did our other *little* matter go?"

Mandy said, "Smoothly, but my heart almost broke sending them in there."

Vaughn nodded then nodded toward Jenny and Mandy offered her hand. "Welcome *home!*" When Mandy and Jenny's eyes met, there was instant connection, and when Vaughn saw it, he vanished.

☙

Stephanie had visited quite a few places all through the day and night but just had to squeeze in one more. But she didn't like that she was being led back up North. North didn't interest her anymore. But even more than that, she was led to her very own little town where she'd grown up. Stephanie *really* didn't want to be *here.*

Memories of Gary and his gang and of her own slovenliness ran through her heart and mind with the expected shooting pains in her chest. *Why Lord Jesus am I* here? But just then a girl, maybe eleven, in long blond hair, bare feet, only in her underclothes, came running through the darkness down the main street. Her fear palpable. Behind her was a group of boys and girls obviously chasing her. A couple of the boys seemed around thirteen and Stephanie grew dark.

One of the girls, a brunette, said to the obvious leader as they ran, "You sure we can chase her down *main street?*"

The leader, a skinny thirteen-year-old with black hair said, "Sure. Why not? No keepers anymore."

The brunette, about eleven, too, said, "I've always *hated* her. That's why I always try to *trip* her when we play soccer."

Stephanie followed them all from the Corridor. There was something familiar about *both* girls. And then the blond went down hard and fell on her face and knee and the pack of dogs surrounded her and began kicking her!

Stephanie materialized right beside the fallen girl and covered her with her body and threw up a forcefield. Then, still covering the blond girl, she looked up at the brown-haired girl, saying, "What is *wrong* with you? Then she caught the other four kids in her glare, saying, "With *all* of you?" She expected to see gray arms reaching into their heads but saw none! This was just their *own* evil, now!

The brown-haired girl mocked back, "What is wrong with you, what is *wrong* with *you?*"

Stephanie stood up and began to glow golden and they all recognized her. The leader said, "Oh *shit,*" and began to run, but Stephanie frowned and he tripped and faceplanted. Stephanie said, "I want you *all* to explain this."

But the brown-haired girl looked closer at Stephanie. "I can't believe it. It's *true!*"

"*What's* true?"

"You're, *Fanie!*" And she started laughing hard. "Oh my *God!* They told me but I didn't believe them. The *slut* that became *queen.*"

Another boy, thirteen, with dirty blond hair, said, "Ain't she da one rescued that lil bitch when y'all small?"

And the brunette nodded with impudence and put her hands on her hips, saying, "OK, whacha gonna do? Burn us all up? Go ahead! Then you'll be *sure* to lose your special *election.* Gonna lose *anyway.*" Stephanie thought to herself, *The way she acts, just confirms my suspicions. Surround people with lies long enough, and that's the* only *reality they know, then they make the mistake that it's the* truth, *the* right *way to act!*

The blond who fell stood up and came to Stephanie's side and their eyes met and the world seemed to disappear. Stephanie remembered looking into this person's eyes five years ago on the playground when she had fallen when Stephanie was only fourteen. When that *bitch* brown-haired girl tripped her back then and Stephanie hadn't even realized she had healed that little girl. Stephanie put her hand to the blond girl's shoulder and the girl glowed and was instantly healed and adorned in a common brown peasant dress. And Stephanie said, "I'm Stephanie."

The girl began to sob, putting her hand to her mouth. Blood still dripped from her nose as well as her knee from wounds that no longer existed. "I'm Leah." And she went down to one knee and bowed, then said, "Ever since that day when you healed me before, I've thought of you, and *you* kept me going. And every time I saw you on the TV, I wept. And when you told us all about God, I *prayed.*"

Stephanie looked over to the gang leader and extended her hand and her *faithwalking* power drew him to her with her hand to his throat. "I asked you a question."

And her hand began to glow red-hot and the boy shouted, "She always thinks she's better than us. We just decided to prove she wasn't."

Leah stood up, saying, "By *gang-raping* me?"

Stephanie's eyes turned black and the ground shook and the gang all fell down, but the brown-haired girl was laughing! "Go ahead. LET THE WORLD KNOW, I Janie Marsh brought the *faithwalker* down!"

Stephanie calmed, and looked again for any sign of a gray arm but saw none. *What if it's not an Alpha doing this?* Stephanie readjusted her spiritual vision and her hunch was verified. A dirty golden hand hovered over the kid's head. Then she heard the Anti-Christ laugh, and his voice appeared in Stephanie's head. "You think it's *me* who controls her? I just polished her a bit." And his hand vanished from above her.

Stephanie looked inside the girl but surprisingly, the Anti-Christ told the truth. She was a little bitch in her *own* right. In similar manner, Lady Stephanie peered deeply into the others. The Holy Ghost spoke within Stephanie, saying, *He that is righteous, let them be righteous still, And he that is holy, let them be holy still, but they that are wicked, let them be wicked still! The Holy Ghost reproves the world of sin and holds the keys to heaven and Hell.*

Stephanie turned to Leah, "Allow me into your mind and heart?" and Leah nodded, opening her eyes wide because of the request. And when Stephanie knew all that had been done to Leah, she turned *very* dark again, then turned to the other kids, and said, "You all think because you're young, you can't die." And to the smug brown-haired girl, she said, "You're *nothing* now but an Earthly demon. Meet a *real* demon!" And Stephanie waved her hand and the girl disappeared!

When the others saw *that,* they began saying various excuses, blaming each other. Stephanie shook her head. "I *know* what you all did. It's too late. *Yes,* I was a *slut.* But I rose above *all* evil and the Lord Jesus saw fit to place in King Vaughn's and my hands the *whole* world's judgment." And she began to glow in rainbow colors and Leah went to her knees and bowed, not feeling worthy to be in such presence. But the others shook from fear and condemnation.

Stephanie waved her hand again and the brown-haired girl returned and collapsed in front of them all, her dress shredded and covered in vomit. "She'll tell you your fate better than I can. The *next* time you see me, it *will* be your last. Now *go!*"

And the kids ran as fast as they could and disappeared except for the brown-haired girl they left behind. She was still shaking uncontrollably, in shock, and curled up, and Stephanie knelt down and touched her shoulder and she stopped shaking. "I only calmed you so you could hear me. I *know* what you are. And now *you* know where you'll end up, because you drove out of yourself all goodness and *every* imagination of your heart is *only* evil continuously. Try and *enjoy* the time you have left." And Stephanie turned to Leah, saying, "Take me to your home!"

And Stephanie took Leah's hand and she looked up at her Queen with a smile that seemed to beam. Down the main street they went then turned left down a small street and into the poorest section of town where the street became rubble. Stephanie shook her head. "I don't understand. The country has been doing so well. Why is this town so *bad?*"

Leah said, "Mommy told me that because the people here are so *very* evil, that when the money came to the officials, they all took it for themselves. And you and King Vaughn outlawed drugs but that gang and others are run by the officials here!"

Leah stopped, and said, "I'm sorry. This is where we live." Stephanie's mouth dropped open. It wasn't exactly a house at all but a small cottage and half the roof was caved in. Stephanie thought where *she* had grown up was bad. But *this* was unspeakable poverty. Leah said, "You don't have to come in. I understand. You're a *Queen. Our* Queen." And she said it with true pride in Stephanie.

Stephanie said, "I most *certainly* would *love* to come into your home. It would be an honor!"

Leah said, "I don't see any honor in this at all. All the kids and even adults make fun of us living here. Sometimes they even come to our front door and bang on it saying they'll give us a cent if we. . . well, I don't want to say those words."

Stephanie held her anger in check but the Holy Ghost began to bring something much different to her. Leah took a key and unlocked the door. Inside, to the left was a broad woven tapestry that hung down from the ceiling at an angle that gave the floor more area than the ceiling, clearly designed to give them every single inch of floorspace they could muster. But what really caught Stephanie's eye were the designs of beautiful birds and other animals. It was *so* beautiful it reminded Stephanie of Appendaho art. Then Stephanie realized why the tapestry hung slanted liked that. *This matches how the roof caved in.*

Leah said, "Mommy made that herself!"

On the other side was the kitchen. An old gas stove, small sink, and small refrigerator. The paint had long ago peeled off the cabinets, and the walls had lost their paint completely, yet the house was free of dust *everywhere*. The old wooden table was covered in another beautiful tapestry like the larger one. "What does your Mom do?"

"She's a seamstress. Her *hobby* is tapestries. But they don't pay her much at work and not for these either because, well, she's not like everyone else." Then Leah went over to a walk in closet and proudly opened the door. This is my bedroom!" And she pulled a string and a single lightbulb that dangled from the ceiling lit up. Though small, every wall had beautiful tapestries upon them, even the floor. Stephanie dried her eyes because of the deep love she felt. And in the corner was a small TV.

Leah jumped onto her bed which seemed to be a homemade mattress quilted together in more beautiful designs but this time they were geometric. The balance of colors was magnificent. Leah said, pointing at the TV and smiling, "This is where I used to watch you on TV."

Stephanie asked, "Where does your Mom sleep?"

"Oh, she sleeps where the tapestry in the living room, meets the floor. She takes her mattress out from another closet."

Then they heard the front door open and her Mom called out, "Leah, who are you talking to?" And Stephanie turned around to see a woman with a white cane coming in the front door. Stephanie's mouth dropped open. "Leah? Someone is in the room with you, Who is it?"

Her voice was kind but also concerned but Leah sprang up and took her Mom's hand and led her to the table to sit in one of the two chairs. She seemed quite tired. Her hair was already all gray, her face drawn, but her spirit. . . Leah said, "Mom, you won't *believe* what happened."

And Leah told her Mom the story until her Mom asked. "Is that who's in the room *now*?"

Stephanie spoke up. "Pardon my intrusion, Ma'am, into your *beautiful* home, but yes, I'm Stephanie."

Leah's Mom's hand went to her mouth and she began to cry, but she went to her knees and bowed to the floor, and said, "My Queen. You shouldn't be here. This isn't fit for you."

Stephanie said, "A home is *fit* where a *lot* of love is. I feel *quite* comfortable her. May I ask? I see you've lost your sight. But how could you have done such beautiful tapestries?"

Leah helped her Mom back into a seat, and her Mom said, "In my work as a seamstress which I learned as a child, every color was given three numbers relative to its brightness and warmth and position on the rainbow. I put colors together based on numerical relationships that seemed right!"

Stephanie was in awe. "But… but… how did you create the animals, the shapes?"

Leah laughed, saying proudly, "That's *my* doing. I loved stuffed animals and its's the one thing Mommy would buy for me, and she would feel the shapes."

"And from the shapes I understood about animals."

Stephanie's heart pained her suddenly, so she asked, "Where's your husband?"

There was silence, so Leah spoke up, "I don't have a Dad. Never did. Mommy said. . ."

"Leah," her Mom scolded her. "Don't trouble the Queen with such things."

But Leah insisted, and looked Stephanie in the eye. "Mommy told me that to get the job she had to have sex with the boss. It was the *only* place that would hire her. That's how I came about. But we live *here* for so long because Mom has been saving all the money she can to send me away. But I told her, I'm *not* leaving her. And anyway, someone broke in yesterday and stole it all."

There was banging at the front door and hollering. "Come out and *play*. Bring your blind Mom. She won't know what we put in her mouth." And many other things they said.

Leah ran and locked the door then threw a piece of two by four into a slot to lock it further. But the banging increased and the door began to break from its hinges. Leah's eyes went wide. "They've *never* been *this* bad before."

A young lady's voice came loud and clear. "Where's your Queen *now?* If you don't come out and *play* we'll burn your house down with you *in it!* And all those weird rugs on the walls will burn, too!"

Leah said, "How did she know? We never had *anyone* in here?"

Leah grabbed her Mom, saying. "We have to *go!*" Then she turned to Stephanie, saying, "The back of my bedroom has a secret door. We get out there and the woods are close by."

Stephanie said, "I thought you watched me on TV?"

Leah said, "Well, the local channel didn't like you very much so they only played little bits to make fun of you but I *loved* it. Seeing you, I mean. They were just *wrong.*"

Stephanie said, "Where will you go, if you go into the woods?"

"I found a cave and kinda fixed it up just in case this happens."

Stephanie shook her head, then said. "There's a lot you don't know about me, but you're about to find out. Let's start with this." And Stephanie placed her hand on her Mom's head and said, "Lord Jesus. You gave me an open door of prayer and told me that *anything* I ask of you, you would grant. Give this woman her sight and strength!"

And she lit up so brightly the light shined through every crack in the house and the people outside saw it. The woman straightened and looked up at Stephanie and her eyes blinked three times and she saw her Queen and her hands went to her mouth, but she said, "You are so *beautiful.*" Then she looked upon her daughter for the first time, and Leah, crying now, fell into her mother's arms. "*Mommiieee…*"

Stephanie waived her hand and the door shattered into pieces, many of which struck the people outside. But when she came out, she was shocked at what she saw. It looked like the whole town had gathered. The brown-haired girl was in front with her gang. Stephanie panned the few hundred people that were left in this God-forsaken place. No gray arms, no Anti-Christ hands either. It was just *them.*

Stephanie turned dark and said to the brown-haired girl, "I told you, the *next* time you saw my face, it would be your *last.* But I didn't expect it to be so soon nor like *this!*"

The Holy Ghost turned Lady Stephanie, *Judge Stephanie,* even deeper black, and she said, "In ancient times God sent angels down to the wicked towns of Sodom and Gomorrah to see if they really did according to the cry of evil that reached even up to Heaven. But God no longer needs to send *anyone* down now. You know *why?*"

They laughed. They mocked even more, saying, "Oh *destroy us* Queen Stephanie." Then they began to chant, "Jargono, Jargono, fulfil your promise. Vanquish our enemy!"

Stephanie reached out her hand and the Staff of God appeared in it. Leah and her Mom's eyes went wide. "He's not coming because he *knows* he can't interfere with the Lord Jesus' Judgment. God no longer needs to send angels down here to see because the Holy Ghost is now *Judge* of the Earth, and *particularly,* the Lord Jesus has given that task to King Vaughn and his Queen. And Stephanie slammed the staff down and it thundered and the whole town fell, including every building *except* the little house they were at.

And when the people lifted themselves up from the ground, behold, they were blind. Stephanie turned to Leah and her

Mom and brought them back into the little house, and said, "Are there *any* in this town that were kind to you?"

Leah thought for a moment, then said, "*Waverly!* He used to chase away the bullies from me."

Stephanie was shocked. That was Vaughn's best friend here and who sent her the letter about Vaughn dying. She was about to ask where he lived but then they heard a man's voice calling Leah's name, "Leah." Then urgently, "*Leah.*"

Leah called out, "We're in *here*. We're OK."

And then, stepping upon some bodies still on the ground and pushing others aside, Waverly, now quite tall with light brown wavy hair and green eyes, burst through the doorway and swooped Leah up in his hands and spun her around, "You're OK," he said. "When I saw all the people coming here and heard what they said I was so worried," He put her down, then said, "And ashamed. Because what could I do against all those *people*. I'm not a King Vaughn or Queen Stephanie! And then that *earthquake!*"

Stephanie cleared her throat, sent the Staff away, and said, "But I am! Queen Stephanie, that is."

And when Waverly, who looked exactly like he did when he was younger, but just a *bit* older, but even taller, broader shouldered, but still gentle, when Waverly saw Stephanie, he couldn't believe it.

Leah said, "That wasn't an Earthquake. *That* was our *Queen!*"

And Waverly realized he wasn't just seeing a vision like he had when Stephanie came to heal Vaughn, though she was now still glowing golden. But Stephanie, crying now, opened her arms and they joined in a wonderful hug and Waverly lifted her off the ground and spun her around, too. When Waverly put her down and she looked deeply into his eyes, she said, "I've often thought about you, wondering how you were. I should have come *way* sooner. If it wasn't for your letter, Vaughn would have *died.*"

Waverly was speechless, and then Stephanie turned *very dark* as the Holy Ghost was prodding her. She held out her hand and the Staff of God reappeared in it and Waverly's eyes went wide and he swooned a bit. Stephanie said, "I'm sending you all above, but *this* time, unlike those that fled from Sodom, you get to *watch,* because you covet *nothing* that is here." And she slammed the foot of the Staff down again and the little house with them in it disappeared.

But Stephanie stood where the front door used to be, facing the blinded crowd, and she said, "Lord Jesus, give these wretched human beasts back their sight. I want them to *see* what shall befall them" And they immediately received their sight. "The Lord Jesus, after I showed him *everything* about you, has given *me* through his Holy Ghost, your *Judgment.* Stephanie raised the head of the Staff up to Heaven and deep dark clouds formed, darker than the darkest night, *oppressively* dark, and angry thunder boomed but then fell silent. Then a small fiery object fell out of the sky. Then another, and another. And whatever it touched, it burst into a blaze as if lighting a match. And the people began to scream and run but the fiery hail increased greatly and Stephanie went up into the Corridor.

Leah, still in the house with Waverly and her Mom, said, "I guess you're gonna lose the election?"

But Stephanie shook her head. "Not for this. Anyway, God first."

And they all said, "Jesus first,"

In the next moment, the little house was settled back on Earth. Out their front door was the view of a castle, and they were on a little hill in a clearing to itself. Stephanie waved her hand again and the cottage was restored, the roof no longer collapsed. Food also filled their cupboards, and their refrigerator was larger and also full of food. In fact, the whole cottage was larger, with three bedrooms now, and a living room with a couch and a large modern TV. "All of you come to my castle tomorrow morning." And Stephanie disappeared.

# Drastic Times
# Drastic Measures

*The Father called an impromptu meeting. No warning, no hints, no gossip. Everyone, every single Alpha and even all underlings were in his deepest darkest room crammed in so tightly they couldn't help but tail up against each other. Now, if you know anything about Alpha, they hate to be touched by another Alpha. It causes an immediate reflex of aggression, so everyone kept raising up as if to consume then repressing the urge, then raising up again. . . It almost reminded you of certain exotic birds on Earth during mating season except this would be consuming season.*

*"Quiet," was the soft spoken one word command that came from the Father, and, remembering the consequences of the last time they ignored such a command, everyone became still. Except for one underling who tugged on his Master's eye right there in the Father's room, because he wanted to ask his Master a question. The total insult caused his Master to reflexively rear up against his underling whereupon the Father's massive tail lashed out so fast no Alpha could hardly see it. The next moment,*

*his Master was gone and he now became the Master! Except, without consuming his Master, so he was a Master that was, well, quite small by Alpha standards, so Great Eyes began to drool over consuming him and taking his domain for themselves.*

*"Quiet," the soft spoken command came again but every Alpha wondered. We're all perfectly quiet. Why did the Father order it again?*

*And the Father said, "I can hear everyone drooling!"*

*Great Eyes twisted. No one ever knew you could hear drooling and no one knew how to stop it or drool in silence.*

*The Father said, "It's not a very large phenomenon in the larger scheme of things. But this has only happened one time before, and granted, that one was sizable, but I want explanations!"*

*Every Alpha quaked, which meant they kept bumping into each other even more, which meant they had to suppress their urges even more. . . They could hardly even think under such duress. The underling who got his Master eaten raised his small tail and kept waving it in the Ethereal no air, so much so that everyone noticed, including the Father! Great Eyes became sad because they knew the Father would consume him.*

*But the Father said, "Master. . .ACJ?" The Father asked as he checked the roster he kept engraved on his tail, and everyone had the same question. ACJ?*

*"Yes, your Highest, most Darkest, most Feared. The last time this happened was in the ancient cites of Sodom and Gomorrah. All those souls we had counted on consuming literally disappeared, bypassed our right to consume. There was much speculation as to Truce violations per soul, but no Alpha found*

*any proof as to where they went so no grievance could ever be filed. However, I have it on good authority. . ."*

*Every Alpha couldn't help sneer, both at this underling's arrogance and even possibly having a source they didn't have, but also saying he had a good source. No Alpha ever used such vernacular.*

*ACJ knew all their thoughts but raised up in deep Alpha pride, even floated above all the rest! And said, "I have it on good authority that all of those in the past and all of those that just disappeared have been sent directly to what is referred to as The Lake of Fire that Burneth with Brimstone!"*

*There was true silence in the Ethereal. This was dire, indeed. It shook the very foundations of Alpha reality, but it made sense to the Father. The Father said, "Reveal your source. Ahhh," and he looked at his tail, again, saying, "A. . .C. . ..J?"*

*The underling nodded with pride but also knew it was against Alpha code to reveal sources of information.. But the Father couldn't stand it anymore. He had mindlessly recorded the name on his tail without thinking, but now. . ."*

*The Anti-Christ cleared his throat, being, yet, still in human form. "Father," and he bowed low, "His source is me. I am privy to things on Earth none of you are. I was there, having been called by my faithful for help. But as I arrived, I witnessed the faithwalker Stephanie call Fire and Brimstone out of Heaven and then I tracked the Fire and Brimstone and all it consumed, both soul and body as well as the whole town as it vanished. It was sent to a place beyond our orbs' reach but I was able to stand, as it were, at the border and behold it!"*

*The underling smacked his tail hard on his arm in delight and the Father's Greatest Eye bore down on the annoyance, and the Father said, "What is ACJ?"*

*And the Anti-Christ said, "Well, Father, it's short for Anti-Christ Junior. . . of course!"*

*The underling spoke up on his own, now. This wasn't part of his Master's plan. "Father, this changes everything. Threatens our very existence. We must all band together and fight for our rights like never before!"*

*It was actually a fairly rousing speech and many Alpha found themselves newly inspired! The Father narrowed his Greatest Eye at the upstart, then turned to the Anti-Christ, saying, "You really have good use for this one?"*

*And the Anti-Christ said with surety, "I do! He's going to be my running mate on Earth!"*

Stephanie laid in Vaughn's arms in bed weeping, the covers pulled up tight. They had shared all their current experiences and the love Stephanie had for the people was so intense it tore her apart. "Vaughn, we haven't done anywhere *near* good enough. There are *still* too many good people up North, How can we get them out?"

Vaughn hugged her and stroked her head, her fiery red hair not in braids but falling naturally over him and her. "Stephanie. . . we can't."

And when she heard *that*, she bawled all the more, then said, "Jesus gave me an open door of prayer."

But Vaughn shook his head. "Even *that* has parameters, Stephanie! God won't force himself on *anyone's* free will. They've made their choices."

But Stephanie shook her head and leaned up from Vaughn's bare chest, saying, "But *you* saw, too. What *choices?* Many of them just can't make it South, or are bound by something they can't leave."

Vaughn's thumbs caressed her tears away from her cheeks then held them tenderly. "My dear wife, my Queen, I think the ones that are left understand but they've just decided they would face whatever comes."

Stephanie practically yelled at Vaughn, "But they *can't* face what's coming. They. . . *can't.*" And she collapsed back onto his chest again being flooded by prophetic visions that she rarely had. Arlupo was a true prophetess, but Stephanie only had a smattering of the gift. But that *tiny bit* was in full force now and she didn't know how to deal with it. Then she thought about Arlupo and all she knew but hid, how she *knew* her and all her people would die protecting Stephanie but Arlupo just carried on with her normal life. Stephanie said, "I don't know *how* Arlupo could have managed it. I *don't.*"

"I don't, either," Vaughn simply said. "But at least we have each other." And when Stephanie heard that, she clung to Vaughn even tighter but her visions and her weeping increased. Vaughn said, "I think Arlupo cried alone!"

Lynnara walked into the bedroom, waved her hand, and little Michael appeared beside her and they both climbed into bed with Lynnara on top of the blanket beside Stephanie but

Michael wormed his way atop the blanket between his mother and father.

Stephanie was instantly comforted, but fearfully said, "*Michael!* Lynnara? What have you *done?* Michael must *stay* on the Holy Mountain." And Stephanie concentrated to send him back but he didn't go!

Vaughn calmly said, "Stephanie. I think when the Lord gave you to burn up our home town, I think that the season has *changed.* Different rules apply now! Let the children be where they're *supposed* to be! I think we need them, now more than ever!"

And Lynnara, petting her third and bestest Mommy's head, said, "You do, Mommy, because we *love* you more than *anything,* well, except for Jesus."

Little Michael relished being in between both Mommy and Daddy, being with them at the same time as both his parents' arms encircled him. He began to feel whole in ways he hadn't felt before and he began to glow a light blue from joy! When Vaughn and Stephanie saw *that* they deeply wondered but each kissed him on a cheek at the same time, and Michael squealed in delight.

Laying on his back between Mommy and Daddy, little Michael raised his hands and a vision opened up above them all.

Stephanie's eyes went wide and tears streamed down her cheeks while her heart pained. "It's so *beautiful,*" she whispered and Vaughn merely nodded in silence.

A city, of sorts, bejeweled in the roads, the walls, the very small *side streets* with twelve manner of precious gems, each their own unique color that glowed. But the cement, or whatever it was that held the jewels together, was the color of milk mixed with honey, a golden cream. The people there were all shining, each with unique glows and colors, no one was the same, yet everyone was one. And there were *no* perverse there, no evil *at all*, but holiness, itself, lit up the city, a presence as if it were air to breathe.

And the trees were magnificent, as if ancient, being hundreds of years old. Squirrels and birds and other animals played within and between them and even the animals had soft glow to them. And an immense fountain shining with golden water splashed in the center of the city and spilled over its receptacle with the water guided by silver gutters throughout the city down the center of broad sidewalks filling smaller fountains which then gushed upwards only to spill over and fill more silver gutters.

Around the fountain in the center of the city were seven magnificent trees, one of which was the Tree of Life. But there was also a Tree of Love, a Tree of Truth, a Tree of Justice, a Tree of Peace, a Tree of Wisdom, and a Tree of Understanding, and the people in the city ate of the Holy Trees as often as they will. . .

Little Michael became sleepy and as his hands withdrew from the vision, it faded and he fell asleep. Lynnara asked her Mommy and Daddy, "Why are you crying?"

Stephanie looked at Vaughn because she couldn't speak the answer, and Vaughn said, "Our daughter, every day we see you, is a day filled with more joy than the day before!"

Stephanie's eyes watered with different tears now, because Vaughn had used Arlupo's father's favorite saying, but Lynnara scrunched up her nose, then said, "Daddy. . . that's *too much* joy!"

But Vaughn said, "Not if our hearts keep enlarging!" And Stephanie looked deeply into Vaughn's eyes because she'd *never* heard nor thought of that response before but she knew it was definitely right.

Lynnara said, "Oh! Well, *that* makes sense, Daddy. That's the way it's *supposed* to be!"

Stephanie touched Lynnara's cheek but she disappeared then reappeared, but this time she was on her back between Mommie and Daddy and little Michael was sleeping in Lynnara's arms with Lynnara's cheek against the top of his head.

Stephanie and Vaughn rolled on their sides to face each other and threw their arms over the children.

Stephanie said, "When it's our time, I think I might remember this *exact* moment. I can't tell you how much it fills me."

Vaughn said, "When it's our time, we're going to feel and see a lot more than just this. But right *now,* seeing *you* like this, and the children like *this,* is all the joy I could ask for."

Lynnara said, "Daddy, you'll have even *more* joy tomorrow," and she kissed the top of Michael's head.

Stephanie said, "Lynnara, the *world* we live in is going to be darker, more evil than it ever has been. *You* are going to see suffering the likes of which has *never* been before. You need to be ready for that. Even though you're still a little girl, you're *also* a *faithwalker.* We *have to* be able to bear the pain."

Lynnara kissed the top of Michael's head again, then said, "I understand Mommie. I've already hurt really bad before. But I have Rebecca and Lana to help me, and *together*, we can beat *anything!*"

Vaughn and Stephanie looked deeply into each other, then at Lynnara, and laughed together, both saying, "We believe you!